blue bird
yellow bird

rachel nameika

Auctoris
Press

Norwell, MA

Published By

Auctoris Press
P.O. Box 274
Norwell, MA 02061
www.auctorispresspub.com

Printed in the United States
Edited by ReviewYourBook.com
www.bluebirdyellowbird.com

For Joshua

One of these mornings
You're gonna rise up singing
You're gonna spread your wings
And take to the sky
Lord, the sky

-George Gershwin, Ira Gershwin

Joshua,
It is my greatest wish that you live your life dreaming big
and acting accordingly.
- Love, Mum

acknowledgements

First and foremost I would like to thank my parents for giving me the best sister in the whole wide world. Without her, this project would not have come to fruition. It is my sister who helped me to see that anything is possible. It is my sister who worked so hard to make my dream happen. My sincerest gratitude is for you, Laura!

Thanks also to Julie for your enthusiasm, support, and hours and hours worth of help. You are truly an above and beyond kind of friend!

I am also eternally grateful for my readers: Brunnie, Patty, Denice, Mrs. Feeney, Jessie, Erica, Bonnie, Alison, Holly, Elena, Lisa, and Jan. Thanks for your time and input!

Last but not least, I would like to say thank you to all the ladies at meditation... thank you for sharing and for the inspiration you offer... Namaste!

the end

The beginning is something you don't remember, except for, perhaps, at the moment of your birth. A vision may still be there, not of the grisly particulars, but of the watery womb, of odd appendages, such as fingers, legs, and knees. Muffled noises pass through all of the barriers into the newly forming tympanic membranes in the baby's ears. A mother's voice may be heard first, then a father's. Comforting sounds drift through the amniotic fluid. Startling ones pierce, causing knee-jerk reactions which the mother will feel, placing her hand on her growing, stretching belly. Maybe, just maybe, the baby remembers these things for a short time after it is born. Perhaps it remembers more than that, too, like where it came from in the first place: somewhere ethereal and eternal, someplace where knowledge is a whole, complete thing. The baby may recall what its soul must do after it is born, what it must overcome, how it must evolve throughout its life on Earth, however short or long. Perhaps it is remembered and then forgotten, and, hopefully, remembered again.

part one

the nest

Baby Caroline remembered. She remembered for a short time. Of course, this was without language, since babies don't have language. It was more like a knowing, having something to do with being up high and then coming down fast into the womb. Before that, the coming down, there was something about knowing what she would have to do in this life. It had something to do with overcoming and forgiving, healing. Baby Caroline also remembered that there was another soul up there with her. This one would be coming down at the same time. It was the strangest thing, though. One moment, these two souls looked like birds, a fluttering of blue and yellow wings. The next moment, they looked like people. An instant later, they were bodiless and faceless, looking only like air. Baby Caroline remembered about this other soul, and she knew that they would have the same purposes in life. However, the other soul would have a much shorter life on Earth than her soul would have. She knew, also, that their lives would intersect, somehow, and that this intersection would allow each of them to fulfill their purposes. They would have to be open to it. They would have to be ready for it. It all had to do with a forgiveness that would have to reach back and go forward. Baby Caroline knew, in a baby sort of way, that others would enter her life to help her fulfill her purpose and that, in doing so, she would be helping them to fulfill theirs... without even knowing it. With a fluttering of blue and yellow wings,

2

Caroline, as well as this other soul, was born on March eleventh, 1964; they were born to different mothers in different towns. Caroline would remember, and then she would forget.

The night Caroline was born, her father, Will, had a dream. It made no sense, but it made perfect sense. In the dream, he was standing at the edge of the marsh, the one he and his pregnant wife, Rose, lived on. The usual marshy smell was not in the dream--that muddy, putrid smell that Rose liked. She said it smelled of the Earth. Will said it smelled of decay. Instead, in the dream, the air was laced with the smell of mountain air. It was the same air of his childhood where he grew up in Oregon. It smelled like clear, fresh water, silvery fish, and wet rocks. However, there was another smell that made no sense. It was sweet and juicy... the smell of peaches. Will stood with his back to the house, the one he himself had built. Beside the house was the barn with his workshop neatly tucked inside. His shoes were sprinkled with sawdust. He had a beer in one hand and a cigarette in the other. The cigarette burned dangerously down toward his fingers, its long ash curling around and around... much too long for real life. The beer made sense, the cigarette, the house, Rose, the barn, the marsh. Even the mountain air made sense, however out of place. The part that didn't make sense was that there, on each of Will's shoulders, was a small bird. One of them was blue, the other yellow. Will had never liked birds much. He had always imagined them infested with small gnat-like bugs, the kind that could get on you and send you scratching. These birds were shining and clean, glowing even. Soon the sky took on the same glow, an Aurora Borealis of blue and yellow. Will felt, at that moment, to be like a tree, holding still for these two birds. He stood like this for a quite some time, enough for the sky to begin to darken with the encroaching night. Finally, he had to move, to get to Rose, for she sat at the kitchen table waiting, reading. He moved slightly, and the birds took off, fluttering over the marsh. He watched until he could no longer see them and turned to go to his wife. He noticed something slick under his left foot, and he picked up his leg, looking at the bottom of his shoe. There, he saw that he had stepped on a peach. Its scent filled his nose, the air. He scraped it off before going into the house and asked his wife.

"Rose? What do peaches mean?"

She looked up from her book, paused, and said, "Peaches are the fruit of life, I suppose."

When he woke, Will remembered the dream, unlike most of his other ones. He remembered the peach and the two birds and concluded that this meant Rose would have twins.

The night of Will's dream, Rose went into labor, and it was quick. It took four hours all together, as opposed to the forty-eight hour horror stories she'd heard. In between contractions, her husband told her about his dream and was convinced that it meant they'd have twins.

She told him, "Don't be ridiculous, Will. The doctors would have been able to tell."

He'd said, "Maybe one was hiding."

Then another hard contraction hit, and the conversation was over. Rose was right. It was just one, a girl named Caroline.

What do new parents know, really? This is what Rose and Will thought: They thought that they would just keep on with their lives as they knew it, except that they would have this beautiful, precious baby to show off, to moon over.. to love. They did all of these things. They did. What they didn't know was that they would lose more sleep than they thought was possible. Their child would be colicky and then, when older, would cry out in the night with mysterious terrors. The child would cling constantly to her mother's leg, leaving it sweaty and snotty. Caroline's red-faced tantrums left her parents mute, unable to decipher where such outbursts had come from. Caroline began to have strange thoughts, like thinking she had a twin sister named Birdie. "What does she know?" thought Will and Rose. She's just a child, after all; perhaps a lonely, only child given to whims of thoughts and fantasy. Will and Rose tried for more children. Negative pregnancy tests and unwanted periods left them frustrated, empty handed in the face of their daughter's supposed loneliness. When brought to neighborhood playgroups, Caroline would gravitate to the perimeters. At the playground, Caroline often found the most secluded areas to tuck herself into. By the time she was three, Will and Rose had decided to leave the problem of their daughter's self-imposed isolation be. "She's just shy," they said. "She's perfectly happy all on her own."

However, it worried them. Rose worried while cutting up vegetables for beef stew. Will worried while planing planks of pine wood in his workshop. The act of worrying separately, and not together as they had always done, left them in their own separate worlds, outwardly smiling from within their respective bubbles. It was better that way and, at the same time, worse. It was better, because the less they worried together, the less they fought. It was worse, because the energy-charged fretting had been replaced by a chasm of unsaid things: like the times Rose listened to her daughter speaking to Birdie in her bedroom, like the time she and Caroline stopped at a field of wild flowers to pick some for their kitchen table. Caroline had frozen in the middle of the field. Purple flowers rose up to her knees as she peed in her pants, screaming that she didn't like fields... didn't like them at all. There was also the time they'd gone on vacation in Maine. Will slept the day away in the cabin while Caroline and her mother went exploring in the mountainous forest. They were at the foot of a dense, craggy, wooded hill when Caroline got onto her hands and knees and began to dig. Not playfully, not curiously, but frantically. "Bones, Mum. I have to find the bones," panted Caroline.

They saw a moose wading in a murky watering hole later that day. They watched in silence as it stuck its long, beastly nose into the water, coming up munching, then plodding forward for more lily pad snacks. Seeing the animal made Rose feel strange, similar to the feeling she often had when watching her own daughter, though she would never say it out loud. Rose felt as if she'd stumbled upon an alien... a wild, beautiful thing. Then, Caroline broke the silence when she started crashing through the brush, saying that she wanted to go into the water to find bones. The moose startled, escaping into the woods with surprising grace.

Rose told Will about none of these things, nor about Caroline's tendency to incessantly straighten her toys and collectibles. One time, Rose asked her why she did this. Caroline replied, "It has to be perfect." "Why?" Rose gently inquired. "Or else," Caroline answered. Rose had quietly walked away and, with a shaking hand, put a pot of water on to boil for tea. One evening, Rose had to stop Caroline from her straightening ritual, only to find her up in the middle of the night picking up where she'd left off. Rose had let her continue until she was done, then heard her say, "See Birdie? Now it'll be just fine." No, Rose told her husband none of these things, lest they break their unspoken vow of silence, which had become an entity of its own, like an invisible person between them. Besides, Will had taken to the workshop as if it was his new home, drinking his way through the evenings, leaving him cranky and remote. Rose had seen this in her husband before; even before Caroline, but to a much lesser extent. She wondered, at the oddest times, if her

7

husband was an alcoholic: while reading a book, or coming up out of a heavy, sweat-soaked sleep. She wondered if she'd have to live in a lonely, airless bubble forever, if her daughter would.

While Rose wondered, Will wondered... silently ruminating, tasting the flavor of his thoughts over and over. What had gone wrong? Why couldn't he seem to understand his daughter, who was far too pensive for a four-year-old? He could sometimes hear her talking in her bedroom, the one that overlooked the marsh, late at night. He knew it was Birdie she was talking to, but he could never make out the words.

One bright, sunny day, Will was walking the perimeter of the house, inspecting the foundation, when he spied something small and bright blue on the ground. He inched up to it. A breeze came and kicked it up off the ground. It settled back down slowly, resting gently on the blades of grass. A feather. Will picked it up and inspected it, but could not place what sort of bird it could have come from. He looked up and saw only sky, that and Caroline's bedroom window. He looked back at the feather and remembered, for the first time since Caroline was a baby, that long ago dream he'd had of the birds on his shoulders. Will chuckled at the remembrance and its silly foolishness, its ignorance, its hope. He went back into his workshop, slipping the feather into his jeans' pocket and promptly threw back three nips of Vodka in quick succession. Caroline came in moments later in her red paisley dress and pig tails.

"Hi, Daddy," she said.

8

Will's eyes filled with tears at the simple greeting. She watched him.

"Oh. Here. I've got something for you." He reached into his pocket and came out with the feather, handing it out to her.

Caroline smiled, rubbed it against her cheek and giggled. "It tickles, Daddy." She reached out with it and rubbed it against his cheek. He laughed and took it back from her, trailed its delicate edge against her neck, her shoulder. Caroline laughed, and the sound was like music, like angels.

"Daddy, I don't have any pockets."

"Here, I'll keep it in my pocket for now to keep it safe," he said. Will asked her if she'd like to stay with him and work in his workshop. She said that she would, but soon announced that she was going back to the house to play with her doll, Sara. After she left, Will forgot about the feather in his pocket but kept remembering Caroline's greeting... "Hi, Daddy." He smiled and teared up again. It was something about the Vodka. It always made him emotional, which was, sometimes, preferable to feeling nothing. Will reached down into the bottom drawer of his workbench and got three more nips, which he made quick work of.

At three o'clock that morning, Rose came into the workshop. She saw him, not for the first time, sprawled out on the floor on his stomach, snoring loudly. There, by his foot, was an empty nip bottle. She picked it up and saw one drop left. Tipping her head back, Rose let a drop roll out of the bottle onto her tongue. It felt like stinging acid. It felt like something you might appreciate if you were trying to feel alive when, of course, it was really making you dead. She bent down and rested the bottle next to his head, right before his eyes. She wanted him to be confronted by his choice the minute he opened his eyes.

The next morning, Will woke up and spied something in his direct line of vision. It was small and clear. He could see right through it. He reached out to touch it, and it rolled away from him, coming to a stop just before the edge of his workbench. He sat up and touched the side of his face. It was wet with drool. Saw dust and grains of dirt stuck to his cheek. Will wiped it all away and stood up. He shuffled over to his work bench, kicking the nip bottle on his way. He had so much to do; including fashioning a tool shed he'd been commissioned to do for the local hardware store. Instead, Will set about making a keepsake box for Caroline. He used the best of wood he had, cherry. When he was done, he reached into his pocket and took out the feather, the one he'd promised to keep safe. Putting it in the box, he closed the lid. Will ran his hand over the box's surface, over the smooth edges. Satisfied, he went on with his day.

The following week, Caroline and Rose sat at the kitchen table, finger painting.

"Mom, I'm scared," said Caroline.

"Of what, my love?" asked Rose.

"Of the wind chimes," replied Caroline.

"The wind chimes? Those things?

"Yes," said Caroline, "I don't like the sound." Caroline raised her little hands to her ears.

"Honey, but it's really a pretty sound. Don't you think? It's the sound of the wind."

"I don't like it, Mum. Make it stop!"

Her mother went out the kitchen door and took them down. "Okay, honey? Here, see?" Her mother touched them with her hand. "See honey? It's just a sound. Like little bells. Here, you touch them."

Caroline reached out and touched them with her finger, the one she had been using to finger paint with moments earlier. "Please, Mum. Make it stop! I don't like it!" screamed little Caroline, rocking back and forth with her hands covering her ears.

"Okay, okay, honey, it's all right. I'll put them away, okay?" Her mother put them inside a drawer in the pantry. She returned to find Caroline's chair empty. "Carly? Honey?" she called. She found Caroline in her bedroom, lying on her bed. She was clutching her favorite doll, Sara. "I really didn't like that sound, Sara."

Caroline's mother watched her daughter for a moment. At times like these, her daughter was a mystery to her, a stranger. "Carly? Come with Mummy. Let's go have a hot chocolate together."

They returned to the kitchen where Rose prepared hot chocolate with a practiced hand, the way only a mother can do.

"Here, Sara. You have some, too," said Caroline, moving the doll to the edge of the mug. They drank quietly until Caroline moved into the living room to watch her favorite afternoon show.

11

Rose stepped out to have a cigarette, to think. As she smoked, she was remembering how last week Caroline had come to her while she was doing laundry and asked, "Mum, what happens to your body when you die?"

Rose looked over at her. She supposed that this question was normal for a five-year-old, but she was unprepared for it, just as she had been for parenting in general. "Well..." She folded a pair of jeans, buying time.

"Mum?" said Caroline.

An answer. She must have an answer. "Well, it goes to heaven of course," said Rose. Caroline stared at her. Rose knew her daughter doubted her. She could almost see her daughter's thoughts. They were big and snarly, demanding to be answered.

"But how can that be if your body is in the ground?" asked Caroline.

"Okay, then..." Rose noticed that she'd been folding and unfolding the same pair of pants over and over. "Your body stays in the ground, and your soul goes to heaven. Your soul is..."

"I know what a soul is," said Caroline impatiently, "but your body, does it just stay like that forever, in the ground?"

"Well, yes, I suppose it does."

"But what if bugs get in there?"

"They can't. The body is put into a sealed box. Nothing can get in."

"But what if there is no box?" asked Caroline, intent on following through her train of thought.

12

"Well, then, I guess there would be bugs. Then, too, the body would become food for the grass and flowers."

Caroline's brow pinched up, then relaxed again. "Flowers?" she said, "Then I'm glad I don't have a box." Satisfied, Caroline skipped upstairs and disappeared into the kitchen.

Rose leaned up against the warm dryer. She surveyed the basement with its clutter; its useless items that had once had a purpose. She felt profoundly confused by her daughter. What had she meant by not having a box? And, then, in an instant she let the thought go.

Rose's thoughts returned to the present moment. She sighed out heavily as she stubbed out her cigarette. Children can be so nonsensical. She decided to leave it be: the thing with the wind chimes.

Will came home late that evening. Caroline was already in bed. She heard her parents talking... a voice answered by another voice, muffled parent voices talking about the day. She heard clinking and clanking in the kitchen. Her father wanted to know why the wind chimes were in the pantry. Her mother told him.

"You're making it worse, Rosemary," he said.

"You didn't see how scared she was," said Rose.

"Well, I wouldn't have taken them down," he said, "She's got to get over her fears."

"She's only five, Will."

"Still," said her father as he strode out of the kitchen, the screen door slamming behind him. Caroline knew he was in the barn, in his workshop. She knew her mother was sitting quietly and still at the kitchen table.

Caroline didn't like Halloween time. She pretended the best she could to like it because, if she didn't, her parents would fight. It was the dark she hated, and the crowds roaming the streets. It wasn't the costumes that scared her, it was the big people. The year she was five, she wore a cat costume. Her mother had stayed up nights and nights sewing it. It was like a celebration when it was all done. Her parents took her out trick-or-treating. Caroline was glad for the cat face covering her own, because she'd had tears. She was relieved when they got home. She shared some candy with Sara. Caroline's parents discussed her that night. She could hear them talking while she was lying in bed. The sugar was coursing through her veins, speeding up her heart, making her thoughts jump about before giving them a chance to complete themselves. Her parents didn't think she could hear them, but, of course, she could. Parents think they know everything, but they don't.

Her mother was saying, "Why don't we just scrap Halloween from now on. She doesn't like it, Will."

"What kind of kid doesn't like Halloween?" he asked. "When I was a kid…"

"This isn't about you," interrupted Rose. "She is not you. She is her own person, and she doesn't like Halloween."

"Our daughter will not be raised as a quitter, Rose," he'd said, "If she's afraid of something, she'll face it and get through it. How else is she going to get through life?"

They were silent for a bit. Caroline heard sounds: the sliding of a drawer, the opening of a cabinet, the clink of a glass on the coffee table.

"Remember when we brought her apple picking?" asked her father in a clipped voice.

Her mother remained quiet.

"She'd wanted to go, up until she got to the orchard."

"Of course, I remember. It was only last month."

"Okay, so you remember how she kicked and screamed when we got there. She was afraid to go into the orchard, right?" he said.

Still, her mother said nothing.

"And what did you do? You let her have her tantrum and told her she didn't have to pick apples if she didn't want to. Pick apples? What kind of kid is afraid to pick apples?" he hissed through his teeth.

"She's not just any kind of kid. She's our kid," her mother said levelly.

Caroline heard the clinking of ice within a glass. She imagined that it was lemonade. She was suddenly thirsty and wished she could go downstairs and get a drink.

"Yes, and if she had been made to go into that orchard and pick the damn apples, she wouldn't be afraid of it anymore, would she?" hollered her dad. He slammed out of the house. Caroline could hear her mother sniffling. She heard voices on the TV, and she clutched Sara closely to her chest.

The next week, while Will was working, Rose took Caroline back to the orchard. Caroline was nervous, but she tried not to let it show. Her mother was nervous, too, but she didn't think Caroline noticed. They put dollars in a box and grabbed a pail. Caroline thought it strange that they gave their money to a box and not to a person. "What if someone comes and steals the money out of the box?" she asked. "Who would steal money from an apple orchard?" replied her mother. They walked into the rows of trees. It was cooler in there and very quiet. A breeze came along and rustled the leaves. Caroline clutched onto the handle of her pail. It swayed and squeaked as she walked. Her mother clutched onto her hand.

They went further in. Caroline turned and saw their car getting further behind. When she turned back, she saw that the orchard went on and on, deeper and deeper. Her left arm began to tingle, the way it had when she and her mother had stopped at a field to pick wild flowers for their kitchen. Caroline began to feel sick to her stomach, but she didn't tell her mother.

"Here's a good one," said her mother.

They turned to face an apple tree. It really was not a good one, Caroline knew. Most of its apples had already been picked, just as it was with most of the trees. But, still, there were some, so Caroline began to pick. She dropped one into the pail, and it landed with a thud. She picked another and another. She was determined to bring home a bunch to show her father. Caroline saw movement deep within the orchard, a flash of color, the distant thud of an apple being dropped into a bucket. Caroline's head began to throb. Her temple felt as if it was bruising, a mysterious ghost bruise forming all by itself. Caroline stepped on an apple. Her ankle twisted, sending pain shooting up her leg.

She cried out, gasped, and choked. "Mum? Mum?"

Her mother came in front of her. "It's all right. It's all right," she said.

Caroline began to gag. She began to shake. She began to run.

The following year, Caroline was a princess for Halloween. This time, Rose bought the costume at K-Mart. She hadn't had time to make a costume, because she'd had to get a job being an operator at the telephone company. Caroline was six. She still hated Halloween, but her father had insisted that she take part. This time, she had nothing to cover her face, and she was a little nervous. But she was older and pretty sure she wouldn't cry. However, she did cry, because she suddenly got a bad stomach ache. They had to go home early. She wasn't lying. She did get a stomach ache. Her father thought it wasn't true. She was getting stomach aches a lot at school now, too. She'd been to the doctors a lot, but they couldn't find anything wrong with her. She'd been made to drink this disgusting molten liquid that was supposed to taste like bubble gum but didn't. They took pictures of her insides as the liquid traveled through her body, a body that kept saying something was wrong. The doctors kept saying that all seemed in perfect order. Even Caroline's teacher and the nurse knew about this. They were told to ignore her complaints. "She can't be spending all her days at the nurse," said her father.

At seven-years-old, the doctor told Caroline's parents to bring her to a different kind of doctor. That caused lots of fights. Her mother said that it was all her father's fault. Her father said it was all hers, the withdrawal, the compulsive straightening of her toys. Will spent most of his time in his workshop then. Sometimes he invited Caroline along. She liked that. She didn't get stomach aches in there. She liked the smell of the sawdust. She liked watching her father work. Sometimes he let her make something. One time, she made a little stool. Her father let her paint it however she wished, and she did so with blues and yellows.

Rose and Will did take Caroline to a different kind of doctor--
the talking kind. Mostly, there, she just played with dolls and
drew pictures. Sometimes she talked about her parents: that
they argued, that her father spent most of his time in the
workshop, that sometimes she would find him wiping a tear
away for no reason at all, that her mother seemed mostly
cheery, except for when she thought Caroline wasn't looking.
They talked about Caroline's need to count the steps from the
bus to her front doorstep. There had to be an even number of
steps or else she'd have to go back and do the walk all over
again.

The doctor told Will and Rose to arrange some play
dates. They planned for her to go to a classmate's house down
the street. When Caroline refused to leave the house, her
parents had the girl come to their house instead. The girl's
name was Trish, and Caroline liked her. She was bold in a way
that Caroline was not. They made up dances together. They
performed them for Caroline's parents, who seemed very
pleased.

One day, Trish wanted Caroline to come to her house
to show her parents a dance they had made up. Caroline
agreed and thought nothing of it. It was Christmas time, and
she wanted to go there anyway, to see Trish's tree. She
imagined it to be perfect, like Trish. Caroline's mother
dropped her off after school one bitter winter day. Trish
pulled her through the door and up to her room, which had

wallpaper and a perfectly made bed. Also, there was a bird in a cage. Trish wanted to show Caroline the bird, to show her that it could talk. But Caroline just felt very sad looking at it. Suddenly, she wanted to go home. She felt as out of place as that bird in its cage.

Lucky for Caroline, Trish was onto something new, some new idea, and she pulled Caroline back downstairs to the kitchen where her mother stood putting cookies on a plate. "Hello Girls. How about some cookies?" They ate their cookies while Trish chattered about this and that. Next, Trish planned to show Caroline the Christmas tree, which stood proudly in the living room. Trish was pointing out all of their ornaments when Caroline heard footsteps coming up from the basement. She heard a jingling, too, coming up and closer... like keys or a chain bouncing about. Caroline's stomach lurched, and she started to sweat. The jingling and the footsteps seemed to go on and on before Trish yelled, "Daddy!" Trish left Caroline there to greet her father as he came through the door leading from the basement. Caroline wanted to bolt, to run home, and her mind quickly mapped out the route she would take to get there. It was too late because Trish's father was now in front of Caroline, crouching down and saying something. Caroline burst into tears. She did not like this man, this stranger, or his wallet chain, or their tree, or Trish's bird. Trish's mother called Caroline's mother, who took her back home.

Caroline grew older. Christmases, Easters, days and nights came and went. She became tall and awkward with long, waving red-brown hair. And, of course, she hated it. At ten, Caroline's friend, Trish, helped her straighten her hair with a straightening iron. At eleven, Caroline stole her mother's blonde hair dye, and she and Trish dyed each other's hair while Caroline's mother was taking a nap. When they were done, they both cried, because they were scared about how they looked. Caroline's mother was not mad. She was just relieved that Caroline had a friend to make stupid mistakes with. Trish's mom, however, was mad, and Trish got grounded for a week. This made them famous in school, though. They became known as the blondsy twins, and it was because of this that they made a few more friends. They would all meet on Blanchard Drive, a small nearby road with a cul-du-sac. That was back when kids could walk around neighborhoods by themselves and spend hours and hours without their parents knowing exactly where they were. Both Caroline and Trish loved a boy named Bobby. He was the first boy Caroline ever kissed, each with their mouths full of Hubba-Bubba bubble gum. Trish had kissed him, too, but then she was always kissing boys.

When Caroline was fourteen, the Blanchard Drive group became more adventurous. The first joint made its appearance... a curious, strange newcomer. The first bottle of booze came along, too, sneaked out of some parents' basement cupboard. There were lengthening spring days spent together on the hillside. Bobby drank too much and threw up in the woods. Trish smoked a joint and laughed for hours. Caroline smoked one and became paranoid.

Summer days came. They played Chicken on Blanchard Drive. Caroline always wanted to go on Bobby's shoulders, but sometimes it was Trish or Tina who got that spot. Whenever someone showed up with Hubba-Bubba, they knew it was time for Spin the Bottle in the woods.

One summer night, they had become so carried away with each other that it was dark by the time they'd disbanded to go home. Caroline used the path through the woods between Blanchard and her house. Summer beetles buzzed and sang from deep within the woods. She stumbled over a root and adrenalin coursed through her body. Her airways constricted, and she breathed in asthmatically. Her throat closed up. She began to run. Someone was running behind her. Whoever it was would soon be at her heels. He came upon her and wrapped his arms around her from behind.

"Get away from me!" yelled Caroline. "Get away! Don't hurt me! Please! I need... I need..."

"Carly!" shouted Bobby in her ear. "Carly, it's just me. I'll walk you home. You seemed so scared when you left. Are you okay?" he said looking at her.

"No," she said, shaking uncontrollably, "I hate the dark."

After that night, Caroline thought of the idea of locking the doors and windows in her house. She began to do it three or four times a night. She began, also, to miss summer evening outings with her friends. From up high in her bedroom window, Caroline would watch them on Blanchard Drive, their bodies visible through a line of trees: Trish chasing Bobby, Tina and David wrestling. Caroline watched all of them lying on their backs on the embankment looking up at the emerging summer night sky.

It wasn't until Caroline began to spend more time at home that she noticed something had changed. It was barely noticeable, really, but enough to notice that it was something. Her father still spent all his time in the workshop. It was her mother. Where before she had always pretended to be happy, she now no longer pretended. She drank her tea every morning, but no longer smiled when Caroline came into the kitchen. She made hot dogs and beans for dinner and served herself but told Caroline to get her own. She no longer sewed or knitted, but read books behind the closed doors of her bedroom. Caroline often heard, through her mother's bedroom door, the clinking of ice in her mother's wine glass. Rose hadn't even noticed Caroline's nightly ritual of locking the doors and windows.

Yet, Caroline hadn't disappeared completely from her friends' lives. She spent some summer days with them, the kind that send the beetles into their intermittent buzzing, their long drown out calls begging for a cool breeze. She listened to her friends' stories of King of the Mountain and of eating cotton candy at the Marshfield Fair while riding high on the Ferris wheel, touching the night sky. They were their stories and not hers.

Just before entering High School, Caroline came down with a bad case of pneumonia. Her mother came alive then, bringing her cold face cloths to cool her feverish skin. She brought her Vicks and homemade soup. Caroline slept and dreamed a lot. She had dreams of shivering in a shower with her clothes on. She dreamt of a man, strong and foreboding, tearing a necklace off her neck. She awoke that time with her throat on fire and called for her mother in a weak, odd voice. Her mother came and rubbed Vicks on her throat, tying a bandana around her neck. Caroline's skin burned there where her mother's fingers had touched her throat. The fiery spots could have burned holes right through the red paisley cloth. Caroline could hear her mother saying something. It sounded like, "Your father's leaving.", or "How is your breathing?" Caroline wasn't sure which. The next day, Caroline woke screaming. Her father was there beside her.

"Caroline! Caroline! It's all right! I'm here."

"What, Daddy?" she said, unsure what he was talking about.

"You were dreaming. You were yelling. It's okay; it was just a bad dream."

"What was I yelling?" she asked.

"You were saying, 'I need my boy' over and over. But it's okay now. I'm here. Go back to sleep."

"Dad?"

"Yes, love."

"Are you leaving?" asked Caroline. He either said, "Yes. I'm sorry.", or "No. Don't worry." She couldn't tell which.

Because of the pneumonia, Caroline missed the first ten days of her freshman year, which had put her even further out of the loop. Bobby had moved away, and Trish had started up with a new group of friends. Caroline's father had indeed, left- moving back to his home state of Oregon. This was preceded by a brief and uncomfortable conversation in the workshop. The conversation included something about the drinking, sadness, and forgiveness. The whole time her father spoke, Caroline stared at his hammers displayed on the wall. Hammers would, from that point forward, remind Caroline of being left behind.

Caroline had cut her own hair that winter. Her hair stuck out in odd angles and spikes, the blonde long gone. Some members of the drama club noticed her then, thinking a little purple lipstick and black nail polish might make her a perfect addition to their motley crew. But Caroline had no interest in joining this group, or any other. She was not a joiner, had never been.

At sixteen, Caroline's old friend, Trish, got her license, and she bought a dark blue Ford Falcon from her grandmother for a dollar. Each morning, groups of kids crammed into the Falcon on their way to school. Not Caroline. There was no room for her. Even if there had been room, Caroline would not have gone. She didn't like for people to be so close to her.

Caroline, however, did not get her license. She'd had no desire or need to go anywhere. School was all she could manage. Getting good grades wasn't the problem; it was getting through the day. The masses of people around her, passing her in self-absorbed clusters in the halls, gave her headaches. Each group that approached her was like an obstacle to be mounted, a precarious foothold on a mountain. Her days were an obstacle course. The school bell, which rang at the same times every day, never failed to make her jump.

Gym class was the worst. There was too much socializing to avoid in the locker room, although the girls left her alone for the most part. They knew to stay away. Occasionally, a girl might approach her with some sort of comment or question, such as: "Who do you like?", or "Hey, I saw you at the pit the other night. You were so wasted!" Caroline silently nodded her head in agreement, even though she had never been to the pit and had never been wasted.

There was this one girl who, for some reason, liked Caroline. Her name was Suzanne, and she was one of the popular girls. She had braces and big hair, Homecoming Queen material. She and another girl named Paige were rivals. Paige also had braces, but her hair was smaller and she had lots of freckles.

Suzanne once asked Caroline in the locker room, "I love how you do your makeup. How do you do it?"

Caroline had said, "Me? I don't wear makeup."

"I hate you," replied Suzanne, playfully slapping her on the shoulder.

Another time in the locker room, the girls were categorizing each other: jock, freak, frock (jocky-freak), popular, geek, slut, druggie. Suzanne was a self-admitted frock. Caroline suddenly felt dread descending upon her. She sensed their thoughts turning toward her the way a dog might sense an approaching storm. Her senses heightened and the pungent smell of the locker room came into sharp focus, the smell of sweaty bras and crotches, disinfectant and dust.

"Hey, what's Caroline?" asked one of the girls.

"Druggie. She's a druggie," said another.

"No way," replied Suzanne, "She's smarter than that. You watch. Some day she'll be the most successful of us all."

While in high school, Caroline got a job at a restaurant called The Fairview. It was her first job. She was a dishwasher there. Her mother would drop her off at four in the evening and pick her up at eleven at night. The cook was crude. His name was Steve, and he yelled and bellowed at will, calling the girls "bitches" and cracking them in the

27

behind with a wet dish towel. The girls just laughed, but Caroline didn't see the humor in it. Despite this, Caroline had become adept at her silly little job, and it gave her a sense of accomplishment. Forks and knives are easy to deal with. They require nothing of you. Plates know nothing of shaking hands, unless you drop them. Which Caroline had, plenty of times. Much to her relief, though, no one had seemed to notice, which only proved that no one ever noticed her anyway.

It was a perfect job, until Suzanne came along. Caroline had been stacking plates one night when she heard a voice behind her, "I didn't know you worked here!" Caroline turned to find Suzanne behind her. Her hands were on her hips, and she was chewing gum.

"Yes, I do," replied Caroline.

"Goody! I do too, now! We're going to have so much fun together!"

Caroline taught her how to run the machine, where to stack plates, when to deliver bins of pasta to the chef, Steve.

"You're so smart!" squealed Suzanne.

Caroline began to wonder if Suzanne was a little retarded.

Suzanne made quick friends with the bus boys and even Steve. She advanced to bus girl and then to salad maker. But she always included Caroline in on her jokes, always remembered to talk to her, and continued to ask her questions: "Are your parents divorced?", "Are you going to college?", and "What kinds of music do you like?"

One night, Suzanne invited Caroline down on to the beach in front of the restaurant after work. She and some of

28

the bus boys were going down there for some beers and a bon fire.

Caroline had stammered. "I can't. My mother's going to be here at eleven to pick me up."

"So call her. Tell her you're going to hang out with some friends, and I'll drive you home."

"She'll worry," said Caroline.

"She's probably more worried about you not hanging out with friends more often," returned Suzanne.

Caroline doubted it. Her mother never seemed to worry about her much in general. She became angry then and used the office phone to call home. "Oh sure," her mother had said, "You have a good time, Honey."

By the time they reached the beach, the bon fire was already going. It sizzled and popped in the summer ocean air, sending fiery ashes reaching up into the blackness. The bus boys were there, and they were soon joined by Steve, who sported a case of beer. Caroline crawled further into herself and sat on the warm, dry sand; her arms wrapping around her knees. Someone passed her a beer, and she took little sips. Suzanne danced and hopped around in her animated way. Caroline retreated further inward. The bus boys tried drawing her out, but they soon gave up. Somehow, a boom box appeared, and the Eagles blared out of it with "One of Those Nights", and then Bob Seger's "Night Moves."

Suzanne ended up on the other side of the fire, which had grown higher and higher. Caroline hadn't budged from her curled up position. Her arms and knees seemed to be deflecting any humanly advances. She could see Suzanne's image through the flames, and she saw that Steve was with her. She saw his head tipping back as he took long swallows of his beer, his Adam's apple bouncing up and down with the effort. Caroline saw him, suddenly, as someone young and blonde, pulling and pulling from his beer. Caroline wanted to get up and run up to the street. She wanted to jump into the surf, except that she couldn't move. She began to worry about how many steps it would take to get to either place. Even or odd? Odd would be bad, even best. Caroline saw Steve with his hands on Suzanne's shoulder. She was laughing, the light from the fire glinting off her braces. The bus boys had retreated down the beach, being swallowed by the darkness. Caroline saw Steve pull Suzanne toward him. She saw Suzanne pulling, backing away, or trying to. She saw Suzanne's mouth twisting up in a tense grimace, her braces gleaming. Suzanne turned her head sharply. Caroline got up and ran to the street, into the restaurant, where she called her mother who came and took her home.

Later that week in gym class, underneath an airborne volley ball, Suzanne came up to Caroline and said, "You left me. You left me alone with that pig!", and strode away. Suzanne had quit her job. So had Caroline.

Graduation came shortly thereafter, and Caroline chose not to participate in the ceremony. She had her diploma mailed to her instead. Shortly after school ended, there was word that a girl from school had disappeared. Her name was Margaret. She was six months pregnant when she went missing. There was talk of her boyfriend, Joey, killing her. There came an investigation and organized searches ensued.

Caroline joined a team of people who had been assigned the task of hanging posters throughout the town. Nailing pictures of a missing pregnant teen could be done, more or less, in solitude. She'd felt bad for Margaret, who had become an outcast. Margaret had been in her biology class, and Caroline hated her until she became pregnant. Before, she had been polished and shining, a star. Afterward, she became a curled up girl with long, stringy hair and a growing stomach. Caroline didn't mind joining the community in her search, not one bit. She spent the whole summer after high school hanging posters and watching news broadcasts with updates: Margaret's parents begging for mercy, begging for information, begging for their daughter.

Caroline decided to go to college. Her father, whom she hadn't seen since he'd left four years ago, had offered to pay for it. Caroline contemplated on what she wanted to go for. She decided to go to medical school, because she liked the sterile environment of hospitals. She liked the science of the body, the pathology of disease. She liked the act of taking something complex and reducing it down to its simplest form. She liked to think that she could use science to fix, to heal.

In college, there was a counselor whose office Caroline would pass every day on her way to the student dining center. She'd wanted to go knock on her door, but didn't want anyone to see her doing this. Not that it would have mattered. Caroline didn't really know anyone at college anyway. Even her roommate, a boisterous girl from Michigan named Ashley, was not really a friend. She spent most of her time with other girls from the dorm, leaving Caroline alone in their dorm room. Although this is what Caroline wanted, she often felt a haunting loneliness whenever she heard the girls cackling down the hall in room 38C. Caroline got good grades, because she used all of her time to study. As a pre-med student, she was ahead of most other students in her class, because no socializing meant all studying. She'd also tested out of many basic prerequisite courses and was quickly immersed in some med classes. Some of the girls came to her for help, which she willingly gave. Once, they had come and invited her to go drinking with them at "The Depot." She'd planned on going until a panic attack so gripping landed her in the dorm bathroom while the girls hooped and hollered at the bar. She'd listened to stories for days about their adventures, about Ashley dancing on the bar, flashing her chest.

There was a boy named Carlin who Caroline was pretty sure liked her. He, too, was a loner. They would study together in the campus library. He kissed her once as their heads bent into a study carol. She pulled away, whacking her head against the back of the partition. Carlin just laughed and told her she was cute. After that, she hid from him throughout campus and in library aisles.

Caroline soon came to realize that the best place for her to be was locked safely in her dorm room. Ashley, however, began to insist on keeping their dorm room window open, which Caroline did not like. To suggest closing it, especially on warm spring days, would have seemed ludicrous. Besides, there was this enormous Rose bush right outside their window and the scent of its big red blooms would perfume the room. This, Caroline liked. However, given the choice, she would have shut out the glorious smell and kept the window locked at all times. Given the choice, she would have checked that lock over and over. Sometimes, the knowledge of the window being wide open would send her out to the campus track, speed walking and counting her steps. If she made it around once in an odd number of steps, she'd have to start all over again until an even number brought her back to the beginning. It was the only thing that seemed to tame the fires of her anxiety over that window. At least, in the winter, she could keep the window closed. One icy February day, she stood at her dorm window and watched the other girls sliding down the hill in front of the dorm. They used stolen cafeteria trays as sleds. Caroline watched and imagined the feel of the cold, fresh wind on her face.

Caroline finally got up the nerve to knock on the counselor's door one late spring afternoon. She went in and talked to the woman, whose name was Karen, and let spill all of her troubles. Karen was young and kind. She told Caroline about Obsessive Compulsive Disorder and about anxiety. She gave her some relaxation techniques to practice and told her of a support group on Wednesday nights for students with similar conditions, right there on campus. Caroline left feeling like a different person. She left feeling a different sort of emotion that she later identified as hope. Caroline planned on attending the group session. She really had.

Caroline attended her classes on Wednesday afternoon and looked at her classmates with new eyes. Would any of them be attending the support group that night? Would any of them be afraid of walking in the darkness to the student support services building? Caroline made it through her classes that day, distracted and uneasy. Afterward, she entered her dorm and walked down the long hallway to her room. It was still light out; a beautiful, warm day. She approached her room, but heard voices from within. They were angry voices. One of them was Ashley's. The other was her boyfriend Dan's. Caroline stood outside the door and listened. She heard the words "stupid," and "don't you ever." She heard slamming, crashing. She heard "son of a bitch." A commotion erupted from within, a struggle. She heard "Let go of me!" A loud thud against the wall shook the floor upon which Caroline stood. She heard crying, wailing. Footsteps approached the door. It flung open. Dan's red, startled face met hers. He looked away and strode past her. Caroline peered in through the open door. She saw Ashley on the floor, her back up against the wall. She had blood on her face, mixing in with her tears, dripping onto her white t-shirt. Caroline turned on her heels and ran. She ran like a hunted animal, out of the building, across the track, to the student services building where she used the pay phone to call her mother, who came to take Caroline home. She never returned.

The ensuing years came and went, each a drip from a leaky faucet sliding down a drain. Caroline tried things, many things: jobs, friends, counselors, apartments. Her hair grew longer and longer. She didn't like to go to the hair salon, so she either trimmed it herself or her mother would trim it for her. Soon, neither one seemed to have the time or the inclination to do it. Caroline stayed around her home town of Marshfield, with its neat, residential streets. Of course, there were the bad parts as well, and she and her mother lived just on the edge of these. Caroline would keep a job long enough to be able to live on her own for a short time, but then lose her job. She'd have to move back home again.

Caroline worked at a Dairy Queen for a short time, but the orders came at her too fast. The patrons' faces flashed at her like a frantic slide show, making it impossible for Caroline to focus. She constantly got orders wrong and dropped blobs of ice cream from the tops of sugar cones onto her feet. She quit before she got fired.

Caroline's next job was at the office supply store in Marshfield center. That worked out well enough until they moved her from the back stock room to the front desk. There, she quickly rang up orders without making eye contact. The bell hanging by the door signaling peoples' entrances and exits unnerved her. Certain customers were COD, but Caroline never had the nerve to tell them that they must pay cash for their purchases. She let them use credit cards. This, she got in trouble for many times. She wished to be back in the stock room arranging reams of paper, boxes of Bic pens, and containers of elastics just so. She thought of the acronym COD, and realized that if you just switch the letters around, it would be OCD; which is what she had. That's what her latest shrink, Sally Stone, called it. Obsessive Compulsive Disorder.

At twenty-five years old, Caroline went back to school, or rather, enrolled in a certificate program to be completed at home. She would become a medical coder, filling out encounter forms with mysterious five digit codes corresponding to various medical diagnoses, right from her own home. She would then send these forms to insurance companies, so the doctors making the diagnoses could be paid for their services. Caroline quickly mastered the medical terminology, their codes, and their abbreviations. DM meant diabetes, CA-cancer, OAG-glaucoma, MI-heart attack, CVA-stroke, HBP-high blood pressure. She would repeat these codes over and over until it became a mantra. It became a fluid, constant stream of codes day and night: 230.00, 230.02, 117.52, 899.46... all meaning something, all representations of someone's fate, which Caroline preferred not to think of. They were, after all, just numbers; apart from the actual people they were condemning. The numbers and codes took on a rhythm that, at times, lulled her to sleep: 104.54, 108.18, 228.22. Hypertension, Gout, Migraines...

208.72. Caroline preferred, however, to leave the odd numbered codes out of her mantra. She didn't like odd numbers. Caroline's mother, who scrubbed, straightened, and cleaned incessantly every day after work, thought that Caroline was getting better. Caroline's obsessive thoughts, however, had turned from counting footsteps, quadruple checking door and window locks, and compulsive showering to habitually rehearsing medical codes. The more her mother scrubbed, the more Caroline rehearsed. It was all unbeknownst to Caroline's mother.

Caroline's newly earned certificate allowed her to be at home alone every day. Her computer, as well as her work, was her best friend, her only friend. Neither of them challenged her in ways she didn't want to be challenged. Caroline's mother would come home in the evenings and do her ritualistic cleaning, and then disappear into the basement. There, she would spend hours hemming curtains, making slip covers, and designing soft, cool pillow shams... both demure and dramatic. She would sell them to her co-workers at the phone company, then to friends, and eventually to complete strangers. Night after night, Caroline's mother would come up from the basement with glue stuck in her hair and burns on her hands and forearms from the hot glue gun. One night, she came up from the basement with her hair in a tangled mess, a long burn along her cheek.

Caroline looked up from her computer. "What the hell are you doing?"

Her mother peered at her through a tangled mess of bangs. "I'm finding myself." Exhausted, Rose then fell into her bed for the night.

Caroline finally saved enough money to rent her own place: a one bedroom apartment above a realty office in the neighboring town of Scituate. Here, she continued her medical coding work, drank endless pots of coffee, and roamed the creaky wooden floors of her apartment in her slippers. Sally Stone told her it was an important step and suggested Caroline try poking into some stores, if only briefly, to slowly desensitize herself to being around people. Caroline would stare out her second story window onto the Scituate harbor below and contemplate on the stores on the opposite side of the street. Should she try the Harvest Moon Cafe? The Front Street Liqueur Store? Charolette's Hair Cuttery? In the end, Caroline decided to start with The Quarterdeck, a small, quirky gift store precariously hanging over the green harbor water on a rickety wooden deck. She knew that some scenes from the film, The Witches of Eastwick, were filmed in this store. Sally Stone thought this was a great place to start, and she even loaned Caroline her 'Witches of Eastwick' video. Sally said Caroline should watch it, to become more familiar with her destination before entering it. Caroline brought it home and watched it one night while a nasty northeaster tore down Front Street, lashing angrily against the salty shutters of her building. She watched on as Cher crafted odd, abstract looking sculptures in The Quarterdeck, which was the setting of Cher's home in the movie. Caroline was immediately enchanted by the small, sea-faring building.

The next day, fresh ocean air came rolling in on the heels of the previous night's northeaster. Caroline left her apartment, not as herself, but as Cher. As she strode down the sidewalk, she imagined herself to be a dramatic woman, dark and defined... as magical as Cher herself. Caroline found that she could make it through, that she could meet the eyes of the sales clerk, that she could browse, touching the odd, curious items: items hanging from the ceiling, teetering on the edges of shelves. Caroline ran her hands along pea green woolen coats, brass sundials, bowls of shells, and polished stones, long, striped knitted stockings, bins full of old postcards, and ancient pictures of Scituate Harbor. She found mason jars of all colors... green, rose, and yellow. She found bowls of beads. Beads and beads and beads. Tarot cards sat for display at the sales counter. Caroline bought a pack of these and several bags of beads, string, and clasps. She left The Quarterdeck unscathed. Her imaginary Cher costume fell away with each step down the sidewalk, restoring Caroline to herself again. She passed a potted plant of pink petunias, wilted and dying. Caroline grazed her hand along the shriveling petals on her way by. Back in her apartment, she spilled the beads into a tray and began stringing them, attaching the clasps. She worked into the night this way, making bracelets, necklaces, earrings. At three o'clock in the morning she went into the bathroom to wash up before bed. When she saw her reflection in the mirror, she saw a girl looking back at her: a girl with long, frizzy hair and dark circles under her eyes. Caroline eyed the matted clumps of hair where she had been poking her fingers, twisting in concentration. She remembered her mother, emerging from the basement, announcing that she was 'finding herself'.

Before bed, Caroline opened her new pack of Tarot cards, but she was too tired to study them. She pulled out one, just one. It was a picture of a man hanging upside down by his ankles... the Hanged Man. Caroline feared what it meant and didn't want to ruin her good day, so she passed on reading about the meaning of the card in the enclosed booklet and went to sleep.

In the morning, Caroline got up and inspected her jewelry. She was quite pleased, so she decided to make more. The Hanged Man card was sitting on her bedside table, staring at her from upside-down. Caroline looked up its meaning, expecting to find some sort of message of doom. Instead she found that it held a different sort of message... one of surrendering to experience. Caroline walked over to the window, overlooking the harbor and spotted her next conquest, the Scituate Music Store.

This time, Caroline pretended to be Susan Sarandon with her pouty lips and gorgeous eyes. She wore a long, flowing skirt and clogs, a black and brown bracelet she'd made the night before, and a white, form-fitting shirt. Upon crossing Front Street, Caroline noticed the pot of petunias she'd passed the day before. Its blooms reached proudly to the sky, open and ready for new life. A bell above the entrance to the music store chimed as she pushed open the door. Musical equipment lined the hallway, leaving just enough room to get through sideways. Guitars hung from the walls at every inch. Racks of music books hid around every corner. CDs and albums spilled out of cubbies and rows. Caroline stood before a rack of guitars. Such beautiful instruments, something that would be nice to have, just to run your hands over, even if you didn't know how to play. She reached her hand up to touch a smooth, blonde guitar, when she heard a voice behind her.

"Do you play?"

Caroline turned to find a tall man standing behind her. The store clerk. She thought.

"You play?" he repeated.

"Me? No. I'm just admiring. You play?" returned Caroline.

A crooked smile came across the man's face. His clothes were the colors of the brown earth. They hung loosely from his frame. "Me? I'm an old folkie. I play all around. You ever been to the Mill Wharf?" He waited for a response, but he got none. "I play there every Wednesday night. You should come see me some time."

Caroline blinked her Susan Sarandon eyes and smiled her Susan Sarandon smile, but her knees shook under her skirt. She gripped onto her thighs. "Me? Yes. That would be good. I could do that. Maybe I will."

Before he left, he gave her his card and said, "You should learn to play. There's nothing like a chick who plays the guitar." Caroline looked at the card. It said: 'Tim Parlay.

Folk Musician for hire. Parties. Weddings and more. Call for bookings: 781-555-2117.' He was from Scituate. The Mill Wharf was right across the parking lot behind her building. As Caroline left to go home, she realized he hadn't even asked for her name.

The first time Caroline tried to go the Mill Wharf, she chickened out. Well, she did make the trip there, but when she reached the door to the restaurant/bar, her hand froze above the door handle, never actually making contact. Her second attempt found her inside the foyer, but that's as far as she went. The third attempt took her half way up the stairs, leading to the bar where Tim would be playing. Sally Stone wrote Caroline a script for Klonopin, an anti-anxiety medication, and the fourth try found her sitting alone at a small table against the wall in the bar area. Tim recognized Caroline immediately, to her relief and horror. He sat with her in between sets, talking non-stop and drinking tea with her. Tim spoke of his music, his tendency to watch the kinds of things he puts in his body, the kinds of chemicals he is careful not to expose himself to. The conversation turned to, of all things, deodorant. It could have seemed a strange topic, but Caroline didn't think so. After all, what did she know of conversation? Tim confessed to using a deodorant stone, a kind of crystal used to rub on your armpits to prevent the musty odor. He rattled off a list of the hazards of regular deodorant, of the mercury that can cause early on-set dementia. Afterward, came a flurry of information, ranging from the deteriorating effects of chemicals on humans to the cellular destruction caused by shampoos, detergents, red meat, and wheat. As Caroline listened, she thought of armpits, musty skin smells, and alternatives.

Caroline took to using a deodorant stone and found that it did, indeed, work. She began using all-natural perfume-free soaps and detergents. She went to the Mill Wharf every Wednesday night, and she regularly took the Klonopin. She accompanied Tim to his gigs and discovered a whole world out there that, before, she'd only just imagined about. Caroline knew, without her Klonopin, this world would assault her senses, causing her to retreat, hide, and disappear. The medication dulled the sharp sounds and turned all the people around her into ghosts, making them easy to dismiss as figments of her imagination. It allowed Caroline to focus on the one thing that had substance, the one thing that mattered... Tim. When she wasn't with him, she waited for him to call. Her phone became larger than life, filling her thoughts and dreams completely. It was her savior when Tim called and her enemy when it was her mother calling. Those were the only two people who ever rang for her. Caroline told her mother nothing about Tim, for her mother had become a body sinking into the murky waters of 'finding oneself'. Caroline had the sense that her words to her mother were heard as if listening while underwater.

Sometimes Caroline would have to endure long weeks of Tim's absence, only to find herself sailing upon a cloud when he would finally show up, unannounced, at her door step. His absences were unexplained, and never challenged. Caroline began to follow him to the Cape where he played at a pub called The Wooden Nickel. She would sit near him, handing him his musician's tools: capos, picks, and microphones. She learned that no two harmonicas are alike. There's one in the key of C, G, and D. She learned that the invisible chemicals in the rugs at Tim's gigs made his eyes sting and burn. Caroline tried to show no reaction when Tim shoved tissues up his nose on their way to gigs in an effort to prevent the inhalation of the car exhaust all around them.

Tim frequently hosted an open mic in Marion. Caroline especially liked going with him to that particular place. There was something about the town of Marion that spoke to her. She felt less squirmy, more at ease. Marion was really just a town like any other, but its sea-side community was somehow different from that of Scituate. It was anonymous, other-worldly... a perfect fit. The open mic featured other aspiring musicians, cautiously trying their hand at the performing arts. Since Tim was the host, he was the cheer leader, the smooth-talking encourager. Caroline felt slighted when all of his attention went to the other musicians, especially the chicks with the guitars. Back in her apartment, Caroline often yearned to be back in Marion. There she felt, not like Cher or Susan Sarandon, or even herself, but like someone else all together.

Once, when Caroline was trying to install some software on her computer, she called Tim to ask for his assistance. He impatiently told her that he was tied up and rushed off the phone without so much as a goodbye. Caroline didn't hear from him for a month after that. In that endless time, Caroline sank herself into her work. She received one encoding form after another and filled them out with

efficiency. Her medical code mantra began in earnest...
108.28, 642.74, 226.04. Caroline fell asleep rehearsing,
careful to leave out the odd numbered codes. She also began
to delay submitting those ones to the insurance companies,
knowing that doing so would result in some nameless,
faceless people losing coverage for their medical procedures.
Then, she would go ahead and submit them anyway, because
to do otherwise would be wrong.

When Tim returned, Caroline started accompanying
him again to the Mill Wharf, and to Marion. A sense of relief
flooded Caroline, easing her raw nerves. It occurred to her
that this must be the way drug addicts feel when they get their
fix. However, Caroline began to discover a new and unsettling
dimension to Tim. He began unplugging appliances in her
apartment, claiming that the frequencies from them
disrupted his thinking, messed with him, made him sick.
Each time he left to go home, Caroline would plug them all in
again.

One evening, Tim told Caroline over the phone that
he was leaving, moving to Florida to go live with his father.
He thought it might be just the scene for him. After the phone
call, Caroline sank to her kitchen floor, collapsing on its faux
red brick linoleum (reminiscent of her childhood kitchen
floor). Great big sobs tore out of her, perhaps drifting out the
open living room window to the unsuspecting public on Front
Street. Her mother called as Caroline wiped her nose with her
sleeve. Their clipped conversation ended with Caroline
explaining that she had to go, that she had a cold.

Tim and Caroline spent their last days together. This surprised her, Tim's choice to be with her. He made her dinners. He told her that she didn't have to tell him her feelings if she didn't want to, but that he'd had hopes for them. Caroline had not said a word.

Tim left and Caroline began to hold back the odd numbered insurance claims. She did this once, twice, three times... and then she got fired. But before Tim drove off in his red van, he gave her his Gretsch guitar, saying he'd be back for it someday. She waited for one month, then two. She called her father in Oregon, asking if she could come live with him. He told her he didn't have the room. Didn't have the room. Caroline didn't want to go back home where she might interrupt her mother's 'finding of herself'. So she went the furthest she'd ever been from home, to Marion, and rented a small house on the back of a piece of property belonging to an elderly man named Jacob. She took the Gretsch guitar with her, her jewelry, the Hanged Man, and not much else. Caroline was twenty-seven-years-old when she came to live and work in Marion as a bill collector. She lived with her compulsions, fought them, and hid from the world as best she could for the next seven years.

part two

birth

Caroline was thirty-four years old and having a bad day, the kind accompanied by a cold fog and a bad case of PMS. Lacking for anything else to do, she attended a mediation session with her friend Sarna on that particular bad day. She did not really want to go, feeling a fool at the prospect of having to meditate with a group of women who probably knew how to do it. Sarna certainly knew. She seemed a natural at all kinds of deep, murky, transcendental stuff. On that bad day, Caroline seemed capable of only deep and murky. She knew it the moment she opened her eyes that morning and immediately felt like flinging her cat, curled up like a question mark against her leg, across the room. This was a familiar feeling: the savage need for all living things to go away. The feeling came the same time every month and sometimes in between as well. She could understand the PMS-related times, maybe stemming back to a woman's intuitive need to protect her body during her fertile window. As for the in-between times, Caroline had no explanation. She wished she wanted to connect, but lately only wanted, only needed, to connect with her TV. That, and a Baby Ruth bar each night, while in bed, while watching TV. She was a bit concerned about this needing so little, this lack of yearning. Also, Caroline felt as if she was walking through deep, hot sand everywhere she went on that bad day. She was tired, just so tired... eye-stinging, eye-rubbing tired.

Caroline went to meditate in spite of all of this. She found the place easily, not surprising, given Sarna's steadfast directions. It was in the center of a town, two or three blocks away from her own, in a small space above a sub shop. Upon climbing the two flights of stairs to the room, Caroline felt a freezing inside of her. There, behind the door, would be people. She paused and then went straight in. The people inside, only six of them, stopped their discussion and looked at her. Thankful for Sarna's long face peering around an older cross legged woman, Caroline found a space within the circle, but it was the bed in the corner that she really wanted. Introductions went around and instead of making an effort to absorb the names, Caroline noticed and thought on various peculiar things about the room: a Virgin Mary statue, a shelf of books that her fingers tingled to touch, a bowl of stones, and a lit candle in the middle of the circle. Caroline worried momentarily about a woman's feet resting just inches from the flame. Then it was her turn.

"Hi. I'm Caroline. I'm here tonight, because my friend, Sarna, over there, invited me." Caroline paused, glancing at the Virgin Mary statue, then continued. "And I thought it would be fun to try something new." There. She wondered for a brief second if she'd offered enough of herself in her introduction. Should she mention the PMS? Would the facilitator intuitively sense her murkiness? Would her mediation not count if she didn't particularly believe in the Virgin Mary? At least, thought Caroline, it was a comfort that the others looked so regular. No tinkling, dangling jewelry or flowing gowns here. Just jeans, t-shirts, and practical hair styles. Even the facilitator, Lila, could have been her co-worker or sister even. With a crisp white blouse and black pants, she sat just to Caroline's left and right on the floor with all the rest. Sarna had built Lila up so completely that Caroline half expected her to be floating in the middle of the circle with Godly beams of inspiration, light, and love radiating like an umbilical cord to each unworthy soul in the circle. If anything, it was all a bit interesting... so far.

The women were instructed to get comfortable and close their eyes. Caroline did so, wondering how long her folded up legs would take to go numb. Her eye lids began to twitch. She opened one eye a crack to make sure all other eyes were closed as well. Lila's voice was like a languid ocean breeze, and Caroline found herself curiously still as she listened. She was to imagine herself at the edge of an ocean. The water would be still, as if on a late summer evening. There would be a basket at her feet, brown and sturdy. It would be quiet except for the ebb and flow of a lazy current. She would be wearing a t-shirt, so the air could touch the skin on her arms... and jeans, and bare feet. The ebb and flow, the basket. Then, Caroline began to worry a bit. Should her feet be in the water? The sky sunny or gray? The wind blowing her hair or not? Caroline was rescued from her fretting when Lila said, "Let it be however you want, however you need it to be." But still. Well, there was the basket, oval and sturdy at her feet.

Next, the group was instructed to put their worries, their burdens, and their thoughts into the basket. Some time was given to accomplish this, but Caroline was not sure if she could. Her worries seemed like steamy blobs of colors plopping into the basket, blue-gray mists... sort of. She wondered if the others had actually labeled their worries. One might say "job," another "boyfriend," another "mother," or "father." Caroline's were indefinable. It would have to do, because now all baskets were to be floating out to sea. Bobbing, rocking. Going out, out, away, smaller and smaller. It was as if Caroline was watching a movie with the sound turned off. It really was quite peaceful, until Lila said, "Now imagine that God is taking that basket. Taking it up with him and taking care of everything that's inside." God? Who knew God would be here!? First the Virgin Mary and now God! But Caroline did her best to stay focused, and, well, a pair of arms *did* come down from up above and take her basket. "Now I would like you to be still. Just be still and see if you can notice any messages you may be receiving. These messages can come as thoughts, images, or even feelings. Let's take a moment." Now, Caroline's legs really were numb, her eyelids fluttering again. It wasn't until that moment that Caroline realized there was music playing, barely audible. Had it been playing the whole time? A lone flute echoed from somewhere in the room, stretching out its notes, climbing up, sliding down. Heartbreaking, lonely. The beautiful sound of solitude. Caroline lost track of time.

At some point, Lila said, "We're going to bring ourselves back now, slowly...feel your feet and how they rest upon the floor. Feel your legs (which Caroline could not). Feel your breath. Breathe in through our navel and out through your mouth. In, out. In, out. Hear the sounds around you.

Remember the people next to you, across from you. On the count of ten, open your eyes and take another deep breath." Lila counted backwards. On one, Caroline opened her eyes to find people stretching. Someone's knees cracked. Another still had her eyes closed. A woman across from her looked nice enough, pensive, smiling slightly. Sarna was studying her hands. Lila asked if anyone wanted to share. How did it feel? Did anyone receive any messages, any impressions? Everyone looked around mutely.

The woman whose feet could have lit on fire earlier volunteered. "It's funny, but I wasn't alone on the beach. There was someone next to me the whole time. When I looked, I saw that it was my friend who died of breast cancer last year. She was well, not sick, and she just stood there for the longest time. Until she bent down and picked up some sand and tossed it into the air. She never said a word."

Lila commented, "Interesting. What do you think that means?"

The women watched her with an affirming nod.

"I don't know," said the woman. More silence, more nods, encouraging smiles.

"Well," said Lila, "Hold onto that. It'll become clear to you when it needs to."

Lila turned toward Sarna. "And Sarna? Do you have anything to share?" For some reason everyone laughed.

"I don't know," she said. "I just saw the color purple. I don't know what that means."

"Do you know what the color purple represents?" Lila gently inquired. More nods. More stares. "It is the highest form of spirit. You were surrounded by spirit."

Sarna wrapped her arms around her knees, looking absently at the floor. More discussion followed.

One woman felt herself floating, another sinking. Caroline didn't venture to offer her visions or impressions, since she hadn't really had any. Thankfully, no one had pressed her. In the end, it seemed there had been no answers-- only questions... left hanging in the air above the circle like little bubbles blown by a child. Before the group disbanded to go their separate ways, Lila reminded everyone to watch for signs, notice the signs. A stop sign came to Caroline's mind, and a yield sign, triangular, bold, and yellow. What was she talking about? The women shared hugs while Caroline waited by the door for Sarna. Just as she and Sarna were about to leave, Lila came and thanked Caroline for coming and said casually, "It's no coincidence that you came tonight." Caroline couldn't help but feel that Lila was truly glad she'd come.

Out by their cars, Caroline and Sarna hugged. Caroline saw a man watching them from within the sub shop as he took a bite of his sandwich.

"That man probably thinks we're gay," said Caroline.

Sarna turned, smiled at the man, and waved. Turning back to Caroline, Sarna said, "Did you like it? Lila's great."

"It was nice. But I didn't really see anything or feel much."

"That's all right. Look at me. All I saw was purple."

"Well at least that's something. At least you got spirit."

"So do you," said Sarna, "Keep coming. You should come back next week."

Caroline thought that maybe she would. Before driving off into the night, Sarna waved her over. "Carly!" she called, "Do you know how to get home?"

"Yea. I think so."

"Are you sure?"

Snowflakes began to fall between them. "I'll be fine," said Caroline as she drove off.

Yet, driving home did not prove to be so easy. It had really begun to snow, and Caroline took the wrong turn off the rotary. It wasn't the snow that had distracted her, but the thought of breathing in through the navel and out through the mouth. Caroline was trying it out when she took the wrong turn. What was it supposed to feel like while breathing in through the navel? She knew, logically, that the technique was meant to relax, but it had simply unnerved her. The Native American flute, however, was nice. Caroline hit the scan button on her radio, looking for something to train her mind on. Her eyes were stinging again. And now, she was lost. She was thinking of stopping and getting directions when a stop sign suddenly peered out at her, barely visible through the thickening snow. Caroline punched on the brakes, and her back end slid out in one swift, silent movement. Caroline's car came to rest, looking back in the direction from where she had just come. An odd, high-pitched screech came out of her mouth just before the car had come to a stop. She knew it did, because she could still hear it. She'd had no idea she could make such a noise. The thought of it almost made her laugh as she drove forward, back toward the rotary, back toward home.

That night, by the blue luminescent light of the television, Caroline dozed. She was having watery beginnings of dreams. There was something moving there just behind her eyelids; something blue and shifting, soundlessly shifting. Something nonsensical, as dreams often are. A voice other than her own spoke within her, "Wake up!" She cracked an eye and noted the time, 11:11. Caroline absently registered that the TV was still on. One of those shows, Forensic Mysteries, was on. Caroline heard the words...fibers, trace amount, victim. Caroline sat up, feet to the cold floor, and made her round of the house, checking the locks one, two, three times, and once more for good measure before going to bed.

By day, Caroline worked at a collection agency, calling and harassing folks who owed Sears money from six, seven, eight months back and further. Their accounts were long overdue and stretched out like an old pair of sweat pants, their only interest in Caroline was to avoid her. Although the pressure was always on to collect, Caroline didn't mind their constant dodging, broken promises, and unreturned calls. Many of them would never, ever pay back. Many of them couldn't.

Some of them did... sometimes. But Caroline had the best record of return of anyone else in the office, mainly because she didn't push. She didn't demand. She understood about simply not being able to give. Caroline was often apologetic: "I'm sorry Mr. or Mrs. so and so; I know that things must be tough for you right now. Oh sure, just send along what you can, when you can." It truly was not a tactic. It was simply how she felt; sorry at having to impose herself into the lives of people who had momentarily, blissfully thought they might be able to afford something they really couldn't.

By night, Caroline made jewelry at home. She liked this, because it was both mindful and mindless at the same time. Thinking of the beads, their colors... sometimes opaque, sometimes icy... gave her something to think about. Arranging them into earrings, necklaces, and bracelets was akin to making a thought, an idea, a real, tangible thing. Each little bead a... nugget of satisfaction. Each piece of jewelry... a reality. Every couple of weeks, Caroline brought her creations, safely packed in an old brown briefcase, to a used book store in the harbor. The owner housed her jewelry in a small glass display case under the register. Some pieces sold, others didn't. Caroline sometimes wore her own jewelry, mostly the bracelets. She never wore the necklaces. She hated the feel of anything around her neck. It had always made her feel as if she couldn't breathe.

The used book store, aptly called The Used Book Store, was where Caroline met Sarna. Sarna was a clerk there, working part time, while working the other part of her time as journalist at the local paper. Sarna later became a notable journalist at the Globe in the city. Seven years ago, Caroline had gone into The Used Bookstore hoping they could order a book for her. She could have gone to one of the bigger stores, like "Borders", but she would have been overwhelmed by the sheer size of the place, by the crowds. The Used Book Store was just anonymous enough for her: kind of creaky and ghostly, not likely to house or even attract too many people at once. Sarna ordered Caroline's book with efficiency, without registering any unusual response, which relieved Caroline. They'd gotten into a discussion about a book they'd both recently read. Their discussion lasted long enough for it to be getting dark by the time Caroline left. She'd had to hurry back home.

The first time Caroline was in love was with her father, who smelled of sawdust and cigarettes. A woodworker by trade, he used to spend long evenings in his workshop, a dusty old room in the back of the barn. It was a curious place, with tools Caroline didn't understand. There was a big, rusty drum her father rigged into a wood burning stove, piped to the outside. On snowy winter nights, you could smell the smoke from the fire as it crept back into the workshop through the cracks in the window panes. A bulb hanging from the ceiling would swing as he walked by it, causing the shadows to move as if they were alive. She'd loved his purposeful movements and how he would talk to himself of measurements, of how this piece of wood could fit together with that piece of wood. Always, by the end of the night, his walk became more of a shuffle, his stance more of a wobble, his words more of a slur. His eyes shone with a wetness that Caroline always thought was brought on by her. She would do anything to dry his eyes. If that was love, then she loved him. It wasn't until Caroline grew older that she found out it wasn't her at all causing her father's tears, but the drink he had hidden in the bottom drawer of his work bench.

The second time Caroline was in love was with a neighborhood boy who could do the best pop-a-wheelies in the neighborhood and could chew bubble gum as long as she could. All the girls loved him, but not like Caroline. She was sure that none of the others dreamed of Bobby as she did. She memorized songs that she knew he liked: Van Halen and ZZ Top. Yet she never had the nerve to sing them around him. She wrote, "I love Bobby," on the back of her bookcase. He'd stuck up for her once when another neighborhood boy told her she had no ass. "Shut up," he said. "She has a nice ass." She really didn't. Caroline had always been thinner than oxygen. But Bobby saw her. He knew she was there. And if that was love, then she'd loved him.

The third time Caroline was in love was with Tim, whose voice was the most satisfying sound she'd ever heard. Her vision went blurry when she looked at him, frantic always to hear his voice on the other end of the line, saying that he was on his way over. Caroline knew that he did not love her, but she didn't care. Being able to hear him say her name, being able to smell his skin, and touch his blue denim shirt was enough for her. If that meant love, then she'd loved him. Sometimes Caroline would see a little nick-knack in a store that she would want to buy for him: a guitar Christmas ornament, or a small railroad crossing sign for his teeny-tiny shelf. She never bought those things, because she knew he wouldn't want anything from her, except for her occasional company. When he told her he was leaving, moving to Florida, she went to the Abby and bought him a St. Christopher pendant to protect him in his travels. She thought he would not accept it, or just take slight note of it, maybe even leave it behind before leaving her apartment the morning of his departure. Instead, he was truly surprised, even grateful. He'd asked her if she was Catholic, and it struck her how little they'd known of one another. "Yes," she'd said, "but I'm not really religious." He hung it on the rear view mirror of his red van and left her with his Grestch guitar, saying he'd be back for it someday. That someday never came.

After Caroline's first attempt at meditating, Sarna called her at work. "Are you coming to mediation tonight?"

"I don't know," said Caroline, trying to think of an excuse. She didn't like being out at night. It was a fluke that she'd gone last week; that she didn't remember she'd be out in the darkness.

"Come on. I'll come get you, and we can go together. Besides, you have to come. Lila gave me a message for you."

"For me?"

"Uh, huh. She said she was glad you came and that your toes are in the water."

"What? What does that mean?"

"Just come, alright? I'll be there at six o'clock."

So, Caroline hadn't had much choice. By the time Sarna arrived, Caroline had scoured the kitchen, cleaned the bathroom twice, disinfected all the door knobs, and locked, unlocked, and locked the doors and windows four times. She knew she was in trouble. Going to mediation could be disastrous, given her condition. She was remembering a time when, in college, she and her housemates were getting ready to go to The Depot, and Caroline couldn't step foot outside the dorm. After her housemates left, Caroline spent the night in the bathroom getting sick, breaking out in cold sweats. She then cried herself to sleep in her dorm room-- partly out of relief for not having to be out in the night, in the crowds, and partly out of sorrow for having missed another night out with the girls.

The book Caroline ordered that time was called <u>Obsessive Compulsive Disorder: There is Hope</u>. It was yet another attempt at helping herself. Before that, it was therapy, doctors, medication. None of it had worked. She was still afraid of the dark, still locked her windows and doors four times each night, still came to pieces around too many people, still needed small enclosed places like a blanket wrapping around her. She was the opposite of claustrophobic. She was habitual, redundant, her neural pathways firing again and again. Lock the door. Do it again, and again, and again, and again. Germ-phobia was not typically her thing but when she was feeling particularly anxious, her obsessive thinking migrated into new areas.

Sarna came as promised at exactly six o'clock and saw Caroline's pale face and shaking hands. "You're going to be fine," she said, "You're coming."

"I might throw up."

"Then, I'll pull over."

"I mean in meditation."

"There's a bathroom."

"But people will hear me."

"Then, run the faucet."

They went. Caroline did get sick, but it was in the car on the way there. At meditation she recognized a few women, especially the one whose friend died of cancer. And Lila, of course, and the Virgin Mary.

When they arrived, Lila hugged Caroline. Again, Caroline felt that Lila was grateful she'd come. But then again, Lila hugged everyone else as well... so who knew? Caroline noted Lila's credentials on the walls: a Masters Degree in psychology from Harvard, a certificate of completion from the Angelic Therapy Workshop, Reiki Master. If she was smart enough to attend Harvard, then why was she into all of this other hocus-pocus? Caroline was feeling cynical, even angry. Why had Sarna insist she come? The women took their places on the floor. Again, there was music playing softly: this time a woman's voice rising and falling with a soft echo. They were to say their names again. Maryanne was the one with the burning feet. Laura, the one with the dead friend. Caroline was the one with the fear of everything.

Again, there was to be more letting go of worries. This time they were to put their worries inside balloons. Let go. See them go up. You are in a field. Breathe in, out. In through the navel, out through the mouth. You are surrounded by a blue light, a white light, whatever color you want. See them go up, the balloons; they are dots now, specks, being taken care of. This time Caroline's worries were a little more specific. A lock was in one, the black of night in another. Her heart began to race because she didn't like being in a field, so she took herself and her balloons into a clearing in the woods. Her heart went from a gallop to a trot. But then one of her balloons got stuck in a branch and popped. Black-blue unfathomable darkness flowed upon her and her heart sped up like a freight train. She could not stay, so she ran out, leaving seven bewildered women behind. The bathroom in the hall was the best place for her to be, since she could not go out into the night. Sarna came in a moment later to find her in a ball on the floor. Sarna took her to the car. The ride home was mostly silent except for Caroline's apologies, and then Sarna's for having forced her to come.

Back at home, Caroline put towels on the windows so as to keep the night out, scrubbed her hands, and did the locks exactly four times. Sarna watched.

"I'm sorry," she said again.

"Sarna, it's my fault. And, besides, for punishment now you have to stay the night."

"I know. Because the house has been secured," said Sarna.

"And I can't break that," said Caroline.

"I know."

Before bed, Caroline scrubbed her hands again. This time little sores began to appear. Scrub. Scrub. Do it again. The sores felt good, like something inside her was trying to come out. Caroline took a Klonopin and lay in bed while Sarna settled on the couch. It felt good that someone was there. She wished Tim would show up for his Gretsch. She wished Bobby would show up at her door blowing bubbles. She wished she was in her father's workshop.

"Sarna?"

"Yes?"

"What do you think Lila meant when she said my toes are in the water?"

"I don't know. We'll think about it later."

"Sarna?"

"Yes."

"Why do you put up with me?"

"I like talking about books with you."

"Thank you. Good night."

"Good night."

Caroline's little house wasn't really hers. It belonged to an elderly man, Jacob, who lived in the main house on the front of the property. She rented it for $700.00 a month, which worked out since she only made $1,600.00 a month from her collections job. Some months she made more, depending on how much she was able to collect from the people who owed. Jacob had learned to leave her alone. One time he had come unannounced with his ladder to clean her gutters. Caroline was at her kitchen table, a small, sturdy thing with a red linoleum top, when she heard a scraping against the back side of the house. Startling like a cat, she jumped, sending beads of all colors to the floor, ran out the door, and hopped into her car. By instinct, she gunned it in reverse and immediately rammed into something behind her. Turning to see what she'd hit in a moment of surreal confusion, she saw that it was Jacob's pick-up truck there behind her, whose front end was now in a tangle with her bumper. Jacob had come running around the side of the house and found Caroline in her pajamas, apparently in such a rush to get out that she hadn't even looked behind her. From then on, he always called before coming over. When Caroline went back into the house, she'd forgotten about the beads strewn upon the floor. When her heels hit them, she fell hard to the floor on her hip. Those were among the prices she paid for all of her fears: a landlord's truck smashed up, a bruised hip, few friends, and a college career abandoned.

Caroline's memory of the mishap with Jacob's truck was strolling through her mind the day after her failed attempt at meditation. Caroline could not attend work that day, for her compulsions, those maddening, unwanted guests, had their claws in her. She had to tap the garbage can six times before opening it. She had to vacuum each section of the rug an even number of times before moving on to the next part. She had to sit down and stand up eight times, equal to the number of letters in her name, before finally coming to rest. Caroline laughed out loud. "I cannot take this anymore. I've got to do something," she sighed.

Later that day, Sarna called. "I think I know what Lila meant about your toes being in the water."

"Oh? What?" Caroline was reading a book by Stella Maze about a sister who was conceived for the purpose of donating her kidney to her older sister who had chronic kidney failure. Caroline was at a good part and wondering if she'd had a sister... could she take away her sickness, too?... when Sarna called.

"I think you're about to make some discoveries, you know, take a chance."

"Sarna, remember, I've done all that? I've been to counseling. Made peace with my father's drinking. Been to Al-Anon. Taken pills. Joined support groups. I don't know what else to do."

"Lila said she wants to see you. Just you and her. She's not like a regular therapist. She's..."

"Let me guess, quality," interrupted Caroline.

"Yes, quality."

"Okay, I'll try," said Caroline before hanging up. She went back to her book, to the good part. The part where the older sister has just found out her white blood cell count has gone up, and the younger sister has begun to question her existence.

The phones were driving Caroline crazy. It was only 8:50 in the morning, and already they were chirping like birds. "These phones are driving me crazy."

"It's only 8:30, pumpkin," said Barry, peering at her from his cubicle. "Let's go get a drink."

"I don't drink Barry, you know that."

"Maybe you should start."

"Are you saying I need to lighten up?"

"I didn't say it, you did."

"Well, I think I'm light enough. I only weigh ninety-seven pounds."

"Soaking wet," Barry quipped.

"How would you know?"

Caroline's phone rang. "Collections. Oh yes, Mr. Fitzgerald. Yes. Let me get up your account. One moment." Caroline tapped on the computer keys. "Okay, here we are. Yes. I see you're late on your last installment. Are you able to pay anything at this time? ...Oh, okay... I see...you've had a death in the family...your son? Oh, no. Yes, I completely understand...I am so sorry. Oh my gosh... Yes, please take your time." Caroline hung up.

Barry's voice came from behind the cubicle wall. "You actually believe that crap?"

"Why shouldn't I? Maybe it's true."

"I hear that all the time. My son died, my mother died. One time a woman told me she was in a car accident and had her leg amputated."

"Maybe she did," returned Caroline.

"No. I know the woman, went to high school with her. I saw her a few days later jogging in the park."

"Oh, well," she said, "People get desperate." Turning back to the computer, Caroline stared at Mr. Fitzgerald's overdue account. She arrowed up to the box she was looking for, the one that said 'satisfied', clicked, and watched Mr. Fitzgerald's worries disappear.

"I took a chance today," said Caroline on the phone with Sarna from work that day.

"Oh?"

"I deleted a man's account whose son died."

"Deleted it?"

"Well, I felt bad for him, because his son just died and couldn't make his payment. I just felt like helping him out, so I did. I lied. I told the computer that his account was satisfied. The whole thing, $7,500.00 worth."

"Jeez, Carly. That's not the kind of chance I was talking about. Besides, you actually believe that crap?"

"Well, people do die, you know."

Speaking of death, Caroline had yet to experience any in her thirty-four years of life-- except if you count the death of your parents' marriage, or the death of friendships, or the death of a college dream. When she came home from work the day she deleted Mr. Fitzgerald's account and couldn't find her cat, Dart, she was beside herself with confusion. Why isn't Dart sitting at the window? Why isn't Dart waiting at the door for me? Why is Dart's cat food still in the bowl? Why isn't Dart coming to me? Then, there was the question of what to do with him once she found him...still as a teapot, not yet put on to boil, lying on her bed. Do I wrap him up in a bag, a blanket, a box? Do I bury him, just as he is with his long, gray fur with the little white patches? How deep the hole? What will I do without Dart tucked into the crook of my legs at night? What will I do when I don't have to remove him from the sink each time before I brush my teeth? In the end, she called Jacob who came bumping down the road in his pick-up truck with a shovel clanging in the back. He came in with a pillowcase printed with little fading blue flowers and left with Dart. The pillowcase would be Dart's coffin, she surmised. It was fitting, seeing as though what he loved most was to sleep. She could hear Jacob digging out in the woods: the clanging of metal against rock or root, the muted thud of dirt hitting the ground. She couldn't look. She wished she didn't have to hear either. She sat and listened to every last shovel-full.

Later that day, Sarna called Caroline wanting to know if she could go see Lila on Saturday at ten in the morning.

"Saturday?"

"Yes. She sees clients individually on Saturdays."

"Oh, so I'm a client now?"

"Well, not yet."

"Besides, I can't. My cat just died."

Sarna had given Caroline Dart as a kitten years ago, so that she could have some company. They both laughed and cried at the same time. At least the appointment would be during daylight hours.

Caroline got to Lila's without incident. She was having one of her better days, despite Dart's dying. Something about it had made her feel free, as if death frees you up somehow. The ground was slushy, the air cold but new, as if in early spring. The hem of her skirt became wet from the slushy puddles. She climbed the stairs up to the top floor and passed the bathroom she had crouched in only days before. Caroline caught a glimpse of her reflection in the bathroom mirror. Her long sugar-cinnamon hair had gone wild, waving in frizzy ribbon-candy lengths away from her face. Her cheeks were flush from the cold and her long black pea coat gave her the appearance of an eccentric Bostonian, or a homeless person--depending on your frame of mind. Although the band aids on her hands from the ceaseless scrubbing in the days prior may have indicated the latter. Caroline put her hands in her pockets, but then took them back out again, thinking that Lila might hug her. Lila did hug her, that neutral kind of hug where only the upper parts of your bodies touch. Caroline noticed how beautiful Lila was, with shoulder length bouncy black hair sweeping away from her face... and a big toothy smile, but not too big. Everything about her was crisp, from her white pressed cotton shirt to

68

her black pants, to her porcelain teeth. She could have been of some Spanish or Portuguese heritage, but not quite.

"I'm so glad you could come," said Lila.

"Me, too," replied Caroline, although she wasn't so sure now. What was she supposed to say? Was she supposed to just come out with all her problems? Instead, she apologized. "I'm really sorry for the other night. I just... It was just..."

"It's okay," said Lila kindly. "There's no judgment here."

They sat down across from each other. Caroline wished, again, that she could lie on the bed in the corner. That way she could talk without having to actually look at her. "I have OCD and anxiety, and I think I've done everything I can about it. Nothing's helped. I suppose you think you can help me," blurted Caroline.

"Well, I think I could."

"How?"

"We can talk about it. I also offer hypnotism and Reiki services. We can work on affirmations, meditation techniques, changing your archetype. Things like that."

These terms were as confusing to Caroline as the tools in her father's long ago workshop.

"We can talk a little today. Maybe next time do some Reiki. Do you know what that is?"

"I haven't a clue."

"It's an ancient Japanese technique that's been alive for thousands of years. It's a laying on of hands of sorts where I channel energy into various parts of your body, clear out energy blockages and balance your chakras." Caroline had heard of chakras, although from where, she could not now remember. They had something to do with invisible little metropolises of energy within the body. Lila was explaining all of this, about how different metropolises can become veritable ghost towns, others booming at full speed like New York City on New Year's Eve. "An overloaded chakra or under functioning chakra can cause physical pain, mental or emotional pain, and overall unbalance."

Caroline had to admit that she was unbalanced. She suddenly felt like a dirty dish towel in a gleaming kitchen. "Can I lay down in that bed over there?"

"Sure."

Caroline lay on top and looked up. A crystal hanging in the window caused triangles of light to dance across the ceiling. "I'm afraid of everything."

"Everything?"

"Well, not everything. Mostly... the dark, people, wide open spaces, anything that threatens to take me out of my cocoon."

They talked about her reactions, her securing of the home, her compulsions, the things she has missed out on: dances, proms, college, things she didn't even know she was missing out on. Caroline didn't mention the sores on her hands, but she did tell her about how the jingling of the janitor's wallet chain at work fills her with a sense of panic and fear that she can't explain. She told her about how the sound of a bird's call fills her with a loneliness that stretches so far back that she loses its thread. Caroline told her about

70

her father, who is now sober, who always had a gentle quality, even in his drinking days...and about her mother who lives alone in a row house on Beacon Street who is, at times, as strange to her as Caroline is to herself. She didn't tell her about Dart. Caroline asked, "Could my past really have caused all of my issues?"

"Yes. They could have. Sometimes there's more to a past than you know about at this time."

Caroline didn't know what to say to that, so she asked, "What you said before about my toes being in the water. What did you mean?"

"You'll see in time."

"I won't drown, will I?"

"No. We'll make sure you know how to float on your back."

Before leaving, Caroline made an appointment for the following week. They'd do some Reiki and talk some more. Also, Caroline was given homework. She was to practice meditation using a CD Lila gave her for ten minutes a day. She was also given an assignment to discover her archetype, or as Lila explained, the deep rooted image that she portrays to the world. Again, before leaving Lila said, "It is no coincidence that you have come here.", and "Watch for signs." And then, one last thing; "Did you know you're not alone? There's a cat with you. Came in with you, and he's leaving with you right now," she said with an amused smile.

That night, Caroline dreamt again. This time it had something to do with a small, round-faced boy who she was chasing through a crowd of people. She was on Blanchard

71

Drive, her old stomping grounds. The crowd was oblivious to her frantic attempt to reach the boy, whose little black jacket was now nothing but a distant patch dodging about in the thick of the crowd. The boy was getting further away, and she was getting further behind. A man strolled peacefully in front of her. A family with three small children clamored beside her. The children pulled a little red wagon behind them. She realized then, in her dream, that it was a parade she was in, a Halloween parade. Some woman wore a face mask made of colorful feathers. A child was dressed up as a cat. The round faced child was out of sight, and Caroline heard a commotion far ahead. People were exclaiming, rushing up ahead to the right, like a river twisting away from her. She followed the crowd and found that it led to a cliff. The people were peering over it. They were talking about what a shame it was. What a shame that the boy had gone over; the small round-faced boy.

Caroline woke with a start. Something had made her wake... some sort of dream. Just a few little scraps of it floated in her mind. There was something about a black jacket and falling; something about colorful feathers. Maybe it wasn't the dream that had woken her. Maybe it was the soft thud that she could have sworn she heard, the one that sounded like Dart's paws hitting the floor, jumping off the bed. She looked at the clock. It was 11:11. Time to check the locks, again.

Caroline was thinking of signs, her archetype, her mother, Sarna, jewelry, and for some reason of Jacob when she was really supposed to be thinking of nothing. That's what the meditation CD told her anyway. Think of nothing. No thoughts, which to Caroline, seemed like a contradiction. Even thinking of not thinking was a thought. The man on the CD sounded like what Caroline imagined God would sound like. He said that at first having no thoughts would be difficult. So, in the beginning, simply hold onto the spaces in between your thoughts. Stay in those spaces for as long as you can, he instructed; which, for Caroline, was approximately one point two seconds. Thinking of this one point two second thoughtless window made her think of the number eleven, which caused her to remember that she'd woken up from a dream at exactly 11:11 twice in a week. Caroline's eyes snapped open from her pseudo-meditation. Was this a sign?

However, Caroline had decided that this was nothing more than a coincidence, even after she'd gone out the next day to deliver more jewelry and collect her check for her portion of jewelry sales in the amount of eleven dollars. She had also decided that Sarna must have told Lila about Dart. They were, after all, friends of sorts and e-mailed each other from time to time. But why would Sarna care to tell Lila about her dead cat? Questions kept revealing themselves like fireflies in the night.

"Barry? What sort of person do you think I am?" asked Caroline from behind the walls of her cubicle.

"What?"

"You know. If you had to, say, categorize me, what category would you put me in?"

"Oh, God. I don't know. Let me think about it, and I'll get back to you, okay?"

She asked Sarna and got the answer she expected: good friend...loyal friend...creative...blah, blah, blah. It wasn't the answer Caroline was looking for. Truth is, she didn't know what type of answer she was looking for, but she trusted that when she found it; she'd know. She called her mother and asked her.

"Independent. Resourceful. Creative. A little lost maybe," Rose said.

"Lost?"

"Yes, but who among us isn't, dear?"

She called her father and asked him. He paused and answered as expected: intelligent, sweet, smart, strong. Caroline chastised herself for asking him. What did he know of his daughter? Caroline wished she knew more people. She wished she knew someone who knew her better that she knew herself. She would have liked to have asked Jacob, but he already thought she was weird. No need to add fuel to that fire. Maybe that was her archetype...weird girl... weird, lost, girl. She was getting closer.

That night, Caroline tried again. This time she sat cross legged, whereas before she had lain on her bed. Perhaps sitting upright would cause her thoughts to run down and out of her head. She put the God voice CD on and followed the instructions. You are in a bubble, a luminescent bubble. Nothing can get in. Nothing. Your thoughts are not enough to penetrate the bubble. It is too strong. It is just you and nothing else. Rest in this space, this gap, this exquisite space. Caroline began to feel something. Something close to nothing. It felt as if her head was not attached to her body, and she held on to that word. Nothing. Just that one word. Although it was a thought, it was just one, and not five. Her real thoughts were shadows prowling the perimeter of her bubble, but they could not get in. This space was hers alone, so nothing, so simple. In an instant, the bubble was pierced by the ringing of the phone, and Dart, who was not really there, leaped from her lap. "Hello?"

"Ah... Caroline?"

"Yes?"

"This is Jacob. I'm sorry to bother you, but I need some help here. Seems I've fallen, and I'm in a lot of pain. Can't get up."

"I'll be right there," she said.

After unlocking her door and sprinting up the driveway and around the corner, Caroline realized it was dark, a smothering, never-ending, silent darkness that was just light enough to let you see the figures of trees and just quiet enough to let you hear a noise that could sound like footfalls. She turned on her heels, ready to run back home or to her car, then turned back toward Jacob's house. She ran as if her life depended on it. She began to breathe sharply and could hear either her blood thumping in her ears or footsteps somewhere behind her. She heard something like a chain snapping. Or was that her sharp, almost asthmatic breathing? Caroline made a screaming noise, lost her footing, and came down on something sharp, onto her knee. There was no pain, nothing. She thought of that word, nothing, got up, and ran.

It was quiet inside Jacob's house. Caroline had only been in the house once when she had answered his ad for the rental of the small house she lived in now. Jacob was quiet that time, soft spoken, with olive green eyes and steady hands. She could tell that he was a man of ritual: a ritualistic coffee drinker, newspaper reader, using the same coffee mug and spoon each morning, placing his coat on the same hook each day kind of man; a slippers under the bed, dressing in his casual Sunday best everyday kind of man. She did not know if these things were so, but she liked to think so. Entering his house that first time had made her uneasy. Tonight it was her island. The only sound she could hear upon entering was the ticking of a clock. She called his name, "Jacob?"

"Here! I'm in the bathroom!"

Caroline approached. "Jacob?"

"It's okay. Come in. I'm decent."

She went in and saw that he was on his side on the floor, his eyes pinched up tight against the pain.

"I think it's my hip," he managed.

"Do you want to try to get up?" Caroline came behind him and tried hoisting him up, but it was no use. The pain was too great.

"I thought you could maybe help me by getting me up, getting my wife's cane that she used to use. In the basement. But, it's no use. It's my hip."

"I'll call an ambulance. I'll wait here with you," she said.

The ambulance came for Jacob. Caroline watched them take him out on a stretcher, his head bobbing along as the men carefully hoisted him down the walk into the ambulance. It struck her how alone he was... so alone... just like her, standing stupidly in his house.

She shouldn't have. She knew she shouldn't, but she did anyway. Caroline wandered about Jacob's house looking in rooms; looking at things, his things, his books. She saw Classics like Moby Dick and Treasure Island and Shakespeare and Little Women. She opened that one and saw that it was inscribed: "For Gretta"... perhaps it was for his late wife, or someone else. The pages had been worn up to a certain point, and then afterward not at all. She saw fishing and boating magazines and a calendar which said "Library" on the first of February, which was only a few days away. Caroline ventured upstairs. The steps were as creaky as she thought they would be, the railing as solid and sturdy as Jacob himself, as he used to be. Once upstairs, she saw an empty room, a bedroom with a twin bed, and another bedroom with a shirt hanging on the bedpost. There were pictures on the dresser: one of a laughing woman at the beach, another of a little girl on a tire swing. A third photo showed the same girl as the one on the tire swing, maybe thirteen or fourteen years old, smiling brightly with long, brown ringlets of hair hanging limply by her face. For some reason, Caroline became dizzy and she stepped away from the dresser. Back downstairs, she locked the front door and proceeded into the basement. There, she found a table saw, a jig-saw, and little plastic drawers full of nails. A lonely workbench to her left caught her eye. Hammers hung on the wall above it, arranged precisely in order from large to small. An unwelcome shadow passed through Caroline's heart. She crossed over to the workbench, running her hand along its surface. Her hand came away with a fine powdering of sawdust. She opened the drawer at the bottom of the workbench and found there a bottle of whiskey, its rusty contents sloshing back and forth. Feeling like an intruder, Caroline went back upstairs. But her snooping didn't stop there. Inspecting Jacob's collection of videos (he had no DVD's), she found one titled "Gretta" in faded handwriting. Caroline went so far as to pop it in the VCR. She went so far as to watch it. Caroline watched a little girl growing up from event to event: a birthday party, birthday candles being blown out, a man's voice in the background, Jacob's, calling, "Come on Mumma. Get in the picture. I want my two little women in this one." A woman's voice came next, laughing. A Christmas enfolded, many years ago: a Hippity-Hoppity, a Light Bright, a Cabbage Patch Doll. Another Christmas came, this time with Gretta older, surrounded by a flurry of wrapping paper, putting on her new roller skates. This was before roller blades, before cell phones, before I-Pods.

"Daddy, help me up. I can't get up." Laughter. A hand reaching out, pulling her up. The tape went black. No more. No more birthdays or Christmases. Caroline rewound the tape, back past all of this. Back to the beginning.

No one had called Caroline on Mr. Fitzgerald's account. Then, that could take some time. Book-keeping would be done, accounts cross referenced... eventually. Caroline would lose her job, she knew. She just wasn't sure she cared.

One morning, Barry found her in the break room getting coffee. "Okay pumpkin, I've figured it out."

Caroline looked up from her mug. "What's that?"

"Your category."

She returned to stirring in the cream. "Do tell."

Barry inhaled deeply. "You are somewhat uptight. Probably a real bitch at times. But sweet, somehow. Very mysterious, kind of scared. But of what I don't know. And I think, but I'm not sure, that you can show some real balls when you need to, sometimes when you don't really need to either."

Caroline stared mutely at him, blinking. "Wow, Barry. You've really given this some thought."

He stood just across from her now, and she saw that he could be handsome, could have been handsome, once. She wanted to step back but couldn't; the counter was right behind her. It was littered with empty sugar packs, coffee stains and sticky stirring sticks.

"I'll have to think about it, your rendition of me, and I'll get back to you."

"How about over a drink with me tonight? I mean a coffee or a dinner or something."

"I can't. I have to take care of my neighbor, my landlord. He's disabled." He stepped closer. "I don't know Barry. I'll think about it and let you know."

Back at her desk, Caroline called Sarna from work. "Did I get you at a bad time?"

"No. I can chat for a minute. Jeez. I was just assigned a piece about a local beauty pageant for children. How disgusting. This is one I am not looking forward to."

"Better you than me. Listen Sarna, I need your advice. Barry, you know Barry, just asked me out on a date."

"A date? Then go!"

"But, Sarna, he's not quality!"

"So what! It's something to do. Think of it like practice. Go. How long has it been for you anyway? Five years?"

"Seven."

"God. You better accept. Go tell him yes, and then call me right back."

Caroline called back a few moments later. "Okay we're going to The Path. I'm supposed to meet him there at six o'clock. I don't know if I'll be able to do it, Sarna. It'll be dark. There'll be tons of people."

"Okay, so I'll be there, too. I'll go and sit at the bar."

"The whole time?"

"The whole time."

"You'll get drunk."

"That's okay. I'll need it after this whole exploiting-children-in-the-name-of-fame-and-beauty thing."

It wasn't a lie that Caroline had to help her landlord. He was still in the hospital, but she had to take his mail in for him and water his plants. Caroline did these things and got ready for her date. The Path was a casual restaurant with a bar in the center. Caroline wore her cream blouse, khaki trousers, and black chunky heeled shoes. She took half a Klonopin as insurance: against panic attacks, against date abandonment and cracked up cars. She decided to leave early, at four o'clock, before it had gone completely dark. She would meet Sarna at the bar shortly thereafter. Once there, Sarna would sip her martini, and Caroline would sip her coke-except that it wasn't just a coke the bartender gave her, but a rum and coke.

"Send it back," said Sarna.

"No. Maybe I'll just sip on it. Besides, I'm feeling really jittery. Maybe this will help."

"Carly! That's not like you one bit!"

"I know. Honestly, I don't know what is like me anymore. You know, the other day I snooped around my landlord's house."

"Oh, please. That is so something I would do. Didn't you know that everyone snoops?"

"They do?"

"Hell, yes! What did you find?" asked Sarna, as she ordered her second drink.

"The most interesting thing is that I found out he has a daughter."

"Why is that so interesting?"

"I don't know. I really don't know why it intrigues me so. Her name is Gretta, or was Gretta. I don't know. I think she's not alive anymore."

"How can you know that?"

"Just some little clues here and there... and a gut feeling, I guess."

Caroline realized that there were people pressing in on either side of her.

"I'm ordering you another drink," said Sarna.

"Is my discomfort that obvious?"

"Yes."

"Great, then how am I supposed to make it through a whole date?"

Barry came right at six o'clock. He actually looked nice with a curly head of brown hair that almost made him look intelligent. He wore glasses, too, which surprised Caroline. Had he always worn glasses?

"I wear these at night, to drive," he announced, moving to take them off.

"No. Leave them on. They look nice," Caroline said, touching his wrist.

They sat at a table and ordered drinks: he a beer, she another rum and coke.

"I thought you didn't drink?"

"Just for tonight," she said.

"Lucky me."

"Shut up," she said, slapping his hand.

Things were going well. Caroline learned that Barry was divorced. His ex-wife turned out to be gay. She and her partner were actually living together in Barry's pre-divorce house. Barry had once been a finance major, and then an accountant, but had fallen into a deep depression after his divorce. He'd lost his job, been unemployed for a year, and gotten the job at the collection agency as a way to get back on his feet.

"Are you back on your feet now?" asked Caroline.

"If you call living in an apartment, making minimum payments on credit card bills, and taking anti-depressants back on your feet... then yes."

"Is that better than a year ago?" she asked.

"Well yeah. I can go out on dates now. That's something."

"And you go out on dates a lot, I suppose."

"Just once in a while with a girl from the office," he said, smiling.

Caroline offered little of herself; just that she lived alone, hadn't finished college because it "wasn't her scene," made and sold jewelry as an aside, and that her parents were divorced. Somewhere in there Barry had ordered her another rum and coke, which she promptly drank. She glanced at the bar, but did not see Sarna. She ate. She talked. She listened. At some point, she noticed a Christmas tree in the corner. It had colored lights.

"Isn't it strange that they haven't taken their tree down yet?" she asked. She told him how she doesn't get a tree for her own place. "What's the use if my father lives in Oregon? The only thing my mother does is go out with weird artsy-fartsy Bostonian friends on Christmas to bizarre expensive restaurants."

"You don't have any siblings?"

"No. I'm an only."

They were quiet for a moment. Caroline noticed they were holding hands across the table but couldn't remember the act of their hands coming together. She scanned the place again for Sarna but found no trace of her. Barry talked. Caroline listened. She talked: about what she no longer knew. They were up and dancing now, on a small, square dance floor that she hadn't known was there. The song they danced to was by Linda Ronstadt... "Blue Bayou." The dance floor was crowded and dark, except for the lights on the Christmas tree: blue, yellow, green. Caroline and Barry were right next to the tree when he put his hands on her shoulders. She stammered backward, into the tree, the needles pricking into her, the little lights hot against her neck. Barry came for her... or at her... coming toward her with a shocked little smile that could have been a tight, angry grimace. His hair, a moment ago soft, brown and curly, was now blonde like the yellow lights on the Christmas tree, flopping over one eye.

"Jake!" yelled Caroline, "Jake!"

The room was dark, so very dark. Caroline sat upright and everything twisted around her. It was as if she was looking through a telescope at the edge of the Grand Canyon or the top of the Empire State Building, panning back and forth. Only it was just her room, and she was sitting still. She needed to get up to check the locks.

"Carly? It's me. It's Sarna. I'm here. Can I come in?" announced Sarna from beyond the bedroom door.

"Yes," croaked Caroline, "What time is it? Where is my voice?"

"It's 12:00."

"A.M.?"

"P.M. actually, and your voice is scratchy, because you were, you were, um..."

"What?"

"Kind of screaming... a lot."

Caroline touched her neck. It hurt there. Screaming? When? Why? "Oh, God." She flopped back down on the bed and fell to the bottom of the Grand Canyon, jumped off the Empire State Building.

"Carly? Maybe you shouldn't drink ever again "

"It also doesn't help that I took a Klonopin before I left."

"God, Carly!"

"What? It was only a half!" Caroline pulled her pillow over her head and moaned, "What day is it?"

"Saturday."

"Oh God, no. Saturday?"

It was Saturday. It was Saturday, and Caroline had a hangover. It was Saturday, and Caroline had to get out of bed because she had an appointment with Lila at two o'clock.

"I'll call her and cancel it," said Sarna.

"You're not going to make me go?" managed Caroline.

"No. I'm not going to make you do anything anymore. Every time I do, it turns into a disaster."

"Well then, since you're not making me go, I'll go. Maybe then it won't turn into a disaster," said Caroline.

Sarna drove slowly. They stopped to get coffee. Sarna swore that it settled a hung over stomach. To Caroline's surprise, it did. It didn't, however, do much for her headache or her sore throat.

"Tell me what happened," said Caroline.

"Are you sure you want to know?" Sarna asked with a sideways glance.

"Yes."

"Do you remember falling into the Christmas tree?"

"Oh... Now I do."

"Okay, well, then you kind of started flailing around."

"Flailing?"

"Barry was trying to help you up."

"Oh, God. Barry," said Caroline, burying her face in her hands.

"You were sort of kicking at him."

"No. Please don't tell me I kicked him."

"And hit and slapped."

"What the hell is wrong with me? What the hell... I have never been assaulted. Never been raped. Why would I react that way? Why?"

"What about your parents?"

"Sarna, I've been through all this. All of it. I've seen three different shrinks. I've been over my past. Over it and over it. I mean, yeah, my parents weren't happy together. My father drank too much, but he was never violent. Never. My mother was remote, sure. But I don't see how those things can cause me to be so fucked up."

"Maybe it was just the booze and the Klonopin."

"Yea."

They drove in silence for a while.

"What about back at home. Was I ... okay?"

"Not so bad. You kept holding onto your neck and would only let go to lock and unlock the doors and windows."

"Four times?"

"Well, no, you actually wanted to do it eleven times, but you only made it to three before you passed out.   I did the rest for you."

"Hm. I'm surprised at the eleven. Usually, I only like even numbers."

They drove the rest of the way in silence. Before getting out of the car to go upstairs to Lila's, Caroline asked, "Did you tell Lila about Dart?"

"Why the hell would I tell Lila about Dart?"

"Forget it," said Caroline before turning.

"Oh, Carly, I forgot to tell you one more thing."

"Can I handle it?" asked Caroline.

"I don't know," replied Sarna.

"Lay it on me."

"You kept calling Barry 'Jake'."

"Who the hell is Jake?" hollered Caroline, as she slammed the door.

"There is something wrong with me. There is something very wrong with me," Caroline complained to Lila. She told Lila everything from the drinking to the Christmas tree, ending with Jake... whoever he was. She told her about her attempts at meditating and her search for her archetype. They carried on that way talking for nearly an hour. Most likely it was the Klonopin and the alcohol, Lila reassured her. But Caroline couldn't help feeling that Lila was holding something back, that there was something dangerous there; something only Lila was privy to. Lila had Caroline lay down on the bed for Reiki. She put on music; something heavenly and beautiful. Lila asked for permission to lay her hands upon her. Caroline said that was fine, just not on her neck. She didn't like being touched there. This lasted a long time; starting at her head, down to her forehead, her eyes and ears. Lila's hands hovered above her throat and Caroline could feel the heat of her hands. Next, Lila went down to her heart, solar plexus, abdomen, legs, and feet. Caroline began to feel herself uncoil. She drifted off. In her semi-conscious state, she heard movement about her: the rustling of Lila's shirt as she moved, the music, breathing. Caroline saw nothing but blackness, and she wasn't afraid.

"What did she say?" asked Sarna on the way home.

"She said it was the booze and the Klonopin, but it seemed like there was more."

"What do you mean?"

"I don't know. Like she knew more than she was telling me. Like she knew something I did not."

"She is very intuitive, you know," said Sarna.

"I'm beginning to figure that out. When will I know? When will I know what I'm supposed to know?"

"When you're ready," said Sarna.

Caroline told her about the Reiki. "You know... I really, really liked it."

"You do look better."

"Hey," said Caroline, "my throat and my head don't hurt anymore!"

"Now we know two cures for hangovers. Coffee and Reiki," said Sarna. They laughed.

"What will I do about Barry?"

"Well, I actually may have taken care of that for you already."

"What do you mean?"

"He called on my cell phone while you were in with Lila."

"How did he get your number?"

"I gave it to him when we were leaving The Path. Don't be mad at me, Carly. He was worried about you. He wanted to take you home himself, but I told him no. That I was a friend of yours, knew where you lived. He was very concerned. I gave him my cell number, and he gave me his. He just wanted to know how you were doing."

"What did you tell him?"

"I told him you aren't used to drinking and that it affected you badly."

"What did he say?"

"He said he'd figured as much. He doesn't want you to feel bad about what happened."

They rode quietly along. "You know, Carly, he's not a bad guy. I think he may even be quality."

Caroline decided to let the Barry thing be, at least for the time being. She needed to go home. She needed to be alone for a while. She needed to get Jacob's mail and, although his plants were probably fine, she just wanted to check them. Damn-it-all, she just wanted an excuse to be in his house. A cold snap had settled in, encasing the world in a fragile glaze of ice crystals. Caroline walked gingerly up the steps onto the porch. The only audible sound was the crunching of her feet upon the frozen film of amazing, miraculous, little crystalline structures; thousands and thousands of them under just one foot. She loved this time of year best. Its beauty could be so stunning... its ugliness so damning.

Once inside, she locked the door, made herself a cup of coffee. She figured that's probably what Jacob would be doing if he could. She sat at his kitchen table, which turned out to be an exact replica of her own, or hers of his, depending which way you thought of it. She went upstairs after a time and stood in the empty room, wondering why it was empty and what it once was. She peered in the small closet and found only two wire coat hangers which clinked against one another and came to rest again. The next room was the one with the twin bed. It was made up with a plain, white cotton bed spread. Caroline pulled back a corner of it and saw that the sheets had a small, blue flower print, the same as the pillowcase used to bury Dart. In Jacob's room, she looked at the pictures again. There they were smiling as before at that timeless beach; grinning in frozen momentum. Jacob's shirt was still on the bed post and, because it was cold, she put it on. She went down into the basement again and saw the trail her fingerprints had left behind on his workbench days before. She saw the bottom drawer but already knew what was in it. Caroline wondered if Jacob had any family, but it seemed like he didn't. A desk was against the far wall that she hadn't noticed before. There, she found some bills, a clean ashtray, and a vertical organizer with slots full of manila file folders. Every one of them was marked "Gretta." She took two files and went upstairs. The fireplace came to life as she turned it on and settled onto the couch, pulling a blanket up over her. She imagined that his wife would have wanted the gas fireplace, which Jacob would have given to her, although his choice would have been a real wood burning one. Caroline opened a file, and there she saw thirty, maybe forty, print-outs of Gretta, all the same; all exactly the same: her brown ringlets hanging down, her smile, one after another after another. At the bottom of each one it read:

Gretta Stills
Age 14: Last seen February 25th, 1978
Wearing: Blue Parka, Blue Snow-pants
Porter Park, Marion, Massachusetts
Green eyes: 5'2" tall: Birth Mark Left Shoulder
Please Contact Marion Police Dept.
Or Missing Persons Division

She knew this, or she knew it was something like this... the reason why Jacob once had a daughter but didn't anymore. Still, that word, "missing," was so shocking, so stark. "Missing" is, must be, worse than death; Death, a relief... "missing," a black hole, or a bottomless ocean, or a never ending night. Caroline began to cry. She cried for every stupid thing: for last night, for her silly little problems, for her father and her mother, for her cat, for Jacob, and for Gretta.

Caroline fell asleep that way, crying, right on Jacob's couch as the fire place hissed softly. She fell into a dream. This one found her in a field. There, she sat cross legged with tall, yellow grass reaching up to her shoulders. A breeze tickled the blades, pushing a strand of hair across her face. Although she yearned to move it away, she dared not stir... for ahead, hopping playfully about, were two birds; one blue, one yellow. She kept her eye trained on them, so as not to lose sight of them. They chittered, chattered, and clicked, bursting forth and then hopping back. Blue chided Yellow and Yellow turned her back on him. Blue circled around to face her, and they made up, pecking at seeds on the ground. Caroline willed them to her. She needed them to come to her. She needed those wild little things like water or air. One moment they would hop two steps closer, the next three steps back A burst of wind came, twisting the grass violently about. Blue and Yellow squawked, fluttering up and away from her another three feet. She willed harder as the grass settled. Another gust came on the heels of the first, more angry this time, bringing with it a sudden and surprising cluster of tall, gray clouds. Her hair whipped around her, rising in protest, covering her mouth, face, eyes. Through the strands of hair, yellow as the grass, she could see Blue and Yellow rising up, up, further, further... glowing blue and yellow specks against the black sky.

"I'll have to let them go." Caroline woke herself up with these words. Or it could have been the hissing of the fireplace that woke her, or the alarm clock chiming somewhere very, very far away. Disoriented, Caroline sat up and the pieces came to her: fireplace, couch, Jacob.. Jacob's house. She stood up, certain she had heard an alarm clock or something like it. She strained to hear, but it had stopped. It was a familiar sound, though. Her mind tried to place it, the way one might try to place the face of someone familiar. She stood there and let that come to her, too. The sound that she knew she'd heard. Caroline walked up the stairs and entered the empty room. She opened the closet and gently touched the wire coat hangers. They played against one another, clinking, chiming then fell silent again.

"I've decided that I don't care," said Caroline to Sarna on the phone the next day.

"About what?"

"About Barry. Or about what I'll say to him tomorrow or about how to act."

"That's probably best."

"I mean, it's so silly to torture myself over something as stupid as a date gone badly when there are far, far worse things in the world like people... kids... going missing."

"There you go," said Sarna.

"But... what am I going to say?" asked Caroline.

"You'll figure it out."

Caroline marched into work the next day with a purpose; which was to appear self-assured, undisturbed. But as soon as she saw Barry pouring himself a coffee in the break room, she escaped into the girl's room and breathed in deeply, out slowly, so as to calm her racing heart. In through the navel, out through the mouth. Or was it in through the mouth, out through the navel? On her way to her desk, she realized that her hands were shaking and her mouth was dry. She sat at her desk and shuffled papers around with no recognition of what she was really doing. She could hear Barry's voice on the other side of the cubicle wall. He was on the phone talking quietly and chuckling. It was a personal call, she knew. She would have liked to have crawled under her desk, thinking that he may have been chuckling at her expense... probably talking about the stupid nut next to him. His call ended. Caroline picked up her phone and pretended to be on a business call. "Yes. Your balance is $2,800.00. That's $600.00 beyond your limit. Yes. Yes. No. That will not do. You will have to pay the excess to bring your account current... No ma'am. You have until the end of the week at the latest... Okay. Then, we'll be expecting your payment." Caroline slammed the phone down. Again, she heard chuckling from next door, this time louder, his laugh becoming more and more hysterical.

"You are so lying," Barry croaked out between laughs.

Unsure whether that comment was directed toward her or not, Caroline moved again to pick up the phone.

"You would never talk to someone that way. I would, but you wouldn't." He was still laughing.

"I wasn't lying," said Caroline, "I was... I was... pretending."

"Same thing," he said, now unable to catch his breath.

They both broke out in a symphony of hysterics, enough to cause others to peek up over their cubicle walls, wondering what all the fuss was about. After their laughter subsided, Barry asked her what she was doing tonight. She couldn't think of anything else to say, so she said, "I'm going to the library." Would he see through that lie, too? She wondered.

"Oh," he said. His phone rang. He answered and was on for a few moments. She heard his chair creek, papers shuffling.

"Would you like to go with me?" asked Caroline.

He was quiet for a bit.

"Although, I don't know why you'd want to," she said.

"Because I think you're interesting. And cute," he said.

Caroline went through the rest of the day thinking that it was actually good that Barry was coming with her. That way, she wouldn't have to go out into the night alone. But then she realized that she wasn't really planning to go to the library to begin with, so it was a useless blessing.

They took separate cars from work and met in the library parking lot. Once inside, Caroline had to figure out why she was there. Barry stood just behind her, his hands in his coat pockets.

"I need a book," she said. There. That was a plausible enough reason.

"A certain book?" he asked.

"I'm not sure. I just finished a good one... and I need another one. I can't go without a book." At least that was true.

"What kinds of books do you like?" he asked.

"Oh, I don't know. Anything that moves me, I guess."

They sat at a table.

"Have you ever read Down South?" he asked.

"Amazing," replied Caroline.

"How about Under the Big Sky?" he offered.

"Sad. Heartbreaking. Incredible," she returned.

"The Seamstress?" he asked.

"Loved it."

"Here's one I bet you haven't read," he said.

"Try me," challenged Caroline.

"<u>The Beginning</u>."

"You've got me there."

"Let's go find it," he said, heading for the computer. Once there, they stood shoulder to shoulder.

"I've got one for you," said Caroline.

"What's that?"

"<u>The Accused</u>."

"Okay, then let's go find that too"

They found their books and turned to the counter. A group of kids came filtering into the library, twelve or thirteen-years-old, with notebooks and textbooks crammed into bags. Ski parkas, braces, and boys with greasy locks covering their eyes abound. The group crept closer to the counter, like a puddle of spilled milk spreading closer and closer to the edge of a table. Caroline's left leg went numb. Her heart strained against her rib cage. Her hands began to tremble, so she gripped tightly onto <u>The Beginning</u>. Caroline and Barry were now surrounded by kids who were young and out of their reach; trying out their crushes on one another. One of them, a girl, applied lipstick, while a boy to her left took an I-Pod out of his deep, fathomless pocket. Caroline heard music, laughter, and smelled a perfume like Teen Spirit or Babe. Barry took care of his book. Caroline watched him do this, because it helped her screen out the chaos of the people around her.

Next, Caroline put her book on the counter. A girl behind her squealed sharply, ramming into Caroline's back. She looked forward and noticed the librarian staring at her.

"Ma'am?" she asked.

"Oh. Yes?" Caroline's mouth could barely move, her muscles there had become paralyzed, as if on a sub-zero degree day.

"Your card?" prompted the librarian.

Caroline managed to fish her wallet out of her pocket book. Her fingers, now shaking uncontrollably, found the card. She slid it onto the counter.

"Okay, ma'am. You're all set," said the librarian, turning from her computer. "Oh, but I see here you have two books on hold," she added. The librarian reached behind her and came up with the books.

"Oh. Yes. Thank you," said Caroline.

The fact that the books were not for her was irrelevant. She grabbed them and pushed her way through the gaggle of pre-teens. She needed to get out, and that's all that mattered. Once outside, Caroline walked quickly toward her car.

"Caroline? Are you all right?" asked Barry.

Caroline dropped one of the books, one of those that didn't belong to her. A square of paper fluttered out of it and skipped across the pavement. Caroline picked it up and saw that it had her address on it. She shoved it back into the book.

"No. I mean... yes. I'm fine. Really. I just have to go. I have to drop these books off to my landlord. They're not mine; they're his," she added, backing away from him, "and he really needs them."

Back at home, Caroline burst into her house, tossed the books onto the kitchen table, and flew from door to window to window to door over and over again like a bird trying to get out of a cage. Only she was locking herself in. She got on her pajamas and crawled into bed. She turned on the TV, turned the volume down low, and flipped through the channels. She felt a numbness overtake her. This was what she needed. She didn't need new friends, or adventures, or courage. She needed only to be left alone. No wide open spaces, she hoped, not even in her dreams. Her stomach growled. She realized that she hadn't eaten dinner. Such a simple need. You get hungry. You eat. So simple. She got up and looked in the fridge... nothing there. She looked in the cupboard and found only a package of Baby Ruth bars. She grabbed three and headed for bed, saw the books strewn upon the table, and grabbed them. Caroline devoured a candy bar, bits of chocolate spilling down her front. It doesn't matter. She thought. Nothing matters. She looked at one of the books, Jacob's book. It was titled <u>A</u> <u>Scientific Approach to Paranormal Activity</u>. When Caroline opened it, it fell open to the page she had shoved the paper into, right on page eleven. "Damn you number eleven," she said. "Leave me alone."

Caroline didn't go to work the next day. She sat around in her pajamas instead. Squished globs of chocolate dotted her top, but she didn't care. "I don't care," she said out loud. She ate two more Baby Ruth bars for breakfast and thumbed through Jacob's books. The other book was called <u>The Paranormal Phenomenon</u>. Caroline tried to guess at why Jacob would want these books, but she didn't really care. "I don't really care," she announced to no one. She made three bracelets and a necklace, but nothing about them really spoke to her. It doesn't matter. She thought. She read the summary of <u>The Beginning</u> and found that it was an inspirational book written by a man in his dying days. "Oh who gives a shit," she said. At around twelve o'clock, she was hungry again. She had no food and didn't feel like getting dressed to go to the store. Caroline headed up to Jacob's house. She knew he had food. She saw plenty when she was being a dirty, no good, filthy snoop. She popped open cupboards like she lived there, got some crackers, peanut butter, and some pickles out of the fridge. She crunched away at a pickle. A drip of pickle juice trickled down her chin. She didn't move to wipe it away.

"Mmm. I forgot how much I like pickles," she said.

Caroline heard it then in her right ear, barely audible, but unmistakable... a whisper: "Me, too."

Caroline sat up straight, her eyes darting to the right... nothing there... nothing but air, space, the kitchen counter. She shot up, overturning the chair in her wake, and ran back home.

Back at her house, Caroline read. She went back and forth between <u>A Scientific</u> <u>Approach to Paranormal Activity</u>, and <u>The Paranormal Phenomenon</u>. She read about how souls, or spirits, don't die. How they go on and on. How they can be all around, just like how furniture or air can be all around you. How they are comprised of energy. That energy is real, may be the only real thing that there is since everything has energy, was made from energy. That you can see this energy or hear it or sense it. That it can manifest itself to the living. That souls come back and back and back to complete their work. Some souls tag team each other through lives. Some want your attention. Some want to be left alone. Some don't even know you're there. Caroline read about personal accounts of supernatural experiences. About people who chase ghosts, people who capture them on video and audio.

At three o'clock, Caroline rummaged through her storage closet. She was looking for her old mini tape recorder, the one she used to tape lectures in college. Caroline came upon boxes and boxes of old pictures, books, clothes, tapes, and CDs. She found Tim's Gretsch guitar and plucked a string. She found a picture of him turning back to look at her, a slight grin on his face. She unearthed an old Nanci Griffith CD Tim had given her before he left and a Van Morrison CD that had been with her through high school and college. Remembering how much she used to love music, she grabbed these. As she turned, Caroline's foot hit something, sending it skipping across the floor. She bent down, feeling along the floor with her hands until she came to it. It was a white stone, just the right size to fit comfortably in the palm of her hand. Caroline turned it over and over. It was smooth and polished; as if it had been carried and held a lot. Caroline placed it in her pocket and continued with her business. There was the keep sake box her father had made for her so long ago. She knew this was filled with images of him, and she longed to see him again. The lid creaked as she opened the box. Something moved inside, popping up and then coming to rest again on the bottom. Caroline reached her hand inside and felt something whisper against her finger. It was the feather, the blue feather her father had given her so long ago. Caroline took it out and trailed its edge along her cheek. She remembered laughter. Next, she found her little rag doll, Sara, the one she slept with, played with, and cried on growing up, long since forgotten. Suddenly, she missed her mother. Caroline turned on her heels and felt something hard beneath her foot. She bent down to inspect. Whatever it was slid out to the side. Caroline picked it up, finding that it was yet another rock... this time black. It was smooth and worn like the white one. She slipped this one in her pocket as well. At last, Caroline found the tape recorder. She pushed a button and Dr. Wolnik's voice came to life in her closet... talking of abdominal hemorrhages. Caroline remembered furiously scribbling notes during this lecture. Now Caroline remembered that she had once wanted to be a doctor. Caroline walked up to Jacob's house, tape recorder in hand. She had rewound it, ready to tape over Dr. Wolnik's voice with whatever was there, or wasn't there.

Jacob's kitchen was as she left it. There was the overturned chair, the half eaten pickle on the table, and the peanut butter and crackers. She had planned on leaving the tape recorder on the kitchen table and scooting out, but instead she went to the basement first. Moving quickly, Caroline grabbed the rest of the folders marked "Gretta." Before leaving, she carefully placed the recorder on the kitchen table and pressed "record."

Caroline figured the tape would run for a few hours, so she spent that time reading the contents of the folders. This is what she learned: Gretta had been sledding at the park. It was 1978. Gretta was fourteen years old. So was Caroline. Caroline may have been watching re-runs of the

Brady Bunch or Gilligan's Island when Gretta disappeared. It was late afternoon, around four o'clock. Gretta's father, Jacob, had left her there with her two friends and their babysitter to run to the store. He told them he'd be back in ten minutes. The store was right around the corner. He was cold and would gather up Gretta when he returned and give her hot chocolate in their kitchen. When he returned, he pulled into the parking lot and saw the babysitter's car in the same place it had been when he'd left to go to the store. His trip to the store didn't really take ten minutes. It took thirty, because he was gabbing with the clerk who had a plumbing question. Jacob was a plumber. He was forty-five-years-old. Everyone in town knew him, and he knew everyone in town. When Jacob returned to the park, he approached the bottom of the hill and peered up. The white that was blinding before he'd left was now dimming. The sun was going down. The hill was empty. He turned on his heels, because he heard voices in the woods, up high, to the left. Why they were in the woods, he couldn't guess. He headed up. He huffed his way up because he was a smoker. His breath became clouds before him, gray like the sky. He reached the top and strained to hear the voices. They were further into the woods now. He called for Gretta. He called for her friends. He called for the babysitter, Janey. She was a nice girl. He knew her father. They didn't seem to hear him, so he picked his way through the dense trees.

"Gretta!" he called again. He heard a desperate sounding holler, high pitched. Jacob picked up speed. His coat got caught on a branch and tore.

"Gretta!"

"Mr. Stills! Over here!" he heard.

He saw them up ahead through a thick stand of trees.

One of the girls frantically called out, "Gretta!"

Jacob stumbled over to them. He expected to find her there lying on the ground or down a gully lying there hurt, but ready to be rescued by her father. He expected to find her there, but he didn't.

Jacob was interviewed by the investigators. The babysitter, Janey, was interviewed by the investigators. So were the girls. They went over it and over it: How they had gone down, and Gretta had stayed at the top. She was going to meet them below. Janey and the girls had gone into the car, rummaging around for the snacks they brought. They'd returned to the foot of the hill, all three of them with their hands up to shield their eyes from the sharp angle of the sun, straining to see Gretta. They couldn't see her but waited for a bit, thinking that their vision had simply been blotted out by the setting sun. When she didn't come down, they called for her. The girls knew Gretta well enough to know that she was always fooling, joking, hiding, and playing practical jokes.

"Come out, come out, wherever you are!" yelled one of the girls, Angela. "We've got Cheez-Its for you!"

When there was no reply, they filed up the hill with some urgency. They found her footsteps, just hers at the top, leading into the woods.

"Gret!" they hollered again.

They followed the footsteps further in where they came upon her blue sled, its rope lying limply upon the ground. There they saw a disturbance in the snow, a tangled mess of footprints, and then a single, larger set of prints leading away from the sled... toward a paved road that led down and away from the hill, away from Porter Park, away from the girls and the babysitter, Janey, and away from Jacob.

There were pages and pages of the following investigation: The babysitter's car had been combed through. There, they'd found a high school biology text book, a shopping bag full of various snacks, cassettes, and a pack of cigarettes. In Jacob's car, they'd found plumbing supplies (all itemized in the report), a carton of cigarettes, and a newly purchased bottle of whiskey, still in its brown paper bag. They'd interviewed scores of people. No one, not one person, had seen or noticed anything or anyone unusual in the area at the time or at anytime beforehand. They took footprint impressions in the snow, measured tire tread marks, collected bits of things from the site- including a piece of Jacob's jacket from the branch. Police flooded the area and areas in surrounding towns. They wanted to know if Gretta had a boyfriend, enemies, or emotional problems. They wanted to know about Mr. And Mrs. Stills' marriage. Was there any discord there? Infidelity? Abuse?

Caroline read on and on. The investigation ended after sometime. First, swamps had been trudged through, woods scoured, people lowered into the depths of ponds. Friends, family, strangers, and communities organized search parties and vigils. On and on and on. It had to end sometime, and, eventually it did. All Caroline could do was lay down. It's all she could do. She listened to her clock ticking. She was thinking of Margaret, the girl from high school who disappeared, but was never found. She thought of Gretta, who was never found, while she, Caroline, was trying to find herself. The clock was ticking, chopping up the silence into perfectly equal bits. Caroline stared, lying on the couch. She stared, without even the need to blink. Her breath was a wave, coming again and again. She was in a dome. She was in a bubble. She was at the edge of the ocean, and there was Gretta beside her. She was smiling, bending down, picking up sand, tossing it into the air. Caroline got up, feeling pain in her hip. Her hand went to the spot, feeling two hard lumps there. The rocks, she had forgotten about the rocks. Caroline pulled them out of her pocket and threw them into the trash can on her way out. They plunked to the bottom as Caroline left to retrieve the tape recorder from Jacob's house. She brought it back home and sat in the kitchen. She rewound it, back past whatever was there. Caroline tentatively pressed play and listened to silence; the sound of silence, almost. Except she could hear Jacob's clock ticking, as well as her own. Caroline sat like this for an hour or more, never once moving. Her clock and Jacob's became synchronized. Caroline breathed in and out exactly once every eight seconds. She thought of nothing, of the word "nothing." Within her came a stillness as still as Jacob's house. This place within her was a sturdy place, a sure place, completely untouched by anything, ever. She had never been there before, or maybe she had. But silence does have a sound.

Caroline heard it then. It said, "Daddy?" The tape recorder said, "Daddy?"

Caroline was waist-deep in water and being struck by lightning, at least that's how she felt. Her nerves crackled with electrical impulses as she stood up and backed away from the kitchen table, the one that looked exactly like Jacob's. She heard, at that moment, a jingling somewhere outside her house, and she dove under the table. There was the crunching of footsteps in the snow, and the jingling came closer. There came pounding on the door, but it was really just a light rapping. Caroline's throat burned like the time she had pneumonia, like the time her mother put Vicks on her throat, leaving behind little fiery spots.

"Carly? Carly? Let me in," said Sarna.

Caroline bumped her head on the table's bottom as she tried to get out from under. She looked up and noticed, written on the underside, some scrawling which she strained to see. It said in faint red crayon, "Gretta was here 11/_1/70."

"Carly! Please let me in!"

Caroline came out from under and let Sarna in. Sarna surveyed her cautiously. Caroline looked down at herself and saw that she was still in her pajamas which were smudged with chocolate and stained with pickle juice. Caroline touched her hair and felt thick snarls there.
"It's okay Sarna. Really, I'm okay. Come on in. Sit down."

Caroline told her everything. She played the tape for her and showed her the writing under the table. They figured out, together, that since Caroline's little house came furnished... this table had probably been Jacob's; that it was once in his house. Caroline's twin bed may have even been Gretta's, once slept in and dreamed in by her in the now-empty room in the big house.

Caroline went to work the next day. Barry acted as if nothing had happened... that she hadn't really run away from him in the library parking lot. Maybe she hadn't. Maybe she had just scuttled away, the way someone might when they've suddenly realized they had something important to go do. He told her he liked the book so far, The Accused. She told him that she liked The Beginning so far, even though she hadn't even begun to read it. She resolved to start that night.

That night, Caroline opened the book while in the cocoon of her bed. It was one of those with a texture to it like old papyrus. There was an introduction by the author himself. He started by saying that he was a struggling survivor of cancer, but that his prognosis was bad. He described his death sentence as a blessing. Through such a sentence, he had discovered the riches of life... all having nothing to do with material possessions or wealth. He went on to say that if you wish to know about such riches... then open the cover, settle into your favorite chair, and read. At the bottom of the introduction, was a favorite saying of his. It was this "The secret to life is to fall seven times and to get up eight times." Caroline thought on this. How can a man who is about to die get up that one last time? Then, she thought of this: Isn't death the final fall? She rubbed at her eyes, yawning. She put the book back down, unsure if she wanted to know about the riches of life, or about falling down and getting back up again.

On Saturday, Caroline went to see Lila. She told Lila about Gretta. But she'd worried over telling her. Would she think her a bad person for snooping? Would she think she was crazy, listening to ghosts?

"I believe," said Lila, "that souls go on forever. Bodies may die, but souls don't. A soul's purpose is to continually evolve."

"How does a soul do that?" asked Caroline.

"A soul comes back through many lifetimes to learn its lessons. Only though learning its lessons can it evolve. My soul's lessons in this lifetime may be different from yours, or they may be similar... who knows? A soul can hang around before it is born into another body. That's what some people call ghosts. I call them souls, or spirits."

"Why would a spirit want to hang around?" ventured Caroline.

"It depends," said Lila. "In Gretta's case, it may be to comfort the living, or to communicate something to the living."

They talked of lessons and of soul purposes. Lila explained that to identify your lessons, it can help to think of themes or challenges that keep reoccurring for you in your life. Caroline reflected on these: Fear, night time, people...

"Dreams, also, can be powerful messages for you."

Caroline thought about her dream of the birds and of the small round-faced boy. Caroline told Lila about the number eleven and how it kept surfacing for her.

"The number eleven represents angels," said Lila. "You are being surrounded by angels."

They talked more about Caroline's obstacles and about how she'd been over and over her past, but how her sometimes strange reactions and fears keep haunting her.

"Let's do some Reiki," said Lila. "Maybe next time we'll do some hypnosis and see if that reveals anything."

Caroline settled down on Lila's bed for Reiki. Lila moved to put on some music, but Caroline stopped her. "Actually, Lila, would you mind not playing the music this time? I've discovered that the ticking of the clock works better for me."

Lila agreed to this and began. Again, she started at the top of Caroline's head and worked her way down, careful not to touch her throat. Caroline's breathing became an ocean, coming in and going out with the seconds as they passed. She felt a pressure and a tingling everywhere Lila went. In some places, it felt as if something was coming out of her and something else coming in. She felt this keenly around her solar plexus. When Lila was at the crown of her head, it felt as if her whole head might have floated right off her body. After a while, Caroline entered a state that felt like sleep, and although she felt very much out of her skin, she also felt very much in it. When the Reiki was done, Caroline sat up.

Lila said, "I'd like to do some more work on your solar plexus chakra, next time maybe."

"What is that chakra?" asked Caroline.

"It's the seat of your personal power. You need some work there."

"Okay," said Caroline.

"And also, who's Tim?"

"Why?" asked Caroline.

"It's just a name I picked up on."

"You did not!" said Caroline incredulously.

"I did."

"He's a guy I used to see."

"Well, there's some work to be done there, too," said Lila. "I look forward to doing some hypnotism with you. I think you'll respond well to it."

Caroline had to go back to Jacob's to put everything back as it was, because he was coming home. She put the Gretta folders back in their slots on his desk and folded up the blanket on the couch as it had been before she used it. She put his library books on the kitchen table and made sure the chair was placed squarely with the table. She made sure Jacob's shirt was hanging just so on his bedpost and checked the video she'd watched and the books she had touched, running her finger along the spine of <u>Little Women</u> for good measure. Caroline would have liked for her own father to have used such a term of endearment for her. A tear came to her, and she wasn't sure if it was for herself or for Gretta. Caroline left, surveying the downstairs one last time before closing the door behind her.

That night, Caroline settled down to read <u>The Beginning</u>. She didn't particularly feel like it, but she didn't know what else to do. The author, Sam King, started his first chapter by explaining his illness. He'd been diagnosed with pancreatic cancer, a swift killer. He called it "The Eye Opener." Before the cancer, he was an average Joe: an overachieving, chronic accumulating, stingy ladder-climbing schmuck. He had been in a bad marriage and had been estranged from his angry, rebellious children. Caroline read on about his life pre-cancer: about infidelity and empty days, a marriage unfulfilled. She could see why Barry would be drawn to such a story, but wasn't sure if it was the right fit for her. Still... she wondered about falling down seven times and getting up eight.

Caroline asked Barry the next day at work about <u>The Beginning</u>. She wanted to know if he thought it was possible to keep getting up... no matter how many times you fall.

"What's the alternative?" he said.

Caroline thought. "Staying in bed," she returned.

"Forever?"

"Well, yes, I suppose."

"Then, I'd rather keep getting up," countered Barry.

Caroline returned to shuffling papers at her desk. Barry's voice came from behind the cubicle wall.

"You know, Caroline. Sometimes just coming to work day after day, even if it is to a crappy, dead-end job, constitutes getting up."

Caroline ventured further. "But...does it ever get better than that?"

"It depends."

"On what?"

"On you," he said.

Jacob came home the next day while Caroline was at work. When she drove past his house, she saw that the kitchen light was on, and she saw his silhouette in the window by the kitchen sink. She decided to stop in to see if he needed anything. Knocking on his door, she heard him call, "Come in!" Caroline entered and found Jacob leaning at the kitchen counter. A metallic walker stood behind him.

"This is absurd, isn't it?" he said.

"What is?"

"A walker," he said, chuckling. "I'm too young for this shit." Again, he was dressed in his casual best. He looked lesser than before. Caroline saw that his cheeks had a hollow look, and the shoulders of his shirt sagged where before they had been broadly filled out.

"Thank you," he said, "for taking care of things while I was gone."

"Nothing," answered Caroline. "It was nothing."

"Well... Could you just help me with one more thing while you're here?"

"Sure, anything."

"Would you mind opening out the couch for me? It doubles as a bed. I think I'll have to sleep downstairs for a while until I can get up and down the stairs a little better."

113

Caroline agreed, and when she unfolded the bed, an old, compressed Raggedy Ann doll appeared; her red yarn hair fraying across her face... her toothless smile and button nose peering up at Caroline. She didn't know what to do with it, so she left it there. Caroline left Jacob to spend his first night back alone, or not alone, depending on how you look at it.

"Can I come with you to meditation on Friday night?" asked Caroline, the phone cradled upon her shoulder. She felt a long, drawn out brushing against her ankle, like the way Dart used to weave around her legs.

"Of course you can," answered Sarna. "I'll pick you up at six o'clock."

Before Sarna came, Caroline called over to Jacob to see if he needed anything.

"No. I'm all set," he said. "I've got someone from the Council on Aging helping me out, bringing me groceries."

"Do you have any family around?" asked Caroline. "I mean... anyone who can help you out or just hang out with you?"

"No," he said. "I'm pretty much it."

"I wouldn't mind doing anything for you, even if you'd just like some company or anything like that. Just let me know."

"Thank you. I'm sure I'll be fine."

"Okay. Well, then...," Caroline said, ready to hang up.

"Oh, Caroline? Thank you for getting my library books for me." Before hanging up, there was a pause in which neither of them said anything.

Meditation offered the same women who sat in the same places. They started with same procedure: of letting go of whatever needed to be let go of. This time the women were to see themselves before a covered bridge. In Caroline's mind, it was spring; the most perfect of spring days where moths and butterflies and insects lazily bounce and drift about. Sunlight was filtering down on her as she stood still and effortless. Not lifeless, but effortless. She gently lay down her cares at her feet and stepped into the bridge. She was wearing a white sleeveless t-shirt, jeans, and sneakers. Caroline walked further in; just walking ahead, so light and simple. Upon emerging from the other end, she turned and looked at the heap of her cares, now apart from her, other than her. They were simply a heap, a pile... like a load of laundry waiting to be washed. She turned her back on these and saw before her a warm, dusty dirt road: the kind that crunches under your feet as you walk. Tufts of tall, yellow, flowering reeds burst forth along the edges of the road. Unseen spring bugs and crickets busily chattered, hunkering down in the tall grass. Breathe in and out, in and out. You just are. I just am. A blue bird and a yellow bird hopped across the road... careless... hopping and pecking for seeds or worms. Caroline just let them go on their way. What else could she do?

The discussion that night was about each person's life story. Lila explained this as being the story that you keep telling yourself, the story you keep living. "Is it a story you want to live?" she asked everyone. Caroline listened to these women's stories. Maryanne was tired of being single. The only men she was attracted to were "scum-bags," she called them. "All the other ones bore me."

Laura explained, "My husband is a paraplegic. All I do... all I've done for years... is take care of him. I have no life because of it. God forgive me for feeling bitter, but I do."

Sarna added, "My house is a mess. I can barely get through it, it's so bad. I have so much crap that I hold onto. Just crap. Stuff I don't need. Stuff I buy just to buy it. It's driving me crazy, and I keep saying I'll go through it, get rid of it, but I never do. I don't know why I can't let go of it."

Caroline watched her friend as she spoke and saw vulnerability there. Another woman admitted to enabling her sixteen year old son who was addicted to crack-cocaine. Again, Caroline offered nothing, and no one asked her.

"You live the story you keep telling yourself," said Lila.

"So how do you change your story?" asked Maryanne.

"You begin telling yourself a different story," returned Lila.

At the end, Lila passed around a deck of cards. She called them "Angel Cards."

116

"Feel the deck in your hands," she said. "Take whatever one you feel drawn to. Whichever one you take has a message that you may need to receive."

Caroline felt like a twelve-year-old experimenting with a Ouija board. She took a card, one that kind of stuck to the pad of her ring finger. She flipped it over and saw a rosy cherub with wings. The word "Forgiveness" appeared at the bottom, and it reminded her of her childhood or of a time even further beyond.

On the way home from meditation, Caroline said, "I didn't know."

"Know what?" asked Sarna.

"That you were cluttered. That it bothered you so much."

"Well, you've only been to my place twice, and both times I shoved all my shit under the bed and in my closets. I think I must have filled seven bags worth of crap. Those I put in my car. I did it because I didn't want you to see it all," admitted Sarna.

"Oh, Sarna. I wouldn't care! You could be a bag lady or go around with underwear on your head, and I wouldn't care."

"Even if it was dirty underwear?" asked Sarna.

"Even then. I'm so sorry Sarna."

"For what?"

"For not paying attention, for not knowing you as well as you know me."

"Oh please, Carly. Don't you know that it is through you that I can know myself? Really, there is no greater friend than that."

That night, Caroline brought a journal to bed with her... just in case. If she dreamt, she didn't want to forget it before she could write it down. And she did dream. She was standing in a shower, shivering with clothes on. The water was not on, yet she was soaking wet- sweating uncontrollably. There was a yellow and peach flowered shower curtain. Someone reached in, yanked the curtain aside, and grabbed hold of a chain around her neck- not a gold chain, but a silver one. There came a hard yank, and the necklace broke off. Looking down, she saw that something... a pendant of sorts... had come off the broken necklace, landing at her feet. It was a feather, a silver feather. Caroline woke up coughing and choking. Through gasps and sobs, she scribbled down the dream, but the sobbing continued long after.

It was Saturday, and Caroline was at Lila's. She didn't know if she would tell Lila about her dream. She just wasn't sure she felt like it. Ever since, a dark cloud was pressing down on her. Even moving was an effort. When she entered Lila's, she headed straight for the bed.

"I'm sorry Lila," she said. "I'm just so tired. I just need to lie down."

Lila moved the clock next to the bed and started at Caroline's crown; then she went down from there, over to the eyes, and to her forehead. Caroline was reminded of the time she had pneumonia, when her mother had taken care of her. That was the time her mother had returned briefly from whatever abyss she had been in and touched Caroline's forehead with a cold, wet cloth. Caroline smiled and drifted. She thought she might have heard Lila say something, but she wasn't sure. She was just so far away. Again, she was back to the time she was sick. She could hear her mother as she lay in her old childhood bed, as she lay in Lila's bed.

"You are a pig," said her mother from the living room, "a disgusting pig. Look at you. You haven't showered in three weeks. You smell. You're drunk every night. You disgust me."

There was only silence from her father. He was probably sitting in his chair, staring straight ahead. Caroline remembered wanting to hear the exchange between her parents better, but she couldn't. Her head was too heavy to lift. Caroline listened to mother's footsteps retreat into the kitchen. She heard her father getting up. A moment later, she heard the shower running. Caroline lay there breathing for a long time. Her lungs rattled. Finally, her mother came in and pressed another cold cloth to her forehead.

"Your father's leaving," she said.

Caroline lie still, pretending to sleep, unsure whether her mother had said it to her or out loud to herself. She was unsure, even, of what she had said in the first place.

Caroline heard Lila say something, or was it her mother speaking?

"Tim," said Lila

"Tim?" What about him?" Caroline replied, her mouth nearly paralyzed, as if talking in her sleep.

"Tell me about him."

Caroline could feel the cotton of his shirt between her fingers. "Oh, I miss him," she said.

Lila's voice came from somewhere off to Caroline's right. "What do you miss?"

"Him. I love his smell. He smells so good, the smell of his skin. I love seeing him coming up my stairs. I miss his voice. He calls me his one true love, but I know it's not true."

"How do you know that?" asked Lila.

"I just know. He doesn't know anything about me, but I like it that way. I miss him," Caroline repeated. "He sang me a song once."

"What song?" asked Lila, now at Caroline's feet.

"I don't know. Something about a mermaid. I don't know the song. I wish I knew what it was. I've always wondered."

120

Caroline woke to Lila touching her feet. She was pulling at them. "What are you doing?" asked Caroline.

"I am grounding you."

"Did I do something wrong?"

Lila chuckled. "No. You've just spent quite a bit of time sort of floating around in time. I need to ground you."

"What happened?" asked Caroline.

"You introduced me to your mother and your father and Tim," said Lila.

"Was I talking? Was I talking about them?"

"Oh, yes," said Lila, "quite a bit."

"I'm coming over to help you clean," said Caroline on Sunday.

"Right now? Today?" asked Sarna.

"Yup. Stay right where you are. I'll be there in half an hour." Caroline could hardly wait to get there, to be the one helping... for a change. She made it to Sarna's apartment in twenty minutes. It was a long, narrow unit on the top floor of a brown, shingled building. The bottom level housed a store boasting a hanging wooden sign which read, "Wine and Spirits." The sign creaked back and forth in the wind. Caroline climbed the steps and knocked.

"Come in!" yelled Sarna from somewhere up above. Caroline entered and climbed up another set of stairs. She met Sarna at the top and found herself surrounded by heaps of clothes, bags filled with mail and papers, and boxes of CD's. Venturing further in, Caroline found Sarna folding laundry in the living room.

"How bad is it?" asked Sarna.

Caroline surveyed the room. The only thing without piles of stuff in front of it or on it was the computer in the corner. Stacks of books and newspapers dotted the floor. Boxes of Christmas cards littered the bookcase against the wall. Next to the television was a high chair. On top of that lay cases and cases of Coke.

"A high chair?" asked Caroline.

"It was only fifty cents at a yard sale!" said Sarna.

"But you always said you'd never have babies."

"I know, but fifty cents!"

"And the Christmas cards? What are there... eight or nine boxes? Do you really know that many people?" asked Caroline.

"No, but... you know... the sales after Christmas."

"All right, then. Let's just start," said Caroline, heading for a stack of newspapers and books.

"Where?" asked Sarna.

"Anywhere," returned Caroline.

They worked for hours creating piles: one pile of stuff to throw out, one pile of things to donate, and one pile of things to put in places where they actually belonged. They spent all this time in the living room, enlarging the piles in other rooms as they relocated things to places where it would make sense for them to be.

122

"I figure one full day in each room, and we'l be set," said Caroline.

Sarna rummaged through a box. "Ooh. I really don't want to get rid of these. Do I have to?" She turned toward Caroline, proudly pulling up a set of wind chimes. The pipes clanged against one another, and Caroline's hands began to shake. She wanted to go hide in the bathroom or run out of the place. But she stayed put, rooting through a box.

"God, I hate that sound," said Caroline.

"Wind Chimes? Why?" asked Sarna.

"I don't know. All I know is when I hear them, I want to run."

"Aren't you curious about that?" asked Sarna, placing the wind chimes back in the box.

"Yes." replied Caroline. "No," she added.

"That's how I feel when I'm forced to go through my stuff," said Sarna, "all panicky."

"We all have stuff," said Caroline. "Except you know all of my stuff, and I don't really know yours."

Caroline made herself busy with a bag full of mail.

"It's hard to know a person," said Sarna quietly.

Caroline thought on this. "Not really. What's hard is letting a person get to know you." That, they both agreed on. They continued their work in silence for the next half-hour.

Then: "Do you want to know something about me that you probably don't know?" asked Sarna.

"Sure."

"I'm gay."

"Is that all?" asked Caroline. "So, I'm afraid of the dark."

"I haven't paid my student loans in eight months," returned Sarna.

"I once stalked a guy; I was so obsessed with him."

"Who?" asked Sarna.

"Tim."

"Hmm," said Sarna, searching for a notable confession. "Here's a good one... I had an abortion when I was sixteen."

"I was hiding in my bedroom when I was sixteen," countered Caroline.

They returned to their work. There was now a clear opening in the middle of the living room.

"So," said Caroline, "I believe in ghosts."

"Oh, yeah? Well, I'm not sure I believe in God," said Sarna.

"Me neither."

Sarna disappeared into her bedroom and came back out with a pair of underwear on her head. "Do you still like me?"

"Absolutely," said Caroline, "It's the color I'm not so sure about."

Before Caroline left, she asked if she could take the wind chimes home with her. She clutched onto them tightly as she went out to her car and placed them gingerly on the passenger side floor. She eyed them suspiciously all the way home.

That evening, Caroline picked up <u>The Beginning</u> while sitting at the kitchen table. She ran her hands over the rough cover and flipped through the pages. The second chapter was called "Going Back." In this chapter, the author finds himself taking a hard look at the condition of his life... a life filled with unrelenting demands, an estranged wife, infidelity, and children who had become strangers to their own father. Caroline read on, watching Sam King look at his broken life with grace... inspecting each broken shard, no matter how painful. There was the fifteen-year-old son with long, stringy, black hair covering his eyes, conveniently blinding him from having to see anything at all. There was the ten-year-old daughter who hid inside her tortured drawings. There was the wife, seeming to care little, who was filled with fragile fragments of shattered love. Each of Sam's unabashed inspections was a sharp triangle of glass, slicing into his soul, drawing out pain like little droplets of blood dripping onto the floor.

Caroline looked up from her reading, her head filled with courage... like Sam King. She put down the book and ventured outside her door. It was night time. She was hanging the wind chimes. A bitter whip of wind came up and upset the chimes. Caroline stood on her doorstep, turned her back to the chimes, and listened to them as she faced the blackness. She stood like this for a long time, until the chimes settled. Their sounds ceased as the blackness of the night pressed down on her. Caroline stood this way until the gravity of night became too much for her narrow shoulders. She scurried into the house, locking the door behind her. Caroline leaned her back against the door, waiting for the beat of her heart to come to rest. Once in bed, Caroline fell into a deep sleep at last. This took some time, given the fact that she had been listening to the wind and the chimes droning on intermittently for several hours. In her dream, she was in a kitchen... but not her own. She wore a long, paisley shirt and many, many beaded bracelets. She was rolling out dough with a heavy wooden rolling pin. The handles were red. In the dream, a chime outside the door whipped about violently in the wind. She pressed and rolled, pressed and rolled. There was a small radio before her with large knobs. The Beatles were on the radio, singing "A Hard Day's Night", and she hummed along. Pressing and rolling, pressing and rolling. The wind chimes became louder, so she turned up the radio. Behind her, where she could not see, the door opened. She did not hear this. The chimes erupted in a cacophony of noise, and she did not hear the opening of the door. Pressing and rolling and singing. She felt a cool breeze against her back, thinking the door must have opened with the wind, thinking she should have locked the door. She turned quickly, noticing a shadow on the cabinet before her. The rolling pin spun out of her hand, meeting harshly with the wall. It woke her: the sound of the rolling pin, the sound of her scream, the sound of the wind chimes.

Caroline got up and padded into the kitchen. She could see the chimes through her kitchen door window pane. They were still, benign, just things hanging there. It had begun to snow heavily, probably while she was asleep having her dream. She remembered the forecast calling for two inches an hour.

The next morning, the world was snowed in. It would be the kind of day that kids would love. Soon they would be outside calling to one another and screeching, their voices being absorbed by the snow. Sleds and snow caves, snow angels and snowmen were the dreams of children this time of year, and their dreams would come true. It would be the kind of day that grownups would either breathe a sigh of relief while sipping their coffee for not having to go to work, or begin to develop a headache at the thought of all that shoveling. Caroline remembered, then, that she and her father used to shovel together. Their driveway was long enough for it to take hours, and she loved this: the side by side rhythmic motion, those uncomplicated, purposeful hours. They would take breaks to go into the workshop and warm up by the big, rusty wood burning stove. It was in the workshop, by the stove, during a blustery fall evening, that her father told her he was leaving. Caroline was fifteen. Her father was forty-six. He told her why he had to go; that he had a drinking problem, and it was making her mother very sad. It was making him very sad.

"And it's making you very sad too, Caroline, even if you don't know it," he said.

"I hope that you can forgive me."

Caroline had said the first thing that came to mind. "There's not even anything to forgive." Even though that wasn't really true. She wondered now... had she ever really forgiven him? What does forgiveness feel like? How, really, do you forgive?

Caroline was glad for the snow day. She was feeling fragile, so fragile that not even her compulsions could get a grip on her. She went outside to shovel and found the task daunting. Barry might say, "Wait until it's done snowing ... otherwise it's like shoveling shit against the tide." Sarna might say, "Screw it and curl up with a good book." Her father might say, "It's best to keep on top of it." Caroline didn't care what was the right way or the right thing. She just wanted to move. She shoveled on and on for hours and was surprised at how far she'd gotten when she rounded the bend in her driveway. Seeing the stretch toward Jacob's house, she decided to keep going. From there, she made it to Jacob's in less than an hour. Caroline knocked on Jacob's door, not realizing she was going to do this until she did it.

"Hello?" she heard from within.

"Jacob? It's me. Caroline!"

"Come in!"

She entered and found him on the couch-bed in a white t-shirt and red plaid pajama bottoms. The downstairs was a mess.

"I'm sorry for the mess," he said. "I haven't been able to get up and around much."

"Are you all right?"

128

"I have pain killers, but I don't like to take them too much." Caroline looked around and saw empty TV dinner cartons, cinched up bags of trash, and mugs and dishes littering the kitchen counter. She began picking up.

"Caroline. Please. I have someone who comes and helps with this stuff."

"And how often do they come?" she asked.

"Last time was... hmm..." He rolled his eyes up toward the ceiling.

"Exactly," said Caroline, "I'm helping whether you like it or not."

She cleared the kitchen and took out the bags of trash. She took dirty towels from the bathroom and put them in the wash. When she came back up from the basement, Jacob announced, "I have a physical therapist coming three days a week. She's supposed to come today, but I don't think she'll make it... on account of the snow."

"What does she do with you?"

"Some muscle strengthening in my legs. Some range of motion stuff with my hips. It helps."

"If you show me what she does, I could try." Caroline didn't expect Jacob to be receptive to this, but he was. As she lifted his leg, he pushed gently with his foot against her chest. His leg shook with the effort.

"I don't know why I bother," he said. "I'm an old man."

"You've got plenty left in you," returned Caroline, although she wasn't so sure of this herself. He seemed even lesser than the last time she saw him, not just physically, but in other ways too. She remembered hearing somewhere that often when an elderly person breaks a hip, it's all downhill from there... as if the hip bone is directly connected to the mental faculties. She just felt very sad for him.

"How long have you been wearing these clothes?" she asked. Jacob looked up toward the ceiling, thinking. "Three or four days, I think."

"I'll get you a fresh pair of clothes before I leave."

Caroline switched over to the other leg. This one trembled even more so.

"My Gret used to take care of me like this," he said, "but for all the wrong reasons."

Caroline didn't know what to say. A stream of questions ran through her mind. Should I ask who Gret is? Does he know that I know? Is he forgetting that I supposedly don't know? She decided to say nothing and gently pressed on his leg.

"My wife hated me for a long, long time. I didn't blame her. I hated myself, too."

Caroline listened and worked. Her hands seemed to instinctively know what to do. She heard his clock ticking.

"She used to say Gretta came to her. I didn't believe her. Otherwise that would mean she was really, really gone. But she insisted. After a while, she stopped talking about it- about how she knew that Gretta was hiding in the closet. She used to love hiding in there. After Gretta was gone, I never did see her in there. I used to sit on her bed, Gret's bed, and just listen. I never heard a thing."

Caroline worked on, pressing and kneading.

"Your bed, the one you use, is hers... you know. After my wife passed, I decided to get a tenant for the back house, and I furnished it with her bed. She used to play in that house, Gret did. She loved it." Jacob's mind seemed to drift. "I figured there was no use keeping her bed in her room any longer. I could never hear anything the way my wife did."

"Sometimes people hear things in their own ways," Caroline said, unsure where that had come from or even what it meant.

"Did I ever tell you about Gretta's stones?"

"Stones? No. I don't think you did."

"She used to have this white stone and this black stone. She would sit for hours asking questions of those stones. "Should I play with Susan today?", "Should I cut my hair short?", "Will it rain today?"... Stuff like that. She would close her eyes, mix the stones up and pick one. If she chose the white one, then the answer to her question was yes."

"And if she chose the black one, was the answer no?" asked Caroline.

Jacob nodded. "She used to swear by it. So innocent. I miss her innocence."

Caroline remembered the stones she'd found in her closet and knew that those were Gretta's... Gretta's magic stones. She knew, also, that she'd already taken her garbage out, but would have picked through the town dump if it meant she could find them again.

Jacob continued with a sigh. "I used to hear my wife talking in the basement while doing laundry. I thought she was going crazy." He paused, and then added, "I thought we were all going crazy."

Jacob began to drift, closing his eyes. The clock ticked on. "My wife softened over time," he said.

"She started sleeping in our bed again. She seemed to forget, or something. Such a soft soul, my wife was. She couldn't stay hard forever. She did seem to forget. I never did."

Jacob fell into a deep sleep at last. Caroline went upstairs and got him a fresh pair of clothes, laying them next to him. Caroline noticed a bump under the sheet and knew that it was Raggedy Ann. She saw the library books on the end tables next to the couch. Caroline left, closing the door softly behind her.

When Caroline got back to her house, her phone was ringing. It was Sarna.

"Carly. Barry just called me. He wanted your phone number," she said.

"What? Why?" asked Caroline, beginning to feel crowded in by other people's lives.

"I don't know. He said he wants to talk to you. He sounded a little... oh... I don't know... upset or something."

"What? What's wrong?"

"I don't know. Do you want me to give him your number?" asked Sarna.

"Why don't you just give me his number, and I'll call him."

Caroline punched in the numbers. He answered on the third ring.

"Hello?"

"Hi, Barry. It's Caroline. What's up?"

"Ah, are you busy right now? I have to talk to you," he said.

She hated that phrase... "I have to talk to you." The last time someone said that to her, it was Tim telling her he was moving. The time before that, it was her father telling her he was leaving.

"Um. Sure. I mean, no, I'm not busy," she said.

"Actually, I think we should talk in person. I don't really want you out driving in this. Can I come to you?" he asked.

Caroline did not like men in her house. She wished she had a white stone and a black stone to tell her what to do. Yes or No? Instead, she pictured a road, long and clear and straight, leading from him to her house.

"Sure," she said. She gave him directions, took a shower, and waited.

An hour went by, and she realized that it must be very important for him to be coming out in a storm to talk to her. The sun poked out briefly through a hole in the sky, glinting off the wind chimes. This stunned the retinas in her eyes, and she looked away, closing them. When she opened her eyes again, she saw, cast against the wall, a shadow created by the sun on the wind chimes... two long, parallel lines in the form of the number eleven. "Okay. Bring it on," announced Caroline. "Just bring it on." Barry came shortly after, sporting a rugged khaki jacket, black scarf, and work boots. He shook off the snow and stomped his boots before coming in.

"I'm sorry," he said, "Do you want me to take my boots off?"

"Off?" said Caroline.

"Well, you know. Some people are anal about that sort of thing, the mess I mean."

"Oh, no," she said, "I'm not anal... about that sort of stuff."

He stepped further in and stood awkwardly.

"Please, sit down."

"Nice table," he said.

"This?" answered Caroline, running her hand over the red, linoleum surface. She knew that Gretta's writing was just below her hand.

"I like that retro look," he said.

"Is your place retro?" she asked.

"I would say mine's more mish-mosh- being divorced and all. You take what you can get."

"Yes. You take what you can get," she repeated, "not that I would know. About being divorced, I mean."

They sat silently for a moment.

"What's up, Barry?" she asked. He looked at her then. His eyes were so blue.

"They found out at work," he announced.

"Oh."

"They'll probably let you go tomorrow."

"Oh," she said again.

"I wanted to let you know before. Are you okay?" he asked.

"Yes. I don't know why, but I am."

"What will you do?" asked Barry.

"I'll figure it out. There's always a way. Something will come," she said.

And she truly did feel this... that something would come.

Barry stayed. They had coffee and talked about <u>The Beginning</u> and <u>The Accused</u>. Barry was angry with one of the characters for allowing another one of the characters, a young boy, to be raped.

"He'd better redeem himself," he said.

Caroline told him to keep reading. She was skeptical about Sam King's love of life and God in light of his cruel death sentence.

"Just keep reading," he said.

Barry told her about his ex-wife, who was recently diagnosed with a late stage breast cancer. She had already begun treatment.

"Have you seen her?" asked Caroline.

"I was there just this morning, shoveling their driveway."

"You're so good!" said Caroline.

"I try to shovel their driveway when it snows, but especially now that she's sick." Barry looked down at is hands. "She hasn't begun to lose her hair yet, but she's lost so much weight. It's weird. She looks so much now like she did when I first met her."

"How's that?"

"Younger, actually. Like when she used to need me."

"Do you think she will need you again, now that she's sick?"

"I don't know," he answered, breathing out heavily, "but if she does, I'll be there."

Caroline thanked Barry for coming as he headed out. "I guess I'll see you in the morning," she said.

"See you then," said Barry as he walked out into the snowy evening.

Caroline decided to make soup... to distract her from everything that was happening. She felt as if she was trying to gain a foot-hold in an avalanche. She used what she had for the soup, which wasn't much, but it was enough to make a good vegetable soup. Meanwhile, Sarna called. "So?" she said when Caroline picked up the phone.

"I lost my job," answered Caroline. "Barry came to tell me that they'll be letting me go tomorrow."

"Because of Mr... Mr... Mr., what's his name?"

"Fitzpatrick. Yeah."

"What will you do?"

"I don't know, and I don't care right now. I'll figure out something."

Caroline decided on a change of subject. "What are you doing on this lovely snowy day?"

"Just sitting here... staring at my stuff."

"That's good," said Caroline. "I'm just sitting here listening to my wind chimes."

"How's it going?"

"It's going."

Caroline decided to bring some soup to Jacob. It would be better than those horrible TV dinners. As she maneuvered the container of soup into her car, she realized that she hadn't locked the door behind Barry when he left, nor did she feel as fragile as this morning. She remembered the dream too, but she did so as if through the lens of someone else's mind and not her own. She found Jacob still on the couch bed, but he was awake and watching TV.

"I brought you some soup," she said.

"Hmm? Oh! Thank you!"

She set him up with a bowl, seeing that he had indeed changed.

"How's the pain?"

"Not so bad right now."

"Good," said Caroline. "I lost my job," she added.

"I lost a job once, too," said Jacob, "but that was my fault."

"This was my fault, too."

"It'll be all right," he said. "Something will come."

"Caroline?" Jacob said before she walked out the door.

"Forget about rent. I don't need it."

"No, Jacob..."

"Forget about it. Sometimes a person just needs a little help."

"Okay, Jacob. Thank you. I'll see you tomorrow."

"See you tomorrow," returned Jacob.

At work the next day, they told Caroline that they could not allow mistakes of such a scale, $7,500.00 worth...

smaller ones, maybe, but not big ones like that. She did not tell them that it wasn't a mistake. Tapping Barry on his shoulder on the way back to her desk, Caroline smiled. He smiled back and handed her a box.

"A box?"

"You know. Like in the movies... to pack your stuff in."

She chuckled and took it, but she didn't really need it since she had so few things. She used it all the same. "Call me," she said to Barry before leaving.

Barry held out his hand. "Your number?"

Caroline scribbled it down on a scrap of paper, handed it to him, and left.

For the rest of the week, Caroline made jewelry. She called her father to say hello. He didn't have too much to say except that he missed her. He wanted to know if she would come out to see him.

"I don't really have the money, Dad," she said.

"Then, I'll buy you the plane fare."

Had he forgotten about her inability to be around too many people? Had he forgotten about their apparent inability to be around each other? But maybe, thought Caroline, this was just the story she kept telling herself. Perhaps she could change that story. Her father said he'd look into it and get back to her. Next, Caroline called her mother who told her she'd like her to come to Boston for a visit.

"Sure, Mom, I'd love to," said Caroline.

It had been a long time since she'd been to her mother's place, and she didn't know why. Caroline liked her place, with its long winding stair cases, tall, narrow rooms, and steel-applianced bottom floor kitchen. Off of this kitchen was a cobblestone court yard. Her mother had, indeed, become a very talented designer. She had never gone to school for it but had used her raw talent to create environments that were astounding in their feel and beauty. Caroline found that she would very much like to go there. Next, Caroline read The Beginning and followed Sam King into his marriage: a dark, tangled-up place where years of estrangement and, yes, even hatred dwelled. She watched as

Sam began praying for softness, for a shift in perspective. Caroline's eyes went wide when Sam Cook proclaimed to have been answered by God.

"Sam," He said, "All of my children are meant only to be loved. ALL of them."

Caroline read on and observed Sam King softening as cancer cells ravaged his organs. She, again, met his family: each of its members drifting precariously away from one another as Sam tried desperately to maintain a fragile hold on them. Caroline shed a tear as she read about Sam King holding one of his daughter's troubled drawings; a girl with a slit throat lying in a puddle of blood. Caroline's tear plopped onto the page as Sam's tears spilled down onto his daughter's drawing.

Again, God spoke. "Love, Sam... love."

Caroline went to Jacob's everyday that week. The physical therapist who had been assigned to him had not shown up twice in a row, so Caroline took over her duties for the time being. She called the agency to inquire about this and found there had been some sort of glitch, and someone would be out within the next two days. However, no physical therapist ever showed up... so Caroline continued. Again, she found that her hands knew just what to do, and it filled her with a sense of purpose and joy that she had never known. She and Jacob played cards and watched football together, something she had never cared to do. With Jacob, it was fun. She liked watching him get all riled up and laughed when he yelled "Idiot!", and "Dumb ass!" Jacob was doing better, managing a few stairs at time, and getting dressed in his trousers and plaid shirts. He shaved and belted out Hank William's songs while he did this. One night, they sat in the living room eating burgers when there came a jingling from upstairs- from Gretta's closet. They both stopped chewing and listened to the sound, which carried on for a good twenty seconds or more. Jacob smiled. "There she is! There's my girl!"

Caroline went to Lila's on Saturday. This time she brought her dream journal and shared with her both dreams: the one with the necklace and the one with the wind chimes. Lila told her that they both, in a way, may represent change and transformation. Caroline's heavy sense of fear in both dreams may indicate her fear of change.

"Does this make sense to you?" asked Lila.

"Yes, I suppose, but they both seemed so real."

"In a sense they are," said Lila. "Fear can be, or feel like, a very real thing. But you can walk through that fear and actually use it as a vehicle for change."

This made Caroline think of Sam King, of tortured drawings, and of a God who actually answers when you call. "How do you know all of this?" asked Caroline.

"A little from my training. Mostly from reading, from clients, from personal experience, too," said Lila.

Caroline wanted to feel hopeful, but she had been though her fears so many times; it had always led to naught. Caroline told Lila about placing the wind chimes outside her door and forcing herself to listen to them as she looked out into the night.

"Is that what you mean?" she asked.

"That was very powerful, what you did. And don't forget, Caroline, sometimes it's hard for us to see in ourselves the progress we've made. Look, you're coming here. You're helping your neighbor. You've gone to Sarna's and helped her."

"And, I forgot to lock my door the other night."

"That's huge," said Lila.

"But I've done my locking ritual every night since."

"That's okay, too. Give yourself credit for the progress you've made and forgive the rest."

They settled down for Reiki or hypnosis or whatever it was. They used the clock as they had before, and Caroline immediately fell into a semi-awake state. This time she had no images or memories. Her body felt heavier than any of the other times, and it sizzled and tingled around her solar plexus... her throat... her hands. Caroline gave way to this feeling which, at times, produced little zaps like the electrical charges made when sliding into bed on a cold winter night. Her hands especially felt this, and a few times it actually hurt. She knew they were almost done when Lila began pulling gently at Caroline's feet. Lila asked, "Have you been using your hands a lot lately?"

"Why?" asked Caroline, thinking of her recent burst in jewelry making.

"I feel a lot of movement of energy there... energy coming through your hands. A lot."

Caroline remembered that she'd been helping Jacob with his physical therapy and how good it felt. She told Lila.

"That explains it. Do you like it?" asked Lila.

"Actually, I love it."

"I think you're actually doing a form of Reiki when you're doing the physical therapy. I can feel a lot of exchange of energy in your hands. I wouldn't be surprised if you see a big improvement in him."

Caroline thought that she already had.

"And in yourself as well," said Lila.

"How so?"

"Because when you perform Reiki to heal others, you also heal yourself."

On Sunday, Caroline went back to Sarna's. To Caroline's surprise, she'd managed to keep the living room clear of clutter. Yet, the cases of Coke, which had been moved

143

into the kitchen last week, had somehow found their way back onto the highchair in the living room.

"Okay... Why are these back in here again?" asked Caroline.

"There wasn't any room for them in the kitchen!"

Caroline walked down the hallway, dodging bags and boxes, managing to make it into the kitchen with Sarna at her heels. There were stacks of phone books, boxes of mugs, bags full of bags, and canned goods strewn about.

"Okay," announced Caroline, "let's do it."

They got to work stacking and unstacking, tossing and throwing. Caroline moved to throw out some empty cereal boxes.

"No!" shouted Sarna, "don't throw those out. I need those."

"What for?"

"For... for... box tops for education."

"For what?"

"You cut off the tops and...," said Sarna, "oh forget it. Just toss them."

Caroline did so and turned toward the boxes of mugs. "How many mugs do you really need, Sarna?"

"Oh just a few."

"Good. Then, we'll pick out... say four... and I'll take the rest to the Salvation Army."

Sarna placed her finger along-side her chin. "If they'll take them back."

"Back?"

"Well, that's where I got them."

Caroline took out four mugs and opened the cabinet above the stove. She saw before her rows and rows of more mugs. She turned toward Sarna, placing her hands on her hips.

"It's really bad, isn't it?" Sarna asked sheepishly.

"Well," Caroline thought for a moment. "There are worse things."

They laughed uncontrollably while attacking the rest of it. By the end, Sarna had a normally functioning kitchen.

"This feels so good," said Sarna. "I feel like a snake that has shed its skin."

They carried bags and boxes of stuff out to Caroline's car. "Wait! Carly! Would you mind taking one more thing for me?"

"Sure."

"Do you think you have room for the high chair?"

Caroline surveyed her car. "Um... well."

"It comes apart. We can take it apart and squish it in."

They went back upstairs and took the high chair apart as best they could. Before carrying the pieces downstairs, Sarna disappeared into her closet. She bumped and crashed around. Things spilled out of the closet into the hall. Something came crashing down.

"Ow! Damn!" yelled Sarna.

"Sarna... Sar?"

"Yup. Yup. I'm okay. Here, I have something for you." She emerged with a brown, leather pocket book. "I think this would look great on you," Sarna said, smiling proudly.

"Here, throw it on my shoulder," said Caroline.

At last, they shoved the high chair in the car and Caroline drove away, beeping and waving out the car window.

On Monday, Barry called Caroline from work. "There's a fat lady working next to me," he said.

"So?" said Caroline, "don't judge a book by its cover."

"She has a beard."

"She does not!"

"And she's ruthless... worse than me."

"Not possible," said Caroline.

She invited Barry over after work. "What the hell am I doing?" Caroline said out loud after hanging up.

At lunch time, she went up to Jacob's to check on him. As she approached, she saw a car in the driveway. She thought of turning back. That Jacob had a visitor seemed so strange. She felt oddly envious. But her curiosity got the best of her, and she approached. Caroline knocked. "Jacob?"

A woman, maybe in her forties, answered. "Yes?" she said.

"Oh. Um. Is Jacob here?"

"Yes. We're just doing some therapy right now."

Caroline looked down at the woman's hands and looked back up at her face. The woman made no move to let Caroline in.

"Caroline? Is that you? For God's sakes come in! Get out of the cold!" yelled Jacob from within.

Caroline stepped around the woman with the glasses and frizzy, brown hair.

"How's it going, Jacob?" asked Caroline.

"Oh. It's going just great," he said, rolling his eyes.

Caroline turned toward the woman. "You can go now," she said.

"But I'm not done. I'm the new physical therapist," said the woman.

"Her name is Marjorie," said Jacob, restraining a laugh.

"Marjorie. You can go now. You see, I'm the newer physical therapist." Marjorie grabbed her purse from the table and left, slamming the door behind her. They both broke out in a peel of laughter.

"Oh, thank God," said Jacob. "She was awful!"

Just when Caroline was getting used to the thought of Barry coming over, he called to cancel. His ex-wife's girlfriend had called him all upset because his ex-wife had become very ill throughout the day. The girlfriend didn't know how to help her or what to do. Caroline felt relieved and disappointed at the same time. For something to do, she brought in Sarna's stuff and went through it. The high chair sat in a heap on her living room floor. She held up the pocket book, inspecting it. Caroline put it on her shoulder, viewing herself in the mirror. "Not bad," she announced. Feeling something crunching inside, she opened the pocket book and saw a stack of aluminum yogurt lids. She took a pink one out, reading the print: "Lids that care." Sarna must have been collecting them to donate for the cause of breast cancer. Caroline took them out and put them in a zip lock baggie so that she could turn them in.

Next, she picked up The Beginning, opening up to where she left off... with Sam King crying tears on his daughter's disturbing drawing.

"Love, Sam...Love," God had said.

Sam looked up, unsure whether the voice had come from within or from without. Pain, both literal and emotional, ate at his insides as he ventured to ask, "What? Love? That's it? If I love them enough, will my sickness go away?"

"It's that and more."

"More? What more?"

"My love flows through you and is intended to reach through you unto others."

"Bullshit," said Caroline. She hated that God was being so cryptic, so evasive. What is He... a politician? Still, she read on. Sam began the arduous process of loving, which spanned many chapters. Sam King discovered the transformational power of love, which is preceded only by forgiveness. Caroline watched through the lens of her imagination as Sam King's daughter and son melted into the children that they were created to be. Sam began to see his wife as the woman she was... deserving only of pure, unconditional love. He began to see them all as God's children, even himself. Yet there was a period of intense guilt. Who had he been, all those years, to pass judgment on who did and did not deserve his love? Who was he to dole out God's good love in such a miserly way?

The next chapter was titled "Going Back." God had, once again, come to Sam King... this time while he was, of all things, on the crapper.

"There's more," He proclaimed.

Sam had wondered if God was referring to the rather private business at hand, or something else much more profound.

Again, Sam looked heavenward but saw only the bathroom's overhead light. "What?"

"There's more for you to do."

Sam shook his head, sighing out heavily. "I'm not surprised."

"Go back."

Sam looked around him. "Back? Where?"

"In your memory. Look for something long hidden."

"What sort of thing?"

Caroline feared that God would not answer or, at best, answer evasively. She really wanted to know.

"There, underneath layers and layers of memory, exists your true purpose."

Sam was thinking that if God had been reading his mind, he'd been a little off. He was, indeed, in the middle of thinking about purposes. He'd actually been wondering about the purpose of human beings' need to crap in the first place. Why couldn't God have designed us to expel our waste in more dignified ways? That's what he was thinking when God first spoke.

Sam had finished his business on the toilet but dared not move. Who would wipe their ass in front of God? Caroline laughed out loud at this.

"Do you mean that, somewhere deep inside my mind, I actually already *know* my purpose?"

"Of course, you do!"

"Well, how far back should I go... in my memory, I mean."

God replied, "Further back than you can imagine."

"Pardon me, God, but that is of no help to me." Sam flushed. God grew silent, and Sam feared that he'd offended him.

Finally: "Children know. They know without the complications of ego, self-doubt, and worldly responsibilities. A child knows his true purpose before a mysterious force seeps into his life and begins to erase the knowing. "

Sam shook his head, exasperated. I have to remember back to when I was a child... what my purpose was? "Mysterious force?"

"Ego, self-doubt," replied God, "Go back... you will remember."

Caroline put the book down. She felt like Sam... exasperated.

Next, Caroline attacked the high chair... assembling it piece by piece. Why was she doing this instead of getting rid of it? She had no idea, except that maybe she couldn't think of anything else to do. Once it was all together, she cleaned it up and set it up in the corner of her living room. Finally, she settled down to make some jewelry.

Caroline kept eyeing the high chair as if it was a guest in her home. She pictured a child in there with little Cheerios stuck to his fingers, popping them in his mouth. She felt a sort of aching somewhere below her stomach, like a straining pulse. Caroline had never wanted children... had never yearned for them. To her, it had always seemed that there was too much worry tied to them. More worry was not something that she'd needed. Caroline finished up a necklace with alternating green and silver beads, resolving to take all her newly made jewelry to The Used Book Store after her appointment with Lila the next day. She could hear the wind chimes lightly tinkling as she curled up in bed and wondered if she should take them down. She didn't really want a dream like the one she'd had the other night. Once in bed, though, she found that she couldn't muster the energy to get back up, and she drifted off. Another dream began in earnest. In the dream, Caroline was lying in a bed that was not her own, but some other one, a queen or king sized one. She was sleeping. In her dream, a sound from the end of the bed woke her. Opening her eyes, she tried to discern the sound. It could have sounded like the rumpling of clothes or a shuffle of feet. As she strained harder to hear, she realized that it was really words she was hearing- but a whisper of words. She sat up and crawled to the end of the bed. She heard the whispers more clearly and could make out the words "Please", and "Let." She peered over the edge of the bed and found herself looking down onto the top of a child's head. The child had blonde hair... a boy. She heard clearly the word "Don't," and saw that the boy was holding something small and colorful in his hands. He was whispering

151

to it... whispering the words, "Please don't let." She could not make out the rest. In her dream, Caroline peered down even more closely. She saw that the small, colorful thing the boy was holding was a worry doll, and he clutched it between his fingers. He was whispering and whispering. Then, as if in a time warp, Caroline found herself sitting in a kitchen, the same one as in the dream from the other night; the one where she'd been rolling the dough. A baby sat in a highchair manipulating Cheerios into his mouth while she, Caroline, was cutting up apples into perfect wedges. The baby screeched with delight. Caroline turned and said, "Happy boy. My happy boy." She picked up a Cheerio and put it in his mouth. He gummed the Cheerio and blew raspberries, drooling down his chin. "My boy," she said, touching his round cheek. When Caroline woke, she did not remember the dream, but the feeling of it stayed with her. The feeling was like yearning, and it wrapped about her like a cloak. Or it was like despair. Or joy.

Gretchen

Caroline went to Lila's who said, "You are all over the place."

"I know, and I don't know why."

Lila tried leading her in a meditation, but Caroline could not relax.

"Here, let me do some energy work."

Caroline went to the bed, and Lila started her ritual.

"You forgot the clock," said Caroline.

Lila moved it next to her. Lila spent time on Caroline's head, throat, shoulders, and heart... at least ten minutes in each spot.

"Can you move the clock any closer?" asked Caroline.

Lila shifted the clock.

"Closer?"repeated Caroline.

Lila placed it on the bed next to her ear. Lila went to Caroline's heart again, spending a long time there. The solar plexus came next. Caroline heard the ticking. She began to tick within and within. Lila moved to her abdomen and Caroline began to tick there, too. She began pulsing. Caroline felt layers of something there, each one lifting out and up... one layer and then another and another. Until, at last, a deep, deep layer now on top held an image of a girl on a kitchen floor on all fours. It was Caroline, but it wasn't. It did not look like her, but it was her. This girl had long, blonde hair, and she was picking things up off a floor. The girl spoke, startling Caroline in her Reiki-induced sleep.

"What the hell, Owen," *said the girl, feeling along the floor with her hands.*

"Ut da hew," *screeched a boy above her in a high chair.*

The girl stood up. "No, Owen, honey. Don't copy Mumma," *she said.*

"The Cheerios are for you to eat, honey. Not to throw on the floor!"

The girl was exasperated. Tired. A radio in the kitchen was on, but the girl was not singing or humming or dancing. The boy threw more Cheerios on the floor and laughed.

"Owen, no! Daddy will be here soon, and he will not like a mess!" she said.

The girl took the baby out of the high chair. He crawled around her ankles.

"Owen, please. Pick up the Cheerios for Mumma. I have to get Daddy's dinner on his plate."

She stepped on the baby's hand, and he wailed. She heard a car pull into the driveway and scooped up the boy, kicking Cheerios under the table. She rushed the boy into the bedroom, clutching him to her chest.

"Sh, sh," she said, "It's all right. Mummy's sorry."

A man came into the house then, brushing past the wind chimes on his way in.

"Gretchen?"

"In here Jake!" she yelled.

"What's wrong with the baby?" he asked, approaching the bedroom.

"Nothing, he's fine," she said.

He came into the bedroom and saw the baby's red face. He saw the baby clutching onto his hand. The man's eyes blazed into her, bearing into her... so blue. "What did you do to him?" he yelled louder. His blue and red eyes were demanding, pinning her down, not letting her go.

"I... I... stepped on his hand, Jake. That's all. It's no big deal," she admitted, backing away.

"How do you do that, huh? How do you just step on a baby's hand?"

"It was just an accident!" she yelled. She put the baby down on the bed behind her because she knew what was coming, and it came... right alongside her face.

"What year is it?" asked Lila.

"19... 1960."

"And what's your name?" asked Lila.

"Gretchen. My name is Gretchen."

Caroline

Caroline felt pulling on her feet. She felt it but could not move. She heard Lila walking around her, around the room. There was also an absence of sound, and she realized it was the ticking of the clock that was no longer there. Caroline turned her head and opened her eyes.

"Oh, my God," she said. "Oh, my God!"

Tears rolled down onto the bed.

"This can be a very difficult experience," said Lila. "It's okay." She covered Caroline's hand with her own.

"What was that?"asked Caroline.

"You went back into a past life. Today I met Owen and Jake and Gretchen," returned Lila.

"No way. No way!" Caroline was becoming more and more agitated. "That's a load of crap! Past life... I'm just crazy, is all. I have a personality disorder or something. That's all... I mean that's bad enough, but... a past life!" Caroline was hysterical. "Can you... can you fix it? Split personalities, I mean?"

Lila waited for Caroline to finish, then insisted on calling Sarna to come and take her home. Caroline did not want this. She wanted to be alone. She felt like a badly wounded animal needing to drag itself deep into the woods where it would either die or nurse itself to health. Lila compromised by making her stay another hour, sipping apple juice. Caroline thought of the names: Owen, Jake, and Gretchen. She thought and thought.

"Lila, I don't think any of it's true. I think I must have made it up," she announced.

"How's that?" asked Lila.

"Here's how. I got the name Jake, obviously, from Jacob. Gretchen, from Gretta or even from the Gretsch guitar Tim left with me. As for Owen, well, I don't know about that one, but I'm sure if I thought about it, I'd come up with some sort of connection."

Lila thought for a moment. "Or... the name Owen could have come from your job."

"My job?"

"Think about it," said Lila. "You used to make a living from people who *owe* money."

Caroline laughed, relieved. "See?"

"Here's what you may want to consider," said Lila, "Sounds have vibration, energy. Names have vibrations and energy. So do words. They carry on through time, back and back. Forward and forward. Sounds, names, words, energy, can follow us through lifetimes, especially when there is unresolved business around this energy."

"I'm not sure I follow," said Caroline.

"Think of it like a wave," said Lila. "A wave starts way out on the ocean, so far that we can't even imagine. It travels through miles, hours, days, even weather... until it reaches a point where we can see it. That wave has energy. Of course it does, or it wouldn't be a wave. By the time we can see it, it has altered somewhat. Maybe it is bigger than it was, maybe smaller. It is still, essentially, a wave. It needs to keep going until it can resolve itself, until it can meet the land and break. When it does, it is not a wave anymore, but a part of the ocean... itself again with its own energy, but ocean energy, not wave energy. Those names are like waves. They began long ago and have traveled through time into your present life until they can be resolved and turned back into the ocean again."

Caroline sat and blinked.

"Here. Have some more apple juice," said Lila.

Caroline returned <u>The Beginning</u>. She did not care to finish it. She did not care to know how Sam King's quest went or ended, having decided she wanted nothing to do with quests. She took down the wind chimes and threw the high chair into the woods out back. When she ordered Chinese take-out and they told her the pick-up number was eleven, she canceled her order.

Caroline started taking a full Klonopin at night because it helped her sleep. She never had dreams when she took it. When Barry called to ask how <u>The Beginning</u> was going, she lied and told him she'd finished it but thought it was a little dry. He sounded disappointed, and at first she cared a little bit, but then she didn't. Caroline told Sarna about what had happened, but quickly squelched her enthusiasm by telling her to forget it... that it was all fabricated anyway. "I probably have a split personality," she'd said. She called her mother and told her she'd be visiting her in two more days. The only thing she did care about was Jacob. She'd spent the better part of three days with him doing physical therapy, eating meals with him, and watching Jeopardy with him. He knew all of the answers... or questions... and Caroline knew next to none. But she liked the meaningless thinking it required of her.

On the third day with Jacob, he said, "You know, Gret, that cat of yours wants to be fed. You wanted it, now go ahead and feed it. Wasn't that the deal?" Caroline was sitting next to him on the couch when he said this. She turned slowly and looked at him. He sat staring at the TV. "Now go on," he said.

Caroline stared for a moment longer and then said, "I already did."

"Then why's it's hopping around here like it's about to come out of its skin?" he asked impatiently.

"He's just... playing is all," answered Caroline.

"Hm. Well then at least let him out. I can't follow my program."

Caroline got up, dramatically opened and closed the door, and came back to sit next to Jacob. They both sat, staring at the TV.

Finally, he said, "I'm getting tired, Gret. Just going to lay down here for a moment and take a little nap. Help me get my feet up, would you?"

Caroline moved in front of him, lifted his feet, and shifted them over onto the couch. Jacob never took his eyes off the TV.

"That's my girl," he said and fell asleep.

Caroline was going to her mother's, and she was worried about Jacob. He was obviously not doing well, and she didn't feel comfortable leaving him for two days. Caroline called the agency and reported his decline. She told them that she was his primary caretaker and would be gone for two days. They said they'd send out a visiting nurse to stay with him. Caroline didn't have the heart to tell Jacob she was going, especially now that he seemed to think she was Gretta. She, at least, waited until she saw a car pull into Jacob's driveway and watched as a matronly looking woman entered his house. After that, she got in her car and left town.

It felt good to drive away. Many people came to Caroline's small coastal town to breathe in the sea air with visions of lazy, sandy evenings spent on the beach watching the sun go down. Whole families would come and rent the same houses on the same beachy streets year after year, their young children falling heavily into bed at night with sand between their toes. Teenagers would hang out in the beach parking lot together in the evenings, their bare feet prancing about on the still hot pavement. Many parents excused their teenager's late night outings under the pretext that parents, too, deserve to be carefree. Caroline liked summer in her town. She, too, liked the sand under her feet. After a whole year of being pent up in socks and shoes, feet like this. She preferred the beach between the hours of four and seven when all that's left are a few stragglers. Caroline liked to imagine their lives. Were they city people? Country people? Were they really as carefree as they looked? However much Caroline liked summer, she was usually glad for its departure. Being left behind by all those summer folks was, in some way, relieving. Winter in her town, like winter in many coastal towns, was ghostly. Posters and fliers advertising summer festivals, concerts on the green, and yard sales lie crumpled and decomposing along the sides of streets, tangled in shrubs and trees. Discarded wrappers from the ice cream trucks lay frozen under mounds of snow and ice. Townies who complain of the summer people... with their caravans, paraphernalia, and traffic... shut themselves up in their homes all winter anyway. Store owners pray to make it to next summer when they will, again, sell objects that are meaningful only for a short time. A ghost town. Which suited Caroline just fine... a ghost girl in a ghost town. Still, it felt good to be driving away from all of this, where she could go be a ghost in her mother's house, looking out of the third floor bedroom window at all the city passers-by.

Once in the city, Caroline parked at the Charles Street garage (the parker's garage as her mother called it) and walked briskly toward Beacon Street with her overnight bag and her new (used) brown leather pocketbook. As the pavement turned into red brick, turned into gray cobblestone, Caroline imagined herself in an old English village. Although, she had no idea of what an old English village actually looked like.

She approached her mother's door and knocked but then just walked right in. Shouldn't she be able to just walk right into her own mother's house? "Mom!" she hollered. There came no reply, so she poked around: going into rooms, down hallways, up stairs. At last, Caroline went downstairs into the kitchen, finding a note from her mother on the table- saying to make herself at home, that she'd be home shortly. Caroline checked the fridge and found all sorts of foods that she, herself, would never think of to eat: collard greens, humus, strange flat bread wrapped in cellophane, chick peas in a Tupperware container. Caroline turned toward the courtyard and found that it was barren. The last time she'd been there, it was summertime and the courtyard had been perfectly staged with potted plants, petunias, flox, and lavender. Caroline rooted about in the cabinets, finding more things that she'd never consider eating: sesame bread sticks, wheat thins, and rice cakes... a far cry from Baby Ruth bars. At last, she found tea bags, and she put on a pot of water to boil in the heavy, stainless-steel pot. She sat at the kitchen table and stared out at the courtyard, feeling that as much as she'd wanted to come, she now wanted to leave. Maybe, she was thinking, she'd beg off- feigning illness, or better yet, a job interview. This made Caroline think of the task before her of actually trying to find a job. Her little bit of savings would not last more than a few months, and her jewelry business was most definitely not going to carry her. She tried to remember if, as a child, she'd had any desires of what she wanted to do or who she wanted to be, but could recall nothing. Caroline was thinking she'd have to ask her mother when she heard the teapot hissing. Turning, she saw her reflection in the teapot and also the reflection of someone sitting just behind her at the kitchen table... a girl with long, brown ringlets of hair. Caroline spun around, looking at the spot where the girl would have been sitting but saw nothing. Looking back at the teapot, she saw only herself. Caroline quickly got up and poured herself a cup of tea, but her hand was shaking so badly that she spilled scalding water on the black, granite counter top.

Just then, she heard her mother entering from up above. "Caroline?"

She looked back at the spot where the girl would have been... still nothing. "Down here Mum!"

Her mother came bumping into the kitchen, her arms full of shopping bags. "Oh. I've just been shopping," said her mother breathlessly as she pecked Caroline on the cheek. Her mother's hair was completely different from the last time Caroline had seen her. It was cropped short and dyed red.

"Mum, your hair! I love it! Remember the time I cut my own hair in high school? That's what it looks like."

"Oh, I loved your hair like that," said her mother. "Your father didn't, but I did." "Oh, and remember when you dyed it blonde with that friend of yours?"

"Trish," said Caroline, "What a disaster."

"I thought that was hilarious," said her mother.

"Trish's mother didn't think so," said Caroline. "Who needs her, anyway?" said her mother. "You know, her mother called me right up that time and really gave me a way to go."

"About the hair?"

"Yeah. She was all... Don't you watch those girls? And on and on."

"What did you say?"

"I said, 'Girls will be girls. It's not the end of the world. It's not going to kill them.' Oh but she just went on and on." Her mother sat down at the table, in the same spot where the ghost girl had just been sitting. "Finally, I just told her to go screw!"

Caroline was incredulous. "You did not!"

"Oh yes I did, and I never looked back."

"Are you cold?" her mother asked. "I'm cold. There must be a draft here."

She got up and adjusted the thermostat. "Oh, here now. I got you some stuff. Nothing much really. Just some clothes."

"You didn't, mom."

"I did. Now it's not much." Her mother unloaded the bags onto the table. Sweaters, shirts, scarves, and boots came tumbling out.

"Mom!"

"Oh, stop. Can't a mother buy something for her daughter?"

"Well, if you insist," said Caroline, "and, besides, I just lost my job."

"Oh?" her mother said, "Well, something will come."

"Yes. Something will come," replied Caroline.

They had a grand time. They watched old movies and curled up on the couch with big, heavy blankets eating salty, buttery popcorn. Her mother looked so young with her short,

164

pixie hair cut. She could have been a friend. Except that in certain lights, Caroline could see an oldness about the eyes. Her hands, mostly, betrayed her age with her gnarled, arthritic knuckles and age spots. Her skin there looked paper thin. Everything else about her was so young, from her blousy linen pants, to her slim v-neck sweater, to her dangling silver earrings. Caroline thought that in many ways her mother looked better than she did.

"I'm going to get a glass of wine," announced her mother. "Do you want some?"

"Oh, no. But if you've got some Coke or something, I'll take that."

Her mother disappeared into the kitchen and came back up with two glasses, setting Caroline's down before her. Her mother sipped. Ice cubes clinked upon her glass. Caroline was reminded of the murky abyss her mother used to dwell in, back when Caroline was wading through her own.

They settled down to watch an old black and white featuring Jimmy Stewart. They commented on how good looking he was.

"Your father used to look like that when he was young," said her mother.

"Really?"

"Oh. He was a hottie." Rose studied Caroline, thinking. "You look like him," she said.

"Are you saying I'm a hottie?"

"No." Rose studied Caroline more closely. "You have his lips."

"And I have your slight build," said Caroline.

165

"You and I, we have to make sure we get enough to eat, or we'll waste away to nothing," said her mother. "I'll be right back. I'm going to get us some ice cream."

When she came back up with the ice cream, Caroline noticed that she'd also refilled her glass of wine. They watched Jimmy Stewart and rattled off all the other actors that make them chew their nails: Nicholas Cage and Tom Cruise. Kevin Costner and Mel Gibson.

"He looked like Tom Cruise, too," said her mother.

"Jimmy Stewart and Tom Cruise?"

Her mother nodded. "A cross between. Haven't you seen pictures of him when he was younger?"

"No. I don't think I have."

Her mother got up and disappeared again. Caroline looked around the room, noting a potted fern, a painting of a young girl in a floppy hat reading a book, and a small, wooden end table with bowed legs. A book lay on top labeled, Daily Affirmations. Caroline leafed through this and stopped at a page that read, "You cannot discover new oceans unless you have the courage to lose sight of the shore."

At that moment, her mother came in with a picture in her hand. She handed it to Caroline. "Here. See?"

Caroline looked at this picture of her father. He looked to be somewhere in his twenties. He leaned against a car, his arms folded across his chest. He was smiling. He actually did look like both actors. "Wow!" said Caroline. They sat in silence for a bit, both looking at the picture.

"Do you ever miss him?" asked Caroline.

166

Her mother looked at her with glassy eyes. "No. Life with him was too hard."

"Do you miss him?" asked her mother.

"Yes," said Caroline. But even as she said it, she wasn't sure it was true.

Her mother admitted, "I've often wondered if I did the right thing though. For you, I mean. I just couldn't live with his drinking anymore. It took him away from me, from you. It's so awful living with someone who's there but not really there, but a girl needs her father."

They sat and thought for a moment.

"Yes, but if he was there but not really there, then what would it matter?" asked Caroline.

"Hm?" said her mother, staring absently at the TV.

Caroline ventured further. "Did Dad ever hit you?"

"No. Never," replied her mother.

"That's what I figured," said Caroline.

They returned to watching TV in silence. "Are you happy mom?" asked Caroline.

Her mother thought for a moment. "In many ways, yes. I love what I do, decorating that is. I get paid well for it. Enough to afford a place like this."

Caroline's mother looked around the room, and then continued, "And I love the city. I have lots of interesting friends. I would say my life is full. It hadn't always been that way. Your father's illness took up so much of my energy. Trying to protect myself from it. I'm afraid I didn't have much attention left for you. All those years of being absorbed in my own problems. I knew you were out there sort of floating around. I'm sure you could have used a mother, or at the very least, some company."

Caroline said nothing.

"That bothers me still. Being a mother is so hard. You don't just automatically know what to do. To me being a mother is about extremes. It's either intense or it's tender. I've never been good with extremes."

Still, Caroline said nothing.

Her mother changed the subject. "Do you remember how much you used to love giving massages?"

"That's right. I forgot about that," said Caroline, smiling.

"You used to beg to give them to your father and I. Not that you needed to beg. You were so good at it! I used to swear that just the touch of your hands made all the aches and pains go away."

"God. I forgot about that. How young was I when I started that?" asked Caroline, curiously.

"Young. You were very young. I'd say maybe five or six."

Caroline looked down at her hands- thinking of Sam King and of life purposes.

"Do you think you still have the touch?" asked her mother.

"We could give it a try," said Caroline.

Caroline had her mother lay down and began to work her hands over her back. Her hands just knew. They were strong when they needed to be and gentle when they needed to be. They tingled and zapped, more so in some spots, less so in others. Her hands remembered the feeling and, somewhere inside of her, she remembered the feeling too.

"Oh, yes," her mother said, "you still have the touch."

Caroline went up to bed; to her third floor room. The bed looked so much more inviting that her own, than Gretta's. She crawled in and stared up at the ceiling. She could just barely hear her mother somewhere down below. Caroline knew that she was probably straightening and cleaning, because that was what she'd always done- straightened and cleaned, incessantly making things perfect. Caroline felt guilty and, somehow, angry. She should be helping her. After all, it was she herself who had helped to create the mess. Then, she remembered that her mother had never really wanted her help, that it had always been viewed as interference in her pursuit of perfection. Again, Caroline felt alone, angry. Just then she heard a jingling... a clinking, coming from the closet at the foot of the bed. She didn't feel scared, not one bit.

"You don't have to hide from me, Gretta," Caroline said as she dropped off to sleep.

The morning brought with it bright sunlight filtering in through her mother's delicate, white curtains. Laughter rose up from the street. Car horns chattered back and forth. Caroline opened her eyes and saw the silhouette of a bird against the curtains, its little body twitching back and forth as it shifted about on the windowsill outside the window. Caroline watched it until it flew away. Its wings were soundlessly beating in the air. She was glad for it, that it could just get up and go like that. But she also wanted it to stay. Caroline got up and went downstairs to find her mother

169

sipping tea in the kitchen. Caroline's mother had an appointment to meet a client at Fanueil Hall that afternoon. They decided that Caroline would come along and poke around while her mother met with her client. She worried over being around too many people and over how wide open the place would be.

However, she needn't have worried because there turned out to be few people and not a lot of wide open spaces. There were plenty of stores, smaller ones, to hide in. Caroline found that, oddly enough, the city held a certain amount of anonymity. People seemed to be in their own bubbles-floating by one another. She could be walking around bald or bottomless and wouldn't have received so much as a glance. The people that she saw rushed hurriedly about with headphones on, listening to music or perhaps books on tape. She could have been yelling obscenities, and no one would have known it. Caroline thought that, perhaps, the city might be just the place for her: a place where she wouldn't be noticed, a place where she was just as weird as everyone else. Weird, lost girl. Caroline saw her mother and her client through the window of the café, looking for all the world like a weird, lost girl, too. Everywhere she looked, everyone else looked that way, and it occurred to Caroline that maybe everyone in the world is a little weird and lost. Caroline suddenly saw all the people passing by her as reaching back in time and time and time. Each person, perhaps, had been someone else once and before that, someone else... and yet to be someone else the next time around. Caroline stepped out into the midway and walked slowly along, each step one of hundreds and hundreds of thousands she's ever taken. Maybe her mother was an obsessive cleaner. Maybe Caroline was afraid and anxiety-ridden. Maybe Sarna was gay and hadn't yet forgiven herself for it. Maybe her father was absent, drunk or not. Maybe Gretta was a ghost trying to tell her something. Maybe Jacob was losing his mind. Maybe Barry was wasting his time. Maybe it was all just life.

Strolling through the city, Caroline happened upon a bar called The Black Rose. She stopped to look at it and noticed, in the window, a poster of a smiling man with a guitar slung over his shoulder. He wore a cap and a faded, denim shirt hanging loosely from his shoulders. His name was Tim Parlay, and he was playing at The Black Rose in three more weeks. Caroline took a step back. She hadn't seen him in seven years, and here he was staring back at her through the window. She stepped in closer and touched his smile line, looking like a parenthesis around his mouth. She touched the little bit of hair whisping out from under his cap. Stepping away again, Caroline went to find her mother.

They went out to dinner that night to an Indian restaurant. Caroline took a quarter of a Klonopin just in case. She may have been able to walk down the midway with ease earlier that day, but to go out at night may have been a different story. She wore the clothes her mother had gotten for her: a long black cloak and black boots. Caroline looked and felt like someone else. The restaurant was dark inside and sectioned off into smaller rooms for the patrons.

Once they were seated, her mother asked, "Are you okay with this?"

"Yes. Why wouldn't I be?"

"Well, I know you don't like crowds too much or the nighttime- or at least that used to be so."

"I guess it pretty much is still so," said Caroline.

She'd expected some sort of advice or words of wisdom, but then quickly dismissed the notion; her mother had never been one for such words. Instead her mother suggested the lamb wrapped in grape leaves.

Caroline spent the last night at her mother's on her own. Her mother had to, once again, meet with another client who was having an impromptu gathering. Apparently, she needed some emergency interior designing to accommodate the expected crowd. Caroline's mother said she'd be home by ten o'clock. So, Caroline picked through her mother's videos and found "It's a Wonderful Life." She remembered that she and her parents used to watch this movie every Christmastime. An image of her father crying at the end of the movie came to mind, accompanied by another image of her mother rolling her eyes. Caroline watched on as Jimmy Stewart, or George, bought into a life he hadn't wanted and wished to throw away. Clarence, his bumbling angel, came down to accomplish the difficult task of showing him that his life was worth wanting. Of course, in the end, George saw the value of his life- wanting it with a vengeance. Caroline considered this. Is it better to want the life you have, like George? Or to want for a life you don't have, like Sam King? Caroline checked the locks four times before going up to bed. Shortly afterward, she heard her mother come in. She heard her picking up, straightening, and cleaning. Then she heard her below in the second floor bedroom. A clanking came from down there. It sounded like the ice cubes in her mother's wine. Her father had never used ice cubes in his drinks, but her mother did. Her mother always did.

The next morning, Caroline told her mother she'd be back in a few weeks- maybe. She explained that an old friend of hers was playing at The Black Rose, and that she might stop in to visit him. Her mother seemed somewhat distant and preoccupied. She was scrubbing and cleaning in places that hadn't needed it. Caroline wasn't sure that her mother had even heard her.

"Mom?"

Her mother pulled up a chair. "Here, sit down, honey. There's something I want to tell you."

This time Caroline sat where Gretta, the ghost girl, had been sitting only days before.

"I found out I have breast cancer," said her mother.

"Oh, no, Mom. Why didn't you tell me?"

"I just did," said her mother, bending down to scrub at a tile on the floor.

"No, I mean before."

"We were having such a good time. I didn't want to ruin it."

"When did you find out?"

"Last month," said her mother. "I start treatment next week. That's why I cut my hair. I figured I'd let it go in stages."

"How bad is it, Mom?"

"Not the worst. I may be able to beat it with treatment."

"I'll come and stay with you," announced Caroline.

"No. You've got your own life."

"No, I don't Mom. Not really."

"Well, then, you'll be busy getting your own life I'm sure."

"I don't even know where to begin," said Caroline.

"You will. Something will come. Besides, I've got my friend Marta on call. She lives just two doors down," said her mother.

Caroline stayed for a bit longer, trying to fit this new image of her mother into her old paradigm. It felt like trying to fit a sleeping bag into a zip-lock baggie. Finally, Caroline drove toward home with her new purchases in the back seat of her car and her head full of her mother's ghostly image... shimmering, shifting, changing.

Instead of going right to her house, she went to the beach. She parked in the beach lot, the only car there. Bundling up against the wind, Caroline walked onto the beach and sat on the cold sand. The rhythm of the ocean came again and again and again... relentless, but not harshly so... just enough to say... "I'm here. I'm here. I'm here,"... with each wave coming and resolving itself.

Caroline's life became an avalanche, a flood. When she returned home, she found messages from Sarna, Barry, the visiting nurses association, and her father. She was most interested in the nurse's message, so she did not absorb the others so well. They had called just yesterday to let her know that Jacob had to be taken to the hospital, for he had become despondent, his blood pressure dipping down dangerously. He'd been asking for Caroline. She immediately phoned the hospital and found that he was still there. His blood pressure had been stabilized, but he was being held for close observation. Caroline left for the hospital, forgetting about all of the other messages. When she arrived, she identified herself as his neighbor and caretaker. They gave her directions up to his room. She followed the red arrows down a maze of hallways, passing patients with mysterious ailments. The elevator took her up to the third floor where she followed yet more red arrows. She passed a pediatric unit with Goofy and Mickey Mouse painted boldly along the wall. A boy, about seven-years-old, sat up in a hospital bed in his room, laughing. He was bald. A young girl in a wheelchair and a johnny quietly wheeled by. The red arrows quickly veered away from the pediatric unit. Caroline followed these to a nurse's desk where she stopped and asked for Jacob Stills. The nurse directed her to a room down on the right.

The door was open and Caroline entered. She expected to see Jacob sleeping, perhaps because that was how he was the last time she saw him. But he was awake, doing a crossword puzzle. Jacob looked up and smiled.

"There you are," he said gently.

"Yes. Here I am."

"What happened?" she asked, sitting in the chair beside him. She noted that his cheeks were more hollow, his brow line and the bones around his eyes more prominent, making his eyes look as if they were receding. But they were still as green as ever.

"That damn nurse thought there was something wrong with me. Maybe there was... I guess," he said.

"All I know is one minute I was walking along, and the next there were these paramedics staring down at me. It was my blood pressure. It just plummeted. I guess I don't blame her for calling the medics. That happened to my wife once, toward the end. One minute she was fine, and the next she was drooling and not making any sense. That's probably what I did," he said.

"Your blood pressure is okay now?"
"Presumably so. I was also dehydrated and iron-deficient, so they've got me hopped up with this IV and iron shots. Not to mention the blood pressure pills. They say they'll spring me after a few more days."

"Oh, good," said Caroline, "then I can come over and we can watch Jeopardy again."

"Where did you go?" Jacob interrupted.

"I went to visit my mother in Boston," she said, looking down at her feet.

"Oh, good. You should go see your mother. What's her name?"

"Rosemary. Most people call her Rose. She told me she has breast cancer," she blurted, surprised at the lump in her throat.

"Oh, dear," he said. "How old is she?"

"Sixty-seven."

"She'll beat it," he said. "Many women do."

Caroline looked away. "And many don't."

"Try to be optimistic. Sometimes that can make a big difference."

They sat quietly for a moment. Jacob looked toward Caroline... not at her but beyond her. He smiled and laughed.

"There she is," he said like a giddy child.

"Who?" asked Caroline, although she already knew.

"Gretta! I can see her reflection in the window behind you. You brought her back with you!"

A nurse came in at that moment to check Jacob's vitals and asked to speak with Caroline in the hall. She wanted to know if Caroline was family. Caroline explained that she was just a close friend and his neighbor; that she often took care of him. "He has no family left," she added.

"We'll have to get a release signed from Jacob, giving us permission to discuss his situation with you, but I'll just fill you in a little right now. So you know what you're dealing with."

Caroline became nervous. Situation? Dealing with?

"Apparently he became somewhat belligerent before being brought to us. The visiting nurse reported that he had become very agitated, yelling for someone named Gretta. He went into a bedroom in the upstairs and kept staring at a closet, crying for this Gretta. I guess the nurse got him to come downstairs with her where he lost consciousness."

"Oh, Lord," said Caroline.

"We're watching him right now for signs of dementia. He also has an infection in his hip where he broke it, so we're getting that under control, too. But it's mainly the dementia we're concerned with."

Caroline looked toward Jacob. He sat upright on his bed, peering at the window, laughing. This is not dementia. Caroline thought to herself.

After Jacob signed the release form allowing Caroline to be informed of all medical information, she left to go home. She promised to be back the next day. She retraced her steps along the red arrows but took the wrong elevator which brought her to a different unit. Caroline found herself at radiology and almost turned back but instead walked further in. She saw nurses and doctors. There were regular people, too: men in parkas and women sporting pocket books, jewelry, and full heads of hair. One woman wore a pair of earrings that Caroline was quite sure she, herself, had made. A little girl skipped along-side her father, clutching onto a Barbie doll. Caroline walked deeper into the unit where foreboding medical equipment sat against the wall, ready for action. Caroline turned a corner into a hallway that seemed devoid of life. Passing a room, she saw a woman hunched over a suitcase. She wore a beautiful blue scarf over her bald head. A little further in, she spied a woman sleeping in her bed. An

IV line snaked out of her arm. Her long, black hair spread out over her pillow like a fan. A doctor came out from around another corner, bumping square into Caroline.

"Do you need help with something?" he asked kindly.

"Oh, no," stammered Caroline, "I'm... I'm just lost."

She turned around before the doctor could respond and ran down the hall. She began to cry as she turned corners and corners until she reached the elevator, its doors just closing. She reached her hand in just before the doors shut, pushing them open. There, inside the elevator, stood Barry.

"You?" they said at the same time.

"I'm here for my wife. My ex-wife," he said.

"Yes, that. I'm here for my neighbor."

"Is he?" "Is she?" they said all at once.

"She was admitted day before yesterday. She'd gotten really sick and was very dehydrated. They're finishing this round of treatment in the hospital, so they can keep her hydrated. Her girlfriend left her, so I'm here now. You know."

"I know," said Caroline.

"Your neighbor?" he asked.

"Oh, he's fine. I mean not fine, but... He's just dehydrated and anemic, and he has an infection in his hip. He has no one but me, really. So I'm here."

"Good of you," he said.

"And you, too."

They walked off the elevator.

"Oh. You called?" asked Caroline.

"Oh. Oh. That. Yeah. I was just wondering if you wanted to meet me at the cafeteria here and have some lunch with me. It can be kind of lonely here," he said.

"I'd love to," said Caroline. "Let's go."

They sat for hours in the cafeteria. Barry had gone up a few times to check on his ex-wife, whose name Caroline learned was Emily, but each time she was sleeping soundly. Caroline wondered if Emily had been the sleeping woman she saw- the one with the black hair. Barry said that he'd like Caroline to tell him about herself, that he felt he didn't really know anything about her.

"Yes, you do," she said.

"Okay. I know that you like to read, that you live alone, and that you lost your job."

"And that I take care of my neighbor."

"Well, what's his name?" asked Barry.

Again, Caroline felt a crowding inside her. "So knowing my neighbor's name will help you to know me?"

"Yes, actually. Knowing the details about someone's life can help you to know that person, don't you think?"

Caroline thought on this and decided that the smaller details are not like the larger, monstrous ones. "Jacob," she answered.

Then: "What was it you said about me, Barry? That I can be a real bitch sometimes? That I'm afraid of something? That I'm sweet and ballsy? Sounds like you know me pretty well," she said.

"No," Barry countered, "your life. I want to know about you and your life."

"Why?"

"I just do. Do I need a reason, really?" he asked.

"I suppose not," answered Caroline. "But if I tell you, you might not want anything to do with me afterward."

"Give me a shot," he said.

So Caroline told him everything: about her OCD, her anxiety, dropping out of college, her parents, her mother's breast cancer, even about Gretta, Lila, Gretchen, Jake, and Owen. She felt a little crazy, but also like something was being lifted up and out of her.

"You don't believe, do you," she said, "any of this stuff."

"I don't disbelieve. Who's to say that we mere mortals know everything there is to know? That there aren't past lives or future lives or ghosts?"

"I'm not even sure that I believe, Barry. It's killing me."

"You'll figure it out," he said, "and whatever you decide, I won't judge."

Caroline looked at him closely. He was not the person she thought he was. He seemed, at that moment, so much older.

"How old are you Barry?"

"I'm forty-six," he answered.

"Wow. I had pegged you for my age, maybe a little older. Thirty-seven or thirty-eight."

"I've been carrying my age well so far," he said.

"I'd say so."

181

They got up to leave, she to go back home and he to go back up to his ex-wife.

"There are two more things you don't know about me," said Caroline before leaving. "I never really finished <u>The Beginning</u>. It was just too much for me to handle right now."

"Ah," said Barry, looking down at his shoes.

"But... can I ask... Did Sam ever discover his purpose?"

"Yes, he did," replied Barry.

"What was it?"

"I won't tell... in case you want to finish reading it someday."

Caroline ventured further. "Did he die...? Did Sam King die?"

"Yes."

"So, he wasn't cured of his illness?"

"Actually, he was," said Barry.

At Barry's cryptic answer, Caroline turned to leave.

"Caroline?" called Barry, "what's the other thing?"

"Oh, that," returned Caroline, "I give a mean massage."

When Caroline got home, everything seemed different: everything from the air she was breathing to the light of the setting sun to the manufactured light of the light bulbs in her little house. She noticed that it was getting lighter later, the slant of the sun more forgiving, the tint of the snow more blue than white. It was the rotation of the earth, or the shifting of the people in her life, or the movement within her. Or it was all of these. She pressed the button on her

182

answering machine and listened with new ears. Her father was saying that he had some information about some flights from Boston to Oregon. Sarna was saying that she'd cleaned out her bedroom and that the kitchen and living room were still in perfect order. Caroline felt a sense of pride or gratitude well up within her like a spring bubbling up and filling itself into a hole in the earth with good, clean water. Caroline moved to call Sarna and her father back but then stopped. Instead, she settled herself down on the living room couch, placing her small, black, battery-powered clock on the table in front of her. She sat and sat. Listened and listened... until she found a place within her so new, so old. It was a place but not really a place, a feeling buy not really a feeling. Old, new. Lost, found. Surging, sitting, waiting, still. Back and back to something unfathomable, or to nothing. Nothing. But it was a nothing made of fabric, and she was one of its threads... breathing, ebbing, flowing. When at last Caroline opened her eyes, she looked at the clock, seeing that it was 11:11. Five hours had passed during the time that she was in a place that had no time.

Caroline went back to Lila's with the intention of meeting Gretchen. Instead, she met with Tim again. This time, she found herself in her old kitchen in Scituate, seven years ago... on the phone with Tim. He was telling her he was moving to Florida. When Caroline hung up, she slid down onto the floor, wailing. A few hours later, he showed up unannounced at her door as he often did. Again, her heart felt like a balloon filling up and rising, as he walked up the stairs into her kitchen. Gone was his jovial sing-songy expression, replaced by a naked look upon his face. He said nothing but wrapped his arms around her; his long arms which fit his guitar so well, wrapping around her almost twice. "No hug has ever felt as good as his," Caroline told Lila. They went back to his place, already packed, save for the reel to reel recording equipment upon a makeshift table. He made her something to eat. He let her listen to his recordings. He wanted her to sing a background vocal on one of his tracks. Caroline did this, blundering through it. It took hours to lay down that track. In the end, it was really no good, but it didn't matter. She was with him. She saw a picture of him when he was younger. He was heavier then, but she liked him as the thin version she knew. Caroline spent the night with him upon his mattress on the floor. He fell asleep, but she didn't. She cared not to lock the door as the moonlight illuminated the room.

The flood continued. Caroline went to see Jacob every day, doing physical therapy behind the doctors' and nurses' backs. Jacob's infection went away. His blood pressure stabilized. They hadn't seen any signs of dementia. His B-12 shots restored the iron in his body. He'd be going home soon, but not before scheduling a slew of appointments first. Barry came over to help Caroline install a hand railing up to Jacob's entrance, since Jacob was becoming even more unsteady on his feet. Caroline gave Barry a back massage on Jacob's couch as payment, and he swore it had alleviated the pain in his right knee, which always gave him trouble from an old hockey injury. Emily came home after a week's worth of intravenous chemotherapy and radiation. Barry moved back in with her. Emily had begun to lose clumps of hair in the shower. Barry aged five years in a week. Sarna invited Caroline over to meet her new girlfriend, a co-worker who Sarna had always wondered about. Her name was Julie, and she'd been wondering about Sarna. Caroline liked her and could see that they, most likely, were in love. She watched them as they moved freely about Sarna's newly purged place. Caroline had her father book a flight for her in another month, when spring would be real and not just a feverish wanting. Her mother began her treatment, the kind where she could take pills at home- their toxic chemicals killing both the bad cells and the good ones along with them. So far, her mother felt fine... if a little tired. Also, Caroline went back to Lila and met Gretchen again.

Gretchen

Lying on Lila's bed, the clock took her back.

"What year is it?" asked Lila.

"It's 1958."

Lila quickly did the math... it would be six years before being born into Caroline's current life.

"Where are you?"

"I am at a dance."

"What are you wearing?"

"I'm wearing a puffy white skirt and a pink sweater. My hair is in a ponytail. I'm wearing lipstick and eye shadow and blush, but I had to wait to put it on 'till I got to the dance, otherwise my parents would kill me."

"They don't like for you wear makeup?" asked Lila.

"No. Sarah and I put it on at the dance."

"Who's Sarah?" asked Lila.

"My girlfriend."

"How old are you?"

"Nineteen."

"What's going on around you?"

"There are a lot of people. All the girls are wearing skirts and sweaters, like mine. There's loud music. Sarah and I are standing against the wall. She sees a boy she likes from town. I don't like anyone from town. I like the boy from across the orchard."

"What's his name?"

"Jake. Jacobson, I think. I think that's his real first name. He's here. He's coming up to me, calling me Blondie. Blue, very blue. A light blue t-shirt, khaki's, loafers. Sky blue eyes. I can see them even though it's dark. Blonde. His hair is so blonde, like mine. I'm leaning against the wall trying to play it cool. I like him so much. I want to dance with him."

"Do you?"

"Yes. Oh. I like him so much. He's the best looking boy here. He's so gentle. Even his voice is gentle. I love his voice. We are dancing, twisting. No. No. Now we are slow dancing. His touch. His voice. So gentle. I like him so much."

"Where are you?" asked Lila.

"A dance."

"What state?"

"State? Virginia. In a town, Cedar... No, Cedarville."

"Where is Sarah?" asked Lila.

"She's dancing with a boy. Not the boy she likes, a different one. People are all around us. They are leaning in, calling us the Blondsy Twins. That's funny. I like that."

They were silent for a while, Lila and Caroline.

"Oh, okay. Now we are going somewhere."

"Where are you going?" asked Lila.

"A bunch of us. We're going to the clearing in the woods by the apple orchard."

"Do you want to go?" asked Lila.

"Yes. But my parents will be furious. But I want to go, so I go. We are there, and there's a kettle drum in the middle with a fire in it. There are already people there. I sit on a log next to Jake. My skirt will get dirty. I'll have to fix that before I get home."

"How will you get home?" asked Lila.

"I'll walk with Sarah. We walked to the dance. We'll walk home. It's not far."

"Are you afraid?" asked Lila.

"No. I feel good. I'm next to Jake. He has his arm around me. Everyone else is pairing up, too. Oh, God. They're all necking. I'm so embarrassed. I've never done that before, but Jake isn't pressing me."

"What's he doing?" asked Lila.

"He's talking to me. He's telling me about his father's automotive shop. I know this already. My father brings his Chevy there to get it fixed. His father has blonde hair like him. Jake is telling me that he works at his father's garage. He likes it, he says. He says he makes a lot of money. Jake is passing a big bottle of something to me. He takes a swig. I take a swig."

"What is it?"asked Lila.

"I don't know but it's gross. It burns my throat. I think it must be what my parents drink at Christmas and at our family parties. I am drinking more, and he is drinking more."

"Are other people drinking it, too?" asked Lila.

"Yes. The bottle is going around. Sarah has some more too. The boy she's with has his hand under her sweater. I can't believe it! I can't believe she is doing that! But it's not the boy she likes."

"Is Jake touching you?" asked Lila.

"No. Just his arm is around me. He's telling me he lives with his father and grandmother in his grandmother's house. He says his grandmother lives in an apartment in the basement. I think he said his mother died. Is he saying she had red hair? I don't know. I'm not following him so well. But I think I know the house he lives in. It's the one on the other side of the orchard. Over by the garage where he works. It's small, brown shingle. They found my dog in their yard once. They called. My father and I went to get him. His father, Jake's father, handed the dog to us. My father thanked him, but he just handed the dog over to us, unsmiling. Their house is small. The grandmother is very old. The father looks old, too. I got my dog."

Again, they were silent for a while.

"What's happening now?" asked Lila.

"I think... I think I'm telling Jake that I'm going to go to typing school. Where I can learn to type and be a secretary. It's a good plan for me. I'll be a secretary, get married, have babies... like my mother. But then I'll stop working and raise my kids. I can't tell if Jake's listening. He's staring at the fire. Now I am, too. Sarah is on the other side, laughing. I can't tell if the boy she's with still has his hand up her shirt. But they're both laughing."

"Is Jake laughing?" asked Lila.

"No. He's very serious. He's saying that he will someday be running his father's garage. His father is not well. He has breathing problems or something. I'm trying to follow him. It's hard."

"Why is it hard?" asked Lila.

189

"I don't know. I'm all fuzzy. My body feels so heavy. I will not drink anymore of that stuff. It's making me feel sick."

Silence enveloped Lila's room. Lila waited for more.

Finally: "I don't know what's happening. Something is happening. All the people are running out of the clearing. Jake is pulling me up. He's telling me we've got to go, there's someone coming. People are stumbling and laughing, crashing through the woods. Is it my parents coming? I'm scared. No, says Jake. It's probably just old man Fitz. Old man Fitz is worse. Everyone says he's crazy. That he kills cats just for the fun of it. But I don't believe it. No one would kill cats. I'm telling Jake this. Or maybe not. Maybe I'm just thinking it. He's picking me up. He's crashing through the woods with me."

"Are you scared?" asked Lila.

"I'm scared to go home, but I like Jake carrying me like this. He is fast. I can't make out anything. It's all blurry. He's putting me down in the woods. I'm getting sick. He picks me up again but he's not going as fast. Where are we going? I ask him. To your house, he says. I want to know how he knows where I live. But I can't tell if I actually say it or just think it. He says, 'I know where you live. I've had my eye on you for a long time.' I put my head into the crook of his neck. It fits perfectly."

Again, Lila and Caroline were silent.

"I don't know how he gets me home, but he does. My parents are up. I am in big trouble. Probably, Sarah's in big trouble too. But I'm too sick to care right now. I fall into my

bed. I see the lace curtains. I see my poster of James Dean. Good bye James, I am saying. I'm no longer in love with you.

In the morning, my parents call me down. Gretchen, they say, you are not to see that boy again. I say okay, but I've got different plans."

"Do you continue to see him?" asked Lila.

"Yes. I go to his garage after school every day. He picks me up in his pick -up truck, a blue Ford. He smells of oil and grease. And something else that I can't place."

"What do you do when you are at this garage?" asked Lila.

"I watch him fix cars. I think he's good at it. He usually gets it right. Except for once when he couldn't figure something out, and he got mad and threw a wrench. It hit the garage door and put a hole in it."

"Did this scare you?" asked Lila.

"I figure this is what men do sometimes."

"Did your father ever do this?" asked Lila.

"No. But he's a salesman. Salesmen don't have to figure things out and fix them. It must be hard for Jake to have to fix everything all day long."

"Is Jake's father ever there?" asked Lila.

"Sometimes. He really does have a hard time breathing. He's very quiet. Mostly it's just Jake."

Time ticked on, the seconds spilling out into Lila's room.

"My parents found out."

"About going to the garage after school?" asked Lila.

"Yes. They figured out I wasn't actually going to drama club meetings. They had high hopes for me getting the lead part in the school play. Instead I was coming home smelling like grease."

"What did they do?" asked Lila.

"They talked about it. I could hear them while I was in my bedroom doing homework. They said that maybe I was old enough now to go steady, that maybe it was only natural. And they liked that Jake has a good, steady job."

"So they let you go?" asked Lila.

"So they let me go."

Caroline

Caroline was remembering things from another life while she helped Jacob with his physical therapy. He was home now, and she was remembering. She remembered a touch, gentle but hot, and it felt like spring: all green and blue. She remembered skin and a tickle of hair. Jacob was oblivious to her remembering. He seemed to be oblivious of most everything. The happiness that Caroline had expected upon his return had not come. He hadn't noticed the hand railings, hadn't cared to watch Jeopardy. Caroline was disappointed and worried. She hadn't realized how much she'd enjoyed his company, their banter. As her hands ran along his calves and rotated his ankles and loosened his tight, stubborn hip joints, Jacob lay there registering no response. Not even pain.

At last he said, "Please. Can we be done?"

Caroline stepped back. "Jacob?" she said, "what is it?"

"I don't want you to touch me."

Tears pricked her eyes.

"Every time you do, I get better, and I don't want to get better. I want to let go. I see her, Caroline. I do. I see her more and more, just like my wife did. I wish we could have seen her together. I don't know why. I don't know why it's taken so long."

They were quiet for a moment.

"I think maybe before I couldn't, because I was too much in a fog. I was drinking heavily. I even drank a lot while Gretta was alive. A lot. She used to make sure I got up to bed all right. If I hadn't gone to the store that time. If I had stayed. I never would have let her go into those woods. Never," Jacob sobbed. "I can see her, but I can't hear her. She's trying to talk to me, but I can't hear her. I see her in the windows, sitting in a chair, reflected in the TV. I even see her in you," he said, turning to look at Caroline, "but I can't hear her."

Caroline was crying now, too, tears rolling down her face, forming little puddles in the hollow spaces of her collar bones. Jacob continued.

"Did I ever tell you Gretta's favorite story?"

Caroline shook her head.

"It was the story of Narcissus, a youth who visited a lake daily to peer in and admire his own beauty. One day he fell into the lake and drown there. A flower had grown in his spot, which is now called the Narcissus. A Goddess appeared then at the lake and asked why it was crying so. The lake replied that it was crying for Narcissus. The Goddess said that it was no surprise, for Narcissus had been so beautiful. The lake asked, "Narcissus was beautiful?"... to which the Goddess replied, "Well, yes, of course. Didn't you see his beauty every day?" The lake replied, "I never noticed that Narcissus was beautiful. I weep, because I could see in his own eyes my own beauty reflected."

Caroline blinked, thinking that she didn't even know what a Narcissus looked like. She resolved to find out.

"Ah... she loved that story. We used to tell it over and over. I got so sick of it. Now... I tell it to myself at night. It helps me fall asleep." Jacob went on. "Such an imagination... Gretta had. I think her imagination served her well. She was lonely, being an only child. For a while there, she had an imaginary friend. Actually, no, Gretta said it was her sister, her imaginary twin sister."

Caroline's head swam with memories of her own imaginary twin sister, long since forgotten. She knew what Jacob would say next.

"Gretta called her Birdie."

As Jacob began to drift, he added, "It's been a long time. A long time without her. All these years I've kept going, because God asks me to. I don't want to keep going anymore."

Caroline spent the night. She couldn't bear to leave him, so she stayed in the spare room upstairs, the one that his wife probably stayed in... all those years that she couldn't bear to share a bed with the father of her missing child. Caroline dreamt of three girls: Gretta, Caroline, and someone else, circling around one another... talking to one another, but she couldn't hear what they were saying.

Gretchen

Caroline went back to Lila's. She expected to pick up where she left off, sitting in Jake's garage, but she didn't. This time she found herself sitting on the arm of the sofa in her parent's living room.

"What year is it?" asked Lila.

"1959."

"What's going on around you?"

"There are a lot of people in my living room. Jake is sitting on the couch to my right. His father is there, too. And my parents. And my cousins. My aunt and uncle."

"Is it a party?" asked Lila.

"Yes. For me and for Jake. We're engaged. It's a big deal, but Jake's not happy with me."

"Why?" asked Lila.

"Because of what I'm wearing."

"What are you wearing?"

"Long pants. The waist comes down low, and they're flared at the bottom. I'm wearing a long brown and pink striped sweater, form fitting, a turtle neck. And a scarf around my forehead. It trails down the back of my hair, and I like it. I thought Jake would like it, too, but he doesn't. He likes me in skirts. 'We'll talk about this afterward, Gretchen,' he says to me. Now he's been quiet all night, and I feel funny. At least he's talking with my father."

"What about?" prodded Lila.

"About Eisenhower. My father likes him, but Jake doesn't. He says he's useless. That we ought to be going into

195

Vietnam. That he would go if Eisenhower would just send us. My father thinks it's none of our business to be there."

"What do you think?" asked Lila.

"I don't know. I don't really know anything about it. I just want to go to typing school. I don't know anything about war. I don't want Jake to go, so I guess I don't want the war."

"Do you love him?" asked Lila.

"Yes. I'm going to marry him and have children with him. I'll be the wife of a mechanic and the mother of his children. We'll live in his grandmother's house."

"When will you get married?" asked Lila.

"In two more months. In June. I can't wait to be his wife. Our children will be so beautiful. Blonde like us. We can visit him across the street at the garage. I'll make Shepard's Pie for dinner and have candles lit when he comes home. My mother's been teaching me how to cook and bake. I'm picking it up quickly."

"So you're liking this? Being engaged and thinking of the future?"

"Oh yes. I love Jake."

A pause came. Lila got up and got herself a cup of tea, blowing on it in an effort to cool it down. Steam came off the top, dissipating in the air. She waited, then: "We haven't done it yet you know."

"Done it? You mean... as in sex?"

"Yea, that. We're waiting until we're married. Jake feels very strongly about that. So do I, but my mother already talked to me about that. About... intercourse. She said it hurts the first time. She told me about the bleeding."

"Are you nervous?"

"Yes and no. I know Jake will be gentle. He's always gentle. Even when he fixes cars. Except when he throws wrenches."

Again, silence.

"Are you still at the party?" asked Lila.

"Yes. Everyone is drinking a lot. Well, not everyone. Mostly my father and Jake. Also Jake's father and my uncle. The men are in the kitchen drinking and smoking. They're making quite a ruckus. My father only does this on special occasions. They're playing poker, the men. Jake's father is getting all blurry. His speech is slurring. I want to go outside, to be away from him. I've seen him do this before. Once his speech goes, it's all down-hill from there."

"How so?" asked Lila.

"He gets all angry. Once, he flipped over the kitchen table, because he couldn't find his boots. He's always doing that, misplacing things. Then, be blames everyone else. He tried to blame Jake for his missing boots. Jake and I, we knew it was he who misplaced them. Now, at the party, he's getting all worked up. He's lost some money in poker, and he's challenging my uncle. 'Damn hand,' he says, 'Can't get a break. You know something about these cards I don't?' he says to my uncle, 'You countin' cards here?' I can hear an edge in his voice. Like he's begging to be matched. My uncle doesn't seem to notice. He's just laughing. But me, I'm waiting for the table to fly."

"Does it?" asked Lila.

"No. Because Jake steps in. He smoothes it over. Tells his father that no one in this crowd is smart enough to count cards. Tells him he'll win him his money back. Everyone laughs. I watch them. They have no idea of the disaster that's just been avoided. My mother, aunt, and I go on the back terrace to smoke. I have never smoked with my mother before. I am almost a woman now, so I can do this."

"How do you feel?" asked Lila.

"I feel good. Like a grown up. Like my life is under my feet. From where I stand, I can see Jake through the window. He and my father are laughing, uproarious. The radio is so loud. It's playing "Hound Dog," so me and my mother and my aunt start dancing. Oh, it's so fun. The stars are out. It's warm. I can hear peepers. We're singing along, yelling. My mother says, 'Praise the Lord for Elvis Presley.' We're all gyrating. My father and Jake watch us through the kitchen window. They have their arms around each other's shoulders. My father is smiling. He looks so proud. But Jake is not smiling."

"Why?" asked Lila.

"I don't know, except that I think maybe he doesn't like my dancing. The dancing and the clothes. That must be it. I stop. Maybe it's not proper for a girl about to be married. I go inside and start picking up, because I don't know what else to do. Jake is angry, I think. He's done this before. One minute he's warm and glowing like a lit candle, and the next it's as if the flame has gone out and the candle is all cold and dark. That's what he's like sometimes."

"What's that like for you?" asked Lila.

"It's not so bad. I have to admit, it makes my hands shake and go cold. But men will be men. They have a lot of pressure. I just wait. It passes, it always does."

Lila sipped at her tea and patiently waited for more.

"Afterward, we go home, to Jake's. His father goes right to bed. He's had too much to drink. Jake is sitting on the couch. I am getting myself a glass of water and bringing Jake one too. 'No', he says. 'I want a beer.' I get him a beer. I am bringing it in to him. He's still cold and dark, and now I'm cold and dark inside too. He's pulling me down onto his lap. I'm sitting on his lap. His breath smells like booze. His eyes are not blue, but gray. 'You are so beautiful,' he says. He starts touching me all over. I let him. We are about to be married. He is touching under my sweater. His other hand is down my pants. He is kissing my neck. The TV is on, and it's flickering. There is no sound. He is kissing under my shirt. My pants. He is trying to get them off. 'No, Jake,' I say. 'Yes, Gretchen,' he says, 'Gretch, you are almost my wife. You are so beautiful,' he says again. He is on top of me now. He is moving. He is hurting me. It hurts so bad. So bad. I don't think I can take it. His breath smells of booze. His eyes are gray. He does this. The TV flickers. He is finished. 'You are so beautiful Gretch. But Gretch? Don't ever dance like that again,' he says.

Jake drives me home. We're both quiet. We don't say anything. I can't stop shivering. I can't stop. These clothes I'm wearing, they seem so ridiculous now. I left my scarf on his couch. I'm thinking of Sarah. That's all I can think of. I *invited her to the party, but she never came. I miss her. I wish I was with her right now, sitting in my bedroom, mooning over James Dean. He drops me off at my house, my parent's house. 'See you tomorrow,' he says. That's all he says. I go in. Everyone is still there. Still drinking. Still having a good time. My mother playfully slaps my father on the shoulder. 'You dog,' she says. Everyone laughs. They don't notice that I've even come in. I go upstairs into my bedroom with the lace curtains. BoBo, my teddy bear, is propped up on my bed. I tear down the poster of James Dean and fall into bed for the night."*

Caroline

"At least he redeemed himself," said Barry of <u>The Accused</u>. "I have to admit, I had my doubts, though."

"You mean the guy who allowed that little boy to be raped?" asked Caroline.

"Yeah, that," returned Barry.

"There is no redemption for such things. At least, that's what I believe," Caroline spat. She changed direction. "But, Barry? How could Sam King have died if he was cured of his illness, as you said?"

"I told you... finish the book if you really want to know."

They were sitting in the hospital cafeteria again. Emily had been admitted once more on account of a bad lung infection. Caroline's thoughts returned to <u>The Accused</u> and to Gretta.

"Is there truly redemption if someone does something really bad, in real life I mean?" asked Caroline.

Barry thought for a moment. "I think so. Look at killers. Serving life, or on death row. Some of them even find redemption."

"Is it really redemption or just them trying to make themselves feel better for what they've done?" asked Caroline.

"I don't know. I guess true redemption lies with God, so who are we to know?" he said.

"Maybe it's us humans who can forgive and God who can redeem," said Caroline. "But, really, I don't know how any human can forgive a person for taking the life of someone they love."

"I think it happens sometimes," said Barry. "It's the only thing the person who's left living can do to set themselves free."

"How do you know?"

"I don't, really. Haven't you ever watched "Locked Away?" Caroline shook her head.

"Yeah. It's this show on Friday nights. They go into prisons and film the inmates. Some of them are just fuckin' crazy. But some of them really grapple with what they've done. They even have programs in prison where the offender can meet with the families of their victims, so they can explain themselves. So they can say they're sorry. It's pretty intense. Sometimes the families say they forgive them. Sometimes they say they'll never forgive them. The offenders get to sit there and see their fury. The ones I've seen, they just sit there and absorb it. I guess more than anything, it's closure."

"They don't deserve closure," said Caroline.

"Maybe not. But the families do."

Caroline was feeling angry- a red and yellow shoving anger.

"Are you okay?' asked Barry.

She told him about her last regression, about Jake and her innocence lost.

"I still don't know if I believe it, Barry. What if I'm making it all up?"

"No one could make that stuff up," he said.

Gretchen

"What year is it?" asked Lila.

"1959. We've gotten married. I'm now Jake's wife... Mrs. Jacobson McAuley. It's definitely not what I thought it would be."

"How so?" asked Lila.

"Well, for starters, I haven't seen much of Jake, and I'm so lonely for my parents."

"You don't see them anymore? Your parents?" asked Lila.

"Not really. It's just that I don't want them to see me like this. The other day, I was eating dinner alone, a meatloaf I'd made with my mother's recipe, and I just started crying. I couldn't stop. I cried right in my meatloaf! Also, there's something else."

"What's that?"

"Jake's grandmother died, and it's been so awful around here. Now Owen, Jake's father, won't come out of his

room, except to use the bathroom or get a plate of food. One night, Owen didn't like the spaghetti sauce I made, and he came crashing out of his room, dumping it in the garbage pail. He scowled at me and said, 'This shit is disgusting,' and slammed back into his room. Jake has been very remote. He comes home at midnight or sometimes even later, drunk. He's either quiet or angry. I tried telling him it's okay, about his grandmother... that she lived a good, long life. 'Long, maybe,' he said, and walked away.

Once, when Jake got home from work and passed out, I walked over to the garage. It was dark out, and I could see my breath puffing out as I walked across the street. There was a chill in the air, so I put my hands in my pockets. I used Jake's key and let myself into the garage. I was looking for booze. We keep beer in the house, but never the hard stuff. I needed to see what he was drinking before coming home. I don't know why I needed to see, but I did. I went in there and rummaged around. I looked in his office and his tool chests. I looked in closets and drawers, but found nothing. Then, I noticed the oil vat, this underground barrel that he throws old oil into. I pulled the lid aside, but it was too dark down there. I couldn't see. I grabbed a flashlight from the shelf and peered in. There, I saw bottles and bottles of booze, all empty... just tossed down there, piling up. I closed the lid. I saw what I had come to see, so I went back home."

"Were you surprised?" asked Lila.

"I shouldn't have been, but I was. When I saw all those bottles, I felt like... I felt like... I don't know, like I was at the receiving end of a bad joke. Like I was all alone, standing out in a cold fog."

"Also, I'm upset... because I'm pregnant."

"You're not happy about this?' asked Lila.

"No. I should be happy, I know, but I'm not."

"Pregnancy can be a very emotional time," said Lila.

"I didn't know that. I thought... I thought..."

"You thought what?' asked Lila.

"I thought I would want to have Jake's baby, but now I don't know."

"Why?" asked Lila.

"He's so moody. Sometimes I'm afraid of him. He can be so gentle, but then, it's like he's always trying to restrain himself or something. Like he's always trying to stop himself from exploding. Maybe that's what it is... restraint. Not so much gentleness, but restraint. With his grandmother dying and getting married and all... It's a lot of changes. I'm wondering if he can handle another big change, having a baby."

They fell into a comfortable silence. Lila's clock ticked on.

Finally, Lila said, "How do you plan on telling Jake about your pregnancy?"

"Eventually, I do."

"Do you want to go to that time?"

A breeze came through Lila's window, gently pushing the white, gauzy curtains into the room. A corner of the curtain tickled against Caroline's cheek, but she felt *nothing. A smile played against the corners of her lips as a laugh escaped her.*

"Yes... Oh yes. When Jake comes home, I tell him. I sit on his lap at the kitchen table. He sighs and shifts his legs. I say, better do it now, because in a little while I'll be too heavy to sit on your lap. He says, 'Hmm?' I say it again. He looks at me and touches my stomach and smiles. He smiles and the light is back. His eyes are blue again."

"Is this what you expected?" asked Lila.

"No. Yes. I don't know. He goes in and tells his father, who comes out of his room. I haven't seen him for weeks, and he looks gray and gaunt. He pours a drink for himself and for Jake. They have a cigar together and laugh and clap each other on the back. I call my parents and tell them. Everything is going to be all right. Oh, I'm so happy I could cry. I call Sarah and tell her and she screams. 'Auntie?' she squeals, 'I'm going to be an Auntie?'

"What month is it?" asked Lila.

"Summer. It's hot. Jake and I go down to the pond on summer evenings. There's a little sandy part there just big enough for the two of us. He fishes, and I swim. It's my favorite spot. Sometimes I go while he's at work, and I like that best. It's so quiet. I love the hot sand on my skin. I love swimming down and then surfacing. I like going together, too. When he catches a fish, we bring it home and fry it up. We have that for dinner, and sliced cucumbers, and tomatoes from the garden. Especially now that I'm pregnant, that's all I want. Cucumbers and tomatoes He's so good to me. He always makes sure I have fresh cut

cucumbers and tomatoes. He sings to the baby. Did I tell you he has a beautiful voice?"

"No. I don't think you did," said Lila.

"He does. Sometimes he makes up his own songs. He also loves to sing Frank Sinatra to the baby. He says I've never been so beautiful. And, truth is, I've never felt so beautiful. Even Jake's father comes to life. He talks more, and because the smell of coffee makes me sick, they both give it up, which is not easy for either of them."

"How far along are you at the end of the summer?" asked Lila.

"Three, almost four months and I'm showing. I've just begun to get some energy back so I've been cleaning non-stop. I can't stop cleaning. My mother says I'm nesting. And it pleases Jake."

Lila noticed that her smile began to relax, and then, it disappeared completely. "Is everything alright?" she asked.

There came no answer, only time slipping by. Lila busied herself by taking notes, detailing the particulars of the day's session.

Finally: "Oh."

Lila returned to her side, gently pressing on. "What's going on?"

"He calls me up from work one day."

"Who? Jake?"

"Yes... 'Gretch? Can you send my father over? I need some help,' he says. I go quietly into Owen's bedroom. I've only been in there once, to gather his laundry. He grabbed *me by the arm that time, told me to never, ever go into his room again. He had a lit cigarette in his mouth and a burning ash fell off, landing on my arm. He just held my arm there and let that ash burn me. I'm terrified to go in his room, but I have to; Jake needs him. My hand pauses before the door handle, but then I press ahead and go in. It's very dark in there. 'Owen,' I say. I can see him in bed, but he doesn't stir. 'Owen?' I feel like there's something wrong. I just feel it, like the time my cat, Frick, disappeared. I knew that Frick wasn't going to come back, that he was dead. Then I found him way in the back of the orchard. He'd been ravaged by something. Anyway, I call Owen's name again and go further in. I go up to the side of his bed. He's very still. 'Owen?' I touch the side of his face. It is very cold. I rest my finger under his nose and wait, but I feel nothing. I back out of the room. I don't know why, but I shut his door behind me. I stand in the kitchen for a second, or maybe longer. Then, I run out the door to the garage. That's when everything changes."*

Caroline

Lila said to try to send Jacob some healing energy. Caroline asked how to do this, and Lila told her to imagine white and green light bathing his body. She said that it would be best to get his permission first.

"How am I going to do that?"

"You'll figure something out, and if you can't, just ask his angels for permission."

What? Angels? Oh for God's sake! But, still, Caroline tried.

"Jacob, please, you need to eat something," pleaded Caroline.

"I don't want anything," he said.

"Just stop this," she said. "You're acting like a stubborn old man."

"I am a stubborn old man," he said, a chuckle escaping him. Caroline tried to suppress her own chuckle, but to no avail.

"Aw, hell," he said, as he took the plate from her.

"No, up here, at the kitchen table. You're going to get bed sores if you don't get off that couch."

"Aw, hell," he said again. He really looked awful, all crumpled and shrunken. As he sat at the table, Caroline went over to the couch-bed to fold it back up.

"How about some physical therapy today?" she ventured.

"That?" returned Jacob, shaking his head. "Only if you can do it without touching me."

Caroline smiled. "I can do that."

She watched him with his back toward her as he ate. She closed her eyes and imagined a tunnel stretching from her forehead to where he sat. It carried a vortex of white and green light, twisting and dancing toward him, fast, fast. She felt a sucking pressure at her forehead, and she had to grip onto the arm of the couch, as she felt that she, herself, could be sucked up into the tunnel. All at once, Caroline believed it and doubted it; belief and doubt, belief and doubt, the curse, or the blessing, of human nature. Up and down, in and out, yes and no, ying and yang... the rhythm of life. Caroline opened her eyes and saw, for a brief instant, the back of Jacob's head and, off to his right, Gretta sitting on the counter top, her legs crossed, bouncing forward and back, forward and back. The next instant this image was gone, leaving Jacob alone eating his sandwich.

Later that day, Caroline had to bring Jacob to a doctor's appointment. Jacob got dressed while Caroline waited. They went out onto the porch.

"My car or yours?" asked Caroline.

"Mine," said Jacob. He went in front of her down the steps, gripping onto the railing.

"This?" he asked. "How did this get here?"

"Must be a fairy put it there," said Caroline.

"A fairy for the old and lame... or an angel," he added. Getting into his pick-up truck Jacob said, "Feels like spring." Again, Caroline smiled. "Yes it does."

Gretchen

"Jake rarely comes home before eleven o'clock."

"Why is that?" asked Lila.

"Ever since his father died, he's been like a different person."

"How long ago did he die?" asked Lila.

"Two months ago. He doesn't talk to me. He doesn't touch me. He doesn't sing to the baby anymore. Every night he comes home smelling like booze. One night, I was in bed sleeping and he came in, grabbed me by the arm and pulled

me into the bathroom. He... he... he picked up a towel and pushed it in my face. 'What is this?' he hollered, 'What the hell is this?' 'What? What Jake? It's a towel!' Again, Jake pushed the towel into my face. 'No. This! What is all over it? What is this... nasty dirt? You put a dirty towel in the bathroom for me to use?' I looked at it, but could see nothing there. Maybe a small, old stain, but no nasty dirt. He flung the towel onto the floor. 'How the hell are you going to be able to take care of a baby when you can't even keep clean towels?' He shoved me back. I stumbled backward, tripping over my feet and fell on my butt. He just stepped over me and said, 'I'm sick of this shit!' Then, he passed out on the couch."

"What did you do?" asked Lila.

"Nothing. I went to bed and cried myself to sleep. Now, I always wash the towels, two and sometimes three times before I put them in the bathroom. Also, lately he wants everything to be perfect and clean, so every day I make sure I do certain things before he comes home."

"Like what?" asked Lila.

"Like scrub the floor in the kitchen, check for cobwebs everywhere, straighten the welcome mat, line the canned goods in the cupboard so the labels are facing outward. Stuff like that. It's hard, because I'm so tired. My energy burst from before seems to be gone, and my stomach is getting bigger every day. What else am I going to do? I'm not in typing classes like I had planned. I'm just waiting for the baby. I've got nothing else to do."

"Have you considered going to visit your mother or Sarah?" suggested Lila.

"I don't really want to."

"Why?"

"I don't know, really. I just don't feel like it. Besides, it seems like everything I do is wrong, so it's better just to do nothing."

"How so?"

"Like the other day, I decided to go for a walk. I just needed to get out. I've been feeling lately like the walls of the house are closing in on me. I went for a walk. I passed the garage, just kept walking. Leaves crunched beneath my feet. I could smell smoke, like from a chimney somewhere. Again, I longed for my parents. I miss sitting by the fire with them, trying to figure out cross-word puzzles together. Anyway, walking along, the cool air felt so good on my face, like it had been years since I'd felt it. I just kept walking and walking. I came upon a driveway on my left. A long dirt driveway. There was a mailbox. I looked at the name on it, thinking I don't even know who my neighbors are. It said Fitzpatrick. It dawned on me that this would be Old Man Fitz. The crazy guy who is so famous in town for killing cats. I don't believe it. I don't. I turned into his driveway and started walking down it. I don't know why I did that. I just did. I kept walking. It's a long driveway--so long I began to wonder when his house would come into view. I kept going, because it felt so good to just keep going. Away and away. Finally, his house came into view. Just a little shack really, with a rusting car in the yard, half sunk into the ground.

211

And a torn up couch outside. Just weeds and weeds up to my knees. Then the front door opened, and he came out, Old man Fitz. I'd never actually seen him before. I expected some old decrepit man. He didn't look so old, maybe sixty or so. He wore a white t-shirt and jeans but no shoes, with his hair greased back and long side burns, almost to his mouth. He saw me standing there... this ridiculous pregnant woman in front of his house. 'Hello?' he said. 'Oh, hi,' I said, backing away, 'I'm sorry, I'm just a little lost.' 'Can I help you find your way?' he said, coming towards me. 'Oh, no,' I said, 'I'll just go back the way I came.' I stepped further away. 'You must be the new girl down the street,' he said, 'Jake's wife.' And he came up to me with his hand out. He had a smile on his face. Really a kind smile. I extended my hand. 'I'm Gretchen McCauley,' I said. 'Pleased to meet you.' I saw then that he was just a man, just a person and nothing more. 'You can call me Samuel,' he said, 'I was just heading to my car for my smokes. Left them in there, would you like to share one with me?' he asked. 'Oh no,' I said, 'Tempted as I am. I found that once I got pregnant the smell and taste just made me sick. Perhaps after the baby I'll take it up again,' I said. 'Power to you,' he said, 'I tried once to quit myself. Nearly went out of my mind.' 'Yes. Well. I'd better be going. Nice to have met you, neighbor. Samuel.' 'Yes, you run along. Woman with child such as yourself ought to be careful walking around town alone.' 'Yes. Well, I'll be going. Nice to meet you.' I walked back down his long dirt driveway thinking; old man Fitz is not so bad. When I reached the end of the driveway, a blue pick-up truck was driving by...

Jake's. He pulled over, leaning across the seat and opened the passenger door for me. 'Get in,' he said. I got in and could see that this was bad, very bad. 'What are you doing?' he yelled. 'What the fuck are you doing at Old man Fitz's? You stay the fuck away from him, you hear me? He's crazy, and what are you doing out here alone anyway?' I tried to explain. I tried. Anything I said just came out sounding lame. He hit me across the face, one good hard time, and shoved me in the house. He got very drunk that night. I just curled up in bed until the morning. He slept on the couch."

"It's okay, though. Growing up at my parent's, our neighbors, Mr. and Mrs. Tims, they used to fight all the time. We used to hear them. Mostly Mr. Tims. We could hear him hitting her. Always it sounded like a crack and then a thud or a crashing. Whenever we heard it, we'd all just get quiet. My mother would say to my father, 'Joe, do something.' And he would say, 'It's none of our business. Leave it be.' Sometimes, I would see Mrs. Tims around town. At the drug store or the supermarket. She always looked fine to me, never any marks or bruises. She was always smiling everywhere she went, so I guess it's just the way it is sometimes. I guess. Except one time I saw her do something very strange."

"What's that?" asked Lila.

"I saw her sitting in Bemises, the pharmacy. There was a counter in there where you could get soda. She had a shake or something. She was wearing a pretty pink wrap on her head, like a scarf. And she had on these long white gloves. She looked so delicate. Like a delicate lady. I couldn't

213

believe it, but a colored person came right in and sat down on the stool right next to her."

"How old were you?" asked Lila.

"I think eleven or twelve. Well, anyway, he sat right down next to her, and she started talking to him. Just talking to him like he was a regular person. She was even laughing, her head tipping back softly. People were staring at them, and I could see the man at the counter was coming over to tell him to get up, to leave, that there are no coloreds allowed in here. Just then, Mr. Tims came in and grabbed Mrs. Tims by the arm. He yanked her out of the place. Her scarf had fallen off, and I bent down and picked it up, balled in up in my hand. Mr. Tims shoved her in their car. I could see them through the pharmacy window. He hit her again and again. It was the first time I'd actually seen him hit her. Just like at home, everyone in the place got very quiet. Even the colored man, who got up and walked out. My mom and I sat at the counter and ordered our sodas, but neither one of us said a word. Not the whole time we were there or the whole time on the ride back home. We heard the beating continue after we got home. Then, it just got very quiet there too, at the Tims'. Later, the next day, I went over there and knocked on their door. It took a long time, but finally Mrs. Tims answered. She opened the door just a crack and peeked out with one eye. It was awful, all red and blue and swollen. I couldn't even say anything. I just held up her scarf. I held it out to her and she took it. 'Thank you,' she said, before closing the door. I felt so bad for her, and, now, I'm just like her."

"Anyway, I figure it's better for me to just do nothing. At least for now. At least until things settle down."

"Do you think things will settle down?" asked Lila.

"I think so. Jake just needs time to deal with his father's death. In the mean time, I'll just do what I need to do and not do what I shouldn't do."

"And what, exactly, shouldn't you do?" asked Lila.

"Go for walks. Leave cob webs in the house. Not have everything ready for Jake when he gets home."

"Anything else?" asked Lila.

"Yes. Open or close the windows without checking with him first. Sleep too late. Get up too early. Ask about work. Touch his stuff. Things like that."

"Sounds like a tall order," said Lila.

"It is."

Caroline

It hit her like tsunami. It felt like forever since it had last happened, when in reality it had been only a few weeks. But still. It was always hard to deal with it when others were around, and this time was no exception.

"Caroline? What are you doing?" yelled Jacob from upstairs.

"I'm just throwing in a load of laundry!" yelled Caroline from the basement. Which was true, but she was also hiding. This time, it started with her hearing. A buzzing gave way to a complete blocking of her ears... or almost, as if someone had just stuffed her ears with wet cotton. This gave way to a buzzing and tingling of the arms, a closed up

215

throat, and an inability to move; a panic attack, leaving Caroline looking for a point of reference. Where am I? I am here, standing on this floor, on a Sunday in March, 2008, and it will pass. It will pass. It will pass. She'd learned this technique from a psychiatrist once. Sometimes it helped. Sometimes it didn't. The counting down technique had never worked for her. It stressed her out too much, worrying if she was counting too slow or too fast or if she'd skipped any numbers. She thought of something Lila had suggested. Grab hold of an object, anything, anything at all and hold it in your hand. Just hold it in your hand, and it will ground you. Caroline did this. The closest object was a stapler off of Jacob's desk. She grabbed this and stood with her arms out to her sides; her eyes closed. She saw herself, in her mind's eye, as Gretchen. Images came and went in quick succession, like a slide show: Gretchen giving birth, her feet in the sand at the pond bending down to pick something up, sleeping in bed with her son, running, peering at a pair of birds in a cage, running, crying on the couch, because John F. Kennedy just got shot, her baby boy's warm, wet mouth gumming along her jaw line, big colored bulbs on a Christmas tree... and then...   Feet running on the ground, upon the earth; Feet, Caroline's feet, on the basement floor, cold and hard... on the floor in Jacob's basement, on a Sunday in March, 2008. When it passed, Caroline went upstairs.

"My God," said Jacob, "you look awful. Are you all right?"

"Fine," said Caroline. She went over to the door and locked it. She went over to each window, locking them...

216

doing it all again and again and again. All the while, Jacob looked on.

"Please, don't ask," she said. "I just need to do this."

"Okay," replied Jacob, looking at her the way one might watch a naked person walking down the street. Caroline had been staying there nights to help Jacob, or for other reasons, too.

"I'm going up to bed," she said.

"Okay," he said again, blinking. Caroline went up slowly, leaving Jacob to take care of himself.

It didn't end there. Sarna and Julie came by the next day, unannounced. Sarna had always known intuitively when Caroline was going down. She'd call or stop by, attempting to bring her out of her muck. Always, at first, Caroline resented this. However, she usually came around to see that there was a light beyond her woods, if only briefly. Sarna had a way of reminding her of this without actually saying it. The fact that Julie was with her threw Caroline. It was bad enough that Jacob had to see her walking around like a sick, nervous cat, but Julie, a complete stranger, was a different beast all together. It was nearly impossible for Caroline to pretend that she was well, capable of conversing, listening, and entertaining. Here they were all together at Jacob's house, which made it all that much more strange. Jacob, however, didn't appear to mind the added company. He actually seemed relieved. They immediately fell into a rhythmic conversation which Caroline could not be a part of. She had even retreated to the spare bedroom without the slightest notion of how to

217

rejoin the group. She had used the upstairs bathroom four times to wash her hands, which had grown cold and clammy. She had an insatiable need to be clean. If she could have, she would have run... except that leaving the house was out of the question. Caroline had wanted to lock the doors after Sarna and Julie came in, but to do so would have ignited her queer, repetitive habit.

Caroline heard them downstairs. They carried on as if they'd known each other for years, yet they'd only just met. She envied their ability to chatter this way, with such ease, and she wondered briefly how Jacob would feel if he knew they were gay. You never know with the older generation, how they feel if about that sort of thing. Caroline had a sudden urge to go downstairs and shout, "They're gay, dikes, lesbians!"... just to make them leave. She heard Sarna at the top of the stairs, calling for her. Caroline's cheeks turned red at the thought of her latest impulse. She got up and opened the door. Sarna came in and sat down on the bed.

"Love Jacob," she said.

"Me, too," said Caroline, finding it difficult to make eye contact.

"You're having a hard time aren't you?"

"You can tell?"

"Why don't you come down?" asked Sarna.

"Just give me a minute."

"Alright, but not too long. You'll have to come down soon," said Sarna.

"Why?"

218

"You'll find out soon enough. You'll kill me, but you'll find out soon enough."

"Oh, God. What is it Sarna?"

"Just come down, and you'll see."

They went downstairs, Caroline following Sarna. There, in the kitchen, was Jacob, Julie, and Barry standing around the table which held a birthday cake, glowing with candles. They all broke out into the "Happy Birthday" song. Still... it didn't register with Caroline why they were doing that, why there was a birthday cake, why they were all watching her, smiling.

"It's not," said Caroline when they were done.

"It is," said Sarna.

Caroline turned to Barry. "Barry?"

"Sarna called me, and we sort of put this together."

Next, she turned to Jacob. "Jacob?"

"Sarna came over, and I helped put it all together."

"How did you...," stammered Caroline, looking at Sarna.

"I stopped by here the other day when you weren't home, and he helped me arrange the whole thing."

"I didn't even remember," said Caroline.

"I did," said Sarna.

They had gifts for her. Caroline opened Barry's first which, she could tell from the package, was a book. It was The Beginning.

"In case you want to finish reading it someday," he said.

Next, she opened Sarna's. It was a water color print of a field, yellow, brown, and red. In the sky, hovering over the field, was the form of an angel, barely discernible, its white wings reaching up.

"It just reminded me of you," said Sarna.

From Jacob, she got a book, <u>Little Women</u>. She opened the inside cover where it said "For Gretta." Jacob said nothing but created a temple with his hands, resting his chin upon his fingertips. Caroline came up behind him and wrapped her arms around him. She felt a tear, his tear, plop onto her forearm as she whispered thank you into his ear.

The party moved on, as parties do. It had taken on a life of its own, gentle and easy. Caroline stepped into it the way one might step into a stream or a brook. They moved onto the porch where it was unseasonably warm. Caroline thought she heard peepers, although there really weren't any... not yet. Jacob sat in a green, plastic chair. Sarna and Julie claimed the porch swing. Barry and Caroline sat on the top step, their thighs resting against one another. They all chattered back and forth laughing, learning, sitting. It was getting dark, the sun leaving them behind. Their banter rose up into the night sky like smoke from chimney. Caroline chuckled at a remark from Sarna, something about sandy bathing suits and drunken summer nights. Caroline wished, not for the first time, that she had her own story to add. She looked out into the night where she saw a light, shining just beyond the woods.

Caroline had increased her visits to Lila to twice a week. Before leaving to go there, the day after her surprise birthday party, Caroline's mother called to wish her a happy birthday. She'd reported feeling well, but still quite tired. Caroline asked her if she'd been feeling sick.

"Not at all," her mother had replied. She'd even been able to keep up with work, so far.

"I've sent you a little something in the mail," said her mother, "for your birthday."

"Mom. You just bought me all those clothes. That was enough."

"It's just a little something," replied her mother.

"What did you do for your birthday?" she inquired.

"Some friends of mine threw me a little party."

"Oh, good. See honey? You do have a life."

"More than one, actually," said Caroline before saying good bye.

Gretchen

"Things have been better."

"I'm glad to hear that," said Lila.

"Owen came in the middle of the night... of course. I barely made it to the hospital. He was born on February 11th. He is such a joy! He even brings Jake out of his black moods. Over the summer, we all went to the pond almost every day. Owen loves the water. Jake lets me swim while

221

he wades in the water with Owen. I love to swim. I swear it helps shrink my baby belly."

"Does Jake still drink?" asked Lila.

"Yes. But mostly just beer, and now, he's coming home right after work every day. We all have such fun together. Owen throws Cheerios at him, and Jake doesn't even get mad. He laughs and throws Cheerios back at Owen. I love it. I love being a mother. I like to put Owen in his high chair for lunch. I always put the radio on. I dance around to Elvis, and Owen just laughs and laughs. I knit him blankets and hats. I love doing things with my hands. My favorite thing to do, though, is rub Owen down with lotion after he's had his baths. He's a very active baby. When I rub him down, he becomes so still, and he just stares at me the whole time. I often wonder what he's thinking at these times. If babies don't have language, then what are their thoughts? I wonder. Actually, no, it's not staring, exactly. It's more like looking, like looking right into me. I wish there were words to describe it."

"I think I know," said Lila, smiling.

"Anyway, there was Christmas. We had a tree. We decorated it together."

"That must have been very special, your first Christmas as a family," said Lila.

"It was all right. Jake did get mad at me, though."

"Why?" asked Lila.

"I wasn't holding the tree straight enough when he was trying to fit it into the stand, so it came out crooked. He kept yelling at me to get it right. I was getting more

222

and more nervous, and I just couldn't get it right. Jake was really getting worked up, and I tried to tell him to calm down. He didn't like that at all."

"What did he do?" asked Lila.

"He grabbed me by the shoulders. He was just trying to talk some sense into me, trying to tell me that a wife doesn't say things like that to her husband, and why don't I just listen, why don't I just do what he says? He was shaking me really hard. I lost my footing and fell back into the tree. I screamed, 'No Jake, Jake!' Owen was right there and saw the whole thing.

"That doesn't sound much better than before," said Lila.

"No it doesn't, does it? It really is better. There are good times in between. Did I tell you what I got Jake for Christmas?"

"No."

"I got him a wallet, the kind with a chain that hooks onto your belt loop."

"What did you get Owen?" asked Lila.

"We got him a pair of parakeets. A blue one and a yellow one. They're so cute. They're just like people."

"People?" asked Lila.

"Yes. They bicker. I swear they do. Then, they make up. They clean each other and cuddle. Owen and I watch them for hours. We're trying to get them to come on our fingers, but every time we try, they skip away from us into the corner of the cage. Owen gets frustrated. I just keep telling him that we'll keep trying. It'll just take time for

223

them to get used to us. They do, eventually. It happened by accident. The birds got loose in the house. I was cleaning their cage, and they got out. Owen hobbled around after them, squawking. He kept losing his footing, since he'd only been walking for a month. I ran around after them, leaping into the air. Before long, Owen and I were both laughing, the kind of laughter that makes you cry. At some point, Owen disappeared into the kitchen while I tried coaxing them onto my finger. Owen was calling me from the kitchen, 'Pee, pee!' I went into the kitchen and saw that he'd pulled out the hutch drawer and was sitting on it with his pants down. He was peeing right in the drawer! I couldn't believe he could even do that! He looked so proud, the most proud, innocent look in his eyes. It was his first time peeing anywhere other than his diaper, and so young, too!"

"How old was he when this happened?" asked Lila.

"Eleven months. I was so shocked, so overwhelmed with love. Anyway, I ended up sitting him in the living room. 'Hold very still Owen,' I said. 'Mummy has to get the birds.' By that time, they had shit all over the place. Still, I couldn't stop laughing. Yellow was perched up on the curtain rod, and I was trying to catch her. I heard Owen say, 'Ma?' I said, 'Hold on Owen. Mummy's almost got Yellow.' 'Boo, boo!' he said. I turned around and there was Owen sitting up very still just like I told him to, with Blue sitting on his shoulder. He put his little hand up to his shoulder, and Blue hopped on. I reached out my hand and touched my fingers to Owen's. Blue walked onto my hand,

and I put him back in the cage. Yellow then flew right over, into the cage. Now, Blue and Yellow always perch onto our fingers."

"Sometimes the very best things happen by accident," said Lila.

"Sometimes, yes."

Here, she drifted off to sleep on Lila's bed... Caroline, or Gretchen. She could not hear Lila walking quietly about the room, scribbling down notes, crossing back and forth. She slept like a hibernating bear, its heartbeat slowing to a bare minimum, conserving energy, its body fulfilling inhuman rhythms.

After some time, she said, "Oh!"

"What is it?" asked Lila.

"There's something in the sand."

"Are you at the pond?" asked Lila.

"Yes. I have Owen with me. He's filling his hands with sand and watching the grains sift through his fingers."

"How old is he?" asked Lila.

"He's one and a half. It's 1961. August, I think. There's something in the sand. I bend down to look at it. It's silver. A silver necklace. I see it. I pick it up. It has a silver feather on it. I like it. I put it on. Someone must have been swimming here and left it behind. Maybe I should leave it. Maybe, whoever it belongs to will come back looking for it. Owen turns to me. 'Mummy. Bird. Bird. Wike Boo and Lellow,' he says, pointing to the necklace. It's the feather. 'Yes, honey,' I say, 'Like Blue and Yellow. Do

225

you like it?' He nods and smiles. 'Wike it,' he says, returning to the sand. I leave it on and turn my face up to the sun. A car pulls over to us. I recognize it but can't remember from where. A man is leaning across the passenger seat. He opens the door. For a moment I think it is the owner of the necklace, and I cover it with my hand. This man, he has long sideburns. Old man Fitz, Samuel. 'Awful long walk home,' he says. 'Not really,' I counter. 'Like a ride?' 'Yeah, Yeah, Mummy a wide!' screams Owen. 'No. Really. We're fine,' I say. 'A wide Mummy!' hollers Owen. I look from Owen to Samuel and back again. 'Oh sure,' I say. I sit Owen in my lap. We're driving down the road, passing the apple orchard. 'Nice day,' says Samuel. He has a cigarette dangling from his lip. 'Like one?' he asks. 'Please,' I say. I light up. The smoke is harsh in my throat, but it feels good, good like the sun on my face. 'I've missed this,' I say. His car rattles from somewhere underneath. 'You ought to have Jake look at that.' 'Oh, no. I will not have him look at my car,' says Samuel, looking straight ahead. 'Why not?' 'Don't get me wrong. He's the best mechanic around. The best. But he doesn't like me much. Came to my house that time you'd walked up to my house. After that, told me to stay away from you. 'Stay away from my wife', he said. Except with stronger language that I wouldn't say around a lady.' 'I'm sorry, Samuel. I had no idea,' I say, embarrassed. 'No harm done.' Buddy Holly's on the radio. Jake does not like Buddy Holly or Elvis. He only likes Frank Sinatra. I do, too. I also like the others. 'He's at work?' asks Samuel. 'Yes.'

'Good then. I'll bring you 'round the other way.' Samuel drops us off. 'Take care of yourself now,' he says, looking me in the eye. He lights up another cigarette and drives off."

"I go inside and get dinner ready. I put Owen in his high chair, although I'm thinking that he may not need it anymore. He's big for his age. And smart. Physically he can do things that I think are advanced, but I don't know. He walked at a young age. Always been very steady. He's quite dexterous and sure in his movements. Very thoughtful about what he does. He laughs and pops a Cheerio in his mouth. 'My boy,' I say, and I touch his round cheek. I can hear Jake coming… his wallet chain jingling. I move a bit more quickly, getting Jake's dinner on his plate. He comes in, and I can see immediately that his eyes are pale gray. He's back to the hard stuff again, plus the beer. I don't say anything. Neither does he. My hands go cold and clammy. I wash them. Even Owen gets quiet. 'What's that?' says Jake, looking at me. 'What?' I say. 'That. On your neck.' 'Oh this,' I say. I'd forgotten about the neck ace. 'I found it at the pond.' 'Oh? Or someone give you that?' 'No. No. Jake. I found it there. I really did. Owen was there. Even he'll tell you.' 'Oh yeah?' Jake turns to Owen. 'Owen. Tell Daddy.' Owen begins to cry. 'He's not gonna tell is he? You got him sworn to secrecy? Huh?' He pushes me. Again and again, backwards into the bathroom. He shoves me into the bathtub. My head hits the porcelain, hard. I think I scream, but I'm not sure. I hear Owen crying out. 'No -ake!' I try closing the shower curtain, not that it would help
227

much, but he reaches in, grabs the necklace, and tears it off. The feather falls to my feet with a succinct little clink. Jake leaves. He leaves the house, and I don't know where he's gone. I don't care either. I just want him gone. I just can't take it anymore."

"What do you do?" asked Lila.

"Nothing. I just go to bed. I take Owen with me. We lay there for a long time. It's only eight o'clock, and the sun hasn't completely left the sky yet. We just lie there very still together in bed."

Caroline

Caroline found herself at Barry's somehow. It had started out with her waiting for him outside his work, outsider her old work. She didn't know why she went there. Except that she'd called Sarna who was on her way out to dinner with Julie, and she'd called her mother who was in the middle of a nap, and she'd checked on Jacob who was turning in early... and she didn't want to be alone. She found herself driving the familiar route to the office. Only this time, she hadn't gone in. Instead, she sat in her car and smoked cigarettes. She'd picked up a pack of Marlboro's on her way there. Caroline also didn't know why she'd done that, since she'd never smoked, at least not in this lifetime. The filthy, biting, glorious smoke shooting down her throat like a knife hadn't made her cough. Not once. It did, however, make her dizzy and lightheaded, but she didn't mind that either. She felt like another person all together, and this was okay, too. When Barry came out of the building

228

and she saw him walking toward his car, she suddenly started crying. The old Caroline would have just sat there and watched him drive away. The old Caroline would never have come in the first place. This Caroline, however, this strange new one, beeped the horn. She beeped the horn and cried at the same time, waiting for him to notice, waiting for him to come over. Barry turned toward her, and there was a moment of recognition.. Still, he just stood looking at her, into her, or through her. Caroline just sat. She didn't move to push her hair away, glued to her face with tears. She didn't move to open her door. She didn't move.

Barry finally came toward her. Caroline didn't even roll her window down. Barry peered in at her through her passenger side window. He made a motion with his hand that said, "Follow me." He pulled out, and she followed him down streets, around corners, through neighborhoods... to his own. His house, or Emily's, or theirs, was tall and narrow, nestled in by apple trees and stone walls. Caroline had expected something average, like a split ranch. This, however, took her by surprise. The front door was black, as were the shutters. One of them was crooked. The house itself was white. The paint peeled near the door where they entered. Inside, Caroline saw tall radiators which were ticking and hissing. A large hutch built into the wall in the kitchen housed plates of many colors, tea cups, and neatly folded cotton napkins. A large brick chimney stood in the middle of the downstairs, the only thing separating the kitchen from the living room. A small, pot-bellied, wood burning stove jutted out from the chimney. It was cold and lifeless.

"I always used to keep this going," he said, motioning toward the stove.

Caroline sat on the couch. Barry sat next to her, but then he lay back and pulled her with him, enclosing her in his arms. Caroline's head rested on his chest.

"When Emily and I separated, I used to lie on this couch and cry like a baby. For months. Probably longer. I loved her so much. Or maybe it wasn't love. I don't know. I had always seen her like a little girl. I never saw her as a grown woman with her own self. She always said that I never really knew her. She was right. I never really did. It still hurts me that someone else could know her the way I couldn't, even if it was another woman. And now, she's alone again. Emily is. And it hurts all over again, that I'm the one who's there for her, but I still don't really know her. So I've been crying again, on this couch right here. But that's okay I guess. Someone once told me that tears are the river that carry you forward."

"Who told you that?" asked Caroline.

"Emily," he said. Barry got up and went outside. He came back in with an armful of wood. Caroline watched him fitting the pieces skillfully, with purpose, into the stove. He lit it up and the cold, black iron became a hot, living thing. He lay back down, fitting Caroline back onto him. He rested his chin on the top of her head and Caroline stared at the stove where she could hear the flames, red and yellow, green and orange, licking and dancing within. They kissed, but that's all they did, and the hissing of the fire within lulled them both to sleep.

In the morning, Barry said, "You were smoking."

"Yes. Isn't that strange? I don't even smoke."

"If you have anymore, we could share one," said Barry.

They went outside and shared a cigarette. The bitter chill of the night before had given way to a truly warm and glorious morning. They sat side by side on the front stoop looking out over a small cranberry bog across the street. A surprising mist hung there.

"I used to smoke a long time ago," he said, "I forgot how good it can be."

"I used to smoke once, too," said Caroline. "Well, not me. Gretchen did."

Barry said nothing.

"I still don't completely believe," she said. "What if I'm just crazy? Or what if I have a split personality? What if that's what it is?"

They flicked their cigarettes. Barry held onto her hand, their fingers interlacing. "I don't know," he said, "It could be real. Maybe it's not. Who knows?"

"I've been thinking of something," said Caroline, "If it is real, if it is, then Jake could still be alive today. So could Owen. I could try to find out. I could try to find them.'

When Caroline got home, she found two things. She found Jacob out in his yard, standing there with his boxers on. She also found a check in the mail from her mother in the amount of five thousand dollars. First, she took care of Jacob.

Caroline approached him. "Jacob?"

"Yeah. That cat. That damn cat. Got out. I have to get him back before Gretta finds out. She'll carry on and on. Last time this happened was in a snow storm. I had to come out in the middle of it. Looked all over the neighborhood for Christ's Sake. Oh, but she was fit to be tied. I knew she wasn't going to calm down until I came back with that cat. Turns out he was hiding under the porch the whole time. Now, it's happened again, and I can't find him. Already looked under the porch," he said.

Caroline took him by the arm. "I'll find him. Let's get you in."

She led him into the house. When they entered, she found the kitchen littered with food, a pan on the stove encrusted with something like eggs, and the TV shouting at full volume.

"God, Jacob. What have you been doing?"

"Just the usual."

Caroline sat him down in front of the TV and turned the volume down. She started cleaning up the kitchen, finding that the pan on the stove was, indeed, encrusted with egg and bread. He'd been trying to make French toast.

"The cat?" he said.

"Oh. That. Yeah. I'll go find him now."

Caroline turned to the door and asked, "What does he look like?"

"You know. Grey with white spots. That one."

Caroline went out on the porch and took some deep breaths. She stepped down onto the ground which was, for the first time in months, beginning to soften. She crouched down and peered under the porch. There, she saw a rusty red and white radio flyer tricycle tipped over on its side and a deflated ball. Caroline stood up.

"What am I doing?" She went back in the house.

"Okay. I found the cat. I put it in my house, so it won't disturb you."

"Your house?" he said.

"The house out back," returned Caroline.

"Oh. Good. I'll have to tell Gretta that's where he is, so she won't get upset," he said, staring at the TV.

Caroline surveyed Jacob cautiously. "I'll tell her for you."

"Good," he said, "She's upstairs."

"Okay."

Caroline went upstairs, turned into Gretta's bedroom, and stood there. Sunlight filtered in through the window, creating elongated patches of light on the floor. Shadowy branches from the trees outside the window danced within the rectangles of light. Caroline looked toward the closet door. She became as still and silent as it was. She stepped into a patch of sunlight. A shadow of a tree branch whispered across her leg. Crossing over to the window, she looked out. There, she saw the tree with a tire swing hanging down from it. It swayed gently back and forth, back and forth. Come and go, come and go. For the first time, Caroline thought of Gretchen and how she came to leave her life, thirty five-years ago. She knew, Caroline knew, in her heart of hearts, that it was all true, and how Gretchen had come to leave her life.

Next, Caroline called her mother.

"Mum. Why did you do that?"

"I wanted to help you out. I know you're not working right now, and I wanted to make sure you were going to be all right."

"But... five thousand dollars?"

"I can afford it, Carly. It's not going to hurt me any."

"Mum, I don't know how to thank you."

"You don't have to. Just make sure you use a little of it to treat yourself to something."

"I'll try. How's it going Mum, with your treatment?"

"I'd say pretty well. They're upping the dose, since I've tolerated the dose I'm at so far. I'll be fine."

"Good, Mum."

"Oh, are you coming up this way this week to see your friend?" asked her mother.

"My friend?"

"The one playing at "The Black Rose".

Caroline had forgotten about that. "Oh. Yeah. I think so."

"Oh, good then," said her mother, "we can go together."

Later that night, Caroline and Jacob settled down to watch a movie together. He seemed to have settled down after the whole cat incident, although he hadn't said much.

All he'd said so far all evening was, "Did you tell Gretta about the cat?"

"Yes."

"What's she doing up there?" he asked.

"She's just... reading a book," replied Caroline. It was the first thing that came to her mind.

Satisfied, Jacob said, "Good, she loves to read."

The other thing he'd said, a bit later was, "Go into the other room and fish out that video of mine, "Family Man", will you? I feel like watching it."

Caroline did this. They settled down to watch the movie. Nicholas Cage played a man who was made to leave his current life to live a different life, one that would have been... had he made different choices. It made her laugh, and it almost made her cry, but not quite. Jacob, however, did both throughout. Caroline wondered about this character and about George in "It's a Wonderful Life," and about Sam King. She thought of Gretchen and of herself, all going back and forward, back and forward.

Gretchen

"We think we hear Jake's wallet chain, Owen and I, while lying in bed. There's still some light in the sky, and it sounds like his wallet chain. Thankfully, it's not him. It's just a neighborhood dog running by, his collar bouncing about. We fall asleep. I wake up at three o'clock in the morning, get up, and check the house. Jake's not there. He's not coming home, I know it--at least, not for a while. I go back into bed. I begin to fall asleep, and I'm surprised I can do this. I

haven't fallen asleep this easily in a long time. It's easy to do with Jake not there. I do something the next morning that I haven't done in months."

"What's that?" asked Lila.

"I call Sarah. She's home when I call, and I start to cry. I hadn't planned on it, but I just did... as soon as I heard her voice. She's the only friend I have, and we aren't even really that close anymore. I don't know who else to call. She comes right over. This is really a gamble."

"Why?" asked Lila.

"If Jake comes home and sees Sarah there and me crying, he'll really get mad. He'll suspect that I'm telling her everything. And I do. I tell her every single thing. Sara looks so good, so happy, when she comes in that I just fall apart even more. The more I cry, the more the back of my head throbs. I have a big lump where my head hit the bathtub the night before, and it really hurts. Owen comes over and starts to cry, too. 'Mummy 'k? Mummy 'k?' he asks. 'Yes. Mummy's okay,' I say. 'Mummy's just a little sad right now.' He has dark circles under his eyes, and his hair is sticking up all over."

"What does Sarah say?" asked Lila.

"She's madder than a hornet. She says she'd suspected, but she didn't want to say anything. She's really mad, which doesn't surprise me, since she's really big into the equal rights movement and everything. She says that no one deserves to be oppressed...blacks, women, anyone."

"Do you agree?" asked Lila.

"Well, I always did feel bad for Mrs. Tims, especially the time she got beaten for talking to that colored man. I even felt bad for the colored man. I never really thought of it in terms of oppression. Not even with myself. I just try to get by day to day. That's all I have the time or energy to think about, I guess."

Silence descended upon Lila's room. Lila waited patiently, scribbling her notes. She stifled a sneeze.

Then: "Did I tell you that Sarah's going to teacher school? She also goes to rallies for equal rights. They have them right here in Virginia. She's even gone to Georgia and Mississippi for these rallies. There aren't many white people at these things, so I think she's really brave. She's had rocks thrown at her, flaming torches hurled at her, you name it. She has a scar above her eye where she got stitches from a brick that got thrown at her head. She still keeps going to these things.

Anyway, she's so mad that she marches right out the door and over to the garage. I'm so scared that there aren't words for it. All I can do is pace. My hands tingle and the back of my head throbs. Owen follows me around. The birds, Blue and Yellow, squawk. Even they seem agitated. They are in some sort of frenzy, flapping around furiously. Little wisps of feathers come popping out of the cage. I'm so nervous; I turn on the radio just for something to do. Except I turn the dial all the way up, and "The Twist" comes screaming out. This startles Owen, and he begins to cry. I turn off the radio. I wish I had a cigarette. I decide to go into Jake's father's bedroom, where I never go. Even though

237

he's gone, I'm still afraid to go in there. It's like he will pop out of his closet any minute, a cigarette dangling from his mouth. It's very dark in there. Jake hasn't touched a thing in that room since Owen Sr. died. I quickly open the top dresser drawer where I know he used to keep his cigarettes. I find a pack of Camels and take one. I light one up, and just as I'm coming back out of his room, Sarah comes in. 'What happened?' I say. 'He wasn't there,' she says, 'Not there. It's locked up. His truck's not there. No one's there. Except some guy who pulled up. He wanted to know where Jake was, said Jake was supposed to take a look at his engine. I told him that Jake got into some sort of trouble and had to leave town. The guy got all pissed off and peeled out. His tire kicked up a stone, and it flung up and hit a window. Then, I picked up another rock, a bigger one, and threw it at another window, smashed it to bits.' Sarah laughs. I laugh, too, a little at first, and then I can't stop myself. Owen joins us, too, and before long he's in hysterics, although he has no idea why. Sarah tries to get us to leave, to go to my parents' house or something, but I say "no". To do so would be to admit to my mistake. Also, I'm not completely convinced that it's not my fault... that there are still not things I can do to prevent it. True, the list of things that I should do and shouldn't do is getting longer, but I still think I can manage it."

"What happens next?" asked Lila.

"Jake doesn't come home that day or the next. They are two glorious days. I crank the radio, listening to Elvis. I smoke right there in the kitchen which, for some reason,

238

Jake does not like for me to do, even though he smokes in there. I wear whatever I want. Jeans, bandanas, a long, paisley shirt that Sarah gave me, beaded bracelets going up my arms. Sarah calls them love beads, although I have no idea what that is. The second day, I go into Jake's father's dresser drawer again for more cigarettes, and I find a stack of letters in there. I pull them out and see that they are addressed to a Marjorie McAuley, who lives in West Virginia. She is Jake's mother. I open one, although I know I shouldn't. It's something about the bracelets. The love beads make me feel I can do this. It's like they make me brave. The one that I read finds Owen wishing that she is well. Wishing that she would come back, promising that he would never, ever, touch her again except in the most loving of ways. She is not dead as I have been told. She is only dead to them, or they to her--even her own son. This fills me with a hatred for her and a tenderness for Jake that I don't want to feel. I would never, ever leave my son except in death. Never. Ever. I put that letter at the bottom of the pile. I don't need to read more of them, but I flip through them with my thumb and find that they all say 'Returned to Sender'. The last one, I see, is dated only eight months ago! I need to get out and stretch my legs, get fresh air into my lungs and into my thoughts. Owen does, too. He's bouncing off the walls the way Blue and Yellow are bouncing around in their cage. Since Jake has our only car, the only way to get anywhere is to walk, and that's what we do. Mostly, I carry Owen, but sometimes I put him down so that he can inspect little things on the edge of the woods... pine cones, sticks, rocks. A

239

flowering Magnolia surprises us as we turn a corner. Through the woods in the distance, I see a horse farm that I'd vaguely known was there but had forgotten about. The smell of horse is strong as the wind comes off the farm. We keep going. It is hot and humid, but it feels good, even the humidity does. I can smell something sweet in the air like apples or flowers or both. We have already passed the garage, and I didn't even look at it. Now we are approaching Samuel's driveway, and I turn up it. 'Where goin' Mumma?' asks Owen. "We're going to visit a friend,' I say. We continue up the driveway. Summer bugs lazily curl through the air before us. A mosquito bites my neck, and I slap at it. A hot wind picks up and trails my hair and my bandana behind me. We approach just as Samuel comes from around the corner of the house with a large wicker basket full of something. 'Well hello,' he says, 'Who have we got here?' 'I just wanted to come and thank you for the ride the other day,' I say. 'No trouble, here have a peach,' he says, taking two peaches from the basket, one for each of us. 'A couple of peaches for a couple of peaches,' he says, smiling. 'Do you have peach trees?' I ask. 'Do I have peach trees? Gretchen. Gretchen. Come see my peach trees.' We round the corner of the house where a stand of peach trees comes into view. Row upon row upon row of peach trees. Beautiful and fertile, bearing fruit. 'This is the Shenandoah Valley, my dear. Peaches and apples and grapes abound.' 'This surprises me. I don't know why,' I say. 'Us humans are easily surprised,' he says, 'Here. Take a basket.' He hands us each a basket, and we follow him down the rows. He

240

teaches us which ones to pick and which ones not to pick. Owen and I are in a row when Samuel disappears into another row. I see a colored man cross by further down, silently carrying a basket of peaches. I hear Samuel speak somewhere off to my left. 'Thomas. You take a break now. You've been working since six o'clock. Go get yourself some water or something.' 'Yes sir,' says the colored man, now somewhere off to my right. I hear him walking away from us. Then, I hear a screen door creak open and slam. Samuel comes up behind me and says, 'I take care of my coloreds,' into my ear. I startle, spilling peaches at my feet. 'Oh, it's okay now. Didn't mean to scare you,' he says, bending down to help me pick them up. 'Surprises and unexpected things are the fruit of life,' he says chuckling. 'Me, I much prefer the expected, the mundane,' I say, standing up. 'We've got to be going. Thank you again for the peaches.' 'Anytime,' he says, 'Now, wait here a minute. I've got something for the little one.' Samuel disappears into the house, the screen door slapping shut as it did with Thomas. I hear them saying some words. They laugh. I look out over the peach orchard. Beyond that is the horse farm, big and wide and open. Beyond that, the Blue Ridge Mountains... way, way off in the distance. A mosquito bites Owen's arm, and he squeals. Samuel comes back out, bends down, unfolds his hand, and puts a colorful little doll in Owen's hand, no bigger than my thumb-nail. 'Here, my little man. You have this here worry doll. You can tell your worries to it. It'll listen.' I look down at my son. 'What do you say Owen?' 'Ank you,' he says. 'Good now,' says Samuel, turning, 'You two go on.'

"Sara comes back over the next day. She says she's taking us out. 'Out where?' I ask. To Woolworth's. Let's go get ourselves some unnecessary objects. 'What on Earth for?' I ask, confused. 'Because it's fun! Haven't you ever gone shopping just to go shopping?' I thought. 'I don't think so.' 'You don't know what you're missing!' So we go to Woolworth's. We browse the aisles. Owen runs ahead and touches everything he sees. 'Do you need dish towels?' asks Sara. I nod my head. 'How about batteries?' I nod again. 'Ooh, I know, you could use a new shower curtain!' says Sara, proudly holding up a curtain. 'I don't think so.' 'Soap? Socks? Underwear?' 'No. No. No,' I tell her. 'Well, what then?' says Sara, shrugging her shoulders. 'Didn't you say un-necessary objects?' I ask, smiling. So we go around, scooping up ridiculous things, things I don't need: a mini pot of fake daisies, a pair of panty hose, a plastic truck for Owen, and a hula-hoop. I pick up a tube of burgundy lipstick and ask, 'Is this a necessary object?' 'I think it is,' replies Sara. 'I don't,' I say, tossing it into my basket. Next, I grab a toothbrush. Sara inspects my selection. 'A toothbrush?' 'What? I need a new one!' 'Then, it's not unnecessary. Put it back.' I do. We see the record bin on the other side of the store. We look at each other. 'Is music necessary?' 'Absolutely.' 'Can we break our rule just for this?' I ask. 'Let's go,' replies Sara. We race over to the record bin and feverishly pick through the albums. I grab Buddy Holly and Elvis. Sara gets Chubby Checker and Bobby Lewis. We take all our stuff home and spread it out on the living room floor. We put on our records and sing

242

and dance. The birds hoot and holler. We take turns using the hula-hoop. Owen runs in circles until he gets dizzy."

Caroline

Caroline thought of asking Barry to come with her to The Black Rose but then decided against it. She wanted to go alone, which would be very difficult, she knew, but it's how she wanted it. Being alone in the city at night was not her thing exactly, but every time she pictured herself going, she pictured herself alone; that's how it would have to be. Even her mother coming along somehow did not quite fit. Caroline didn't have the heart to tell her. She'd planned on driving in and taking a cab from the parking garage over to her mother's.... alone. First she made herself bracelets with many small beads of all colors. She put these on her arms, grabbed Tim's Gretsch guitar, and left. She thought of putting in the Nanci Griffith CD Tim had given her, but, for some reason, she decided against it. She tried clearing her mind. She tried breathing eight times a minute. All of it was of no use. She ended up taking out the Nanci Griffith CD and popping it in, going immediately to number ten, a song called "So Long Ago." After Tim had left, Caroline listened to this song over and over, wearing it out. She blushed at the thought of such drama, such foolish idiocy. When the song came on, she remembered its poetic beauty, its wistful nostalgia. She listened to this song about lost love all the way into Boston.

Once in the city, Caroline stood with the guitar on the sidewalk, waiting for a cab. It was a chilly, windy night, and the moon hung full and bright above the city. Her breath escaped her mouth like little ghosts chasing each other down the avenue. She fingered the beads on her bracelets. A man with a scarf hurried by, tipped his hat, and smiled at her. A black man and a white woman walking arm in arm nearly plowed into her. The man gently touched her elbow. "So sorry ma'am," he said. Caroline thought of Sara. She thought of Tim and his voice and, for some reason, Adam's apples. Luckily for Caroline, a taxi arrived, and she slipped in, pushing the guitar in first.

When Caroline entered her mother's, she noticed how quiet it was, yet the whole place was illuminated. Lamps dotted the hallway. In any other context, it could have been obnoxious. Not the way her mother did it. Caroline called for her mother to which there was no reply. She looked in the kitchen and in her mother's room. She tried to decide where to look next, but there were so many rooms she couldn't decide; so many rooms in her mother's house. Caroline heard a little cough, just a little one, and followed it to the TV room... the one where she and her mother had watched movies weeks earlier. There was her mother on the couch under a white cotton throw. Caroline could see the outline of her body, small and childlike. Her red, spiky hair grazed the pillow. Caroline knelt next to her.

"Mum?"

She opened her eyes. "Oh, honey. What time is it?"

"It's seven-thirty."

"Oh, dear. I must have fallen asleep. I'm just so tired," said her mother, her eyes closing again.

"I'm staying with you, Mum," announced Caroline.

"No, you're not. You're going to see your friend. What are you going to do? Sit here and watch me sleep?"

"Mum!"

Her mother opened her eyes, then, and they were as clear as ever, more than ever.

"You are going," she said. "You are going to live your life. That is what I want. That is what's important here."

So Caroline went. She took the guitar with her, got into another taxi, and went to The Black Rose. From the sidewalk, she could see into the place. It was packed with people relaxing after work, or with others trying to hook up with appealing strangers, or people trying to get drunk, or people trying to pace themselves. Or even people who really wish just to be at home... and with someone whose voice Caroline could already hear from outside, muffled but unmistakable. Caroline went in, guitar in hand. The voices were a wall of sound as she wound her way through the crowd to a small table toward the back. A candle on the table flickered before her. She heard Tim say, "Thank you. Back in a few." She saw him place his guitar down and move toward the bar. She noticed his shirt, just like the one in the picture. He'd always been particular about his clothes and would wear the same few outfits over and over. He was not wearing a cap, as he often used to, and she could see that his hair had become thinner. His long arm reached out toward a waitress, and she felt a pang of jealousy or yearning, just as she had seven years ago. The waitress laughed and threw her head back. Caroline could not hear Tim's laughter, but she knew just what it would sound like. He was still, of course, tall and thin, and still sported a goatee coming off of his pointy chin. He sat at the bar, and the waitress brought him a plate of something. Tim ate and chuckled, talking to the man next to him. He sipped a drink. She knew that it was not alcoholic. He did not drink. It was probably a coke. For all of his health food fanaticism, he'd never made any bones about consuming lots and lots of caffeine and nicotine. That he smoked the Native American cigarettes, ordered in from a reservation, eased his mind and somehow made it acceptable. But he wouldn't eat white bread or red meat or anything that was not organic. A waitress came over to Caroline and asked if she'd like anything.

"I'll have what he's having," said Caroline.

"Who?" asked the waitress, looking around.

"The musician."

"Sure," she said as she hurried off.

Caroline's food came a moment later; a veggie wrap with a side of guacamole dip. Tim would pick out the veggies and leave the wrap. He got back to his guitar on stage and started up.

"Good evening, everyone. I'm Tim Parlay. Thanks for coming out tonight. You keep having a good time, and I'll keep playing. Oh, and remember to drink responsibly."

Tim had always said this.

He played songs she knew and songs she didn't know. He sounded the same and looked the same. Caroline knew, too, that he would smell the same if she could get close enough. He asked for any requests and drunken people shouted out song names. Caroline had a request, but her voice wouldn't work. He picked up on a request for Jimmy Buffett, whom he'd always hated doing, but always did graciously. The waitress came over and asked if she needed anything else. Caroline said 'no, but would she mind taking a request over to the musician for her'? Caroline wrote it down, the name of the song, one that he'd written long ago; the one she'd miserably failed at doing a background vocal for in his little apartment shortly before he left.

"I'll be leaving soon," said Caroline.

She paid up and asked the waitress to pass on the guitar to him as well as the slip of the paper with the request, unsigned. The waitress agreed and brought these over to him. First, she slipped the guitar behind him. He hadn't even noticed. Then she gave him the paper. Tim looked at it, and then looked out into the crowd of people.

"Seems there's someone here who knows some of my older stuff. I'd be glad to play this... Whoever you are, but please make yourself known."

He looked around. Some other people did so as well. Caroline looked straight on, confident that she couldn't be seen from his vantage point. Tim began to play. It all came back to her: his voice, him, his arms. She wanted to be wrapped up in them. By the end of the song, Caroline had moved over to the door and slipped out on the last note. It was comparatively quiet outside, and the cold air shot into her lungs. She stood for a moment, her feet clinging to the ground like a snail clinging to a rock in an outgoing tide. She turned on her heels, flipped her collar to the moon, and hailed a taxi.

When Caroline got back to her mother's, she was wrung. She just wanted to climb into bed and let go of everything, just to lie there effortlessly. Her mother was still on the couch, but she was watching TV.

"How did it go?" she asked.

"Just the way I'd planned."

"You look sad."

"I am," said Caroline.

"This friend of yours, is it someone you loved?"

"Yes."

"The first person you loved?"

"Yes, I think so."

"There's nothing like the first," said her mother. "It stays with you forever. You never forget it. Every little nuance, every little detail. You could be on your death bed, and you'd remember every little thing as if it was yesterday."

They were quiet for a bit, remembering.

"This person. What's his name?" asked her mother.

"Tim."

"Is he playing there again?"

"Yes. I think in another couple of weeks," said Caroline.

"Will you go back?"

"No."

"Maybe I will. Maybe I'll go check him out," said her mother.

"Why would you do that?"

"I want to see. I want to see about your life... all the things I never saw before."

248

Gretchen

"Did I tell you what they did?"

"No," said Lila.

"They sent a chimp into outer space. An actual, honest-to-God chimp!"

"How amazing," said Lila.

"I wish they would send me into outer space."

Caroline

Caroline saw Gretta three times the following week. The first time, she was on her tire swing. The second time, she was in her closet upstairs, but it was really just her curly wisps of hair Caroline saw in there. The third time, she was sitting, clear as day, next to Jacob's bed as he slept. Jacob had been in and out of reality, and Caroline switched back and forth with him. She couldn't bear to tell him that what he was perceiving wasn't exactly the truth, so she played along with him. "Yes, Jacob, I will tell Gretta you're going up to bed." "Yes, Jacob, I will fetch the cat." Except for when he thought she was Gretta and asked her to go get his bottle of whiskey from the basement and bring it up to him. To that she sternly said no. One day, Caroline sat at Jacob's bed-side. Gretta was across from her. Jacob stirred, woke up, and looked up at Caroline.

"Caroline," he said, "there you are. Caroline?'

"Yes?"

"I know I'm not doing too well. I know that."

"You do?"

"Yes. Of course. You have to promise me you won't send me back to the hospital."

He looked at her in that moment the same way her mother had when she'd told her to leave, to go see Tim.

"Promise me," he said.

Caroline looked up at Gretta, whose serious face turned to a gentle smile. "Yes, Jacob. I promise."

Gretchen

"I can't believe it!"

"Believe what?"said Lila.

"That a man went into outer-space! His name is John Glenn. I wonder what the world looks like from way up there."

Caroline

Caroline saw Barry many, many times over the next several weeks. She decided to take a break from going to Lila's, from Gretchen. She felt a piece of Gretchen inside her... small, but there. She and Barry ate at the hospital. They kept Jacob company together. They held hands. They kissed. Caroline began to become attached to his boxy, rough, canvas jacket and his slow smile. She liked the way his body bent backward in laughter. She liked his quiet, gentle moods, his surprising insights, and even that unapproachable place that he would slip into sometimes, because she could identify with that.

One night, they had dinner with Sarna and Julie. Sarna had told her parents that she was gay, and they

250

weren't too happy about it. Sarna was upset, and it was Barry, and only Barry, who was able to make her smile and then laugh. Caroline gave Barry massages which always led to kissing and cuddling but never anything more. Neither of them was ready to open up that space within themselves. Caroline learned that he'd always wanted to study Marine Biology and was thinking of going to school for it. She learned that he preferred tea over coffee. He learned that she loved spring peepers, turtles and frogs, tulips and daffodils. And that she had a tendency to breathe in deeply the smells of things from food to objects to traces of all scents in the air. Caroline's mother called her and told her that she'd gone to see Tim play at "The Black Rose". She'd loved him, and she thought he was a 'hottie' and quite intelligent. "Did you talk to him?" asked Caroline. "Well, yes. I introduced myself. He said, of course, he remembers you. He wanted to know all about you. Where you are. What you're doing. He said for you to come back next time. He also said thanks for the guitar." Eventually, Emily came back home from the hospital. She'd lost all her hair and both of her breasts. Her sister came to stay with her, and she and Barry shared many late nights together, helping a very weak Emily. Caroline called her father and postponed her trip to Oregon for a few more months. She didn't want to leave Jacob, or her mother whose main side effect, so far, was being unable to get up off the couch for increasingly longer periods of time. Caroline went on three job interviews, which all led to nothing. Jacob took to the couch again.

Gretchen

"Sara and I decorated the house for Owen's birthday party. While decorating, we sang along to "Up on the Rooftop" by the Drifters. We always do this, Sara and I. We love to listen to the same song over and over. It's as if we just can't get enough of it... if it's a song we really like, that is."

"When was this?" asked Lila.

"1963. Owen was turning three. You know, in certain lights he looks like his father, but everyone says he looks like me. Samuel says that I must have spit him right out of my mouth. The resemblance to his father is in his stance and mannerisms. He bites the inside of his lip when he is concentrating on something, just like his father. Of course the blonde hair, but that's from both of us. Owen's hair, though, curls around his ears and neck like Jake's. In some lights, his hair looks red. I think Jake once told me that his mother had long, red hair. I'd like to ask Jake more about his mother, if she really did... or does... have red hair, but I won't."

"Why?" asked Lila.

"Why? I don't really know, except that I'm not supposed to know that she's alive."

"Does it bother you that Jake lied to you about that?"

"I don't know if it bothers me. In a sense, I feel like it's his business. If he wanted me to know she was still alive, he would have told me. I wonder about her. What does she look like? Has Owen inherited any of her looks?"

252

"Is there anything else you wonder about?"

"Actually, I wonder how she got the nerve to up and leave. I wonder if I'll ever have the nerve. I wonder how she could have ever left her own son. I don't get that. And then... I think... I wouldn't want to know her anyway."

A hush came to Lila's room, and then: " Anyway, at the party, Owen was sitting in the living room with Blue on his finger and Yellow on his shoulder. "Puff the Magic Dragon" came on the radio, and Owen yelled, 'Puff! Puff! Puff!' At that moment, my parents arrived for the party. They were early, of course, but I didn't mind. They walked by Sara and I, going straight for Owen in the living room. 'He-llo?' Sara asked sarcastically, 'What am I, chopped liver?' My dad came back into the kitchen and kissed Sara on the cheek. I looked down at my watch, expecting Jake any minute."

"How is Jake doing?" Lila questioned.

"He hasn't drank for a year and a half, so I guess that means he's better."

"You guess? What do you mean by that?"

"He's like his father more than ever now. Very unto himself, quiet. In many ways, this is worse than before."

"How so?"

"He's...he's... unapproachable. I remind myself everyday that I do love him, even though the challenge to keep loving him wears on me every day. How do you continue to love someone when they can't be reached? When simple conversation ceases to exist, never mind anything that would require him to pay attention to me or Owen? I

253

can't seem to stop walking on egg shells. Even though it has been a year and a half, I'm still waiting. Always waiting for him to lose it, come home drunk, or notice something I've done wrong. Now, it's the opposite. Jake doesn't notice anything, good or bad."

Lila gently inquired, "Do you want to talk about it?"

"Well, for example, last summer, Sara and I went to an equal rights demonstration. When I got home, I expected Jake to be upset, but he wasn't. He didn't even respond, not a word. I wasn't even sure that he heard me."

"What was the demonstration like?"

"It was amazing, and terrible. Sara and I were in the minority of white people, I'd never seen so many coloreds gathered in one area before. We all marched down the street holding signs that said "Freedom Now." The police lined the sidewalk of our parade with their batons in hand, ready to whack anyone if they got out of line. Fortunately, nobody caused any trouble, even when onlookers heckled and harassed us as we held our heads and signs high. We just walked, staring straight ahead. One man in our group had gasoline thrown right on him, but he just kept on walking without pausing. Someone else tried to throw a torch on him but missed. We sang songs as we went, "Amazing Grace" and others that I did not know the words to. Part of the parade stopped at a white's only diner. The police tried pulling them away from the door, tried dragging them, too. More and more joined in deliberate entrance. Soon the police were using their batons. Hitting and whacking and striking and hurting innocent people,

254

black and white. Not once did a single colored person, man or woman, fight back or make a sound. The police were losing the battle, so they hooked up a fire hose to the hydrant and started spraying the whole mob of people. The water was so powerful that it pushed them down the sidewalk like bugs. Some got taken away in the paddy wagon, some ran, some rejoined the march."

"What was your reaction to this?"prompted Lila.

"Sara and I, we reacted differently. I cried. Sara got mad. By the time Sara and I drove home, I was mad, too. I'm not even sure why, just a blinding madness. I wanted to go out and chop down a tree. Whack! Whack! Whack! I couldn't shake the image of those people tumbling down the sidewalk. Even now, I see it like it was yesterday. I have never witnessed such strength and pride in people, and yet they couldn't stand up to the water."

"Do you think you are strong?"

A pause ensued, filling up Lila's room, interrupted only by the ticking of the clock.

"Yes, in some ways. No, in bigger ways. I think I'm getting stronger. Going to the rally, seeing a cob web on the ceiling and walking right by, taking Owen to see Samuel. These are all things I never would have done before, because I was afraid."

Lila gently interrupted, "How do you feel about spending time with Samuel?"

"Owen has taken a liking to him. Samuel and I have coffee together. We chat about everything and nothing. We smoke cigarettes. I'm lonely most of the time, being home with just Owen and the birds. Even when Jake is home, I'm still lonely, sometimes more lonely when he's there. Jake doesn't offer much. I don't even know if he knows that Owen and I spend time at Samuel's or how he would feel if he knew. Anyway, there's something good."

"What's that?" asked Lila.

"It is at Samuel's that I discover Hemmingway."

"Ernest Hemmingway?"

"Yes, him. Samuel has a book by him, "The Sun Also Rises," it's called. He let me borrow it. I think I'm drawn to it, because the main character's name is Jake. I love following him in his travels. He roams France and Spain. I love picturing these places. It seems to me so intriguing... that there are so many different places in the world. Different from here. When I'm reading, I can get so lost in the images. It's like I get to leave my life for that short time. In a way, it saves me."

Again, silence, the ticking of the clock, an abrupt change of subject.

"Owen's party was good. Owen got a tricycle and a big yellow Tonka truck. Jake gave him a model car that he promised they would build together. I hope he comes through. Already, Owen has learned that Jake's promises cannot be counted on. At some point during the party, an unexpected knock at the door interrupted the festivities. When I opened the door, Samuel was standing there. I was frozen, couldn't move if there was a fire under my ass. 'I have a gift for Owen,' Samuel announced. I could not seem to find my tongue. I noticed something moving under his coat, just as Sara came up behind me. 'Who's this?' With Sara's presence, I finally found my voice and my legs, 'Sara, I'd like you to meet our neighbor Samuel.' 'Well, don't just stand there, let him in!' Sara didn't seem to notice my shock or fear. What will Jake do? I moved aside, and Samuel entered my house. I'm not sure I was breathing. At first no one noticed him except Owen. Owen ran up to Samuel and wrapped his arms around his legs, obviously pleased by Samuel's surprise arrival. Then Jacob walked in. He stood very still. His eyes locked with Samuel's, unblinking. Samuel stared right back, unmoving. Blue and Yellow broke the silence by letting out a series of loud squawks. Jake finally stepped forward, extending his hand, 'Samuel.' 'Jake,' responded Samuel, grasping Jake's hand. Sara's eyes caught mine, a puzzled expression crossing her face. I waved her away, my face telling her I would fill her in later. Samuel bent down to Owen, parted his coat, and revealed a small kitten. 'Kitty! Kitty!' shrieked Owen. I was touched and angry by Samuel's gift to Owen: That he thought of Owen on his birthday and brought him such a gift, and that he thought naught of me in asking for permission for such a special gift.... but More angry that he must know I would catch hell from Jake for this. Suddenly, I felt a distrust for this man, an uneasiness I could not explain. Samuel stood up, ruffled Owen's hair. 'I thought you would like her.' He walked past me, toward the door, leaned in close and whispered, 'Surprise,' arching his eyebrows. For the rest of the party, I was shaken. I could not read Jake. He was quiet and withdrawn, although that's not new. Owen *chased the kitten around. My dad and Jake discussed JFK. My father for him, and Jake against. JFK announced that he wants to send American troops over to Vietnam. Jake said he'd go. I'm ashamed to admit that I wish Jake would go. Jake began telling my father about how he turned a Negro away at the garage the other day. My father chuckled. Sara's face turned red, as did mine. Patsy Cline's, "I Fall to Pieces" was playing on the radio. That is just how I felt, how I always feel... like I am falling to pieces.*

Jake doesn't like the cat, or the birds, or JFK. I like them all. Myrtle, the cat, curls up with Owen and me when we take naps. Blue and Yellow chatter and keep us company with their banter. Also, JFK has sent the Russians away from Cuba, stood up to US Steel, and has kept inflation down. Not to mention that JFK is handsome, funny and supports civil rights. I like him most, because he keeps us all safe. Sara tells me about the bomb drills in the school system. The kids huddle under their desks. I do not want Owen to huddle under a desk when he goes to school. I know he would just panic and worry that I'm not huddled under a desk with him. He'll wonder if I'm huddled under the kitchen table at home."

A hush descended upon the room. Lila allowed concurrent life times to exist simultaneously, unfolding like the petals of a flower.

"In November, 1963, everything changed."

"For better or for worse?" asked Lila.

"Dare I say-- for the worse."

"What happened?"

258

"It's awful. Just awful."

"Would you like to go on? If you wish, we could take a break."

"Go on. I want to go on."

"I'm listening," said Lila.

"Well, JFK was shot, leaving me feeling unprotected, vulnerable. It was like we were all in a boat way, way out in the ocean, and the motor just died... leaving us drifting without direction."

"How did you find out?" asked Lila.

"My father was the one to tell me. I will never forget that moment. He walked through my front door one day, crying. I wondered... Could it be my mother? What did Jake do? I was wrong on both counts. My father sat me down on the couch and turned on the television. The picture came on, and we watched over and over the footage. Myrtle was lying on top of the TV, her tail swishing back and forth before the picture of JFK slumping forward in the motorcade car. There was some sort of commotion. Lots of movement in the car. Jackie Kennedy reached around for something in the back. There was a rush and a crowd of confusion. My father and I cried. We cried. We couldn't believe it."

Caroline

Caroline had a dream that had nothing to do with Gretchen or Jake or Owen or birds. It had to do with her father. In the dream, Caroline approached her father in his workshop. His back was toward her. She stood and watched

259

him. The light bulb hanging from the ceiling swung back and forth, illuminating him every other second. In those illuminated seconds, she could see that he was crying, his shoulders moving up and down rhythmically. She looked down at herself and realized that she was wearing a paisley dress. Her hands reached up, and she felt pig tails. She watched him bring something to his lips. He tipped his head back. He did this again, again. Like a clock ticking, like the light bulb swinging. He threw it aside, the bottle. It smashed to the floor. He opened drawers in his workbench, drawer after drawer, getting more agitated, coming up empty handed. Caroline ran out into the driveway. It was snowing. There was snow up to her knees, under her dress. She climbed into her father's blue van. Inside, it was littered with wood, cigarette butts, and trash. She went to his hiding place, the place where she knew he kept it. She grabbed what she was looking for and brought it into the barn. The hallway to the workshop was long, much longer than in real life. She got to the workshop and found her father standing in the same spot. The light bulb was still swinging. She could see him, and then she couldn't. Then she could, and then she couldn't. She called to him, "Daddy?" He turned to her. She took it out from behind her, the thing she went to get. For a second, or less than a second, it was a bottle. Then it was a gun, then a bottle again. She handed it to him. He smiled. "My Carly," he said, "you always take care of me."

Caroline woke, but not with a start. She woke slowly, like rising from the depths of a swamp to its surface. She got up and padded downstairs, pausing to watch Jacob asleep on the couch. A lightning storm flickered somewhere in the distance. The speed of light is so fast, faster than anyone can imagine. Caroline realized that the bulb swinging in her dream had been inspired by the lighting. As she watched Jacob, she felt pricks of anger. The random images from the dream assaulted her: the bottle, the gun, a little girl taking care of her father. As these thoughts were arousing her adrenaline, she spotted headlights coming down the driveway. Headlights? This late? Why? The sound of wind chimes ran through her mind, yet there weren't any and, with that, no sound. Someone came to the window and peered in. Caroline suddenly wanted to throw something at the shadowed person. She wished she had a big wooden rolling pin with red handles. Red handles. As the gears in her mind clicked into place, she recognized the curly hair and glasses and knew it was Barry. Only Barry. Caroline went to the door, opened it, and met Barry on the porch. She was wearing just her pajamas. This time, the peepers really were out, their song calming her raw nerves. The sky lit up again, but the stars were out, their light reaching her eyes in an unconceivable amount of time.

"She's not going to make it," Barry stated flatly.

The peepers, unaware of their humanly dilemmas, sang even louder now.

"How much longer?"

"Any day now. Weeks. Months at best."

They sat on the porch swing and leaned against one another, swinging back and forth. Barry cried and wiped tears away, only to have them come again.

"I wish I could have known her," Barry confessed.

"You do know her, maybe more than you think."

"No, Emily's girlfriend came to see her tonight, her ex-girlfriend, the same one who left her when she got sick. Right away, I could see that they shared something that we never did. It's not fair."

Barry sighed heavily, his chin dropping down onto his chest.

"This girlfriend, she won't even be there when Emily dies. She won't be able to handle it, but I will. I'll be with Emily until the end. I will see it."

As Caroline watched him, a knowing, uninvited and unannounced, came to her: "Maybe, just maybe, the ultimate knowing of a person is to be with them when they die," she said.

Gretchen

"A lot happens in 1964."

"What kinds of things?" asked Lila.

"Well, around the country, Lyndon B. Johnson started sending American soldiers into Vietnam. Jake enlisted. Also, Sara moved to Boston, Massachusetts. She made this move after going to a big civil rights march in Washington."

"D.C., right?" clarified Lila.

"Yes, D.C... Sara said that she loves that area of the country. She said it's so much more progressive up there, whatever that means. Anyway, I had watched that march on TV, which was the first time I saw Bob Dylan or Joan

Baez. That was in August of '63. They had performed at the rally. I had never seen so many people in one place."

"Did you want to go with Sara?" Lila questioned.

"I did want to go, desperately, but it was a long trip. I couldn't take Owen with me. I never considered it an option to go. Anyway, while Sara was there, she started looking into a teaching position in the D.C. area. Who knows how, but she landed one, instead, in Massachusetts, which is more thrilling to Sara. She said that Boston is even more progressive than Washington."

"How did you feel when Sara moved away?" Lila already knew the answer to this.

"I didn't want her to go yet I couldn't hold her back. She's my only friend, and I will miss her terribly, but what could I do? It's what she wants, and, so, it's what I want for her... even if I don't want it for me. Does that make any sense?"

"It makes a whole lot of sense," returned Lila.

A stillness ensued, allowing more memories to surface, like driftwood popping up to the surface of a lake.

"She calls me a lot, almost every day."

"You mean Sara?" asked Lila.

"Yes, Sara. She told me all about her apartment, right down to where each knick-knack is and where each picture was hung. She's still the same old Sara, but just further away. She started reading Hemmingway... "A Farewell to Arms." When she calls, I tell her all about "The Sun Also Rises," and she tells me about her book. We're careful not to tell each other too much, though. When we're each done with our books, we're going to swap. Sara has it all planned out. When we're done with Hemmingway, we're both going to read *Rabbit Run* by John Updike."

"That sounds enjoyable!" said Lila.

"It is. Also, I guess there are a bunch of people her age in the same building. They all get together and listen to Bob Dylan and the Beatles. They smoke hash, whatever that is. I wish she wouldn't worry so much about me, but I'm glad she calls as often as she does. Before she left, she told me, 'Don't ever forget this Gretchen: When a man stands up straight, nobody can ride him.' I asked her if she made up that saying. She's always coming out with all sorts of sayings like that. 'No, you dummy!' she laughed. 'Martin Luther King Jr. said that!' It makes me wonder how close I am to standing tall.

Anyway, I went down to Woolworth's after a phone call with Sara to find two records: "Beatles for Sale" and "Times They are A-Changin" by Bob Dylan. I rushed home and listened to them. Although Bob Dylan has a weird voice, "Boots of Spanish Leather" was my favorite song on the record. The Beatles record is my new favorite of all time. I especially like, "I'll Follow the Sun." It reminds me of Sara.

Lila changed direction. "When will Jake be leaving for Vietnam?"

"I've spent so long trying to prepare myself for saying good-bye to Jake. I began thinking that I would be like all the other wives in waiting. I'd wear long white gloves and carry tissues to the bus station when he went.

My mother told me about her friend's daughter, whose husband had already departed to Vietnam. She thought that I should get together with her, so we could support one another. Her name is Josephine. People call her Josey for short. I'm thinking I don't want to sit and wait with her. I'm thinking I'd rather be in Boston with Sara listening to the Beatles and smoking hash, whatever that is. I want to be free of Jake. God help me for feeling that way, but I do. It's just that living with him is like walking on nails, or it's like living in a gale force wind all the time, every minute. It's like I just want the wind to stop so that I can hear the silence."

"Do you ever get a break from him, from Jake?" inquired Lila.

"Well, when he goes to work... but then the whole time I worry about him coming home. Did I tell you that he fell off the wagon one time?"

"No. What was that like for you?"

"Well, there wasn't even anything to trigger it. He spent a great deal of time trying to pick a fight with me."

"Over what?" asked Lila.

"I hadn't yet put away the clean dishes from the strainer, and Jake didn't like that at all. He tried starting an argument with me, but I wouldn't participate. 'I'll get to it when I get to it,' I said."

"That was very brave of you," said Lila.

"Yeah, well... It didn't go over too well. He trashed the kitchen, then left. He didn't come home for four days that time. I still never know where he runs off to and, to be honest, I don't really care. It's crazy, but I sometimes wish for him to lose it, just so he'll take off. I started to feel a sense of relief that Jake would be leaving for the war. I imagined the type of clothes I would wear, the friends I would invite over--even though I don't really have any, except for Sara. As for Samuel, I haven't seen him much since Owen's birthday, haven't really wanted to."

Lila interrupted to ask, "How did Jake treat you after Samuel's surprise visit?"

"After everyone left, Owen and I were sitting on the couch with Myrtle. Jake came in and picked up the cat by its neck and dictated, 'If that man ever comes to this house again, I'll take this cat out back and shoot it!' He dropped the cat onto the floor and slammed into the bedroom. I got off easy. Owen on the other hand, did not. Owen looked up at me and asked, 'Does Daddy have a gun, Mum?' 'No, he does not have gun.' At least, I don't think he does. Of course, I didn't say that to Owen. Then I thought... what if he did have gun? I thought how, if Jake did have a gun, I'd like to take Jake out back and shoot him."

"What has become of Samuel?" prompts Lila.

"I see him around town sometimes. I saw him at the pharmacy one time. I was looking for a card to send to Sara. I could tell someone was directly behind me, so close I couldn't even turn around to see who was there. 'Surprise,' he whispered in my ear. Later, I thought I knew it had been Samuel even before he spoke. I hadn't even startled. Another time, Samuel surprised me was over the summer. I went outside onto the porch to shake the hall rug out and there,

266

on the threshold, was a basket of peaches with a note saying: *Some peaches for my peaches. I get sick to my stomach when I think what would have happened if Jake had come home before I shook the rug, or if I hadn't gone out when I had. I took the basket of peaches over to the apple orchard, the one between my house and my parents'. This orchard is enormous, more than tripling Samuel's peach orchard. I went way into the back and left the basket of peaches, note and all."*

"What else happens in 1964?" prompts Lila.

"It's not a good thing. Not good at all."

"Do you want to tell me about it?"

"Yes. Yes, I do. Jake was working one day, and I was home with Owen. Owen and I were putting a puzzle together."

Lila interjected, "Owen would have been four years old?"

"Yes. And I, twenty-five. Anyway, it was a hot, sticky day. Owen and I were miserable. We had decided to go to the pond when we finished our puzzle... to cool off. Out of nowhere, I heard an explosion outside in the distance. I ran to the front door to see what had happened, and heard the screams. It was Jake. I grabbed Owen and ran to the garage. Jake was on the floor next to the tire machine. His arm was covered in blood, the machine and floor bathed in it. Owen started to panic. I had to put him in the office, so he wouldn't have to see anymore. I used the office phone and called for help. After endless minutes, the medics arrived and rushed Jake to the hospital. It seems that Jake was using the tire machine when a piece of metal broke off and drove right through his arm."

Lila commented, "That certainly is bad. Is there more?"

There came no answer. Lila waited; knowing that time for the woman lying on her bed was moving soundlessly. That movement contained snapshots of a life unfolding.

Finally, a single tear rolled onto Lila's bed. "He didn't go to Vietnam."

"Who? Jake?" asked.

"He didn't go. When I realized, I felt like I was wading in quick sand instead of walking on air, as I had been."

"Was it his arm?" asked Lila.

"Yes. It was too badly damaged. There's no way the army could have taken him, no way. Here's what happened: While Jake was in the hospital, he asked me to do something, something unusual."

Lila waited for more.

"He said to me, 'Gretchen? I need you to do something for me.' I said, 'Anything Jake, what is it?' 'I need you to go to Samuel. I need you to ask him to take over at the garage for me. I can't stand the guy, but he's the only person I know who can fix cars almost as good as I can. We can't afford to close up shop while I am out of commission.' Jake winced in pain, then continued. 'Maybe the guy is good for something.' Was this an apology? I wondered. Jake made me promise to go over there that same day, so we did.

Owen and I made our way over that evening, when it had gotten cooler outside. Owen was afraid to go, 'What if Daddy shoots Myrtle?' I reassured Owen that Daddy told us to go; he wouldn't be mad, and he wouldn't hurt Myrtle either. I knocked on Samuel's door, no answer. I knocked again, waited. Finally, I heard movement on the other side. Samuel answered the door, and I could tell that he had been sleeping. 'Gretchen, Owen, my little peaches,' he said, smiling, 'What brings you over on this fine day?' I took a deep breath and pushed on. 'Jake would like to know if you would take over for him at the garage for a few weeks,' I said quickly. 'Ah...I heard about his accident. It's a shame, really. So now he needs my help, does he?' I swallowed hard, the mountain air suffocating me. I heard voices out in back of his house... people picking peaches. A mosquito buzzed in my ear. I waved it away. Samuel turned on his heels, thinking as he looked up to the sky. 'Well, that would be a trick. I do have my crew to look after.' Someone out back laughed, maybe Thomas. I quickly volunteered, 'I could come here and look after your crew for you.' Where had that idea come from? Samuel looked at me, the smile disappearing from his face. 'I have to be honest, Gretchen. My inclination is to say 'no'. I worked for Jake once. We did well for a while until he got to drinking and became all prickly and nasty. I, myself, don't drink, not much anyway.' We were silent. Owen squirmed at my side. Samuel's face changed expression in thought. 'All right. Keep in mind that I will be doing this for you and for Owen, not Jake. I

269

wouldn't want to see the two of you going hungry. I'll start tomorrow.'"

"That's how it started. Jake was in the hospital, Samuel at work in the garage, and I at Samuel's peach orchard. Fair trade. I knew his work was a lot harder than mine. All I had to do was make sure that four men took their breaks. Samuel told me that they would work themselves into heat exhaustion if they weren't forced to stop. He was right. In all my life, I had never met the nicest group of men, black men at that. I made them lunches and lemonade every day. Owen and I always sat and ate with them. I'm certain Jake would not have liked that. What Jake didn't know didn't seem to hurt him... or me. I took full advantage of the enjoyment we had, eating lunch with other adults. John, the oldest, took the strongest liking to Owen. He would lift Owen up on his shoulders and have him pick the peaches up high. John lived at the edge of the horse farm and helped with the horses there. He said he had been working on farms and orchards since he was a boy. He said he doesn't want for a better job, that this is all he's ever known. John told me about his son who was going to college in Boston; therefore he did not have to go to Vietnam, which relieved him. At the mention of Boston, I thought of Sara. Mitchell, the youngest, adamantly refused to believe that he would be picking peaches or apples all of his life. He had gone to the freedom ride back in 1961. He rode the bus with the other blacks and whites. The whole bus had gotten smoked out, and all the blacks got arrested. Tears pricked my eyes as I broke up the lettuce for our salad."

270

"Who were you crying for?" asked Lila.

"Maybe for Sara, or for Mitchell, or Jake... or for myself."

Lila let her rest, re-group, collect her memories.

"I would like to tell you a little secret."

"Go on. It's safe to tell secrets here," said Lila.

"Well, Jake can never know this, he can never ever know this... but during my days at Samuel's, I kissed someone."

"Who did you kiss?"

"Mitchell, I kissed Mitchell."

A giggle escaped her before continuing. "We were working in the orchard, picking peaches, and we got into this peach fight. First, he whipped one at me, and then, I whipped one at him. We kept going on and on like that. Eventually, we ended up rolling around on the ground, trying to smush peaches into each other's hair. I got him first, and then he got a hold of me and squished a peach all through my hair. We were laughing so hard. I don't think I've ever laughed like that, at least not for a long time. Suddenly, he was on top of me and our faces were so close. I saw his eyes. Such beautiful eyes. I couldn't believe I had never really noticed them before then. Then, he leaned down and just... kissed me. You know what? I kissed him back. I kissed him back, and I liked it! God help me, but I liked it."

"That certainly is quite a secret," said Lila.

"Then, I heard John coming, and I hopped up, brushing the dirt off my pants. I looked up at Mitchell, and he was smiling at me." 'You are beautiful,' he said. I could feel myself blush. He reached out and touched my cheek. I could hear birds up above. I could hear their wings flapping. I reached out and touched his cheek. 'You, too, are beautiful,' I said."

"That night, I went home, but I kept thinking about that kiss. I could still feel it on my lips. Poor Owen, I never heard a word he said to me the whole night. After he went to bed, I sat at the kitchen table, thinking about that kiss. I touched my lips, and they felt hot. Then, I went downstairs to busy myself, to do laundry. Still, I couldn't stop remembering. I touched my lips again, and they were still hot. When I came back upstairs, I went outside, just for something to do. And there, across the street, was Mitchell... just standing there. He saw me and walked over. Again, he reached out and touched my cheek. I realized then that his touch was gentle in a way that Jake's had never been. He kissed me again, and we went inside. The house was all lit up, and he went around looking at everything. He went around touching things: a lamp, the handles on the cupboards, the kitchen table cloth. He said, 'So this is where you live. I've wondered.' He came over and touched my waist, my thigh. 'So this is what you feel like,' he said. I didn't stop him."

"We did things. Things I have never done with Jake. Things that should have felt wrong but didn't. Things that didn't take away from me, but added to me. I had never felt that way before. Never. Afterward, we sat together in the kitchen. 'There's something. There's something about you,' he told me. "Yes. There's something,' I said, but I looked *away. I couldn't find the words. I couldn't stop touching him. I just needed some small part of me to be touching him at all times... like my hand against his wrist, or my foot against his. Time loomed, enveloping us. He talked of his travels around the country-side, of orchards, and horse farms far away from here. He detailed the smells of every place he's ever been: The smells of earth, fruits, and horse manure. I swear I could smell all of those things as he told about them. He told me about sleeping in barns and using a book as a pillow. He told me about leaving his abusive father behind when he was just thirteen, about climbing trees, and bathing in ponds. I asked him what he was going to go to school for in Boston. 'I don't know yet,' he said. 'Well, what do you like?' I asked. As he thought, I studied his profile, seeing youth, seeing perfection... despite the purple scar along his neck. I longed to touch it. 'I like to be up high,' he answered, looking directly at me. I thought. 'Hmm. Up high. Well, then... a pilot. You should be a pilot.' Mitchell smiled, 'Then pilot it is,' he said. 'And you?' he said. I wasn't sure what he meant. My plans for the future? I didn't have any. Then: 'Have you ever been up high?' I shook my head. 'Ever even climbed a tree?' Again, I shook my head. 'Then, let's go. Let's get you up a tree.' We went outside, and Mitchell searched the back yard for the perfect climbing tree. He found one and motioned for me to go up. 'Alone?' I said. 'Yes. Just you.' 'I can't!' 'Why?' 'I... I'm scared. I've never climbed a tree before.' 'All the more reason to do it now,' he said. His eyes wouldn't let go of mine. So I started up the tree. I was more nervous to climb that tree than I*

273

was about anything that had happened that whole night. But, still, I kept going up, one limb at a time.' 'That-a-girl!' Mitchell yelled from below. The higher I got, the more I shook, but I kept going. My shoe fell off, and he caught it. 'I got your shoe!' He yelled up to me, 'And I can catch you, too, if I have to!' I kept going and going. I could hear Mitchell laughing somewhere down below me. I, too, began to laugh. I lost my footing and ended up dangling from a branch by my hands. I screeched. 'That-a-girl! You can do it!" prodded Mitchell, his voice becoming smaller and smaller. My feet found purchase on a branch, and I went higher up still. At last, I found the top and nestled myself in among some branches. I looked out and saw the roof top of my house, the street, Jake's garage, whose truck was not there. I saw the tops of trees and cars going down the street. I breathed in deeply and hollered out, 'This is unbelievable!' I could just barely hear Mitchell's voice. 'Isn't it amazing what you can see from a different perspective!' His voice echoed into the night."

"Please, don't tell Jake."

"As I said, your secrets are safe here," said Lila.

"Good. I've never told anyone that. It feels good to tell it."

"You never told Sara?"

"No. I never got the chance."

Here, a long silence interrupted time. Lila waited, scribbling her notes.

Then: "We all listened to the Beatles and sang right out loud."

274

"At Samuel's?" asked Lila.

"Yes, there. I discovered Ray Charles, who I decided I loved. We all sang. All four men, Owen, and me."

"Mitchell, too?"

"Mitchell, especially." Again, a smile graced her lips before continuing. "We sang 'Georgia on my Mind" and whatever else came on the radio. Jake would have really flown off the handle at that."

"Jake wouldn't approve?"

"Oh, no. As I have said, he doesn't like the Beatles or coloreds for that matter. Anyway, life was really good at Samuel's that last month of summer in 1964. Until we lost Mitchell, that is."

"Lost him?"

"Yes. He... he... didn't go to college, he went to Vietnam. Lyndon Johnson kept saying that we were kicking their butts over there, but it didn't seem like it. At every turn, you'd hear about someone losing a son, a father, a husband. And I knew, I knew that we would lose Mitchell as well. I mean, I always knew that my time with him was going to be short. I wasn't ready for it to end when it did."

"Did you continue to see each other?"

"Not at my house. That was the only time he ever came to my house. Around the orchard, we were always sneaking kisses, always hiding around a tree, touching one another whenever we could. Anyway, right before Mitchell found out, John's son in Boston got bashed up pretty good at a demonstration he'd been involved in. He had been protesting the war with others, which really bothered those

275

that supported the war. Somehow rocks started to be thrown, people got whacked with sticks, tear gas was sprayed, fires lit. All hell broke loose. John's son got hurt badly enough that he landed in the hospital. I worried about Sara. I pictured her being lit on fire, and I resolved to call her as soon as I got home that day. I worried for Mitchell, and I worried for myself... that I would never feel his touch again. Finally, one day, Mitchell ate his last peach with us, and we all said our good-byes. The last thing he told me before he left was, 'Don't you stop climbing those trees.' He held me so tight. I could feel him sobbing, but it was soundless. I took it hard, but I kept it well hidden... I think. Thomas, also, took it hard. He retreated into the orchard, and we didn't see him again until the end of the day. After Mitchell left, I would sit on my doorstep and look up at the trees. A few times, I almost climbed one, but my heart just wasn't in it. Mitchell would scold me for that. He would make me do it. Without him there, I just didn't seem to have the strength. Besides, I enjoyed just sitting on the step, listening to the wind in the trees. I tried not to imagine Mitchell out there. I tried to remember him as he was."

"And how was that?" asked Lila.

"Young. Strong. Beautiful. Climbing trees."

"Do you think what I did was wrong?"

"Wrong? Well, what do you think?" replied Lila.

"Actually... no. I don't think it was wrong. It feels like something that is mine, and mine alone. I feels like something that Jake can't touch, can't ruin."

"That is good," said Lila. "Good for you to have something that has given you joy. You're right, no one can take that away from you."

Lila continued. "And Jake? What's going on with Jake?"

"Jake didn't come home from the hospital for a little more than a month. He kept getting infections in his blood. The doctors called it a staph infection. I guess it's pretty serious. Eventually, he did get well enough to come home. I tried to enjoy my last days at Samuel's, but it was very difficult."

"Why was it difficult?"

"I was nervous about Jake coming home. I knew I would miss the peach orchard. Missing Mitchell has been awful. Keeping it to myself, even worse. Mostly though, I knew Jake would not have approved of me being at the orchard if I didn't need to be. Jake thought he'd get right back to work when he got home from the hospital. I wasn't as confident. He would still need to be in a brace for a long time. On my last day working at Samuel's, I went into his bedroom. I don't know why, except that it was the only room in the house I'd never seen. There was nothing in there except a bed and a dresser. The bed had no blankets and the dresser had only a record player on it. There was a Jerry Lee Lewis record already in place, so I put the needle down and turned the power on. "Great Balls of Fire" screamed out of the speaker. I startled, spilling the glass of lemonade that was in my hand. I turned off the record player and returned the needle to its holder. I opened Samuel's dresser drawer *and saw boxer shorts and boxes of cigars. Something pink caught my attention. I immediately recognized it as my scarf, the one I'd left at the pond last summer. When I had realized that I left it there, I went back to retrieve it, but it was nowhere to be found. I quickly backed out of Samuel's room and got home as quickly as I could. When I got home I realized that, in my haste, I forgot to close the dresser drawer... Samuel's dresser drawer."*

Caroline

Caroline's mother called. She finished her first round of treatment and was on a two-week vacation.

"I'm having a get together tomorrow night with some clients and some friends. I'd like you to come."

Caroline stammered, "I don't know, Mum. My friend Barry's wife, ex-wife, is very sick."

She almost let it slip, the name of Emily's illness. "I need to be here right now."

Her mother sighed. "That's too bad. Your friend Tim is going to be here."

"Tim? My Tim? What are you talking about?"

"I hired him to be the entertainment for my party."

"God, Mum! Are you guys... buddies now?"

"I told you I liked him, didn't I? He gave me his card when I saw him at "The Black Rose." I called to see if he could play for my party. As luck would have it, he was available. He asked if you would be there."

Caroline began to pace. "When is this get together?"

"Tomorrow night"

"I'll try to be there Mum, no promises."

Caroline made a mental note to have her Klonopin on hand just in case.

After speaking with her mother, Caroline met Barry at the hospital. He looked awful. He had dark circles under his eyes. His laugh lines drooped, and he needed a haircut, or, at the very least, a comb. Caroline's heat raced in spite of this. She hugged him; feeling his low, depleted energy through her clothes. They went up to Emily's room together. Caroline stayed in the hall while Barry entered Emily's room, leaving the door open. Caroline could see Emily across the room in her hospital bed. Her bald head was elevated, and she was hooked up to a respirator. Caroline could hear the rhythmic hums, beeps, and clicks of the various medical apparatus, all being used to keep Emily alive... who was not much more than a skeleton still covered with skin. Caroline looked away, feeling like an intruder. She looked up when she caught movement out of the corner of her eye. A woman was in the room with Emily and Barry. She looked to be in her forties with long, dark hair, a woman who, perhaps, resembled Emily before the cancer. This must be Emily's sister. Thought Caroline.

The woman came out of the room and introduced herself, "Hi, I'm Eliza, Emily's sister." Her voice was soft and heavy, and she smelled like a nurse. "I'm glad to meet you."

Had Barry told Eliza about her?

"Do you want to come in?" asked Eliza.

Caroline stumbled for an answer. "No, I'll give you two your privacy; I'll just wait for Barry."

"Okay, but come in if you want to." Eliza turned to leave, but then paused. "Emily and I are truly happy for Barry. He's a good guy. As good as they come. All that Emily ever wanted... all that she wants... is for Barry to find someone." Eliza peered in at Emily, then turned back to Caroline. A slow smile graced her lips.

"It looks like he has," added Eliza before returning to her sister.

Caroline thought of sisters. Some shimmer of a distant memory flickered, igniting a memory of a childhood fantasy... an imaginary sister named Birdie.

When Caroline returned home, she again found Jacob outside in his boxers. She approached him as always, yet he looked at her as if he had never laid eyes on her before.

"I'll get the cat," Caroline promised. "Let's get you inside."

As she helped him up the steps and through the door, her hand burned and sizzled where it made contact with his arm. There was something wrong inside him, not just in his mind, but in his body as well. She struggled over whether or not to take him to the hospital. Remembering her promise to him, she took him in and made him coffee. His hand shook as he lifted the cup to his lips.

"When are you going to find someone?" he asked.

Caroline stopped in mid-wipe of the counter, wondering if he meant what she thought he meant.

"I already have."

"Good. A nice girl like yourself ought not to be going around with an old man like me forever."

That was the only thing Jacob said for the rest of the night.

Caroline was conflicted. One moment she planned on going to her mother's. The next moment she had resolved to stay home. She did not want to leave Jacob or Barry. Her anxiety and panic attacks, thankfully, had been held at bay, yet they were always lurking, like wolves prowling just at the edge of a forest. In the end, Caroline decided to go. Sarna offered to stay with Jacob while Caroline went to her mother's. She gave Caroline her cell phone in case Barry needed her. Caroline called Barry to give him Sarna's cell phone number. Barry said he was glad she was going, and if she wimped out, he would kick her ass. She didn't tell him about Tim. Barry reminded Caroline that Emily's parents had flown in from California, and he would be with them at the hospital all night, in vigil. "Don't worry about me. It's not like I'm here all alone," he said. Caroline took a half of Klonopin, and then moments later took the other half. She followed her usual route to the parking garage, hailed a taxi, and arrived at her mother's doorstep unharmed and mostly in control. She heard voices from within and felt the same freezing sensation she'd had when she went to her first meditation session. Breathe in. Breathe out. At last, Caroline entered her mother's house. Her feet knew the path down the well-lit hallway. Small groups of people were clustered together here and there. Everyone was dressed alike: skirts, boots, blousy pants, scarves, and funky hats abound. Caroline looked down at herself. She felt to be a drab girl. She hadn't even put on earrings, never mind make-up. She headed into the kitchen where she saw Tim talking with a tall woman, crane-like with closely cropped hair. The bird woman was laughing at something Tim was saying. Caroline remembered that he always had been a talker. She was not ready for this yet. She turned away from him and went to find her mother. There she was, her mother, as flamboyant as the rest. She was in one of the small groups, looking thinner than before but otherwise looking well. She looked happy. While Caroline looked at her mother, she thought of Emily in her hospital bed and couldn't help but wonder why some people make it and others don't. Caroline's mother sensed her in the room, disengaged from her group, and went to Caroline. She began to lead her to Tim. Caroline instinctively pulled back. Her mother took hold of her arm. "Don't be silly, Caroline. He's just a man."

Tim looked up and saw Caroline coming toward him. All expression left his face as they looked at one another. His eyes looked like an old friend. She saw a vein in his forehead that hadn't been as prominent before.

"Get over here," he said, opening his arms to embrace her. It was the same hug, the exact same hug.

Caroline had changed and maybe he had, too, but the hug was the same. She relaxed into his chest, swimming in his familiar smell. The conversation started immediately, as if they had never lost touch... but had years to catch up on. Tim had left Florida to come back to Massachusetts almost a year ago. It had taken him that long, seven years, to realize it wasn't his scene. He had even gone to Nashville for a short time to try and make it there, but no one had wanted him.

"New England is the only place for a folkie like me."

He told her that one of the first things he had done when he returned was go to her old apartment.

"You weren't there anymore. I had no idea where to even look for you."

Caroline said nothing.

He went to his gig bag and took out a CD. The picture on front was identical to the poster on the front of The Black Rose.

"Hold on, now," he said. He retreated, opened the CD cover, and began to write. As he handed it to her, he explained, "My buddy helped me produce this. It has the song on it that you requested at The Black Rose.

"Isn't that the one I tried to sing background vocals for?" Caroline asked, obviously knowing that it was.

"Yeah, that was pretty bad." They both laughed. She always loved his laugh. Tim was the type to laugh with his whole body. He continued to talk, and she listened, forgetting about her earlier attempt to escape. He filled her in about Florida and Nashville. Tim had bought a car, an old beater, when he returned to Massachusetts. His other beater wouldn't have made it another mile. Tim, also, told her about his place in Somerville, no bigger than a postage stamp, and that she should come and see it. After a while, he excused himself, because he needed to go play, since that was what he was being paid for. Caroline leaned against the wall and listened to him play his guitar. He played the song she'd requested at the club. Remembering the girl she used to be, Caroline chuckled to herself. He went on to play: "Angel from Montgomery", "Highway 66", and "Speed of the Sound of Loneliness"… all the ones she had known from before.

Caroline's mother came up beside her. "You have good taste."

Caroline smiled, "Yes, I do."

Tim finished the set and came back to her. He talked about his new guitar and his newest cleansing diet. Caroline felt such affection for him at that moment… he hadn't changed a bit.

Tim played another set, returning to her to talk about a new song he had written about old train tracks gone rusty and useless. He also talked about other stuff that she couldn't follow. Her cell phone rang. She excused herself and answered.

"Carly?" Sarna sounded apologetic.

"What's wrong?"

"Oh, nothing. Nothing at all, I don't think. Jacob and I have been watching Jeopardy. I'm giving him a run for his money. He is used to you never knowing any of the questions. Me, I know as much as he does. Boy, does he get competitive, almost angry. He's just in his boxers, though. He won't put any pants on. Is this normal?"

Caroline could hear him yelling in the background, and then Sarna yelled out, too. "Damn! He got that one first!"

Caroline smiled. "Don't worry about the boxers. I can't get him to wear anything else lately."

"How's it going?" Sarna hedged. "Do you want to come home?"

Caroline looked over at Tim. "Yes, actually, I do."

"Good, then tell them your elderly neighbor just crapped his depends, and I refuse to change him."

Caroline laughed out loud and hung up. She did not use Sarna's excuse. Instead, she begged out, saying that she didn't feel well. Of course, she was feeling just fine. The ease with which the white lie rolled off her tongue surprised her. When she told Tim that she was leaving, his shoulders slumped. He hugged her, and it still felt good. He gave her his card and told her to call him. She said good-bye to her mother, who tried to hide her disappointment.

Then she whispered into Caroline's ear, "Is it your social anxiety again?"

"Yes, Mum. Yes, it is."

Even though, for once, it wasn't.

In the taxi, Caroline looked at the CD Tim had given her. She opened it and saw that he had inscribed: "To Carly, Love Tim." Love? What kind of love? The 'I-adore-you kind', or the kind where you want to be adored? When she got back to Jacob's, Sarna and Jacob were both yelling and screaming at the TV.

"Jeopardy's still on?" Caroline asked.

"It's a marathon," they answered in unison, obviously pleased with their luck tonight. She joined them on the couch as they rattled off questions: Who is Macbeth? What is the House of Representatives? Who is Jack Kerouac? Caroline enjoyed watching the two of them. She enjoyed more the next answer that came over the TV; she knew the question and screamed it out, "What is Golgi Apparatus?"

"Golgi Apparatus?" Sarna was incredulous.

Caroline beamed. "What? I remembered it from college biology!"

Gretchen

"Sara is going to New York."

"What is she going there for?" asked Lila.

"She's going to see the Beatles when they arrive at JFK Airport. I wish I was going with her."

Caroline

The next day, Caroline was in her little house. It felt like ages since she'd been there. She put on Tim's CD and noticed daffodils outside her window. She listened to two songs and took the CD out. She put in Van Morrison, the one she found in her closet ages ago. Her favorite song was "Crazy Love" which she listened to over and over again, as was her habit. Caroline opened the windows, swept and dusted her cottage. She kept eyeing her beads and jewelry supplies, contemplating, but she did not really want to touch them. Her phone rang. It was Barry.

"She's gone." Such a simple statement, two words only.

"Do you want me to come to you? Do you want to come to me? Just tell me what you need," said Caroline.

"Can I come over later today or tonight?' asked Barry.

"I'll be here," returned Caroline. She went outside, looked at the sky, and then, went looking for more daffodils. When she found a bunch of them, she cut them and arranged them in a vase. She placed the vase on the kitchen table and waited for Barry. Because she didn't know what else to do, she lay down on the couch where she promptly returned to her earlier dream of the three girls in the field. Somehow, she willed herself to wake. Lila had once told her that we can control our dreams. Caroline always wondered what that meant: Our literal, night time dreams? Our wishes for ourselves? Why hadn't she asked Lila to explain? She picked up the phone to call Sarna, thinking if she didn't ask someone now, she would forget later.

Sarna answered on the third ring, "Hello?"

"Hi Sarna, do you have a minute?"

"Of course, I do, Julie and I are just hanging out. Is everything all right?"

Caroline decided to start with Barry. "Emily died today."

"Poor Barry, how is he?"

"I'm not sure. He didn't say much; just that he would be over late today or tonight."

"If I can do anything to help let me know."

"I will, but I think he just needs a shoulder; I have two. Can I ask you something?"

"What's up?"

Caroline quickly tried to gather her thoughts. "Lila once mentioned in a meditation class that we can control our dreams. What do you think she meant by that? Do you think she meant real dreams or our dreams... like goals... for the future?"

Sarna was quiet for a moment. "If I remember correctly; we were discussing letting our night time dreams guide us in achieving our life's dreams, our goals. I think. Why?"

Caroline heard Julie laughing in the background and suddenly felt a weariness overtake her. "Just wondering I guess. Forget it, it doesn't really matter anyway."

Sarna let out a huff of breath. "Caroline, it matters, it all matters. Even when it matters to nobody but you, it matters. I'm going to call Lila and find out."

"You don't have to do that Sarna. She might be busy or with a client."

"She might just be watching TV."

Caroline smiled, remembering that even if she, herself, was going to let it go, Sarna would not.

They said good-bye. Sarna would call after she spoke with Lila.

Caroline made some potato pancakes for Jacob. She had learned that he loved them, and she was happy to have something to do while she waited. Of course, he would need something to go with the pancakes, so she made a big salad with radishes, grape tomatoes, and cucumbers. Caroline separated the meal, some for Jacob, and some for her and Barry. She waited some more. Dusk was finally cresting when her phone rang for the second time that day.

Sarna's voice was breathless with excitement. "Caroline! I'm so glad I called Lila. She had been thinking about you all day. She said it was good karma that I called her."

"Well, don't keep me in suspense. What did she say?"

"She said, number one, that all dreams, both asleep and awake, are controllable. You only have to desire the control."

Caroline sighed, "Great, that's as clear as dirty dish water."

"Wait, there's more. Lila said that fields represent choices, freedom."

"Choices about what?" Caroline was not sure she liked the direction of this.

"I don't know. I'm willing to bet that Lila would ask you to answer that very question yourself. Does this make any sense?"

Caroline's first thought was- no this doesn't make any sense. Instead she said, "Let me think about it. I'll talk to you tomorrow."

"Caroline, remember if you need me, call."

"I will, and thanks for calling Lila for me."

"Any time. See you later."

It finally got dark. The hands moved around the clock. Caroline checked on Jacob again. He was sound asleep on the couch, snoring lightly. She returned home to wait some more. Finally, Barry arrived at ten o'clock. He hadn't slept for days. Caroline made him lie on the couch to rest before they had even had a chance to say hello. Barry fell right to sleep and woke a solid two hours later. He shot up, looked around him, looked around again.

He started to cry. "I hate sleeping. Every time I do, the pain gets away from me. When I wake up it hits me two fold."

Caroline sat next to him and took his hand.

"Have you ever seen someone die?" Barry asked.

Caroline shook her head.

"It's so strange, it's like… it's like…" Barry paused to translate his racing mind. "It's like when a clock is ticking, and it just stops. You expect it to go to the next second, just like the one before. It doesn't; it just stops. There's no drama, no event, no nothing. Just stopping. That's what dying is." He breathed out heavily and started to sob again.

"Do you want me to get you anything?"

"Coffee. Please. I would like some coffee. I don't want to sleep again."

Caroline went to the kitchen to put the coffee on. She caught a glimpse of Barry on the couch. A wave of sorrow washed over him, and he began to sob again. Caroline made herself busy in the kitchen until it subsided. When the coffee was done, she brought it to him.

He sipped greedily then asked, "Did you have a nice time at your mother's?"

Caroline could not believe he would be thinking of her at such a time. "It was okay. I just really wanted to come home, to be at home. My mother assumed it was my social anxiety, but, for the first time, it wasn't."

Barry looked at her with such care at that moment. "Do you have social anxiety?" he inquired.

"Hell, yes!"

"That makes two of us," he said, looking down at his lap.

"You, too?" Caroline couldn't believe it.

"I didn't always. It started about three years ago. I just wanted to be alone most of the time. I tend to get nervous around people. Oh yeah, it's great fun."

"I didn't notice that about you. I guess I was too wrapped up in my own anxiety. I'm sorry."

They continued chatting about social anxiety disorders and the related disorders while they ate their salad and potato pancakes. Hours passed like minutes until Barry fell asleep on the couch. Caroline put a blanket on him and went to bed.

Gretchen

"Jake came home from the hospital. He had the brace on his arm. He did go back to work right away, just like he said he would. He doesn't get home from work until late at night, on account of the brace on his arm. As expected, when he does get home he is drunk... again."

291

"How does this make you feel? Are you surprised?" Lila questioned.

"No, I fully expected it. Owen and I do so well all day until Jake comes home. Owen will suddenly get moody and sullen. Then, I have two of them moping around. Jake gets frustrated with Owen. He thinks Owen is misbehaving, and he is. His entire personality changes: he won't eat, he has tantrums, he clings to me, and then rails against me. Jake just can't see that his mental state affects Owen, that Owen is reflecting Jake's behavior. I have tried repeatedly to speak with Jake about this, but he won't hear it, or can't."

Lila encouraged a change of topic. "Have you spoken to Sara recently?"

"Sara still calls me every day. The stories I hear from her! She and her friends go around protesting the war. They wear colorful clothes with peace signs plastered all over them. Just walking down the streets of Boston, you see people with peace signs painted on their cheeks. Sara said that she has a friend with a VW bus that they plan to paint with huge peace signs. Then, they want to drive from Boston to California next summer. They want to spread the message of peace all across the country."

"Has Jake had anything to say about Sara's opinions?" Lila questioned.

"I don't tell Jake of her plans. He is always grumbling about the peacers, that's what he calls them. He says they should go out and get real jobs. I'm thinking that fighting for peace is a job you don't get paid for. I would never say this to him. It would start our own Vietnam right

292

at home. I wonder if Jake had gone… if he had… would I worry? At first I think that I would. He is, after all, a person. But after what happens next I think, no. I would not worry, not one bit."

"What happens?" asked Lila.

"He comes home one evening, and he's in a tear. He's carrying on and on about the birds. He's decided he can't stand them, says he's going to get rid of them. I say, 'no you are not'. 'These are Owen's birds, and he loves them. You will not get rid of them'. Jake would consider this talking back, so I am really skirting the line. Instead of flying off the handle, he goes into the living room and watches TV. I go down into the basement to do some laundry, thinking that I can't believe I've actually gotten away with talking back to him. Owen's upstairs playing with his Tonka truck. I'm folding Owen's little socks, his little pants. I take a blanket from the dryer and drape it around my neck. The heat on my skin feels good. I separate more laundry, Jake's from mine. I always have to do his clothes separately on account of the oil and the grease. I climb upstairs when I'm finished. It's very still and very quiet in the house. I go into the living room, thinking I will find Jake and Owen where I left them, but they are not there. Not Jake, not Owen, not the birds.

I approach the kitchen door and look out. I see them there. Owen is standing behind Jake. The bird cage is on the ground before Jake and the door is wide open. The bird cage is empty, save for their food and water. Jake and Owen are looking up at the sky. I walk out. Owen says,

'Daddy, let the birds go.' Jake says, 'I let them go free, Owen, free.' I bring Owen inside. He is not crying, but he looks dazed. He says, 'I thought Daddy was going to kill them.' I go outside. Jake is still staring up at the sky. I grab him by the arm. I scream, 'You mother fucker!' I scream things I don't remember screaming. I scream, and I spit, and I see stars. Every vile thing comes out of me, and there's nothing I can do to stop it. But I am no match for Jake. His fury comes from a different place than mine, from a place that I don't even have. He grabs me. He hits me in the face, the eye. He's done this before, but always with an open hand. This time it's with a closed fist. I do not feel pain. I feel blood, or I taste it. I am down on the ground, and his hands are around my throat. His eyes are colorless, and his lips curl inward. He is saying something, something. This is it. This is how I will die. I'm going to die. I can't believe it. I can't believe it, can't believe it. Right now, or maybe in the next second coming up, I'm going to die. What's it like? Is this what it's like? I can't breathe, and no sound will come up and out of my mouth. So I mouth the words; I need my son, I need my son, I need my boy. Not the other way around. Time becomes suspended. Each second is a nugget, a pearl... a world of forevers. Then... Jake, he gets up, and I can breathe again. Glorious air fills my lungs. Glorious, beautiful oxygen. Jake wipes his mouth with his sleeve. He says, 'I could have killed you if I wanted to. If I do, if I ever do, I'll bury you so far down that no one will ever find you.' He goes over to his truck. I get up. I say, 'When you leave, where do you go?' My voice is hoarse, my legs wobbly. He

says, 'It's none of your business.' Then, before he drives off, he says, 'Maybe someday I will tell you.' I say, 'Don't bother. There will be no some day.' He hasn't heard me. He's already gone.

When I go into the house, I find Owen in my bedroom. He's huddled in the corner. When he sees me, he runs up and grabs onto my legs. 'Mummy, Mummy, Mummy!' He says it over and over. All I can feel is relief. I am alive. I am here. I am breathing. I get a frozen hamburger and put it on my eye. I lie down. Owen snuggles up to my side. When the hamburger slips off my eye, Owen puts it back on. 'No. Mummy will do this. That's not your job,' I say. Eventually, we fall asleep. I wake up and look at the clock. It's 11:11. I get up and scan the house. No Jake. I go back to bed. I wake up again later. Owen is not in the bed. I sit up. I look from side to side. I listen. I hear something from the foot of the bed. It sounds like rustling of clothes or a foot shuffle. I crawl forward, toward the sound. It is whispering that I hear. I peek over the end of the bed. I see Owen's blonde hair, the top of his head. I see that he is holding something small and colorful. I hear the word 'please'. My eyes adjust, the rods and cones doing that they need to do to see in the dark. I see that the object he is holding is a worry doll, the one Samuel gave him. Owen is whispering, 'Please don't let Daddy come home.'

"The next day there is a knock at the door. I open it a crack, just a crack, and peer out with one eye. The swelling has gone down a little there, but it is red and purple. My bottom lip has a big split in it. It is Samuel. He

295

looks at me, at my eye. For a moment, he says nothing, but then he holds up my pink scarf. 'This here is yours. I found it at the pond once. I meant to return it to you, to its rightful owner, but I forgot. All this time.' He holds the scarf up to the crack. I take it. 'Thank you,' I say. I close the door softly behind me."

Caroline

Caroline couldn't leave the house, Jacob's house, for over a week after her last session with Lila. She came down with a fever that, at times, shot up to 104 degrees. She had to miss Emily's service. There was a job interview that she had to cancel. She lost her voice and, at times, hallucinated. Or maybe they weren't hallucinations. Caroline wouldn't let Jacob near her for fear that he would catch what she had. Her throat burned inside and out. Her body shook with chills and then burned up with a sweat and a fever. Her lips became red and chapped, a big split forming down her bottom lip. They burned and Caroline dreamt of a kiss, a long ago kiss... that, and a tree; something about being high up in a tree. She knew she should retreat to her little house out back, but she was afraid to go outside. Caroline asked Jacob to check the locks for her again and again. All she could do was trust that he was, since she couldn't get up. Her voice was not even a croak, not even a whisper. She dreamt dreams that made absolutely no sense, and sometimes, when she was awake, she thought she was dreaming. This went on for two days.

On the third day, Caroline was able to sit up. Looking out the window, she saw Barry out there with Jacob, who was in his boxers. Resting her head back on the pillow, she thought; What a strange dream! On the fourth day, she was able to take a shower, and when she got out, she felt something stuck to the bottom of her foot. Lifting her foot, she saw a little silver feather stuck there, but when she blinked, it was gone.

Caroline got her voice back on the fifth day. She was able to take little sips of soup. When Jacob handed the bowl to her, he told her it was made especially for her by Sarna. "Sara?' asked Caroline. "Sar-na," replied Jacob, over pronouncing each syllable. "Oh, Sarna," said Caroline. She wondered why Sarna had made her soup, and when had she been to Jacob's, anyway? On the sixth day, Barry came over. Apparently, he had been there several times throughout the week. He'd taken care of Caroline as well as Jacob. He'd brought her Tylenol, a humidifier, and Chap Stick for her hot, cracked lips.

The seventh day found Caroline outside. She breathed in deeply and coughed out violently. On the eighth day, she had a panic attack so profound that the left side of her body went numb. She grabbed a spoon, the closest thing to her, and held it. Caroline waited for it to pass, but the spoon had no effect. It took forty minutes for feeling to come back to her body. After it was over, she returned to cleaning up the kitchen. No one had even known it had happened. On the ninth day, Caroline lost her voice again. On the tenth day, she got it back. She returned to Lila's.

<u>Gretchen</u>

"I tie the scarf around my neck, because I've noticed marks there from Jake's hands. I call Sara, because I don't know what else to do. I tell her everything that happened."

"What is Sara's reaction?" asked Lila.

"She tells me she's coming to Virginia, to me. I say no. I explain that I am safe for now, that Jake won't be home for days. She says, 'How do you know that?' I tell her that I just know. So she tells me to go to my parents. I tell her' no way'. No way am I letting them see me like this! She tells me to come to her then. I tell her I will, in two more days. 'By then my face will look better, I don't want you to see me like this either.' Sara sounds resigned. 'Fine then. Promise me you'll go to the police station. I want this on record, what he's done to you.' I say, 'Fine, then. I will.' She tells me to call her right back afterward. She tells me that if I don't call her back within an hour, she'll call the police for me and send them over to me. I get Owen together and tell him we're going to walk up to Samuel's and ask him for a ride to the police station. 'Why?' he asks. 'Are you getting rested?' 'No. Mummy is not getting arrested. Mummy wants to tell the police about what he did to me. It is against the law, and it is wrong. I'm going to tell them about it.' 'Will Daddy get rested?' asks Owen. 'I don't know,' I say. 'Where is Daddy?' 'I don't know,' I say again. If there is a better way to explain any of this to Owen, I don't know it. I am not capable of thinking up clever explanations right now."

"You're doing the best you can do," said Lila.

"I Suppose so."

298

Silence descended upon Lila's room. It stretched out and time uncoiled like a child's slinky toy.

"What's happening now?" asked Lila.

"We... we are walking to Samuel's."

"Who is walking to Samuel's?" asked Lila.

"Owen and I. We are walking to Samuel's, and I can't believe I am doing this. Also, I can't believe I have not done it before now."

"Done what?" inquired Lila.

"Taken care of this. Gone to the police. Reported Jake...you know... left. Now, here I am, on my way to Samuel's to ask for a ride to the police station. We walk by the garage. The truck is not there. I notice, for the first time, the broken windows... Sara's handiwork. I... we... walk on, and I straighten my back as the wind presses against my sore face. I remember Mitchell. I remember about climbing trees. When we arrive at Samuel's, he's already outside. He slowly approaches us. 'Can you give us a ride to the police station?' I ask. 'Of course,' he says, assessing the damage to my face. Without another word, we get into his car and make our way down the driveway, creaking over pot holes. The car is heavily jarred by a rut in the road, and my elbow comes down hard on the door handle. Pain shoots up my arm. I push back my sleeve and see a lump and an abrasion that I hadn't even known was there. We ride in silence until Samuel says, 'I'm glad to do this. It's good to help, to be needed.' He reaches across Owen and gently takes hold of my hand. 'Thank you,' I say, pulling my hand away. I turn my head and look out my window. The smell of stale

cigarette smoke and mold fills my nose. 'We won't be here for much longer,' I say. 'Not much longer?' 'Yes, we're leaving. We're going to stay with my friend in Boston.' 'To live?' he asks. 'Maybe,' I say, 'Probably.' 'You'll be missed,' he says. I don't respond."

"We arrive at the police station. I leave Owen with Samuel in a small waiting area. I ask to speak to a police officer. Officer Pinkney comes and seats me at his desk. It is littered with papers and files. The smell of coffee drifts over to me, reminding me of Owen Sr. and of Jake. My stomach clenches. I feel bile rise in my throat, taste it in my mouth. Officer Pinkney asks me what happened, and I tell him. I look right at him with my swollen eye and split lip. I feel strangely unfaithful, like I am betraying Jake. I feel like we are on opposite sides of a canyon, a great divide, and he is about to fall into it, or I am, or we both are. Officer Pinkney takes pictures of my face, my elbow, my neck, and throat. He then asks my son, 'Who did this to your mother?' It breaks my heart into a million pieces to hear Owen say this: 'My daddy did, Jake did it.' Officer Pinkney escorts Owen to Samuel, so that we can finish the report in private. He wants to know if I want to press charges against my husband, against my son's father. I tell him 'yes'. The next step is to fill out all the necessary paperwork and sign at every X. I am urged to leave the house, to go somewhere safe: my parent's, a friend's, a hotel. I explain that I am leaving the day after tomorrow for Boston, to a friend's. Officer Pinkney is not satisfied. He wants to know where Jake could be right now. Unfortunately, I honestly do not have a clue. He has reassured me that he'll send a patrol car around the house frequently to keep an eye out for Jake... to keep an eye on me.

Before Samuel drops us off at home, I ask him for a cigarette. He gives me a whole pack, and walks us to the door. To my relief he comes in and hangs out for a little while. He seems reluctant to leave, and I don't blame him. 'Come stay with me.' Out of nowhere I have this urge to snap. An anger surges up within me that I do not understand or even want to understand. Everywhere around me people are trying to help: Sara, Samuel, Officer Pinkney, my parents... if I would let them. I just want... need... to be left alone. I'm so damn tired. 'No Samuel, the police will be watching us all night. We will be fine. We are leaving day after tomorrow. Everything will be fine Samuel.' I breathe through my anger, one breath at a time. 'Well, then, if you won't come home with me, then, I'll keep an eye out for you.' 'If that would make you feel better, then fine,' I say. He leaves reluctantly. I sit on the doorstep. Owen sits with me. I am thinking of Jake's mother and of Jake's father, how he did the same thing to her; and maybe Jake's father's father to his wife before that. I look down at Owen: his soft, blonde curls, his round cheek, his still chubby hands with dimples at the knuckles. I talk to him about this, about how it is not normal to do that to a girl; about how he learned it from his Daddy, and he from his Daddy. I tell him that when he grows up, he can be the one to not ever do that. And then, after that, it will stop. Owen cocks his head to the side, looking directly at me. 'Forever?'

'Forever.' 'That's a long time,' he says. 'Yes, yes it is.' We sit for a while, listening to the crickets. Owen asks more questions, and I answer them the best I can. I send him inside and continue smoking. I notice that it is a beautiful day, and it is almost gone. I think... I decide... that I will not miss beautiful days anymore. I will notice them. I make a decision right then... that I have suffered enough. It is as if I have never been surer of anything, ever. Just then, as I am thinking this, a bird plops down three yards in front of me. It is Yellow Bird. She is pecking along the ground, hopping and preening, one small part of this beautiful day. I stay very still but slowly hold out my finger. She is oblivious, free. She is too busy doing what birds do. I want her to come to me, but I don't. I will her to come to me, but at the same time I hope that she finds what she's looking for and flies away. I don't see Blue Bird but I like to imagine that he is up in a tree somewhere, waiting for her. Doing what birds do. After a few moments, Yellow Bird flies away, and I watch her until I can't see her anymore.

All through that night, Samuel parks his car across the street and sits in it. I can see the lit tip of his cigarette glowing, growing brighter with each puff. I cannot see his body. I don't invite him in. Also, it begins to rain. The next day comes, and it is not so beautiful. It is cloudy and rain spits down from above. Actually, though, it is a beautiful day. It may be gray, but gray is a color too, just like gold or yellow or blue are colors. Water sustains life. I am here, breathing, alive. I pack Owen's things. He knows where we are going, and he is excited. He wants to see Sara. I haven't told him that we may not be coming back here, to this house. I figure he's had enough to deal with already. I remember to call Sara to check in. She is relieved that I am packing. She makes me promise again... 'I, Gretchen McAuley, promise you, Sara Doyle, that I am coming to stay with you tomorrow, taking the nine-thirty bus into South Station where you, Sara Doyle, will meet us.' She makes me say it twice. I tell her that Samuel watched the house from his car the whole night and that he will likely do it again tonight. I tell her that the police are watching, although, I didn't see any cruisers the whole night. I didn't tell her that."

"How do you feel about leaving?" asked Lila.

"Mostly, I'm numb. I feel like a robot that's just performing actions. You know, pick up... put down... do this... do that. Get it done. That's how I feel. Anyway, Owen and I take a nap together. We wake up and pack some more. It is getting dark by the time I call my parents. I figure I should let them know that Owen and I are going on a little trip. That's how I explain it to them, as a little trip. They ask how long we'll be gone. I tell them at least two weeks. They offer to drive us there, but I tell them all the arrangements have already been made. They ask and they beg to take us into Boston, saying that it'll give them a chance to visit with us. I am so overwhelmed by all of the details, I feel like a barrel of water that is overflowing. I cannot appease them. I cannot manage to think of anyone else other than myself and Owen."

"Moments later, my parents call back. They announce that they're coming over to pick Owen up. They want him to spend the night at their house, so they can spend time with him before we go. They say they'll miss him and that they're on their way. Before I can reply, they've hung up. They are coming over, and there's nothing I can do about it. I don't know what to do. I look in the mirror. All day I've been fooling myself into thinking that I looked any better. One whole side of my face is swollen. My lip has a gaping split in it, and my neck has odd looking bruises, like hickeys. I get an idea. I throw a few things into a grocery bag for Owen: pajamas, pants, underwear, a shirt, socks, and his Mickey Mouse toothbrush. I set the bag on the table and tell Owen he's sleeping over Grammy's and Grampy's for the night, because they want to spend time with him before we go. I kneel down before him and tell him, 'Owen, don't tell Grammy and Grampy about what Daddy did. Don't tell them about going to the police station. Don't tell them anything, any of that stuff. 'Why?' Owen looks so lost. It is his first lesson in lying by omission. 'Because they will be very mad at him.' 'Will they yell at him?' asks Owen. 'Yes. Very badly. And then Daddy will yell, and I don't want any more yelling. Do you?' Owen's eyes go wide, like saucers, like a full moon. 'No.' 'Okay now. I'm going to jump in the shower. Give Mummy a hug. Grammy and Grampy will be here any minute. Here's your bag. You might want to put Puffy in there.' I jump in the shower. 'Mummy! You already took a shower today!' 'I know, but I need another one.' Satisfied, Owen runs out of the bathroom. I hear the paper

bag rustle. Owen comes back in. 'I put my worry doll in there, too, Mummy.' 'Good. That's good.' My parents walk in the house. I hear their voices and Owen's, too. I yell from the shower, 'Hi Mum! Hi Dad! I'm in the shower! Everything's in that bag for him!' I hear my mother telling Owen they'll make banana splits for dessert tonight. My father stands outside the bathroom door. 'We'll have him back by, what, eight in the morning?' 'Yeah. That's perfect.' 'Jake working late tonight?' asks my father. 'Must be.' Just the mention of Jake's name makes the bile rise in my throat again. I ask him, 'Where's Owen?' 'He's in the car with your mother.' At that moment, I wish I could see my father. I wish I could pull the shower curtain aside and let him see my face. I can't. I just can't. Tears well up in my swollen eyes, making them hurt even more. I try to blink the pain away, to no avail. Instead, I ask him, 'Can you send Owen in for a minute? I want to say good night.' 'Sure thing, see you in the morning.' My father fetches Owen and leaves. Tipping my face back into the stream of water, I imagine my father's eyes, his blue plaid shirt, his suspenders. I suddenly miss my father, painfully so. I want him to carry me home. I want him to make steak and asparagus on the grill. I want to eat dinner with my parents and Owen on the terrace. I want to hear our banter rise into the night sky, joking about my mother's bad cooking. Instead, I stay in the shower, this crappy shower with the tiles falling down. Owen comes in a moment later. I kneel down, and I poke my head out of the shower curtain. 'Hi Baby. You have a good night, okay?' 'I will, Mummy.' 'Remember what I told you about when you grow up.' 'I know,' he parrots, 'If I don't do it, then it will stop forever.' 'That's right. Don't forget. And, also, I love you so much. I always will. No matter what.' 'I know Mummy. Me, too,' he says eagerly, trying to escape. I grab him. I hug him tight. 'Mummy! You're getting me all wet!' he giggles. 'I know, Baby. I'm sorry. I love you.' 'You, too,' he says and runs out of the house. I let the water run over me. I take deep breaths. My heart is thumping hard. 'Calm down,' I tell myself out loud. 'Nothing's going to happen.' I decide to make myself busy. Coming out of the shower, I get dressed, not in pajamas but in clothes. I pull on my long, paisley shirt and my jeans, bell bottoms. I put on my beaded bracelets. Not having to get dressed in the morning will make it easier to just get up and go. The phone rings, and I startle. It is Sara. 'Everything all right?' she asks. 'Yes. Everything is very quiet. Still no sign of Jake." 'Is Samuel still watching out for you?' I look out the window, but I don't see his car. 'Yes,' I lie, 'He's right there in his car outside my house.' Sara heaves a sigh of relief. 'Thank God. Call me anytime you want Gretch. I'll be here all night. I'll see you in the morning.' 'Thanks Sara. Don't worry. I'll be there.' I reluctantly hang up the phone.

I turn on the radio and try to remember the last time I was alone. It must have been before Owen was born. Before Jake. I decide to make a pie, if only to keep myself busy. It will be for my parents, as a thank you for taking Owen for the night. Suddenly, I wish that I hadn't waited to go to Boston. I need time to go by quickly. I peel and slice apples and peaches. As I begin the dough, I knead it with urgency. Time becomes a shooting star, looking slow, but going inconceivably fast. The wind chimes outside the kitchen door come to life. A driving rain beats on the windows, then dies down to a soft patter. After putting the slices in a bowl, I get the rolling pin out from the cupboard. My mother gave me this rolling pin when I got married. It has red handles. Owen likes to play with it. The wind chimes toll again. "A Hard Day's Night" is playing on the radio. I hum along and press the dough. Roll and press. Roll and press. I sing loudly now. The chimes settle but then whip about again, chiming, chiming. I press. I roll. I sing. I think of Sara. I think of cities and suitcases. There is a shadow on the cabinet door before me. A head and shoulders. I don't see it. I am too busy thinking, rolling. The wind chimes are busy chiming. I look up, because I feel cool air on my back. The door, it must have come open. Maybe it hadn't been closed all the way. I should have locked it. I'm thinking I should have locked it, but I didn't. I look up, and I see it, the shadow. I whip around, the rolling pin in my hand, flour on my shirt, my face. The rolling pin flings out of my hand, hits the wall, hard. 'Oh!' I screech. There, before me, is someone. Someone... not Jake. It is Samuel. 'Don't go,' he pleads. His eyes are a pond, a lake, an ocean with no bottom. There are things in the depths of his eyes I hadn't noticed before. Or maybe I had noticed, but chose to look away. He grabs my arm. 'What are you doing?' My voice is strangled, a stranger to me, as if someone else is saying it. 'What are you doing?' I repeat. 'You can live with me. You and Owen. I've got plenty of room. Owen loves me. He loves me. Even if

307

you don't, he does.' His voice is hoarse, as if he's been crying. He jostles me back and forth. I move to run out the door, but he blocks my way. He yanks at my arm, and my shoulder makes a popping sound. There must be pain, but I don't feel it. 'Don't go!' he shouts. Somehow, I manage to slip out of his grip and run out the door. I crash into the wind chimes on my way out.

He comes after me. It is misting out, and dark. I should head toward the garage, but I don't. Instead, I run into the woods. I can make it to the apple orchard. If I can make it through the apple orchard, I can make it to the street. If I can make it to the street, I can cross it to my parents' house, to Owen. I am running and branches are slapping me in the face. I can breathe in, but I can't breathe out--but with a sharp wheeze. Footsteps crash behind me. Samuel is screaming something, but I can't make out the words. His screams are frantic and high-pitched. The branches catch his syllables, holding them from me. All I can hear is my own breathing, and branches snapping. I do not stumble. Not once. Samuel does, and I'm gaining distance. I need my son. I need my boy. I need my son. I need my boy. I emerge from the other end of the woods. There are miles and miles, rows and rows of trees before me. I run into them, the rows. I don't stop. My foot lands on an apple, and my ankle bends to one side. I don't stop. I don't fall. I can't. I don't have a choice. He's there, in a row, but not my row. He is screaming something again. His voice breaks. I think of dead cats, and tall buildings, and of standing up tall. I think of Mitchell and of climbing trees. I think of Owen. My boy. My son. I think I can't go any faster, but I do. It sounds like he's in a row to my left, so I cut over to the row on my right. I don't like that. It's a few feet further away from where I'm going. I stop suddenly, an idea. To my left, Samuel keeps going. He's ahead of me now. I wait, my back to an apple tree. Rain slips down my forehead and into my eyes. I sprint to my left, across three rows. Running forward, I dodge trees. I am not near the house, but I am getting closer. Rain drills down. That is good, because he can't hear my feet running. But I can't hear his either.

I keep going, faster than before. Now I can't breathe in or out. Or I can, I don't know. I think I scream, but maybe not. I do not tire, do not slow. I don't have a choice. My son. My boy. My son. My boy. I am closer now. I hit a tree, hard. I fall back. There is mud under me. I try to get up, but can't. My hair. It is stuck on something. I pull. It pulls back, whatever has got my hair. Backward. I am being dragged backward by my hair. Away, away from the house and Owen and my parents and the street where I know there is a street light. Mud. Mud all over me. Going down my pants. Where are my shoes? Have I lost them in the mud? Did I ever have them on to begin with? Samuel's got me by the hair, and he's pulling me back, further into the orchard. Apples roll under me. Apples and mud, the smell is all over me. I grab onto a tree. I won't let go. Won't. I won't. He's let go of my hair. Will he let me go? Is that what he's doing? But no. Samuel grabs me by the head, smashes it against a tree. Everything goes black.

Silence enveloped Lila's room. The clock ticked, a reminder that there is such a thing as time: a reminder of the complexity of time, speaking of concurrent life times within one body. Caroline. Gretchen. Life. Death.

"We can stop if you wish," said Lila.

"If I wish?"

"Yes. It is up to you. We can stop and return later, or we can keep going. Whatever you are comfortable with." Lila spoke in a near whisper.

"Wish? You know what? I wish to go on."

"Whenever you're ready," said Lila.

"Oh. What is this? Bouncing. I am upside down, bouncing. I hear things. Samuel's footsteps, not mine. Rain. A horse. I open my eyes. No, one eye. The other one is closed shut. It is dark. So black. Things bounce. A barn upside down. Not close. Far. We are in a field. I am on his shoulder, slumped over it. He grips my legs. I try to scream but there is something in my mouth, way in. I think this is the horse farm. John lives somewhere on the edge, John from the orchard. I do not kick. Instead, I slowly reach my arm around and grab his face, dig my fingers into his eyes, scratch, dig. Samuel yells and drops me. I get to my feet and run toward the barn. It is far, but I can run. I can't get this thing out of my mouth. It is big, my jaw open as far as it can go. Something holds it in, whatever it is. A cloth of some sort is tied around my head, pinning this big thing in my mouth. It tastes. It tastes of something. Sweet, sour... it is an apple. I hear a horse whinny. It hears me, it seems. There is a big, wide open space before me. I can do it. I can reach it.

310

I can make it. My son. My boy. My son... The back of my head. There is pain. I feel this pain. I am a tree tipping over, a bird falling from the sky, a scarf floating to the ground. I fall forward into the mud, which fills my nose. A second passes, then another, another, but not the next.

But I go up. I am floating up. Up into the rain. Into the gray, the black. I can see everything. I can see Samuel and what he is doing with my body, putting me where no one will ever find me. Where weeds and wild flowers will grow on top of my bones. Where bugs and peepers and pebbles and leaves will come and play and rest and go. Where rain will fall and sun will shine and an occasional horse's foot will step. My bones. I go up still. I can see, but I have no eyes. I am eyes. I am everything. Everything is me. There is no me. There's a wide open space below me and above me and around me. Beyond me... the Blue Ridge Mountains. Below them, I see Owen making a banana split sundae. I can see Sara, waiting for me at South Station in the morning, which will be a glorious, sunny day. I can see Jake sleeping in the garage right now. Except there is no now, no morning, no time. There is a word. The word is 'forgiveness'. I think, or I feel... No! It is a conversation between me and something else that I can't even see. Is it God? What is it? Who is it? Are you sure? It asks. I see Owen again. He is placing a cherry on top of his sundae. He is safe, yes, but... he will live the rest of his life without his mother. He will receive the news. My parents will tell him, and he will be alone, without his own mother. Are you fucking crazy? No! I cannot forgive! This? How could I forgive this? How can I? It happens inside you. It says. I don't know how. I can't, so I stay. I float. There are others now, too. Oh! Many. They glow. Do I glow, too? There is one near me, another soul. It had a different life than mine. Its body died when mine did, but in a different way. It is going to go back, into a baby girl's body. It will be named Gretta. I know that this Gretta will not have a long time on Earth. This soul passes through mine on its way down. It is the strangest thing, though. For a moment, we are birds, a fluttering of blue and yellow wings. The blue is like heaven, like faith. The yellow is like joy. A whole conversation takes place in that instant. Even though there are no words, and there is no time. My soul and this other one, we will need to forgive in our next life time. That will be our journey, to come back and learn how to forgive. We will help each other in this. Our lives will intersect, somehow, and we will show each other the way. I come down fast, fast. In a warp. In a vacuum. To a different place, a different state, into a different body, a baby body, in a hospital, being born again, to a different mother named Rosemary, and she calls me Caroline."

part three
taking flight

<u>Caroline</u>

Spring. It is glorious, and it is miserable with all of its rain. It pisses you off when it soaks your groceries as you run across the parking lot, looking for your car. It brings with it new, fresh air. This same air carries with it pollen, those dusty little villains; giving people headaches and runny noses. They are also the seeds that grow new life in surprising places; like along the edge of the woods, in the middle of the forest, way off a barely beaten path which leads away from a horse farm in Virginia, sprinkling the Blue Ridge Mountains. Places where no one ever goes. Wild flowers and poppies and weeds and weeds. Spring is new with promise and old with memories, both of which Caroline had plenty of. She did not hide, withdraw, or crumble after her last time with Lila. She did not lock doors or windows; did not scrub her hands. Had no need to create sores on her skin, trying to get the stuff inside to leak out. She did none of these things. Instead, she got busy.

First, she got her hair cut. She did not have a friend do it for her, nor did she do it herself. She got it professionally done.

Caroline walked into a salon and said, "I don't want long hair anymore."

The woman, whose name was Chrissie, cut Caroline's hair inches at a time. Clumps of cinnamon colored hair slid down her black smock. The shorter her hair got, the curlier and springier it got. It was up to her jaw line by the time it was done. A halo of curls bounced when she shook her head.

"You look amazing," said Chrissie, "I finally chopped my hair off when I had my daughter. After I cut it, I wondered why I hadn't done it before. I look much better with short hair. How about you? Do you have any kids?"

"One," said Caroline.

"How old?" asked Chrissie.

"Forty-eight," stated Caroline. Chrissie stared at her in the mirror. "A son," said Caroline.

She gave her a generous tip and left.

The next thing Caroline did was go wig shopping with her mother in Boston. Her hair had begun to thin. She'd found some clumps in the shower and on her pillow. They both tried on wigs: black ones, brown ones, red and blonde... long, short, straight, and curly, pink, spiky, punky. Her mother liked the latter, and that's what she got. However, after lunch, they returned to the wig store, so her mother could get a curly red wig. She said she'd need a sensible one as well.

After their second visit to the store, Caroline asked her mother, "There used to be a school in Southie called the Franklin School. Do you think it's still there?"

"Yes, I believe it is. Why?"

"A long time ago, I had a friend who taught there. I always told her I'd come visit her school, her classroom. I never did."

"Does she still teach there?" asked her mother.

"Oh, no. She's retired by now. Do you think you could take me there? I'd like to see it."

"Sure," replied her mother, "let's go."

They took the T. They switched at South Station where people waited patiently with headphones on, or reading books. A few scraps of paper tumbled and skipped along the concrete, being pushed along by a cool breeze. Caroline had the feeling of arriving, but arriving late... very, very late. They took the train a short way, got off, and walked a few blocks to the school. It was surrounded by pavement and a chain link fence. The school was a red brick building, three stories high, and in need of updating. The pavement surrounding the building featured a white painted four-square and children's sidewalk chalk drawings. The side of the school sported a small spray painted peace sign. They stayed for a little longer and did not say much at all.

Next, Caroline spent time with Jacob. He had, indeed, gotten what Caroline had. It was the same: the fever, the chills, the sweating, being unable to get up out of bed, not knowing dreams from reality. Caroline spoon fed him soup. On the fourth day of his illness, she rolled him over to change his sheets, because they were wet with sweat, except she found that it wasn't sweat, but urine. Caroline knew that this was bad. She didn't forget her promise to Jacob. She changed his sheets, and she lined the bed with a shower curtain. She knew it would happen again... urine or worse.

Caroline and Jacob stayed up nights to watch Jeopardy, Jacob on his couch and Caroline in the chair next to him. Caroline, for once, knew a lot of the questions. She'd gotten the hang of this game show. She shouted out questions, but Jacob just laid there and stared or dozed. She wished she had him as a witness to her brilliance. He'd be proud of her, she knew. As Caroline sat next to Jacob, she did something she knew she shouldn't. She had to. He needed to get better, at least for a little while, so she could do what she needed to do. She touched his legs without his permission. She touched his head, too, and his chest, especially his chest, which rattled beneath her hands. She touched his hip and rotated his leg, went back to his head, then to his chest again. Caroline finished and sat back down. Her hands hummed, and, for some reason, she got up and rinsed them under the kitchen faucet. She came back to Jacob, sat down again, closed her eyes, and imagined the chord stretching from her forehead to him. The light came through and bathed him, going wherever it needed to go. Caroline fell asleep this way, on the chair. She woke sometime later to find Jacob asleep. She made a makeshift bed for herself on the floor, but tossed and turned, so she got up to call Barry.

"I miss you," she said.

"Do you want to come over?" he asked.

"No. I've got to keep an eye on Jacob."

"Well. I could come over there, and we could both keep an eye on Jacob. Between us, that would be four eyes." He sounded tired.

"That's all right. Maybe we can get together after you're out of work tomorrow," sighed Caroline.

"Actually, I quit my job," announced Barry.

"You did not! Why?"

"I enrolled full time at UMass Dartmouth."

"Oh my God, Barry! When do you start?"

"In two weeks," he said.

"That is so great, Barry!"

"I know. I'm excited. We could actually spend the whole day together tomorrow, if you want."

"I'd like that," said Caroline, smiling as she snuggled down into her make shift bed.

She finally fell asleep well after three o'clock. The morning found her swimming up through a deep sleep, trying to latch onto the sounds she was hearing around her: a bang, a shuffle, a sizzle. The smell of bacon awakened her senses. Caroline got up to find Jacob dressed and cooking breakfast.

"Morning, Sunshine!" he said. "I feel great!"

Caroline had never seen an urn. It was really just a box, and it was heavy.

"What will you do with her ashes?" Caroline asked Barry.

"Technically, it's not up to me. It's up to her family. They aren't sure yet."

"Did Emily have any wishes? I mean, about that?"

"Actually, no. She didn't. I'm sure they'll go to California where her parents are. She grew up there. Emily loved it there, too. I don't know."

"How have you been feeling after everything?" asked Caroline.

"Sometimes I feel like someone just punched me in the stomach, like I can't catch my breath, and I can't stop crying. The times in between, everything just feels strange, like I'm in a different world or something. I'll just keep riding the waves, I guess."

There was a plaque for Emily at the cemetery, and they went to visit it. Bunches of fresh flowers surrounded the plaque. A stone angel sat there, nestled in among the flowers. It held a bowl in its hands. In the bowl, was an ordinary stone. Caroline touched it.

"I put that stone there," announced Barry.

"Why?" inquired Caroline.

"Emily carried this stone with her everywhere, all the time. It would be in her pocketbook or her coat pocket, even in the pocket of her pants. For years. I used to ask her why she always had that stone with her. She used to say it was because she just liked it. She never offered more. Never told me where it came from, or why she had it to begin with. I always felt as if it had some sort of private meaning to it. If it did, she never told me what it was."

Barry paused. A grasshopper skipped across Emily's plaque, chirping. "I was the one who mainly did the laundry, and I was always finding weird things in her pockets. Like a leaf or an acorn or a piece of sea glass, a marble. I learned early on not to throw these things away. Instead, I would leave them in a pile in the laundry room. Emily would sift through the pile every now and then and keep some things, throw others away. The rock always stayed with her, always."

Caroline realized that, perhaps, it was Barry who had tried to know her, and Emily who wouldn't let him.

Jacob made them dinner later that night. He was a little rusty at this, but it was good enough, quite good actually. He whistled tunes Caroline didn't know as he shuffled about the kitchen.

"Look at me," said Jacob. "I'm an old man, and I kicked that bug quicker than you did."

They laughed and talked. Jacob took Barry downstairs to show him his workshop.

When they came back up, Barry asked, "Didn't your father used to be a woodworker?"

"Yes, he was actually, and he was good, too."

"Does he still do it, woodworking I mean?" Caroline paused and thought. "I don't know." Have I ever even tried to

319

know him? She wondered. Caroline and Barry sat on the porch after dinner. She told him about her last visit with Lila. She told him about her plan and, although he looked worried, he gave her his blessing. Caroline knew that she'd have to hurry, while Jacob was still well.

The next morning brought with it an unsettled front, accompanied by clusters of slate gray cumulus clouds. Caroline watched the clouds approach as she called Sarna at work.

"I've got a job for you," she said. Caroline told her what she wanted her to do, and Sarna said, "I've been waiting for you to ask me."

Caroline gave her the names and waited.

It took some time- a bit longer than Caroline would have liked, so she kept doing the physical therapy. She kept sending healing light. Then, it occurred to her that she could do the same for her mother. However, she wasn't sure if this could be done if the person to receive the healing light was at a distance. Surely Lila would know. Caroline almost picked up the phone to ask Sarna to call Lila, but thought better of it. She's doing enough for me. I can call Lila myself. Thought Caroline. She called Lila and asked her.

"Yes. It can be done," she told Caroline. "Just hold her image in your mind and send her love and light."

Caroline did this.

Two days passed, three, four, and then came some news from Sarna.

"I found him," she said.

Caroline had been making a necklace when Sarna called. Her hands trembled, sending beads spilling to the floor.

"Which one?" whispered Caroline.

"Jake," replied Sarna. Caroline found that she couldn't speak.

"Don't you want to know where he is?"

"No," said Caroline. "Yes," she added, "He's still alive?"

"Yes."

"Is he still in Virginia?"

"Yes. Now, do you want to know where in Virginia?"

Caroline remembered her conviction. "Yes."

"He's in prison, for murder."

It went like this; Sarna came after work that same day, the day she told Caroline of her discovery. She came over with a printout of an article about a Jacobson McAuley, convicted of the first degree murder of his wife, Gretchen McAuley, age twenty-five. Jake was also twenty-five. The article was dated August 28, 1964. It went on with particulars Caroline wasn't equipped to absorb. There was a high school photo of Gretchen, her long blonde hair perfect and straight. She wore a white cotton shirt with a collar, buttoned up to her neck. Her eyes were smiling and blue, her eyelashes long and curing upward. Caroline noted a hint of makeup, which she knew Gretchen would have put on at school the morning the picture was taken. Caroline touched the photograph. When she took her hands away, her fingerprints glowed there on the photo, as if florescent, just for an instant and then disappeared. Caroline slid the article away.

"What else have you got?"

Sarna slid another paper toward Caroline.

"Here's a printout of the prison where Jake is."

It was a monstrous, concrete building, surrounded by layers of fence topped with curling barbed wire, keeping them all in; even the ones who shouldn't be there. Sarna slid a map across the table.

"Virginia," she said. "We're going."

"Yes. I know," replied Caroline. She'd already decided this.

Next, Sarna held up a card fastened to a lanyard. "This is for you." Caroline studied it. The card said, "New Bedford Globe." Under that it read, "Caroline Stevens: Journalist."

"All we have to do is pretend you're my intern, a journalist-in-training. We'll go there together under the pretense that we're doing an article on inmates serving time for murder. We'll try to get clearance, and we'll go in and meet him, interview him." Sarna's eyes darted back and forth, mimicking her racing thoughts.

Caroline hesitated, fingering the card with her name and her supposed profession. "I don't know... I don't know if that'll work."

"Hmmm. I don't know either. I'm going to give it some more thought," said Sarna, pacing.

Caroline hesitantly looked up. "No word about the others?"

"Not yet," said Sarna, "but I've got someone looking into it for me."

Caroline and Sarna decided they should nourish themselves with dinner. It suddenly seemed crucial that they fuel up- for there, ahead of them, was a journey. When it would begin or how it would unfold was still unclear, but it would come. They asked Jacob what he felt like having, and he said that he felt like Chinese. They ordered take-out. Caroline called Barry. He picked up the food on his way over. All four of them ate in front of the TV. Afterward, they had coffee and stayed up late. They had fortune cookies and took turns reading their fortunes. Jacob's said, "He who makes noise is heard." Sarna's said, "Love thyself first, others next." Barry's said, "No moss grows on a rolling stone." Caroline's read, "Tall people stand up straight." They discussed their fortunes, finding ways to make them suit their lives. Caroline already knew how her fortune suited hers.

Caroline drank a second cup of coffee, which she shouldn't have done. Her nerves sang and her capillaries opened up, sending blood thumping through her temples. Barry touched a ringlet of her hair. "I love your hair like this." Caroline blushed unexpectedly. Sarna went home around ten o'clock. Jacob went up to bed. Caroline brought Barry to her house to show him the article Sarna had left behind. He studied Gretchen. "I love your hair like that, too." He took her face in his hands and kissed her. She made no motion to stop him, even though she knew what would come next. She'd already decided that as well.

The next morning, they shared a cigarette outside Caroline's house. They held hands. His hugs were not the same as Tim's. They were looser. But his hands enfolded hers the way Tim's never had, not loose, but steady and firm.

"I've got to quit this soon, the smoking," he said.

"Me, too."

They walked up to Jacob's to check on him.

"I hope he's all right," said Caroline.

"I checked on him last night while you were sleeping, and he was fine," he said.

Caroline remembered Barry's shoulder up against her cheek in the night. She remembered other things, too, and sleeping dreamlessly.

324

"You did that?" she asked.

"Yes," said Barry, "and I saw her."

"Gretta?"

"Yes. She was sitting by his bed as he slept."

Caroline smiled. "She does that a lot."

Sarna called from work the next day. She was whispering. "I pitched an idea to my boss. I told him I wanted to do a piece on convicted murderers who claim they've been wrongly accused and imprisoned. He's let me do that before, pursue my own journalistic ideas. It's usually a hard sell. He said he'd think about it."

Caroline heard car horns beeping from Sarna's end. "Why are you whispering?"

"I'm at work, you dummy. I don't want my boss to know what we're really up to."

"Aren't you outside?"

"Yeah. I'm standing outside the building, smoking a cigarette," whispered Sarna.

"First of all, why are you smoking?"

"I just started."

"Secondly, if you're outside, then why are you whispering?"

"Oh. Yeah," replied Sarna.

Another day passed, then another. Barry took to spending all of his days and nights at Caroline's. She didn't mind. She liked it. Being together was easy, and they began to fall into little rituals: morning tea, afternoon coffee, and dinners with Jacob. They talked about Caroline's plans, that she had none... other than the fact that she, too, wanted to go to school, perhaps for physical therapy. Barry took her to his house, because he was on-line, and they could look up schools. There were a few, and they printed out financial aid forms. Caroline strolled through the information on the computer while Barry chopped some wood out back. She googled "healing with your hands." Forty, fifty sites popped up, ranging from, 'Use your hands to heal yourself and others', to 'Heal your chapped hands.' Caroline clicked around and discovered that there was a whole world out there of healing arts; a whole, wide world. She found out that the best place to learn this art, the very best one, was in Oregon, where her father lived. She could hear Barry chopping; a chop and a thump, a chop and a thump. She looked at the web site and her heart sang.

"Here's the deal," announced Sarna over the phone one day. "My boss said that I can do it. I went ahead and called the prison, Norfolk County Corrections. I pitched my piece to them. Seems there's a whole lot of legal mumbo-jumbo involved. I'd have to get bunches of legal clearance. They gave me a list of inmates who are fighting their convictions."

"And?" said Caroline.

"Jake's name was not on the list. Apparently he's never claimed to be innocent."

Caroline's thoughts were in a circular frenzy. Murder? Innocent? How? Why? She sought to interrupt her chaotic thoughts. Caroline began to make plans... arranging for she and Barry to go and visit her mother. Caroline wanted them to meet. They wanted to meet each other. Hopefully, it would help to distract her from everything: from trying to figure out why she needed to find a way to see Jake, from wondering about the others. Caroline settled the plans with her mother. Then, Sarna called while Caroline was doing the dishes, staring absently out the window.

"Did you figure something out?" asked Caroline.

"Not yet, but I found something out."

Soapy water ran down Caroline's forearm. "What is it?"

"I found Sara. That one was a little tough. Her last name was not longer Doyle, but Shalize."

Soapy water coated the phone, entered Caroline's sleeve. "You said- was."

"Yup. Sara passed away four years ago. It was cancer. The guy I have helping me, he got into this one. He likes a challenge, likes to investigate. Anyway, he actually ended up meeting with her daughter. Want to guess what her name is?"

"I can't even think right now." said Caroline.

"Her name is Gretchen."

"Oh, God," said Caroline.

"Yes, and that's not all. I guess Sara was a very busy lawyer."

"A lawyer?"

"That's right. After the death... the murder... of her best friend, Gretchen, back in '64, Sara traveled a bit: to California, Europe, South America. When she returned, she went back to school. She became a lawyer, fighting for the rights, protection, and care of battered women. According to her daughter, she was quite a remarkable woman."

An image of Sara waiting at South Station, absently twirling a key chain around her finger drifted through Caroline's memory. "Yes," said Caroline, "she always was."

"She's buried at the Mount Auburn Cemetery in Boston, in case you want to know."

"Yes, I do."

Later that day, Caroline and Barry went to his place to look up Sara Shalize on line. They found her with little difficulty. She became a lawyer after graduating from law school in 1970. She was thirty-one-years-old. She'd married three years prior, to a James Shalize, also a lawyer. They had a child in 1973, just one, a girl named Gretchen. Caroline did the math. She, herself, would have been nine years old when Sara's daughter, Gretchen, was born. The article went on to say that Sara had, at first, been an elementary school teacher but changed her direction in life when her best friend, Gretchen McAuley, was killed by her husband in 1964. Sara decided to become a lawyer and advocate for battered women across the commonwealth and beyond. She'd gone into shelters and offered free legal representation for the battered women. She'd set up the Gretchen McAuley Foundation, which helped to fund over thirty shelters across the region, each of which was staffed with counselors, career resources, and, most importantly, around-the-clock trained guards. At the bottom of her site was a quote from Martin Luther King Jr. that said, "When you stand up straight, no man can ride you."

The next day, Caroline and Barry went to visit her mother. They took the T all the way in, riding with oblivious people, average-looking people, and strange looking ones; all just people all the same. They found her mother well and animated and ate strange foods, like alfalfa sprouts and guacamole atop thin, crusty wheat crackers. They had salad and sparkling water. Her mother wore her spiky pink wig and then changed into the curly red one when they went out for a stroll in Boston Common. Roller-bladers passed them, men in suits, and college students with their arms full of books and binders. Children fed the ducks in the pond. A small boy in a black jacket ran past them. Caroline turned and looked for a parent that might have been following him but saw none. She saw the boy getting further and further ahead of them, his black jacket disappearing. She stretched up on her tippy toes, trying to keep him in sight and saw, in that instant, that he was running into the arms of his mother. Caroline came back down on her heels and relaxed.

They came upon a vendor with a cart, sporting a green and white umbrella, funky hats, trinkets, and tie dye shirts. A bird flew overhead, unencumbered. Not blue or yellow, but still a bird. They browsed the cart, and Caroline bought a necklace with a peace sign pendant. Afterward, Caroline's mother was tired so she went home to rest. As she was walking away, Caroline saw that her wig was slightly crooked. She shouted out, "Mom!" Her mother turned. Caroline pointed to her wig. Her mother's hands went up to her fake hair. She made an adjustment, smiled, and walked away.

Caroline and Barry went to Mount Auburn Cemetery before returning home. It was enormous, with gardens and twisting, paved paths. Being in the cemetery, you felt as if the city you just walked out of was a distant memory. They strolled, holding hands, pausing every now and then to read headstones. Realizing they could never find Sara's grave stone by chance in this expansive cemetery, they headed back to the visitors building. There, they found out the location of the grave. Map in hand, Caroline and Barry wove their way through the paths. It took a good half hour to make it to the other end, but they took their time. They discovered inlets with benches for sitting poked away here and there.

Entering one, they found themselves surrounded by azaleas, lilies, and irises. They sat upon a bench for a bit, thinking on the names they had seen on the gravestones.

"Mordecai. That's a weird one," said Barry.

"How about Moses?" countered Caroline.

"I actually kind of like that one," said Barry.

"I think I like Mordecai better," returned Caroline.

They left their alcove and wound their way along the path. By the time they arrived to the grave site, the sun was beating down; the promise of another season yet to come. Caroline stripped off her coat and tied it around her waist. She knelt and fingered the letters on the gravestone, boldly engraved, like Sara. She sat upon the grass, closed her eyes, and listened. The silence was still and ordinary, like a blade of grass. The air moved softly around her, and it spoke in its own language... I am here. The air became a breeze, tickling a curl of hair along her cheek. Caroline took the necklace out of her pocket and put it on the ledge of the gravestone. "Here I am," she said.

Caroline was quiet for the rest of the day, pensive. She felt that missing Sara's life was like missing your own graduation, or your favorite movie on a night when it would have been perfect to watch it, or leaving your ice cream behind in the shopping cart in the grocery store parking lot. Then, said Barry, if she'd been there for Sara's life, there would be no Gretchen McAuley Foundation.

"Who knows how many women have been helped by this, by her."

Caroline thought to herself that she would like to meet one, just one, of those women.

Time went by; a few days, a week. Barry would be starting classes at UMass Dartmouth. Jacob would begin to lose his faculties soon, so Caroline would double her doses of healing energy. Her mother would report that Tim had stopped by a couple of times, just to say hello. Her mother admitted to enjoying his company.

Caroline said, "Me, too, Mom. I always did, too."

"But you like Barry's more?'

"I like Barry's different."

However, after hanging up, Caroline realized she liked Barry's company better *and* different. Next, Caroline called her father and asked him about the Oregon Center for Healing Arts. He told her he knew of it, that it was about a half hour drive from where he lived.

"Dad, I think I want to go there. It's an eight month long intensive program."

A pause stretched the distance between Caroline's phone and her father's. It swirled with questions and doubts.

Finally, her father spoke. "Good, then. You can come live with me. You let me know when, and I'll go over there and enroll you."

Something settled inside Caroline, like a leaf coming to rest upon the ground. "Yes, Dad. That'll be good."

Then Sarna called with a lot more news. "Here's how it works, she said. "My boss decided against the whole wrongly convicted thing, which is fine, because it wouldn't have worked for us anyway. He came up with an idea that he liked better."

"What is it?" asked Caroline.

"Well, the Globe's been doing a lot of pieces about hope and redemption, the proverbial flower growing in the garbage dump. Things like that. He wants a piece titled, "Hope in Prison.""

"There's hope in prison?" asked Caroline.

"Apparently so. All sorts. Career programs, counseling programs, mentoring programs, religious services, of course, drug rehabilitation, victim awareness sessions. A.A."

"Okay," said Caroline tentatively.

"Yes, A.A. Alcoholics Anonymous. According to the Norfolk County Correctional Institution, Jake is highly involved as an attendee and a sponsor."

"I see," said Caroline. She was having trouble merging this new version of Jake with the old one.

"I've... we've...already got clearance to speak with him."

Caroline would have liked to have said something, but she was having trouble opening her jaw.

Sarna went on. "I'm going to talk to some other people there, too: mediators in the Victims Awareness

333

Program, inmates, and hopefully, victims and families of victims, too. Later, when we get back, I'll be going into other prisons and doing some work there as well."

Caroline's voice found her again. "When are we going?'

"Tomorrow, if possible."

"Yes. That's possible," said Caroline.

And so it was arranged. Barry would stay with Jacob through Wednesday night. They'd have to be back by Thursday morning, because Barry had classes to attend. They'd be leaving Saturday, coming back late Wednesday night or early Thursday morning. That was the plan. They would drive, because neither of them would fly. That would leave them a few days in Virginia to do what they were going there to do.

Caroline explained to Jacob that she was traveling to Virginia to visit family.

"Virginia?" he said, patting her hand. "Good. Good. You go visit Virginia."

Caroline told him Barry would be staying with him.

"Oh, yes. I know him," he said. "He's a good fellow." Jacob was just oblivious enough to not care and just aware enough to respond. Caroline had to leave quickly before she changed her mind.

Just before walking out the door, Jacob said, "You say hello to Virginia to me now."

She promised she would and met Barry on the porch. They hugged and he said, "See you when you get back."

"Just a few days. I have to go before I change my mind," announced Caroline.

They rode, at first in silence, but by the time they reached Rhode Island they were laughing. Sarna brought along fake eyelashes, because she said she'd always wanted to try them.

"I figured this would be the perfect time to try them out." She applied them while driving. Caroline tried on a pair as well. They waved their hands and flirtatiously batted their eyes at passerby, who either didn't notice them or looked at them, bewildered.

By the time they were in Connecticut, they were singing loudly to Fergie, Cheryl Crowe, and James Taylor. When they drove over the George Washington Bridge, Caroline quietly contemplated the tall buildings of New York City, a whole world unto its own; Boston, a baby cousin, a Cessna Hopper; New York City a Boeing 747 or an aircraft carrier.

"Have you ever been to Ground Zero?" asked Caroline.

Sarna nodded her head.

"What's it like?"

"There are no words for it, really. I saw it shortly after the Twin Towers fell. The Globe wanted to get as much of it as possible. When I saw it... it was total devastation. It wasn't so much that my mind couldn't believe what I was seeing, but that my eyes couldn't believe it. To think that kind of destruction is so commonplace in other countries. That, maybe, someone from Afghanistan or Sarajevo might

335

come here and have trouble believing the completeness of things, the lack of ruin. It's true that you can get accustomed to horrible things."

Caroline peered out her window. She saw her reflection and, beyond that, another world. "Yes, it is," she said absently.

When they entered New Jersey, Caroline said, "What a dirty state. Have you ever known anyone from New Jersey?"

"Not really," replied Sarna.

They were in and out of this state quickly, leaving behind the smell of decay and an industrial strength, sooty grime. Delaware had a different feel all together. It was surprisingly clean, given what they had just come from. Caroline noted the license plates of the cars in front of them: New Jersey, New York, Maryland... none from Delaware. They came to a toll. A haggard looking woman took their money. She looked tired with snarly, brown hair, bunching around her face. Caroline wondered if she was from Delaware and what the state was like out there beyond the highway.

"Have you ever known anyone from Delaware?"

"Come to think of it, no. I don't even think I've ever even known anyone who knows anyone from Delaware," replied Sarna. Delaware came and went quickly; a state of tolls and hypothetical people.

Maryland was a bit more defined. You could see that, beyond the highway, there may have been beauty. Colors and trees abound, hiding in neighborhoods. The famous

Chesapeake, something Caroline had heard of but never seen. The sun began its descent in the sky. People were coming home from work, looking forward to seeing their spouses, or going home to be alone, or dreaming about other places, different lives. Caroline pulled into a town called Spartan, its culture a mystery in the swiftly darkening night. Ahead, a gas station glowed like a lantern. They pulled up to the pump. A boy, about eighteen or nineteen, approached the driver's side window. He was thin with dark, shaggy hair. His t-shirt read "Phish" on it. "What can I get you, ma'am?"

"Fill it regular."

The boy dipped his head down a bit and glanced at Caroline, then turned with a chuckle.

"What's up with him?" asked Sarna.

Caroline shrugged. She turned down her window and heard peepers singing, unseen in the dark, inky figures of trees. She heard music being piped out from the gas station, "California Dreamin" by The Mamas and the Papas. Caroline hummed along. "I love this song. Let's find it on the radio."

They did this and paid the boy, who walked back into the station, shaking his head and chuckling.

"What's his problem?" asked Caroline.

As they pulled out, a car pulled in with a Virginia license plate: the dominion state, the state of peaches and apples, grapes and vineyards, horses and people, magnolias and bluebonnets.

They drove in silence for a while. The radio churned out its litany of songs, but it was "California Dreamin" that kept replaying itself in Caroline's mind. Sarna's cell phone rang. Caroline thought for the first time of Jacob and of Barry and worried over them, especially over Jacob. But it was neither of them calling. It was Julie. Sarna spoke in a clipped voice.

"Yes," and "No," she said.

Caroline thought she heard agitation in her voice, or it could have been conviction. The phone call quickly ended.

"Everything all right?" asked Caroline.

Sarna slowly let a breath out. "Julie's not too pleased that I'm doing this."

"This?" asked Caroline.

Sarna glanced at Caroline. "With you."

"Oh, God, then, we shouldn't be doing this," said Caroline.

"Please. Spare me. Julie doesn't get this, and I don't need someone who can't let me have a friend without a guilt trip."

Caroline looked down at her feet. "I'm sorry."

"Don't be. We have much bigger things to think about," returned Sarna.

Caroline looked at her friend. Such a definitive girl, except when it came to throwing things out; otherwise, so sure and decisive. You want to know how to get something done, what to do next, then, go to Sarna. Still, Caroline sensed a very human, very little girl under that skin. This little girl was, at times, highly visible, even when Sarna had no idea of it. Caroline started to laugh, at first with just a bubble, then with a flow.

"What? What?" asked Sarna.

"The eyelashes," said Caroline, "that's what that kid was laughing at."

They both laughed from deep within their bellies.. big, fat tears getting trapped in their dramatic eyelashes.

By the time they crossed the border into Virginia, the sun was rising and Caroline was driving. Sarna was sleeping. Caroline wanted to take everything in, but she was too tired, her senses dulled, her nerves short circuiting. She was sick to her stomach from all the coffee, her head throbbing from the caffeine. Besides, so far, Virginia looked much like the last state and the last. It could have been Massachusetts, except for the slower drivers and the later model cars. She found the Eonolodge they had mapped out. Caroline woke Sarna, who startled out of her sleep. Blinking, she looked around. "Good job." They checked in and stumbled into their room, which came equipped with gaudy, brown print bed spreads and a small end table, which, no doubt, housed the Holy Bible. They each collapsed into their own bed and fell into a deep, exhausted sleep. Caroline's last thoughts before falling off to sleep were of peaches and birds.

Waking up in a different bed in a different state can be disorienting, especially when you think it's the dead of the night, but it is really the middle of the day. Caroline cracked open her eyes. Her heavy eyelids stung. She saw brightness leaking in through the edges of the thick hotel curtains, which matched the bedding. Caroline heard a voice outside the hotel-room door, the one that opened to the parking lot. She turned toward Sarna's bed and saw that it was empty.

The rumpled bedding and crooked pillow were evidence of Sarna's presence. Caroline sat up, listening more closely to the voice on the other side of the door. It was Sarna, and she was on her phone, pacing. It could have been Julie she was talking to. Caroline got up and peeked out the curtain. The sun was blinding, glinting off the windshields of the cars in the parking lot. Caroline let the curtain drop and sat at the edge of the bed. Sarna came in. Crisp Virginia air flooded the room. Caroline decided that it was somehow different from Massachusetts air.

"That was my guy."

"Your guy?" Caroline hadn't known that Sarna had a guy. Her eyebrows pinched up in confusion.

Sarna paced. "The one who has been investigating for me." "And?" asked Caroline expectantly.

Sarna stopped and faced Caroline. "He found them."

"Both?" asked Caroline, holding her breath.

Sarna's eyes held Caroline's. "Yes. Owen and Samuel. One of them is alive, and the other is not."

Caroline shot up. "It's got to be Samuel who is dead. He'd be... what... in his nineties right now if he was still alive? Owen would be forty-eight. Tell me it's Samuel that's dead. Tell me. It's got to be." Sarna watched her, expressionless.

"Tell me!" screamed Caroline.

"You're right," said Sarna. "He died shortly after Gretchen did. He fell from one of his peach trees. Broke his neck."

Caroline laughed at this ridiculous thought. Fell from one of his peach trees?

Then, she cried. "Tell me where Owen is!"

Sarna's expression softened. "He lives in his grandparents' house. The house Gretchen grew up in."

Caroline buried her face in her hands. "Thank God. Thank God." Tears rolled down her forearms.

Sarna continued. "It seems he's done just fine. He served as a fire fighter for the town of Cedarville until he fell from the third floor of a burning building. He broke some bones, some vertebrae, and had to recover for a long time. He had to retire early, three years ago."

Sarna paused. "He's married."

Caroline looked up, smiled.

"His wife's name is Carol, and she's a nurse."

"A nurse? Carol? Do they have children?"

"No," said Sarna. "Let's get up, get these ridiculous eyelashes off, and get to work.

Again, they drove: south and west... toward Cedarville. They didn't have to go to the prison until three o'clock. That left them two and a half hours to do other stuff. They planned on driving through Cedarville and locating Owen's house, just locating it. Maybe the fire station as well. At some point, the Blue Ridge Mountains came into view. Stately, distant, hazy, there through all sorts of coming and going: through the absurdities of human life... animals turning to dust in the foothills, returning to their natural state. Human bones, too...bones and bones and seeds and trees, insects. The simplest of things of all, mountains. The highway took them down, not up. Down into a valley and then further down into another valley so vast it could have been the plains of Iowa. They passed cow farms and horse farms, pickup trucks and silos. They got off the highway and wove their way through towns with names like Garrison and Palmer. For a while, they drove past nothing at all, except for tall, ancient trees. Caroline thought of the big redwoods that are older than Jesus himself.

Eventually, they came into a town called Dayton which opened up into a surprising array of grape vineyards. Caroline opened her window and smelled something both sweet and earthen. Beyond this, they came to a small center built into a crevice of earth. There was a trading post which tilted to the left, but was probably much more sturdy than it looked. A bank, post office, general store, and gas station completed the town. Caroline and Sarna were once again on toward the next town, which was Cedarville. Here, Caroline called Barry.

"How's he doing?" she asked.

"All right, I guess. He's not talking much, and, I don't know, but his chest sounds kind of rattly."

"Okay. Just keep him comfortable. Make sure he drinks a lot of water. Has he mentioned Gretta?"

"No," replied Barry, "I haven't seen her, either. How's it going on your end?"

"It's going." She offered no more than that.

They finally entered Cedarville, a fairly average-looking town upon first inspection. Except that charming little apple orchards dotted the landscape. Mountain laurel,

342

sun drops, and blue bonnets carpeted the ground in some spots, bunched themselves up against fences in others. They came upon an elementary school and a high school, probably where Owen himself went. The fire station approached them on their left, and they pulled over to look at it.

"Do you want to go in?" asked Sarna.

"No," replied Caroline, "I just want to sit here and look."

There appeared to be no activity at the fire station. Caroline imagined that there were men, and perhaps women, inside playing cards, or doing cross word puzzles in solitude. Caroline wondered why men and women become fire fighters except to rescue.

Sarna interrupted Caroline's thoughts. "Well. We'll have to go in. At least I will. I need to know how to get there from here, to the house." In the end, they both went in.

A man was at the counter, young and handsome.

"How can I help you ladies?"

He had a slight southern drawl and a kind face. Sarna told him the address, and he gave her directions. He winked at Caroline as they turned to leave. She paused at a large town map on the brown paneled wall. Beneath the map, was a series of framed pictures of Cedarville Tigers little league teams. The children in each picture changed from year to year, but the coach was the same... tall, blonde, smiling, handsome. Owen McAuley. Caroline looked into his eyes. She could not tell their color by the photographs, but she knew they were blue. Caroline was suddenly filled up with something, something like air, or the blue, blue sky. She

343

didn't even tell Sarna as they walked back to the car. Certain things she found she wanted to keep to herself. Some details were highly private and sacred, like the unspoken bond between a mother and a child, even one that reaches through time and space.

They found the house, Owen's. There was still an apple orchard across the street. The street light, that was there, too. The house itself did not look the same as in her hypnosis-induced memories. It was no longer brown shingle, but a pale, creamy yellow. It was small, still small. A low wooded fence across the front yard boasted pink Hollyhock and spiky Echinacea. An old Ford sat in the driveway.

Caroline looked away. "I'm not ready for this. Let's turn back around and take a left back there. I want to see the other house, Jake's."

Caroline directed Sarna. She knew just what to do, where to go. Keeping the orchard on their left, they took a left and kept on straight. A few minutes later, they came to a house on their left. It used to be brown shingle, too, and still was. An entryway had been added to the kitchen door entrance. The driveway was there to the right, but you could see it had recently been paved. A small child, a boy, rode his red flyer tricycle on the black pavement. This time, Caroline could not look away. The child looked like Owen.

They drove on and came to the spot where the garage used to be. The whole structure was gone. All that was left was the concrete floor. Tall weeds grew up through the cracks in the concrete. Sarna pulled over, and Caroline got out. She stood on the garage floor. Old grease and oil stains

344

blotched around her feet. The harsh thud of Jake's wrench as he threw it against the wall echoed against invisible walls. An old stain over by the spot where the tire machine once was caught Caroline's eye. It could have been Jake's blood. The ghost of an innocent girl in a pony tail leaned against an old Chevy, laughing. Then the image disappeared. Caroline saw the underground vat where Jake used to dump discarded car oil. He used to throw his bottles down there too. Caroline moved to slide the heavy concrete lid aside but decided against it. She inhaled deeply and smelled a mixture of oil, fresh mountain air, and horse. She looked across and down the street where she and Owen used to walk to get to Samuel's.

Walking over to the car, she announced, "Let's go."

They got into the car and drove further down the street until they came to a mailbox post with no mailbox on top.

"Turn up here," she instructed Sarna. They drove up the dirt road, as rutted and pitted as ever.

"What's up here?" asked Sarna.

"You'll see," said Caroline.

At the end of the driveway, they found a dilapidated house, half caved-in. Grasses and weeds grew inside it. Caroline and Sarna got out and stood, taking in the view.

"Samuel's," said Sarna.

Caroline nodded. "Come around back with me."

They picked their way through the overgrowth. Caroline saw Owen as a child, crouching down at the edge of the woods, intent on something. Mountain Laurel to the left stirred in the breeze. They came upon rows and rows of trees, all gone haywire and crooked, gone to seed. "The peach trees," said Caroline. She went up to one of the trees and touched its skin. She looked up. I could fall from that tree and land on my feet. Thought Caroline. They walked down the rows to the other end. Caroline saw herself as a child with her mother trying, bravely, to pick apples to bring home to her father. She saw Mitchell smiling at her from high up in a tree. An expansive vista came into view. There, they saw the horse farm. Horses casually grazed in a field so big your eyes couldn't possibly find its end. Caroline remembered running.

"Somewhere over there," said Caroline, pointing.

"We'll go there tomorrow," said Sarna. "We have to get to the prison now."

It took nearly an hour to get there, to the prison. "Before, this was a pasture, I think. With cows." Caroline remembered an ice cream stand, licking strawberry ice cream, watching cows. She knew this was a memory from a different life, and she knew it was real. She no longer doubted her memories. They entered the building. It was large and foreboding, smelling of disinfectant. Searches of belongings ensued. Verification procedures began. There was no mention of Caroline's phony ID. She had expected a cacophony of noise, but there was none. It must have been embedded, deep within the prison. They entered a small office. There, they met with the warden, a tall, thin man. His hair was slicked back. Introductions went around, and they sat, ready for discussion. The warden grinned. "The ladies form Massachusetts. What interests you in my prison way down here in Virginia?"

"We are doing a piece in our New Bedford Globe about hope in prison," answered Sarna.

"Yes. I am aware of that," the warden replied, "but why ours? Why here?"

"Well, we're gathering information from prisons all over the east coast. We'll use the most compelling material in our article," Sarna quipped.

The warden tipped back in his office chair. It creaked as it rocked back and forth. He laced his fingers before him, cracked his knuckles. "I think it is an ambitious endeavor. I'm not sure who will want to read such an article." He leaned forward, his face inches from Sarna's. "People want tragedy, not hope." He took a tooth pick out of his desk drawer, began prying at something between his teeth. "Maybe I'm wrong. Maybe it is worthwhile. There is hope in prison, I think you will see. At least, ladies, you will be spared the grislier side of life in prison. There is that, too."

Sarna sat up straighter. "Yes. That's not what we're interested in, though."

"If you're ever interested in the other side of life here, I'd be glad to show it to you," he said, grinning, "Well, now. Let's get started."

The warden stood. "First I'll take you to meet with the coordinator of the victim awareness program. She's the best there is, but I suppose they'll tell you that wherever you go. Her name's June Bergamont. She'll talk you through the process, how it works."

347

They followed him around corners, through passageways, into another office. This one overlooked a conference room complete with a long, rectangular table and chairs. June was in her office. She rose to shake their hands. She had a warm smile, a cold hand. "I'm sorry it's so cold in here. I keep telling them the heat doesn't work right in here. Here, let's go into the conference room. It's warmer in there." They moved into the conference room.

June continued. "Usually the victims and families of victims choose to sit at the far end, away from the perpetrator. They're doing the best they can, being in the same room with the person who changed their life forever. It's hard for both parties."

Sarna took out her tape recorder. "Do you mind if I get this on tape?"

"Not at all. I think it's important for people to know that these perpetrators are just people. They have feelings, needs, and desires, too." Caroline felt a spark within her, like little knives coursing through her veins.

For the first time since entering the prison, Caroline spoke. "Don't you think it defeats the purpose of punishment to help them feel better about what they've done?" Sarna moved to speak, but then thought better of it.

June countered, "I see what you're saying, I do. Believe it or not, the most profound release that comes from this program happens within the victims. The perpetrators don't end up feeling better about what they've done. In many ways, they feel worse. In a sense, they're taking ownership for their own punishment." June paused.

"Go on," said Caroline levelly.

"Remember now, the ones who wish to take place in a victim's meeting actually have a conscience. Their minds are heavy with daunting words: manslaughter, rape, murder, and such. It's because they have a conscience, or have developed one while in prison, that going through the process causes them even more pain, more regret. They live it every day. They eat it, sleep it, feel it acutely." Sarna looked at Caroline. Go ahead, her eyes said.

"And the victims? The families?" asked Caroline.

"They get to tell their perpetrators what it's been like for them."

Caroline was sick of hearing that word- perpetrator. She thought of more fitting words such as: dirt-bag, low-life, scum-of-the-earth.

June continued. "The victims and their families get to tell them how much they hate them. How much they pray for them. How much they struggle to let them go, get them out of their nightmares. It is closure, however much there can be. I know it's hard to swallow. Look, I have an inmate I'd like you to meet if you're interested. Just last month, he met with the mother of a girl he murdered. Would you like to meet him?"

Sarna let Caroline answer. "Yes, actually, I would." The knives that were, a moment ago, coursing through her veins were now piercing the surface of her skin, ready.

June got up and called someone from her office.

Sarna leaned over. "Are you okay?"

"Just pissing mad," returned Caroline.

349

Sarna covered Caroline's hand with her own. "I can see that. Just try to rein it in a little, so we can get through this. Okay?"

"Don't worry. I'll keep my cool," said Caroline.

June returned. "The perpetrator's name is James," she said. Dirt-bag, low-life, piece-of-shit. Thought Caroline.

"He's in for the second-degree murder of his girl-friend ten years ago. He's serving life without the possibility of parole. He would like to speak with you about his experience meeting her mother."

James came in moments later, completely shackled and assisted by a guard. He wore a one-piece orange jumper. Caroline guessed that he was around her age. He was bald and had a thick neck and puffy cheeks. His eyes were like the small holes left behind by fingers poked in dough. He sat opposite Caroline and Sarna.

"I killed a girl," he announced, "Her name was Dawn, and I killed her with my bare hands." Caroline cringed at the image.

He continued. "I was so obsessed with her. She was all I ever thought of. She still is. When Dawn started to pull away from me, started seeing me for the sick person I was, I couldn't take it. I thought I would die. One night I went to her apartment. She let me in. She never expected it, what I would do to her. To her it was unthinkable, not even an option. She was wrong." June gave James a look of reproach. James took a deep breath, letting it out with force.

He corrected himself. "Dawn... Dawn was wrong."

June interjected, "We try to encourage the perpetrators to use their victim's names. It makes the whole process more real for them."

Why don't you call *them* by their real name: scumbag, piece-of-shit. Thought Caroline.

James looked down at his shackles. "I could see Dawn wasn't going to come back to me. It was final, and there was nothing I was going to do about it."

He looked up at them, his dough eyes finding Caroline. "Do you want to know how I did it?"

Sarna touched Caroline's thigh.

"No. I'm all set with that," said Caroline.

"That's fine," he said. "I will tell you that, afterward, I felt a sense of relief I'd never known. Like every hurt, every anger, every pain, every burden had finally lifted off of me. I won't go into where it all came from in the first place, the feelings I'd been carrying around all my life. Where it came from was just as disgusting as I had become."

James paused, thought some more. "I think, now, if only I had been allowed to let all of those emotions out when I was younger, Dawn would be alive today."

He choked back little sobs. "Maybe, if I could have cried, screamed, let it all out... I wouldn't have been so messed up. I told the mother all of this, I did. I told her I didn't deserve to feel the release I did when I killed her... Dawn... when I killed Dawn. So I said, 'Put it on me. Pile it on. Tell me everything. Everything.' She did. It took a long time. I wish I could feel the horrors she feels, the anguish. I can't. I don't have children. I can't know what it's like. She can't know the horrors of what it's like to kill someone."

James looked up toward the ceiling. "I hope she's lighter now. Hopefully she, not me, can feel some sense of relief. I don't know. I don't know if that's possible for her."

"Have you had any contact with her since then?" asked Sarna.

"I have mailed her some letters, but she hasn't answered them. I'll keep writing, though. My letters to her only ever contain two words: I'm sorry. There really is nothing else to say."

"Why bother?" asked Caroline. "So you can feel better?"

He thought for a bit. "No. So she can feel better."

After the interview, Caroline and Sarna talked with June for a while.

"You know," said June. "It's very rare, but occasionally a victim's family, usually the mother, actually comes to a sense of forgiveness. It's the ultimate understanding, the ultimate release."

Caroline spoke. "I don't know how such things can be forgiven."

June reached out to Caroline's shoulder. "You'd be surprised, the kinds of things that can be forgiven," she said kindly.

She shifted the direction of the conversation. "Now, I understand you're off to meet one of our most outstanding inmates. This guy's helped so many others."

They were up and walking further into the bowels of the prison. Caroline could begin to hear some of the life within: a banter, male voices, laughter, whoops, long, drawn out vowels... a culture not privy to anyone else not belonging to it. They veered away just when the voices became clear enough to, perhaps, be able to see who they belonged to.

They entered a room with a pulpit and a circle of folding chairs. Six men sat in a circle. Just then they all stood, shook hands and said, "Keep coming back," as if it was the 'peace be with you' blessing at a Catholic mass. They all helped fold up the chairs, stacking them in a corner of the room. The men filed out, their orange suits disappearing through the door; except there was one man left... one shuffling, blonde man. He had a hunched back and a shocking amount of hair for his age. It was combed back off his forehead, whisping at the collar of his jumper.

He went to the corner and lifted some chairs with ease, unfolded them, and said, "Here you are, ladies. Come sit."

Caroline fingered the ID hanging from her neck, feeling like a frightened nineteen-year-old. She could not look up.

"Look at me," he said, "Look at me. I'm just an old man."

Caroline did look up; She saw deep crevices in his forehead, in his cheeks, a scar above his eyebrow that hadn't been there before, or had it? His crooked, arthritic knuckles bulged. His eyes were a clear, vibrant blue: the blue of an autumn sky, a sapphire gem, a piece of blue construction paper. Not the cold, icy gray of a frozen winter pond. He had a moustache and a neatly trimmed goatee, which was not blonde or gray, but a pale, strawberry blonde... a trace of the mother who abandoned him.

"See?" he said. "I'm just an old man. An alcoholic. A murderer."

"You killed someone?" asked Sarna.

He nodded, closed his eyes. "I did. Do you want to tape record this?"

"Yes," said Sarna.

He opened his eyes. "No. You do not have my permission."

Sarna moved to counter him. He stopped her before she could begin. "Not yet. When we talk about what I do in A.A., then you can. But not yet. First, I want to tell you how I got here. But you," he said, pointing to Caroline, "I want to talk to you alone."

"Why?" asked Caroline.

"I just do. I don't want a whole audience. It's bad enough he's here." He motioned toward a guard in the corner of the room. Caroline hadn't noticed he was even there.

She looked Jake squarely in the eye. "I'm okay with that."

Sarna turned to Caroline "You sure?"

"I am," replied Caroline.

"I'll wait right out here." Sarna stepped out of the room.

"You're shaking like a leaf," said Jake. "You're new at this aren't you?"

"Yes, I am." Caroline thought of lost virginity. She thought of innocence interrupted, of the quiet transferring of a young girl from her parents into the hands of her new marital home. She thought of paper, a poster of James Dean being torn off a wall.

"I killed someone," he said.

"You already said that."

Jake pressed on. "Does that make you uncomfortable?"

"No. It makes me curious."

"Curious?" he asked.

"Yes. Who you killed. Why. What drove you to it. If you know the destruction it causes."

Caroline thought of Gretta, of Jacob.

Jake contemplated. "Those are good questions. You'll do well at this job."

They were silent for a bit. He looked away. Caroline did not. She noticed a slight tremor in his shoulders, his neck and head. She saw, there, a despair; a wordless, untouchable despair. It was a look she'd seen before. When he looked up again, his eyes were a frozen pond.

"I killed someone who killed someone I loved," he said. "Then it was I who killed the person I loved as well."

"So you killed them both?" asked Caroline.

"In a sense, yes. I was in a drunken rage one night when I beat my wife, Gretchen. She was too beautiful to be beaten, choked. I did it anyway. I almost took her life that night. I was so close. She couldn't make a sound, couldn't breathe. She tried to say something. She tried, but she couldn't. When her eyes started to roll back, I stopped, took my hands away from her throat. I left."

"Where did you go?" asked Caroline.

This time, it was Jake who could not look up. "I went to my mother's. Gretchen always thought she was dead. That's what I told her. She was dead, figuratively, for a long time. She took off on my Dad and me when I was thirteen, because my Dad used to beat on her. She left us both, even me. She left me behind with him."

Caroline expected to see anger. All she saw was resignation.

"When I saw that I was becoming just like him, becoming an abusive drunk, I would run to my mother. I never told Gretchen where I was going. I just couldn't. I could beat her, but I couldn't bear to break her heart with the truth."

Again, the trembling. Jake's eyes, eyes that have seen too much, looking out at nothing... eyes with a depth too deep for anyone to reach. Caroline realized that, perhaps, she had never known him, never tried.

"I thought my mother could talk some sense into me. I couldn't seem to stop. Maybe she could get me to stop."

Caroline ventured, "Did she try?"

"The first time, yes. But the second time, she slammed the door in my face. She was so disgusted with me that I'd done it again, gone and gotten drunk, hurt my wife. The third time, I passed out in her front lawn. The fourth time, she took me in and tried to sober me up. She told me to never, ever come back again after a fit of drinking and abuse. That was the time I almost killed Gretchen."

Jake buried his face in his hands. "If my mother hadn't left me with him, with my father, Gretchen would be alive today. She would be alive today."

A tear escaped from between his fingers. "At around three or four o'clock that night, I left my mother's house. She was asleep on the couch. I didn't even think to wake her. I just wanted to get home. I just wanted to see my wife. I drove straight through. But when I arrived, I didn't have the nerve to face her, so I went to the garage where I worked. I had bottles of booze hidden in there, and I took all of them and threw them down the oil shoot, then fell asleep."

"I got up when the sun rose and went home. I found the kitchen door open. Gretch and Owen, our little boy, were nowhere to be found. I saw bags and suitcases in the living room. I saw dough on the counter and a rolling pin on the floor, flour all over the place. The radio was on. I couldn't figure out why she would leave all of this stuff behind like this, why the radio would be on, why the door would be open. I thought that maybe she had left me. I thought that maybe she'd gone to her parents. So I went outside to drive to her parents. That's when I saw the cigarette butts all over the ground, across the street. I suddenly knew. I knew. Samuel had been there. He was a guy who lived up the street. Gretchen had befriended him, against my wishes. I was always telling her he was crazy, but she didn't believe me. Then, I was crazy, too. I drove over to Gretch's parents' house. I don't know why. I really wanted to go to Samuel's, but I was afraid of what I'd find. When I drove up to the house, I saw Owen's silhouette in the window. His little profile. So I drove up to his house, Samuel's. You know what I found?" he asked, looking at her with his gray eyes.

"What?" said Caroline, wanting to know, but not wanting to know.

"I found him sitting up against one of his peach trees with blood all over him. Gretch's bracelets were on him arms. He was catatonic. I pulled him up, stripping him of his clothes and shoved him in his shower. I watched Gretch's blood as it washed down the drain. I pulled him out of the shower, dressed him in clean clothes, brought him outside, leaned him back up against a tree and hollered, "Tell me where Gretch is!" He just sat there, unresponsive. I slapped him. "Tell me!" I yelled. I shook him. I kicked him. "Tell me! Tell me! Tell me!" He wouldn't. I pushed him onto his back, down onto the ground, started to choke him. He didn't even fight it. I changed my mind, pulled him up to sitting again. I got behind him and said, "Where is she?" He spoke. "She's gone." I grabbed him by the head, twisted once, and broke his neck. Some peaches came loose from above and landed on him. I scooped up his clothes, rubbed them all over me, and dumped them in the oil vat at the garage. I drove myself to the police station and turned myself in for killing Gretchen."

"But you didn't kill her," said Caroline.

"Yes, I did. If I hadn't been drunk. If I hadn't abused her. If I hadn't left that time, she'd be alive today. I killed them both."

"Why did you tell me all of this?' asked Caroline.

"I figure it's about time," he said, staring out the barred window. The tremor returned, and also something else that Caroline struggled to identify. Perhaps it wasn't a returning, but a leaving of something. Like an invisible fog, escaping through the barred prison window.

Jake answered Caroline's question. "I've never told anyone before, but now I am so old it doesn't matter. I'm never getting out of here, anyway. I don't even want to. My place is here, doing what I do."

Caroline studied him. The setting sun illuminated his blonde hair. She could see that his mustache was too long, its unruly hairs poking into his mouth. He did not look sixty-nine, but more like fifty-nine, save for the facial lines, hunched back, and swollen knuckles.

"This is the only time anyone has ever wished to meet with me, all these years. Not my mother, not my son. Although, I can't say I blame them."

"You don't have a relationship? With your son, I mean?" asked Caroline.

"No, but I keep tabs on him."

"How do you do that?"

"I have my ways. I think he's done well, my son. Better than I have. As I said, I keep tabs. I don't think he's anything like me. In fact, I know he's not."

"How can you be so sure?"

"As I said, I have my ways."

They were both quiet. He turned and looked at her. "You know all the right questions," he said, "questions I ask myself. You are very good at this."

Caroline looked at this other person... this man. "Thank you," she said.

They dared to look at one another, without pretense, without shields. Something passed between them. Caroline wasn't sure if she was the only one who noticed. He asked if she could come back the next day to talk about his A.A. work. He was tired, and he looked it: deflated, empty, just a rag of a person.

Before leaving the room, Caroline said, "Jake? Your wife? Was she ever found?"

"No," he said, "she never was."

Caroline and Sarna found a bed and breakfast just outside Cedarville. They were exhausted, especially Caroline. Sarna was full of questions, needing to know what Jake had said, how he said it, what it all meant.

Caroline did her best to answer: "No, he doesn't want to ever get out.", and "No, he was not threatening in any way.", and "I don't know how I felt. Sort of numb. Sort of like I just came back from a different planet."

Caroline did not tell her that she felt, in a strange but definite way, that she and Jake were, for once, behaving like parents together, watching out for their son.

Night came quickly. Caroline and Sarna sat on the terrace of their B&B room. It overlooked a small valley, the mountains. It was a stunning evening. Crickets sang, and if mountain air had a sound, then you could hear it. Caroline put her feet up on the railing and wiggled her toes; such a simple gesture, but it made her feel so alive, so present. She called Barry, who reported that Jacob had become quite worked up throughout the day, refusing to eat, looking for Gretta. His chest rattled even more so. Caroline told him to hang on tight. They'd be back the day after tomorrow. She told him she'd send Jacob some healing light, and, although she expected a strange reaction from Barry, she got none. He only seemed relieved. Caroline did this. She closed her eyes and sent the light. It bathed him, especially his heart. Caroline and Sarna then went inside and fell asleep with the door to the balcony open, the crickets lulling them to sleep. Caroline woke briefly, not at 11:11, but at 1:11, and she wondered if this meant her angels were leaving her; if she had enough of her own wings, yet.

In the morning, Caroline called Barry. He reported that Jacob was a little better. He wasn't asking for Gretta and was eating, although his chest was still rattling.

Caroline said, "I love you for this."

Barry paused before responding. "Do you love me for anything else?"

Caroline's reply was quicker. "I love you for everything."

She promised she'd tell him everything that had happened when she got back. He wanted to know if she was all right.

"I trust that Sarna is taking good care of you."

Caroline looked over at her sleeping friend. Sarna. Sara. Earth angels disguised as friends.

361

"Of course. Also, I'm taking good care of myself."

When Sarna woke, they had fried eggs, toast, grits, sliced tomatoes, and sautéed mushrooms. It was as if Caroline had never eaten before, never tasted before. It was as if she'd been looking through a dirty window all her life, and it had just been wiped clean.

It was the same as with the eggs. This time when they passed through the prison, sounds were clearer... just simple, uncomplicated things. People were just people, all doing a job: the guards suspiciously eyeing Caroline and Sarna, the woman searching their belongings, the warden combing his fingers through his hair, the inmates bravely facing another twenty-four hours. Caroline and Sarna entered the A.A. room to find more men this time, sitting on the folding chairs, their fannies on those cold, hard surfaces. Jake, of course, was among them. They spoke of the steps, of higher powers, trying to admit they were powerless over their drinking.

"I know I am powerless when I drink, even though it feels the opposite at the time," said one man.

"That's a good start," said Jake.

"I want to believe in a higher power," said another, "but I'm not sure I do."

Jake returned, "I want to believe, and I do believe that someday I will."

Some of the other men nodded in understanding. Caroline nodded as well.

Jake turned toward another man. "What about you, Teddy? You're going to be out in another month. How do you feel about that?"

"I'm terrified. This is the only place I've been able to stay sober. Every time I get out, I start up again, and my life turns to hell."

The men grunted, made eye contact with one another.

"There's A.A. everywhere," said Jake.

"Yea, but I can't seem to keep it together outside these walls. It's like they keep me glued together," said Teddy.

"We're all powerless over it," replied a man who seemed to be made only of skin and bones.

The man to Teddy's left boomed, "That's bullshit! I could drink in here. All that bootleg shit? All that fermented fruit crap hiding everywhere? I could get shit-ass drunk if I wanted to. I don't, because I choose not to--because I have power over it." He shifted away from Teddy, away from everyone.

"Maybe for you," countered Teddy. "For me, the easier part is stopping the drinking. The harder part is staying sober."

Jake's voice was low and soft. "Give it up to your higher power, find a meeting. Hell, find ten meetings if you have to. Find a sponsor. Keep coming back."

They all looked toward Jake.

One man broke the silence. "Higher power," he sneered.

Teddy looked at Jake, his eyes pleading. "But you're my sponsor."

"Find another one. I'm just one of hundreds, thousands even," said Jake.

Teddy wouldn't let it go. "Can't I keep you?"

"Me? What will you want with an old coot like me? Look Teddy. You can move on, can't you? Find a better role model out there--in the real world."

The men talked on, taking turns. One said nothing, nothing at all. Caroline had the sense that this was okay, too. The meeting ended, leaving Caroline and Sarna alone with Jake. They all sat, facing each other.

Jake motioned to Sarna. "You can tape me now." His eyes were blue. Sarna took out her recorder.

"Are you an alcoholic?" he asked.

Sarna blinked, stared. "No."

Jake continued. "Do you love an alcoholic?"

"No."

Jake looked away. "Then you wouldn't understand any of this, anyway. That's all you need to know. That's all I have to say."

Jake turned to look out the window. He stared out, beyond the bars. "It's a Bluebonnet spring," he said. "You two ought to get out there and enjoy it. Get yourself down in the valley, near the mountains. You can smell them, the Bluebonnets. So blue." Again, his yellow hair glowed in the sunlight.

He turned toward Caroline. "I have a picture to show you. You, Caroline. That's your name, right?"

Caroline stepped closer.

"My son's wife's name is Carol. She's a lovely lady. Don't ask me how I know... I know."

Caroline came closer still. He held it out, the picture. She took it. It was a photo of Gretchen at the pond, leaning against a tree. She was blond and smiling, her frail shoulders tipping toward the camera, her narrow chin pointing slightly upward.

"You called me Jake," he said. "No one calls me that anymore. You can keep that. I don't need it anymore."

He never once looked away from that window, from the bars.

Caroline could feel the fabric of her socks wrapping around her feet, the soft threads of her pants tickling her skin as she walked. Caroline and Sarna went along side by side, past Samuel's broken down house, among the twisted peach trees, through a low stand of trees, to the edge of the horse farm. A white horse frolicked in the distance. It whinnied. Another horse playfully skipped over. Its coat was the brown and white of a container of vanilla and chocolate ice cream. A barn stood on the edge of the field, the one Gretchen had been trying to reach so long ago.

"I want to go in," said Caroline.

"In where?" asked Sarna.

"In the field."

"Will we get in trouble?" asked Sarna.

Caroline looked at her friend and smiled. "Who cares!"

They climbed the fence- no barbed wire there. Their feet were running as soon as they hit the ground. Each footfall across the field was a statement: choice... freedom... choice... freedom. Running and running, not away from something, but toward something. The wind pushed back their hair, whistled in their ears. It spoke without words: choice... freedom... forgiveness. Birds set free from a cage. The horses noticed their approach and scuttled off to a point so much further away. Caroline and Sarna stopped somewhere in the middle of the field. A renegade cumulus cloud slid in front of the sun momentarily, but was quickly off on its way. The two girls doubled over, trying to catch their breath, laughing. When they stood up again, Caroline saw that there were three of them together in the field: herself, Sarna, and Gretta--all three of them in the middle of the field. Sarna did not see, but Caroline did. When she blinked, Gretta was gone. Sarna reached out and touched Caroline's cheek.

"You have roses in your cheeks. You look good."

"Thank you," replied Caroline, "for all of this. There is no better friend. I don't feel deserving."

Sarna smiled. "You are. You are deserving."

Caroline looked over toward the way she needed to go. There, standing behind the far side of the fence was Gretta, watching them.

"You can go alone, or I can go with you," said Sarna.

"I'll go alone," said Caroline.

Caroline turned and walked toward Gretta, then looked back toward Sarna. A gentle smile came to her lips. Turning back, Caroline saw that Gretta was no longer there. When Caroline reached the fence, she ran her hand along the wood, gray and weathered. She climbed over it. When she came down on the other side, she spied a carving in the wood, deep and blackened with time. It read, "Owen was here." Caroline fingered the letters, felt their permanence, their intent. She turned and started down a path carpeted in grass, defined by curling, twisting branches and nasty briers. The path took a turn and then another. Caroline kept catching glimpses of a girl who never lived past fourteen.

They came to a straight-away, and the path was lost all together to a field of tall, yellow reeds and small, nostalgic blue flowers. The smells were a mixture beyond identifying. Some birds fluttered up out of the tall grass and dropped down again into the prickly bedding. Gretta ran, her hair swinging behind her, her elbows pumping back and forth. Caroline blinked when Gretta turned into a blue bird, gliding ahead of her. The next instant, Gretta was just Gretta. They ran this way through the field and then into a thicket of trees. Sunlight shone down through the branches in shafts, momentarily bringing to light the ordinary details of this small forest. Gretta crashed through, using her arms to clear

367

the way, thorns tearing at her pants. The briars were like little whips in Caroline's arms.

At last, the forest was done. Gretta walked slowly to a small outcropping of land, almost a mountain but not quite. She approached it, turned, and faced Caroline. Gretta was pale, and her arms hung down by her sides.

"Why do you run?" asked Caroline, but Gretta did not answer.

Her eyes were green. Caroline walked forward to a certain spot and stood. She sat down, cross-legged, and touched the ground with her hands, felt the cold earth beneath her legs. It was just the earth and beneath that, down and down, Gretchen's bones. Caroline closed her eyes and heard every sound, every bird, every bug, every fluttering wing... all about her, life.

And then she saw in her mind a different place... far, far away from here: a small, stumpy pond with blackened water. Its bottom was a silty clay; the result of years and years and decades of fallen, rotted leaves, trees, and branches. Beneath that, all of that, bones. Gretta's. Above, at the surface, water bugs sailed along, geese skirted the water's edge, dipping their heads under the surface for a bite to eat. Along the edges, unseen bullfrogs called out in their deep, throaty croaks. Small, flat frogs stuck themselves to tree trunks, peeping; all nonexistent to those unaware... but there still, life. Caroline's mind returned to her present spot, the burial place of Gretchen's bones. She rubbed her hands along the earth beneath her. She felt, in her palms and fingertips, not a giving of something, but a taking of something. She opened her eyes and saw Gretta, her head slightly tilted toward the sky, smiling. Caroline took out of her back pocket a picture of a girl from long ago, blonde and grinning. She put it to the ground and piled a little bit of earth on top. She stood, turned, and walked away.

Caroline found Sarna off to the side of the farm, lying upon her back. Her face was to the sun, and she was sleeping. Caroline woke her. She sat up on her elbows.

"Did you find it?" she asked.

"Yes."

"What was it like?"

"Just a spot, really. Nothing more."

They made their way back to the car in Samuel's driveway. Caroline studied the house one more time.

"It gives me the creeps," said Sarna.

Caroline paused, cocking her head to the side. "Not me, really. He's gone now. He was just a sick, sick man. He just wanted company and, I suppose, love. That's what we all want, isn't it?"

They drove past the missing garage and Jake's old house. Further down the road, they took a right. They came upon the apple orchard and then the driveway, still with the Ford Granada in it.

"What'll I say?" asked Caroline.

Sarna looked at her, incredulous. "You haven't worked that out, yet?"

Caroline shook her head.

"We should have planned that out before-hand," said Sarna.

369

Caroline got out of the car. The figure of a person appeared in a window. Caroline went up to the kitchen door. She knocked. Footsteps approached. The door opened to reveal an older woman.

"Yes?" she said.

"Hi. Um... I'm looking for an Owen McAuley," stammered Caroline.

"Oh dear," replied the woman, "he doesn't live here anymore."

"No?" said Caroline.

Something within her heart broke, like the string of a guitar snapping with the harsh twist of its tuning peg.

The woman continued. "We're renters, my husband and I. Owen rented this place to us... what... oh, a month ago?"

"Do you know where he's gone?" asked Caroline. Why hadn't Jake mentioned this? Had he really been able to keep close tabs on their son as he claimed?

The woman thought, placing her finger aside her temple. "Well, last I heard he was in Montana. He and his wife got themselves a Winnebago. They wanted to travel, see the world-- or, at least the United States. They'll be gone at least a year. That's how long our lease is."

"Oh," said Caroline, looking down at her feet.

"Every so often they let us know where they are, and we send along their mail. I just sent a batch the other day. Seems they'll be in Montana for a while. They like it there," she added.

Caroline looked toward Sarna, still sitting in the car. She wished Sarna could tell her what to do.

But Caroline got her own idea. "Well, then, if I give you something to send along... could you do that?"

"Yes, of course," said the woman.

"It's just a letter, really. I'll just have to go get it. Will you be here for a bit?"

"Oh, yes. We're not going anywhere tonight. Tomorrow night, however, we're going to the pig roast in town. Do you live here in town?" she asked, peering at Sarna's car.

"No. Actually, we're from out of state."

Caroline glanced back at Sarna, who waved at them. "Yes. Well. I'll just go back to the B&B to get that letter. Then, I'll be right back."

The woman's hands came up to her face. "How lucky for you! What a lovely place the B&B is. My uncle used to own that, you know. Until he got divorced, that is. Then he lost everything." She shook her head. "Shame. Why couples can't just work it out these days, I'll never know. We all have our trials, Lord knows. If you ask me, a promise is a promise. A vow is a vow, and that's that. No matter what the problems are. How about you? Are you married?"

Caroline stepped back. "Me? No. God, no."

"That's another thing. All the young people today. They stay single forever. Don't know what they're missing out on."

Caroline stepped further away. "Yes, well... I'd better be going to get that letter. You sure it's okay?"

371

"Heavens. Yes, of course it is. Now go on and get it," replied the woman.

"I'll be right back," said Caroline as she escaped into Sarna's car.

Caroline sniveled and cried like a toddler all the way back to their room. She pounded the dashboard. She kicked the car door.

"Just don't hurt yourself," said Sarna.

"All I wanted was to see him! That's all I wanted!" yelled Caroline.

"Maybe you will, somehow, someday." By the time they reached the B&B, Caroline had calmed down and apologized.

"No need," said Sarna. "It's better to let it out."

Caroline apologized again anyway. Once they got to their room, Caroline settled down with paper and pen. She stared at the blank page. It mocked her. "You'll never be able to do it, you fool!" it said. She got up and paced, sat back down, then got up and paced some more.

"Damn it!" she hollered. "I don't know what to say!"

Sarna disappeared and came back in with a cigarette for both of them. She held one out. "Here. I keep these in my glove compartment in case of emergencies. This'll help you think. It helps me."

Caroline took the cigarette. They went out on the balcony to smoke. Caroline tried not to think of the letter, lest her mind would become a tangled-up mess, rendering her immobile.

She looked at Sarna. "Is there a significance to your name? I've always wondered."

Sarna studied the mountains. "It was my grandmother's name."

"Did you know her?"

"No. But there have been stories. I've heard tell that she was quite a woman. Ahead of her time. She wore men's jeans when it was unheard of for a woman to do so. She, at some point, refused to live with my grandfather. They lived in separate houses on the same street. Before that, they fought like they were in a war all the time. Pots and pans would fly through the house. They dumped food in each other's laps. She once threw a brick at their TV and smashed the screen."

Caroline thought of her own childhood home, of the straining silence.

Sarna continued, "Afterward, when they lived separately, they behaved like a couple of love birds. She was a pianist and singer." A dog howled in the distance.

"What did your grandfather do for a living?" asked Caroline.

"At first, he was into historical restoration, an artist, really. He used to restore old paintings in churches. He restored a famous painting on a church ceiling in California. I don't remember which one, though. After that, he got into the steel worker's union. I had always imagined that he must have been miserable... an artist-turned-steel-worker. That must have been torturous. Anyway, my grandmother, she used to let my mother and her sisters stay home from school whenever they wanted. They used to sing all day and at night the neighbors, and my grandfather would come over. They'd all sing into the night. My grandmother used to let my mother drive the pickup truck on the roads when she was just fourteen. As I said, she was way ahead of her time. Or crazy, who knows which."

Caroline and Sarna sat in comfortable silence.

"I don't think my grandmother would have minded me being gay."

"She probably would have invited your lovers over for sing-ins," added Caroline.

"That would have been nice," said Sarna.

Caroline thought of families and their mysterious lives.

She finished her cigarette, went in, and stared at the paper. It no longer mocked her, but stared mutely back at her.

She shouted out to Sarna. "How should I address this? Mr. McAuley, Owen, Mr. Owen McAuley?"

"How about Mr. Owen McAuley!" shouted Sarna from the balcony.

Caroline started to write, then stopped. She got another sheet of paper. It sneered at her, snickered.

She silenced it with her pen. 'Dear Owen McAuley.'

Caroline crumpled up that page and got another. She ran her fingers through her hair, wiped a line of sweat off her forehead with her sleeve. She tried every greeting, pacing back and forth before the pages, observing how each one looked. Finally settling on one, she began to write:

May 17, 2008

Dear Mr. Owen McAuley,

You do not know me, but I am a woman who has been helped by the foundation named after your mother, the Gretchen McAuley foundation. I will not go into the specific details of my prior life of abuse, but let's just say that my life today is so new, so different, so promising that I find myself, at times, choking up with gratitude.

The Gretchen McAuley Foundation housed me, fed me, sustained me, nurtured me, and inspired me when I needed it most. I understand that this foundation was created by a woman named Sara, whoever she is. I am not sure of this connection between your mother and Sara, but I am equally grateful to this woman. I have sometimes thought of your mother's legacy, and, believe me when I tell you, that it lives on... in me. Nothing about her life was in vain, nothing. I hope this letter finds you well and thriving, happy. For some reason, I would love to hear back from you, if you are so inclined.

Gratefully Yours,

Caroline Stevens

Caroline had Sarna read it.

"But it's not true," said Caroline.

"So what," said Sarna. "What are you going to say... Hi! This is your mother speaking?"

"Do you think he'll write back?" asked Caroline.

"I don't know. Hopefully. If not, at least you know you've voiced yourself to him. At least, you know that he's alive and doing well. At least, you know he's had a good life."

"Good?" said Caroline. "You call losing your mother in the worst possible way good? You think it's good that the last time he saw his mother was in a shower with her head poking out of a shower curtain? That he had to pray to a little worry doll that his father would never come home? You call that good?" screamed Caroline.

She watched Sarna watching her. Her tall, strong friend looked small and stricken.

Caroline flopped down on the bed. "What's wrong with me? What's wrong with me that I would strike out at you like this?"

Sarna sat down at the edge of the bed, moved a cluster of hair that had fallen into her eyes. "It wasn't at me. It was just in my general direction," she replied.

"I am ugly. I am an ugly, ugly person," said Caroline. "No," said Sarna, "you are human. You are imperfect, like all of us. You feel what we all feel, at times. Why shouldn't we let it out? Show it all? The anger, the frustration, the fury, the joy, the pride... all of it? What is it about us humans that we feel we must hide from one another?"

Caroline covered her eyes with her forearm. "You're right. You're always right."

"Not always," said Sarna, "just sometimes."

They drove back to the house to deliver the letter. The same woman answered, but there was a small boy wrapping himself around her leg this time.

"Oh, sorry," she said. "This is my grandson, Ollie. He spends a lot of time here with us. It's a good environment for a small boy like Ollie." Caroline hoped this was so.

"Would you like to come in?"

Caroline peered over her shoulder into the small kitchen. She knew what was beyond that and beyond that.

"No, thank you," said Caroline. "I've got to get going. I've got a long drive ahead of me." She held up the letter. "Do you mind?"

"Heavens, no. I'll put it in the mail to him right away."

"Thank you," said Caroline.

She turned, got into the car, and they drove home.

Caroline and Sarna got back just in time for Barry to go to class. They hadn't even had a chance to talk about anything that happened. Barry told Caroline that Jacob had been insisting there was some sort of cat creeping around.

"I thought he was crazy until I saw it myself," he said.

"What did it look like?" asked Caroline.

"Gray with white spots."

Caroline smiled. "That's Dart. Is he in or out right now?"

"He's in. Last I saw him, he was on top of the fridge."

Caroline glanced at the refrigerator. Dart was no longer there. She and Barry went outside on Jacob's porch. Barry pulled her toward him. His familiar lips against hers filled her with warmth. Afterward, when she was alone with

Jacob, she realized there was something different about that kiss: that it made her lips burn.

Jacob knew Caroline right away. He even asked her how Virginia was.

"It was great," she said.

"Did I ever tell you that I was once in the service there? That was during the Korean War, I guess," he said, absently staring at the TV. "Or was it World War II?" he added, puzzled. "No, no. I guess it would have been during the Korean War. That was when the blacks couldn't use the same water bubblers or go into the same establishments. I remember the first time I went down there. I was just a kid, really. What did I know? I saw all these signs, you know... "Whites Only"... "Blacks Only." That sort of thing. I was just a kid from the north. Had never seen anything like that before."

He thought on this for a moment. "Did I tell you I was stationed in New York during the war? That's right, I guarded the city. That was my job."

The coming days were uneventful. Jacob seemed okay, except that his chest was rattling away and, also, he was forgetting things: such as having just gone to the bathroom, or having just eaten, or having just sat down, or stood up. He would drink a glass of water, and then ask, "Caroline? What happened to that glass of water I asked for?" His memories of the past were clearer, more accurate, even if they did take time to come into focus. Jacob told Caroline of his wedding day, of their first big fight, which, like with Sarna's grandparents, involved flying pots and pans. He told her of his first drunk, his last drunk- but nothing about Gretta.

Barry came over to Jacob's most nights after school. He came bursting with information about, of all things... snails. The three of them ate dinner together and talked about nothing in particular, which felt good to Caroline. She had filled Barry in on her experience in Virginia He was amazed at her courage in facing Jake, and thought it was ingenious of her to write a letter to Owen. Barry cradled Caroline many nights when the thought of never hearing from Owen in this lifetime rendered her incoherent. Caroline was inconsolable at these times, but still, Barry tried. However, Caroline reserved some of her Virginia experiences for herself. She and Barry fell asleep together on Jacob's couch often, only to wake to a stiff neck and a new day. Another evening, Barry came over with more snail news and something about horseshoe crabs; something about how ancient they are.

One morning, Caroline took Jacob outside. It was the first truly warm day in Massachusetts, edging seventy degrees. They sat on the lawn overlooking the tire swing and, further off, the small house out back.

"This is nice," he said. "To think, I used to break my back on this yard, this house. Houses all over this town, plumbing people's toilets, sinks, basements. A little know-how and the right tools. That's all it took. Look at this beautiful property, this house. All on a plumber's salary."

Jacob looked toward Caroline. "Know how much I bought this house for?"

Caroline shook her head.

"Six thousand dollars, that's how much."

"Wow," said Caroline.

"It's worth over six hundred thousand now. God, I worked hard. Worked all the time. I used to be young," he said. "I could do anything. Anything."

Caroline studied him. Age spots dotted his temples. A few strands of hair crossed his forehead. His thin, knobby legs jutted out from his boxers. Those legs used to heft hundreds of pounds of wood, bags of loam, grass seed, furniture, appliances. He may have once said things like, "All in a day's work," "Another day, another dollar," and "Better get to sleep before Santa comes."

She studied his profile and looked away, thinking- There's no telling what a man's life has been. She thought of her father, of the smell of sawdust and wood, of long, curling cigarette ashes, chlorine, and tin oiling cans. She thought of fathers, that they are the things we remember. Mothers, the air we breathe.

"What is life, anyway, but our floors, our walls, our ceilings. The air, the grass we mow. Events, one after another. Feelings one after another. Our children's pets we bury."

"Our thoughts," said Caroline.

"Dreams," said Jacob.

"Wants," countered Caroline.

"Days," returned Jacob.

"Nights."

They were silent for a moment.

"Coming back to do it all again," she added.

"If we're lucky," said Jacob.

"We are. We are lucky," said Caroline, covering his hand with hers.

The next day, Sarna came over. She showed up with a bouquet of fresh daisies and a container of black raspberry fudge ripple ice cream.

"I miss you," she said as she stood on Jacob's doorstep.

"And I, you," said Caroline.

They set the daisies up on the kitchen table, with Sarna arranging them just so. Caroline cooked chicken breast and asparagus for dinner. Caroline and Sarna ate, but Jacob wouldn't. He'd been having an irritable, confused day.

He'd yelled at Caroline earlier, asking her, "What do you know about cars anyway!"

There had been no leading conversation and no follow through conversation either. Caroline had just looked at him and resumed her task of folding his underwear, her socks.

After dinner, they cracked open the container if ice-cream, scooped it into bowls, and started eating.

"I love the globs of fudge," said Caroline.

"I like mushing it up all together," said Sarna with her mouth full of ice cream.

When they lifted their faces from their bowls, they saw Jacob staring at them.

"Could I have a bowl?" he asked.

Days and days passed, nights, too. Caroline was having dreams again: Nonsensical ones, but no doubt with all sorts of vague, shadowy meanings. She went back to meditation group and found that she was just like every other woman there, if not seeking answers, then relief; Simple relief from the day's worries, the week's trials. She also found that some of the magic was gone. It had been replaced by a quiet inner knowing that, in and of itself, was magical. She listened and talked, knowing when it felt right to do either. Caroline wanted to tell the women there everything she'd learned: This is life, enjoy it. Forgive the unforgivable. We are all just tumbling along in a circle, and every part of it is something to behold. Look at your crap, and you'll find what's beneath it. Be gentle with yourself. But she said none of these things. She knew it was not her place to tell them... that, perhaps, their lessons were not the same as hers. She knew that their journeys were theirs, and hers was hers.

Weeks more passed. Caroline had to postpone her trip to Oregon, again. She'd enroll in the following semester, the fall one. If she had to, she'd postpone again. Caroline didn't want to leave Jacob or Barry or Sarna. She didn't want to leave. She hadn't even told Barry about her plans, and she knew this was wrong. She also knew she'd tell him when it felt right. Caroline had told Sarna, however, who said she'd be thrilled to come and visit her, often. Sarna had even resolved to get some sedatives, so that she could do the plane ride. Caroline had resolved not to. She wanted to feel every prick of fear. She yearned to know what fear felt like when you're not completely messed up.

Sarna had continued her rounds of prison interviews, and her boss liked what was coming of it. Maybe the world really does want the good news, the hope, the forward motion of life. Sarna, of course, would not be using any material from Jake, since he hadn't offered much. Caroline thought that he had, though, if just to say... "If you've never been there, you're never going to get it." He had offered Caroline so much more than she thought possible: an out, a way to forgive.

Caroline's mother wanted her and Barry to come for dinner, but Caroline was afraid to leave Jacob. Instead, her mother came to them. Barry asked her why she was so nervous for her mother's arrival, to which Caroline replied, "I don't know." Really, she did know. It was because she feared everything wouldn't be perfect enough for her mother.

When Caroline's mother arrived at Jacob's, she seemed out of place: like fine china in a thrift store. She seemed to take note of the cheap, mismatched plates, the Christmas mugs they used to sip their coffee, the rumpled couch; however, a tour of the little house out back, with its cottage gardens, seemed to bring her back to herself. Once again, a sense of ease returned between Caroline and her mother.

After her mother left, Caroline said to Barry, "I don't think my mother approved of Jacob's house or his things. Then, it feels like she doesn't approve of me."

Caroline was surprised by the well of tears that came to her eyes.

"I don't think that was it at all," said Barry.

Caroline looked up at him. "You noticed something, too?"

"Well, yeah. I think it had more to do with the fact that Jacob was... he was drooling."

"Drooling?"

"Yes. Right there at the table. Didn't you see?"

"Oh, God. No."

"Don't worry. I wiped it away," he said.

Sarna stayed at Caroline's cottage for a few days, because she couldn't stop crying. Unlike Caroline, who preferred to cry in private if at all, Sarna liked to have someone with her while she was doing it. Despite her earlier bravery in the face of her recent problems with Julie, Sarna was crushed when their relationship ended. She required an almost constant vigil to her rehashing of the end: someone to pat her hand and hug her shoulders, someone to pass her tissues and discard her used ones. It went on for days, in the middle of the night, first thing in the morning. Caroline took care of Jacob and of Sarna, wiping his drool, tossing her snot-filled tissues. When Sarna asked for black raspberry fudge ripple ice cream, Caroline went to get some at 10:30 at night. As she was driving past Jacob's house to get the ice cream, she saw him half way out the door in his boxers. She got out of her car, guided him back into the house and yelled at him to get in and stay in. When she grabbed the container of ice cream at the grocery store, it slipped from her hand and landed on her foot. Caroline huffed and puffed her way through the checkout line and to her car. Once inside, she screamed, "Damn you, Sarna! Just get over it!" Then shame wrapped around her like a cloak. She remembered what Barry had told her about tears being the river that carry you forward, and she thought she could stand a dose of what Sarna had. Then, on her way home, Caroline remembered Samuel and that some people would kill to be loved, to be needed. By the time she reached home, she would have spoon fed Sarna if it wouldn't seem so bizarre.

Then, on the fourth day, it was over, just like that. Sarna woke up smiling. There was not a splotch on her face, not a tear-induced puffy eye. Not a single mention of Julie, or a single 'why me' crossing her lips. She showered, dressed, and left for work. Sarna called Caroline two times on her way there: once to tell her that she thought she'd be able to get Jimmy Buffett tickets for Labor Day weekend and once to say thank you.

Then, Caroline told Barry. She wasn't so sure it felt like the right time to tell him, but it felt like the wrong time not to tell him. So, she did. Caroline had been giving him a back massage on her living room couch. They were talking about her ability to take pain away, to heal. When she told him she would be leaving for Oregon, he didn't say anything. Beneath her hands, she felt a shift, a deadening, a coldness. Like a limp handshake. Caroline continued to massage until she couldn't go on any longer. Barry sat up. Caroline suddenly felt the way one might feel when they've realized they are lost in a forest. Or the way one might feel when they've realized they've swam to far from the shore.

He did not look at her, but he asked, "Is this the best place for this type of program?"

"Yes. I believe it is," replied Caroline without looking at him.

"Then, that's where you should go," he said.

They didn't mention it for another week, and even then it was in short phrases like: "What's eight months,

386

anyway?", and "Different state, different coast... doesn't matter.", and then finally, "I'll wait." That's what Barry said.

Lessons never end. They never, ever end. On the morning of May 30th, Caroline learned an important one: That the universe isn't there solely for her benefit, that there are no signs, no preparations for some things, that to be human, among other things, is to be caught unawares. To be caught unawares is to feel deeply, for there is no time to put up walls. When Caroline woke up that morning, she found Jacob still in bed, breathing shallowly. In his chest, was not a rattle, but a drowning, liquid sound. At first, his breaths were regular, and then sporadic, and then regular again, but very far apart. Caroline thought to call Sarna, and then thought to call Barry. Then, she realized she didn't have time for either call. She sat by his bed and held his hand. His eyes were closed, his lids thin like paper. His legs stirred for a moment, and Caroline feared that he was feeling pain. She whimpered and said, "Oh, God." She wanted to be a little girl. Wanted to run and get her mother. But she wasn't a little girl, just a woman who felt like one. Caroline tried to remember their last exchange, but couldn't. Clutching his hand, she ran her other hand along his forehead. Her hands felt nothing, nothing. It was very quiet in the room--except for the ticking of his little wind up clock. Jacob's red plaid shirt hung on the bedpost. The heels of his slippers poked out from under his bed. Caroline waited, holding his hand. "I love you," she said. She said it again. His breaths became very, very far apart. Then, Gretta appeared on the other side of the bed. Her cheeks were pink, flushed. She watched Caroline watching her father. Her father... the things we remember most. Jacob turned his head toward Caroline. He opened his paper thin lids, looking at her with his green, green eyes. Green like olives. Gretta smiled warmly at Caroline.

Jacob spoke, "My Gretta."

Caroline saw then, in an instant, all of his days: His gray ones, his bright ones, his youth, his love... a human with a few dark places like all of us.

"Gretta," he said again, rapture on his lips.

Caroline looked up at Gretta. In her eyes, was a reflection of herself.

"Go on," said Gretta to Caroline.

"Daddy. My Daddy. I love you. I forgive you," said Caroline.

The rapture spread into his eyes, and he closed them. There was a breath, then another, and that was it. Then Gretta was gone, and so was Jacob, leaving Caroline alone, listening to the ticking of the clock.

Grief is its own thing, its own living beast. It breathes, eats, and drinks. It rests with one eye open and wakes again, new and raw every time. It brings with it waves and storms, tornadoes, hurricanes, northeasters. It builds you up and then breaks you into a million grains of sand. It renders you useless and then inspires you. It changes you and then restores you to your most basic self: A self whose heart can break at the glorious feel of a hot shower, but whose tongue cannot taste a single food you try to get down. It stays as long as it pleases only to leave and then come back again.

Time passed and Caroline recalled her last exchange with Jacob. She remembered it one evening while in the grocery store's freezer aisle. This was the last time they spoke: "What was that ice cream we had the other night?" Caroline was in the middle of scrubbing the kitchen floor when Jacob said this.

"The black raspberry fudge ripple?" returned Caroline, looking up from the bucket of soapy water.

"That, yes. I liked that."

"Do you want me to go get you some?"

"No, really... I just wanted you to know I liked it."

Jacob then promptly fell asleep. Guttural snores escaped from his mouth. Caroline returned to scrubbing the floor, making mental note to pick up a gallon of the ice cream for Jacob. She never did.

When the memory of their last exchange hit, Caroline had to leave the grocery store without getting what she'd come for. She made it to her car and broke into a million pieces. Tears sprung from her eyes, soaking her shirt, dripping from the end of her nose. This lasted an hour, and then her face was too puffy and splotched to go back into the store. She'd loved him. She'd loved Jacob, as much as she loved her own father... if not more. At that moment, Caroline hated this, this love. It hurt too much, but what is life without pain? Without pain, there can be no joy. Without forgiveness, we cannot love... for humans are fallible. Without love there can be no magic. Without loving others, we cannot truly know ourselves. Strangely, Caroline's thoughts turned to Sam King. She suddenly knew his life's purpose. Also, she knew what Barry meant when he said Sam had been cured of his illness. Still, she could hardly wait to finish the book.

Caroline went to the services and saw, for the first time, Gretta's grave marker. Jacob was laid to rest next to her, or next to the empty earthen space that represented her. Her real bones were somewhere very, very far away; her soul, who knows where... maybe already born again. Perhaps Gretta's soul and Jacob's were hanging around together, making up for lost time. This is what Caroline chose to believe.

The estate, Jacob's estate, was to be liquidated and all proceeds were to be set up as a foundation to help fund the recovery of missing children: to help counsel, heal, and bring together the families of these children... The Gretta Stills Foundation. He'd named Caroline Stevens as its director. She was angry with him for not discussing this with her, for she knew nothing of how to direct or oversee such an endeavor. Then she realized she knew everything about it, about how to fill the void left behind by missing persons. Caroline was just mad at Jacob, and she needed a reason to be. Lila told her that anger is a normal grief emotion. This confused Caroline. How could she be mad at him for dying? Her confusion only made her angrier. The emotions came and came in circles: anger, despair, denial, release, sadness. The sadness was the worst. Somehow, all of it was something to behold, but the sadness drenched her. It was unbearable. Barry said the worst for him since Emily died had been the anger. Sarna said she didn't really know, since she'd never been through such grief, not this kind. She did her best for Caroline anyway. Still, Caroline's best crying was done in private.

Then, one day, something happened. It was a hot, buzzing June afternoon when Caroline went to the mailbox to get her mail. Underneath a Stop & Shop flyer and some bills was a letter... a letter addressed to Caroline from an Owen McAuley. Caroline's hands shook as she placed the letter on her red linoleum table, the one with Gretta's writing underneath. She picked up the letter again and read the return address. It was from Montana, a post office box in a town called Running Falls. Caroline's mind automatically constructed the scene: A quaint valley town with tall, brick buildings and a main street running through. Pick-up trucks dot the sidewalk. Sounds echo off the surrounding mountains. Owen walks down the sidewalk, and people call out to him. He waves back... But it was just an image, a fabrication of the mind, created to fulfill a wish. Caroline considered waiting to open it, but then she realized that she'd waited long enough to hear from her son.

June 20, 2008

Dear Caroline,

I cannot begin to express how grateful I was for your letter, how grateful I still am and will always be. I have never received such a letter from any woman helped by the foundation named after my mother. Although, I know there are many such women. I know this, because I oversee its progress, its functions, its health. It is alive and well. My Aunt Sara and I used to do it together, but now that she is gone, it is my wife, Carol, and I who keep it going, resting our fingers always on its pulse. Domestic abuse is a horrid, horrid thing, as I can attest to. As can you. My mother once told me when I was just four-years-old that when I grow up, I'd be the man to put an end to the cycle of abuse perpetrated through the generations of my family. It was the last thing she said to me, the last time I saw her... and I remembered. Of course, my Aunt Sara was there through all of my years to remind me as well. After my mother was gone, she spoke through Sara. She never left me. My mother never did. Now she speaks through you. It is my mother and my aunt Sara who have changed the course of my life forever, and also yours as well. They were both amazing, courageous women. I visit my mother often in the air, the earth, the trees, and in my dreams. Of course, I visit my Aunt Sara's grave every year. Your letter has brought me a sense of completeness, of closure. Also, a sense of continuance, for I know that my mother's life was a pebble tossed into a pond, sending out ripples that go on and on and on, gently, but with purpose. Again, you make my heart sing! Please feel free to write to me any time. I will be here in Montana for at least another couple of months, and then, after that... who knows where. Then again, I have your Massachusetts address as well, and perhaps I will write you again.

Forever Yours,

Owen McAuley

June 25, 2008

Dear Owen,

Your letter found me shaking and giddy. I had not expected to hear back from you, though I really did want to. You sound like such an upstanding man, the kind any mother would be swelling with pride to have. I don't even know you, and I feel proud. I have become a very curious person, now that I have the freedom to be curious. I looked up your mother's foundation on-line. I wanted to learn the particulars, and through my research, I learned of this Sara. What a lovely, ingenious woman. I think that even I might like to visit her grave. Although, meeting her in person would have been better. Also, I wanted to pass on my new address to you. I will be moving to Oregon in just two weeks to enter a degree program there. If you wish to write back, please find my new address on the enclosed card. In addition, if you are willing, perhaps I could get some advice from you on how to run a foundation. I will be heading one called 'The Gretta Stills Foundation for Missing Children and their Families'. It is something that has sort of landed in my lap, and I don't have a clue about it. Although, I am honored to do it. It seems that we have some things in common! Maybe it is because of this that I take great joy in corresponding with you. Please, do write back.

Yours,

Caroline Stevens

June 30, 2008

Dear Caroline,

I wanted to get this letter to you quickly before you were off to Oregon. My wife and I have decided that Oregon should be our next destination. We have done our research and have found that it is quite a dynamic place in the world. Besides the majestic Mount Hood, did you know there are actually rain forests there? What an unsuspecting place for such a thing! We could actually meet each other and discuss the particulars of heading a foundation, such as the one you mentioned. Let's not think of it as a business meeting, though. My wife and I have decided that we are done with business-y things, or at least as much as can be helped. We prefer peace and discovery with a hint of adventure Perhaps meeting with one another will bring with it all three. Once you become settled in Oregon, you can write me back in Montana, since I will be here for another two months or so. Then, we can arrange some plans.

Yours,

Owen

Over the next week, Sarna helped Caroline pack. Barry was heavily into his studies. He'd been assigned a research project about horseshoe crabs. One evening, they went up to Hull, Massachusetts together to an area on the bay where horseshoe crabs are known to come up to the sandy shore and breed. They found a spot secluded from the rows of houses lining the edge of the bay. Taking off their shoes, they rolled up their pant legs and sat at the water's edge. Tall sea grass swayed gently in the water. Beachy summer noises drifted across the bay toward them: a child's excited screech, a man's laughter, cars cruising the strip with their windows down, pumping out music. Someone, somewhere across the bay, played a saxophone. The sun and the moon began their dance of trading places in the sky, reminding Caroline of a child's bedtime wind-up toy; the kind where the sun and the moon twist around one another as "Twinkle Twinkle Little Star" plays... teaching children the reciprocity of life.

"A full moon and a high tide," said Barry, "perfect for spawning. Watch and you'll see them coming up."

Caroline watched the water's edge. Her eyes played tricks on her as the water rippled, like little tongues lapping at the moonlight. What she thought was a horseshoe crab was really just a stone, a rock, a piece of driftwood. Bunches of sea heather populated themselves among the sea grass and Caroline yearned to wade in among all of it, if just to feel the prickle against her calves. Then, she saw them creeping soundlessly up the sand: a horseshoe crab on the back of another, and then more over to the left.

"There!" exclaimed Barry, pointing.

"I see!" said Caroline. They watched as if they had never seen such a thing, such a miracle.

"The female is the bigger one," explained Barry.

The air cooled momentarily, and Caroline felt a burn in her cheeks, the kiss of the day's sun. Little grains of sand trapped themselves in her curly hair and clung to the back of her neck.

"I'd like to go to Delaware to see this," said Barry. "It's the world's largest breeding ground."

Caroline remembered her and Sarna's trip through Delaware: the state of tolls and hypothetical people... the state of horseshoe crabs.

"Then, you should. You should go to see that," she said.

Caroline scootched up next to him; fit herself right into him.

"Did I tell you that their blood helps protect us humans from infection?"

"Is that so?"

"They collect the crabs, put them in labs, and blood-let them." Barry paused, and then continued. "It doesn't hurt them, though." He rested his hand upon her thigh. "They take just enough blood and then return them to the ocean. They carry on just as before."

Caroline thought on this: how all sorts of living things can give of themselves, and then go on... through the ages and years and decades. Through all of time.

She looked at the vast bay, that wide open space, teeming with life underneath, yet so peaceful at its surface. She heard a plane flying overhead and looked up, a silver bullet slicing through the sky. She thought of the bags she had already packed, especially the one sitting open on her bed, on Gretta's bed. It held clothes and her copy of <u>Little Women</u>, and, of course, <u>The Beginning</u>.

"Did I tell you that horseshoe crabs predate man, dinosaurs, and even flying insects?"

"Yes, you did," said Caroline. "I believe you did."

www.ingramcontent.com/pod-product-compliance
Lightning Source LLC
Chambersburg PA
CBHW050900250626
47155CB00001B/44